THE DAY THE FALLS
STOOD STILL

Cathy Marie Buchanan

For Maryann,

Enjoy the Niagara Core.

Best,

Catty Buch

voice

HYPERION   NEW YORK

THE DAY THE FALLS
STOOD STILL

A Novel

Library of Congress Cataloging-in-Publication Data

Buchanan, Cathy Marie.
   The day the falls stood still / Cathy Marie Buchanan.
      p. cm.
   ISBN-13: 978-1-4013-4097-1
   ISBN-10: 1-4013-4097-0
   1. Rich people—Fiction.   2. Niagara Falls (Ont.)—Fiction.   3. World War, 1914–1918—Ontario—Fiction.   4. Hydroelectric power plants—Ontario—fiction.   5. Domestic fiction.   I. Title.
   PR9199.4.B825D39 2009
   813'.6—dc22

                                                          2009017732

Hyperion books are available for special promotions and premiums. For details contact the HarperCollins Special Markets Department in the New York office at 212-207-7528, fax 212-207-7222, or email spsales@harpercollins.com.

FIRST EDITION

Book design by Shubhani Sarkar

10 9 8 7 6 5 4 3 2 1

FOR DAD,
WHO WALKED WITH ME IN THE NIAGARA GLEN

[We are here at Niagara Falls] to declare that the awful symbol of Infinite Power, in whose dread presence we stand—these visions of Infinite Beauty here unfolded to the eye, are not a property, but a shrine—a temple erected by the hand of the Almighty for all the children of men; that it cannot be desecrated . . . that [we] mark out the boundaries of the sanctuary, expel from the interior all ordinary human pursuits and claims, so that visitors and pilgrims from near or far may come hither, and be permitted to behold, to love, to worship, to adore.

—ORATION DELIVERED BY JAMES C. CARTER
AT THE OPENING OF THE NEW YORK STATE RESERVATION AT NIAGARA FALLS,
JULY 15, 1885

THE DAY THE FALLS
STOOD STILL

Book
ONE

UPPER RIVER

June 1915–August 1915

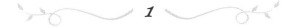

1

Loretto Academy veranda

The stone walls of Loretto Academy are so thick I can sit curled up on a windowsill, arms around the knees tucked beneath my chin. It stands on a bluff not far from the Horseshoe Falls, and because I have been a student long enough to rank a room on the river side, I have only to open a pair of shutters to take in my own private view of the Niagara. Beyond the hedge and gate marking the perimeter of the academy, and the steep descent leading to the wooded shore, I can see the upper river and the falls. Endless water plummets from the brink to the rocks below, like the careless who slip, like the stunters who fail, like the suicidal who leap. I nudge my attention downriver, to clouds of rising mist.

In those clouds I have seen aberrations—flecks of shimmering silver, orbs of color a shade more intense than their surroundings. I have seen them more than once, and I have decided they are prayers, mine and everyone else's, too.

There is a light rap on my door, and then Sister Ignatius, who teaches us English literature, steps into my room. I hop down from the windowsill, wondering why she has come with a stack of books and just minutes before all of us at the academy are due downstairs for the commencement of the class of 1915. "For you, Bess," she says, handing the books over to me. "They're old." But the stack includes *The Hound of the Baskervilles* and *The House of Mirth,* books that are not old at all. There are others— *Wuthering Heights, A Tale of Two Cities, Life and Letters of Harriet Beecher Stowe, The Last of the Mohicans,* and *The Picture of Dorian Gray*—that were written years earlier, but the copies in my arms are new. As I mutter a thank-you, she touches my cheek, and then she is back through the door and in the corridor saying, "Fifteen minutes until you're expected in the dining hall."

For a moment I cling to the possibility that I will return to the academy in the fall for my final year. But Sister Ignatius is yet another example of the sisters having gone soft and sentimental, the way people tend to when they are saying good-bye. It began with Sisters Bede and Leocrita, who teach composition and Christian doctrine, returning a pair of examinations I had not sufficiently prepared for, preoccupied as I was with Father's whereabouts. The comments penciled into the margins were bewildering. "An interesting departure from your usual style." "An original idea." Where were the stern words reprimanding sloppiness and poorly formulated logic I had expected to find?

I mean to get through the evening dry-eyed and respectable, and at the outset all goes well enough. I file into the dining hall with the rest of the juniors, all of us in our white concert dresses, and take my place on the low platform at the front of the room. I stand there, mouthing the words to "The Last Rose of Summer" as the twelve seniors who will form the evening's graduating class make their way up the center aisle.

We had been told that with the war the decorations would be less elaborate than in other years. Still, the platform is lined with potted palms and ferns moved from elsewhere in the academy, and there are large vases of roses and peonies cut from Sister Leocrita's garden at either end. My gaze sweeps the rows of seated parents, moving from powdered nose to clean-shaven face, and finally comes to rest on a familiar navy hat trimmed with silk and an egret feather. Mother is impeccably dressed, though somewhat less fashionably than usual. Her skirt meets her boots rather than ending a few inches above the ankle as do the more daring styles. And her collar is high, stiffly starched. She faces straight ahead, her spine as straight as anyone's in the room, yet she twists the program in her hands. She is sitting beside the aisle, and, though the house is nearly full, the three seats next to hers remain unoccupied. Surely one is saved for Father.

I press on through the singing and then a piano solo, but midway through the violin duet, I am no longer able to pretend Father is merely late. He is not coming. It used to be that I would spot him from my window seat now and then, passing through the large brass doors of the Niagara Power Company, where he is company director. But I have not seen him in the six weeks since Mother and my sister, Isabel, broke with tradition and turned up without him for a Sunday visit at the academy. Ever since I have been steadfastly keeping watch. And while I sat in my window seat dreaming up a dozen explanations for his absences from both the power company and the academy on Sunday afternoons, the empty seat beside Mother tonight rules out all but the most horrible of my thoughts: Father has set out for the battlefields of Belgium and France. I blink wide-eyed, fluttery blinks meant to avoid tears, and slide my fingertips beneath the sleeve of my dress, hoping somehow to discover a handkerchief I know is not there.

The juniors and seniors who do not sing or play an instrument well have been given roles in tonight's morality playlet. And though I am playing Sanctity, a spirit who appears briefly to the main heroine, Rosalba, and points out her folly in seeking earthly glory, I am giving little thought to my role. In the opening scene, all the cast is onstage except for me and Kit Atwell, the girl with whom I have been lucky enough to share a room for the last umpteen years, left alone to whisper behind the curtain strung across the rear of the platform.

Mother Febronie finally finishes introducing the playlet, and True Glory, Innocence, Wealth, and Beauty glide to the other side of the curtain, taking as much time as Sister Bede had insisted real spirits would.

"Kit."

She tucks a lock of flaxen hair behind her ear and leans in close, prepared, despite orders for strict silence backstage. "No exceptions," Sister Bede had said.

"My father, he's gone off to the war," I whisper, my hands cupped around her ear.

"What?" She mouths the word.

"He's not here tonight."

She shakes her head, vigorously. "I promised your mother I wouldn't say anything." She winces. "He was let go from the power company."

It is entirely possible Kit knows yet another bit of news that I do not. Like mine, her family lives in Niagara Falls, and, more than any other girl at the academy, she is privy to the town's goings-on. She is the eldest of six sisters, and though there is an older brother, Edward, he is none too clever and she is treated as the firstborn son. She knows the ins and outs of her father's businesses: the stationery, tobacco, and furniture stores on the west side of Erie Avenue, and much of the real estate just opposite, the buildings housing Connor Bros. shoe store, Louis Fischer cigar store, Clark's Hardware, E. S. Cole Jeweler, W. R. Price Men's Wear, and John Logan Dry Goods.

And Kit would not lie, not on purpose, especially not to me. But what she says hardly makes sense. Isabel is engaged to Boyce Cruickshank of the Buffalo Cruickshanks, and his father is the founder and president of the American company that owns half the powerhouses on the river, including the Niagara Power Company, where Father is no longer employed if Kit is right. "I'm not so sure," I say into her ear.

"My father told me. My mother was there, too. She said that someday Mr. Cruickshank would get his just deserts."

"But Mr. Cruickshank wouldn't let Father be sacked," I whisper back, though even as the words leave my mouth I am remembering a Sunday afternoon visit with Isabel slumped on my bed in the tea dress I was making for her trousseau. We had finished marking the hem a few minutes earlier, and she was turning in a slow circle and going on about how skilled I was and the perfection of the dress, which really did fit her nearly flawless figure like a dream, when she abruptly flopped down onto my bed and said, "Boyce can be so lily-livered. I need a favor from his father and he's afraid to ask."

"The kippered herring?" I said, expecting Mr. Cruickshank had once and for all vetoed the fish being served at his son's wedding.

"No," she said, "but never mind." She stood up from the bed and put on a smile that had struck me as false. "I'll convince Boyce. It'll just take a bit of work."

Then she flipped back to my immense talent and "Oh, Bess, the embroidery!" and it brought to an end my tiny moment of wondering if the favor she needed from Mr. Cruickshank was more important than she was letting on.

Kit puts a hand on my elbow, waits, giving the news of Father a chance to sink in. I had spent a great deal of the last month in the academy chapel on bended knee—an hour each day after lunch, as Mother Febronie had agreed. At the outset my mind had often drifted to the term paper I had not yet written or the examination I had not yet studied for, and it had begun to seem senseless, the tired knees, the ever more feeble attempts to rein in my thoughts. But I glimpsed another fleck of silver above the falls and prayed in earnest from then on, at first for Father to turn up at the large brass doors of the Niagara Power Company and, when he did not, for God to watch over him at the front. And in return I had felt God knowing and bothering about me. He would not disappoint.

But all those hours, I should have been praying for Boyce to let Isabel have her way, for him to ask, or even beg, his father to reinstate our own, for Mr. Cruickshank to yield to the pleas of his only son. "I prayed all wrong," I whisper to Kit.

I have only the foggiest notion of what an unemployed father means. Would he sell Glenview, our home on the Niagara River, and buy a smaller house? Would we live in rented rooms? Would I be expected to work? As a governess? As a clerk in a shop? All that seems certain is that I will not return to the academy after the summer holiday, which is surely awful enough.

My mind careens from one misgiving to the next until it lights upon a comforting thought. Isabel will not be included in whatever my family might become. She is promised to Boyce. She wears a gold ring set with a small ruby on her fourth finger, the finger once believed to be linked by a vein to the heart. And I know with certainty her good fortune will be held out on a platter to me. Always, she has let me have the larger slice of cake, and she whooped more loudly than anyone when I graduated from the little school and won the prize for sewing. Half-asleep, I have felt her palm smooth my brow, her lips brush my cheek. I have heard whispered words: "Sleep tight, Bess."

Boyce will look after Isabel, and she in turn will look after me.

"Our cue," Kit says, apologetically. "Are you steady enough? I could say you're not well."

"I'll manage."

And I do, though I stumble and miss a line and very likely convince the entire audience I have been hit with a terrible case of nerves.

After the curtain call and the applause and another piano solo and two choral pieces and a string quartet, and twelve seniors accepting certificates and handshakes all around, and a lengthy valedictory address, Mother Febronie announces strawberry shortcake and tea in the parlor. Then there is the shuffle of people getting up from their chairs.

I turn toward Kit across the platform, and she gives me the most solemn of nods. I lift a shoulder, force a smile, and then make a beeline for Mother.

She reaches a hand toward me, brushes a wisp of hair from my cheek, smoothing it into place. I have worn my hair parted in the middle, swept up, and loosely knotted at the back of my head for several years. Gone are the days when I could let it fall as it might, as long as I ran a brush through it from time to time. Now I must fuss with combs and barrettes. I have no talent for hairdressing, no patience for it either, so I am left uncertain of the reason behind the caress. Is she offering assistance to a girl of seventeen who has not yet mastered her hair or apologizing for keeping Father's dismissal a secret when it is my right to know? Maybe it is only her way of showing concern over my case of nerves.

"I know Father was sacked." I look at her coldly.

"Kit told you."

Not wanting to implicate my best friend, I say, "Half the girls know."

She places a palm on each of my shoulders, and I stand rigid a moment, my arms at my sides, until I slouch from beneath her hands. "I suppose you've heard about Isabel, too," she says.

I shrug, stumped.

"Oh," she says.

"Just say whatever it is."

"Boyce Cruickshank called off the engagement."

I stand stock-still, dumbfounded. No one walks out on Isabel. No one can resist her.

The Sunday afternoon visit Mother and Isabel had made without Father had been their last, and I had assumed that it was Mother's doing, that she had decided to steer herself and Isabel clear of the questions I was bound to ask about Father. But I had forgotten that Isabel is not as compliant as I, that she once showed up at the academy when she was forbidden to leave the house after missing her curfew three nights in a row.

I wrap my arms around my ribs, thinking of her home in bed, too heartbroken to rouse herself, even for a visit with me. "I want to go home," I say. "Tonight. And I don't want any cake." It calls for only a small change in plans. Along with the rest of the girls, I am slated to leave Loretto for the summer holiday in the morning. My trunk is already packed, waiting beside my bed. Then I add, "I'm not coming back."

I meant we should take my trunk tonight rather than return for it in the morning. But Mother interprets my statement as a question and says, "I'm afraid you won't be, Bess," a first admission from her that my days at Loretto have come to an end.

I wait for further explanation, and when it does not come, I lash out: "The sisters have made that obvious enough."

She cups my chin with her palms, her fingers spread flat on my cheeks. "I only wanted you to finish your year in peace."

I shake away her hands. "I'm packed, ready to go."

We climb the steps of the north stairwell, my fingers sliding over the smooth wood of the banister one last time. At the first landing, the point where the banister loops back, forming a graceful hairpin turn, Mother says, "I came on the trolley."

I had not considered how we would get my trunk home and say, "We could telephone Father."

"We'll manage on our own."

He is not coming to Loretto, not tonight, not as long as the other fathers, the ones with another year's tuition figured out, are swallowing forkfuls of cake in the parlor.

In my room, Mother sits down on my bed as though I might like to linger awhile, but I position myself at one end of the leather trunk embossed with ELIZABETH HEATH. "Maybe you should change," she says.

Other than the white concert dress I am wearing, my options include two high-collared, floor-length black dresses sure to flag me as a Loretto girl almost anywhere in Niagara Falls, the bloomers I change into for athletics, three nightgowns, and a swimming costume. "I'm fine," I say.

She loops her fingers around the handle opposite mine, counts to three, and says, "Lift."

The trunk is more awkward than I thought and Mother, unexpectedly strong. It is I who slump under its weight, I who pant, as the trunk bumps from one stair to the next, leaving scuff marks behind. My hair is disheveled, a strand or two caught in my mouth. A section of hem already pulled loose, I have shortened my dress by tucking a section of skirt under the sash around my waist. This lack of comportment might be liberating if Mother appeared the slightest bit harassed, but she is as dignified as ever, even under the weight of the trunk.

Usually when I leave Loretto for the summer holiday, Father is here, waiting in his Cadillac at the north door. He feigns impatience, shaking his head with the other fathers as we girls embrace and weep our goodbyes. This explicit testimony of a daughter's happiness, of her popularity, has long provided proof of money well spent. But today as I pass through the doorway, I am unmoved. I give only a cursory glance to the arched window overhead, with its etching of the Last Supper. Jesus and his friends. Peter, who denied him. Judas, who betrayed him for thirty silver coins.

2

Mother and I lug the trunk across the wide expanse of lawn at the rear of the academy to Stanley Avenue. While we wait for the electric trolley, I inspect the string of small blisters forming where the trunk handle bit into my skin and wonder how we will manage the half mile between the trolley's final stop and our house, atop a bluff overlooking the Niagara Gorge and River Road.

As the trolley approaches, we take up our positions at either end of the trunk and stoop to grasp the handles. But then a young man, four or five years older than I am, gets off the trolley and says, "Let me give you a hand," and I remember seeing him a few weekends ago, during one of Loretto's Saturday outings along the Niagara River.

The outing had begun as always, a sister out in front, a tail of paired-off girls trailing behind. The man from the trolley was out walking, too, though in the direction opposite ours. With so few chances to glimpse the local boys, unless of course it was a visiting brother in the academy parlor on a Sunday afternoon, we girls poked one another, chins nudging in his direction. I was struck by the size of him, his shoulders, his height. When the gap between us had closed to a dozen yards, it occurred to me that he would likely enlist, as had 150,000 other volunteers, and be sent overseas. Like now, he was wearing the matching waistcoat and jacket, neckcloth, and flat cap of the working class, though he carried himself well. His hair hung a little long, with a few locks the color of wheat reaching beyond his ears. His skin was bronzed, suggesting he spent a great deal of time outdoors. His eyes were like the Niagara River: green, full of vigor, captivatingly so. He was handsome, but not at all in an aristocratic way. There was nothing to suggest an easy life, or time spent primping and preening. I wanted to speak to him, badly, to say something consoling or maybe hopeful, something to give him courage or peace. It struck me that he might not survive the war, that it would be momentously wrong of me to look away. I said, "Good day," as we passed, causing my classmates to stir, and he tipped his cap.

Afterward I peered around each corner, between each pair of buildings, hoping to catch sight of him. But all I saw was the war, cropping up everywhere, like never before. I would glance toward a pair of surge tanks belonging to one of the power companies and see the barbed-wire barricades guarding them from the enemy, the saboteurs thought to be living in our midst. My attention would drift to a lamppost, to a poster pasted there, an illustration of a little girl with blond ringlets, standing knock-kneed, speaking the words "Oh please do! Daddy. Buy me a victory bond." On the next lamppost there would be another, this time a soldier pulling on the jacket of a uniform, beginning to turn, to rush away, laughing out the words "Come on. Let's finish the job."

All of it had come as a great shock. At the academy it had been easy to forget that Britain, and thus Canada, was at war. Little had changed, other than music practice being shifted to afternoon study hall. In the evening the practice rooms of the music corridor, along with most of the academy, remained in darkness. In an effort to save electricity for the factories producing trench shovels, wound dressings, munitions, and the like, we gathered with our schoolbooks in the library and remained there until lights out.

As always, our procession paused at the falls, and I looked into the water of the upper river, at the round stones of the riverbed, each large enough to resist being torn from its resting place and flung over the brink. Clear water hurtled past the stones, then shattered to white as it plunged to the river below. Standing there at the brink of the falls, I asked for a young man to be spared, a young man for me.

From across the trolley aisle, I sneak glimpses, careful not to give Mother reason to watch. Eventually my gaze meets his, and we both quickly look away. After that I keep my eyes forward and do my best to appear contemplative and elegant, though I have been sweating since I first picked up the trunk. Even as I trail my fingertips along my collarbone, as I have seen Isabel do, I know that I am absurd, that he will forever disappear at the next stop or the one after that, that Loretto girls are reserved for men of a different lot. And, honestly, would not my time be better spent thinking about Father's situation or Isabel's broken heart?

When we reach the end of the trolley line, he stands, and I notice what appears to be bedding rolled up and held together with a length of rope. As I sort through rationales for the bedroll—a delivery, a purchase, likely a camping trip—I focus on the facts. His jacket is pressed, his face clean-shaven, his general tidiness not at all like that of a tramp. "Can I help?" he says to Mother, indicating the trunk.

I notice his use of *can* when *may* is correct and wonder whether Mother will point out the error, but she only says, "Thank you," and steps aside.

"I'll take your bedroll," I say.

He hands it to me. "Where to?" he asks, lifting the trunk from the trolley and effortlessly swinging it onto his shoulder. Introductions have not been made, and I wonder if it is out of deference to Mother, who has not offered her hand.

"Glenview," Mother says. "But don't go out of your way."

"I'm heading to the whirlpool."

"You're camping?" I ask.

He nods, and we set off along River Road, walking three abreast.

"It's late to be setting up camp," I say.

"I already have a spot pretty much set up, a cave in the gorge wall. I've camped there since I was a kid, with my grandfather at first."

As he walks he holds his head in a way that makes it seem he is listening to the river. His intensity is such that to speak would be to interrupt. "It's worked up tonight," he says.

"What is?" I ask, though I am almost sure I know what he meant.

"The river. The wind's from the west."

"I could see the river from my window at the academy."

Too polite to do more than hint, Mother clears her throat.

He smiles, his eyes straight ahead, reflecting pinpricks of moonlight. "I've heard the nuns keep a vigil there, that there's always one of them praying."

Years ago Archbishop Lynch purchased the land on which the academy stands and deeded it to the Loretto community of nuns. He had seen a picture of the falls as a boy and thought it would make an idyllic place to adore the Creator of heaven and earth. The notion of the mist above the plunge pool shepherding prayers along to God stayed with him through the years, and soon enough a sister or one of the girls was always in the academy chapel, folded hands tucked beneath her chin. What better way to honor the archbishop's vision than a continual stream of prayer? Every girl at Loretto knows this bit of history, this lore behind the most sacred of the academy's traditions. "Perpetual adoration," I say.

"It's true then, the nuns believe the mist floats their prayers up to heaven?"

"I've seen what look like bits of silver hovering above the falls," I say.

He nods, seeming to give careful consideration to my flecks, and then says, "Some people can't see much beyond the ends of their noses."

"I've seen bubbles where the colors are brighter."

"Honestly, Bess," Mother says.

"I'd like to see that," he says, quietly enough to rule out defiance, loudly enough to let me know he is on my side.

A ways farther on, I make out Glenview, with its square front section facing the river and its rectangular rear. It stands atop the bluff without a single light lit. But even in darkness, Glenview is grand. The front façade is arranged symmetrically, with two ground-floor bay windows and a projecting central bay capped by a gable pediment. The builder had not skimped, and Mother likes to recite the evidence—the raised quoins of each corner, the hood moldings over each window and door, the keystones cut from single pieces of rock.

"You're lucky, living in Silvertown," he says, "so close to the river."

Mother would be unhappy to hear it said we live in Silvertown, though it is true. Surrounding our house on land subdivided long since the days when it was farmed, a neighborhood commonly called Silvertown houses the workers of the International Silver Company, a stone's throw away.

The presence of the silver factory is likely the reason Father was able to afford Glenview, though I doubt that when Mother agreed she had anticipated the number of workers who would opt to live so close by or the extent to which the polishers, grinders, and burnishers on the payroll would have names like Lococo and Petrullo and Cupolo.

At Glenview he sets my trunk on the veranda and whisks away the hand Mother holds out offering him several coins. He tips his cap to Mother and then to me. I hold my breath, thinking of what I might say other than "Thank you," which I have already said twice.

In the entrance hall I count to ten and say, "He forgot his bedroll." Then I set off across the yard without giving Mother a chance to intervene.

"Your bedroll," I say, when I have nearly caught up.

"I'll be needing it," he says, without seeming surprised to find me on his heels.

"It's a warm enough evening."

"It'll cool off in a bit."

I want to change the conversation from the weather, which is a sure sign there is nothing to say. "I suppose the ground can get pretty hard."

"Yep." He nudges the packed dirt at the side of the road with the toe of his boot.

I want to ask his name, but the courage with which I set out after him has deserted me. "Well, then," I say and pause awkwardly before saying, "Good night."

"Good night," he says back.

Before I have a chance to contemplate our parting, he is walking away from me, toward the river.

In the same four-poster bed I have slept in since I was a child, I am unable to sleep. I do my best to focus on the walk from the trolley stop, and am able to conjure an image of him rolling the stiffness from his shoulder after he set down my trunk. Still, other less pleasant details elbow their way into my thoughts: No maid opened the door and ushered Mother and me inside before hurrying off to fetch tea. The coverlet of my bed was not turned down. Far worse, no father clapped me on the back, welcoming me home. No sister flung her arms around my neck.

Last year Isabel made meringue cookies for my homecoming and we laughed our heads off, I with strands of the cotton batting she had stuffed inside each cookie stuck between my teeth.

Though I am home, in Father's house, and he would not approve, I creep out of bed and lift my rosary from a corner of my trunk, where it is hidden beneath my underclothes. He likes to remind me that I am a Methodist, despite more than a decade of attending Mass each morning. What he does not know is that I sometimes joined the other girls in taking the Blessed Sacrament, that I have kept a rosary deep in my pocket for a half dozen years and sometimes bless myself with the sign of the cross.

Fingers sliding from crucifix to beads, I race through the Apostles' Creed, an Our Father, three Hail Marys, and a Glory Be. I linger on the fifth bead and pray in earnest.

O Father, forgive me, my family, our sins. Save us from the misery and poverty that I do not think we know how to bear. We are in need of your mercy, all of us. I am afraid. Amen.

Then I sleep.

The Reporter, April 7, 1848

NEWCOMER RESCUES MEN FROM RIVERBED

There is a newcomer in town, Fergus Cole, and at least a dozen men owe their lives to him. He came from the Ottawa Valley logging camps, arriving a week ago, March 30, the date plenty of folks are calling the day the falls stood still. It was a curious sight that met him—the cliff face of Niagara's famous cataract with so little water going over it that he was able to walk a good ways out onto the riverbed. Half the town was out there, in the mud, milling around, some with logging carts recovering lost timbers, others digging up relics from the War of 1812.

By nightfall the crowd had thinned and Mr. Cole got it in his head that the river was only blocked at its mouth by jammed-up ice. "I remembered the wind changing directions a day earlier, all of a sudden gusting hard from the west," he said. Though he claims he is not much of a geographer, he knew enough to recall that Lake Erie fed the river and that its axis ran east–west. He decided that thawing ice had accumulated in the middle of the lake, that when the wind shifted the entire flotilla of ice was blown into the mouth of the river all at once, becoming lodged. "I knew the dam wouldn't last, not with the pounding wind," he said. He warned as many people as would listen, and some left the riverbed. "When I felt the earth tremble beneath my feet, I started yelling and scooping up folks and pushing the ones I couldn't carry toward shore." According to several onlookers, he was kicked and insulted, even threatened with a bayonet. James Stephens, a straggler dragged from the riverbed just moments before the Niagara came hurtling down the channel like a tidal wave, said, "He grabbed me by the collar and hollered in my face, 'Can't you hear the river coming back?' I tried to shake loose. Not a single one of us could hear the low rumble Fergus Cole could."

Mr. Cole waves away any suggestion of his arrival putting him off. "That river's something special," he said. "I'll be setting down roots."

3

At Loretto breakfast consisted of oatmeal or farina, and toast. All the meals at Glenview had been prepared by Bride, our Irish cook. If there was oatmeal, it was served with figs and strawberries, and always a second dish: codfish, creamed or in cakes; eggs poached with spinach; fruit turnovers; pineapple flan. The dining room table was set with linen, and Hilde, the housemaid, poured tea and told me to *eat up* so she could get on with closing the bedroom windows and making up the aired beds.

This morning a basket, covered with a cloth, sits on the dining room table midway between the plates at the spots where Father and I usually sit. I lift a corner of the cloth and find biscuits beneath. I head for the kitchen, thinking there might be a pot of tea warming on the range.

Mother turns toward me from the sink, where her arms had been buried elbow deep in suds. "Good morning," she says.

"Where's Father?"

"He'll be down in a minute."

"And Isabel?"

"She takes her breakfast in bed." She looks thoughtful for a moment and then throws her palms upward as though she were at her wits' end. "She hardly eats a thing, only biscuits and only because I threatened her with Dr. Galveston coming again."

"Dr. Galveston's been to the house?"

"She's used to having things her own way, and, well, life at Glenview has changed. I've had to let Bride and Hilde go." She hesitates a moment, wiping her hands dry, watching me. "I'm so glad you're home," she finally says. "Dr. Galveston says Isabel needs rest and sunshine, but mostly she needs to think positive thoughts. And I haven't spent as much time with her as I should. I'm sewing frocks again."

"A dressmaker?" Though Mother is a whiz with needle and thread, a skill picked up way back when Father was only a clerk, it is difficult to imagine her bent over a sewing machine rather than ambling about the garden with Hilde in tow, carrying a handful of freshly cut peonies.

"I've made seven dresses and have orders for nine more. Mrs. Atwell convinced me I could earn a decent wage, and then she ordered the first three."

Mrs. Atwell is Kit's mother, and though I have known her for years, I cannot recall ever having seen her in anything that was not a good decade out of date.

"The dresses really are marvels compared to her usual frocks," Mother says. "And every time she gets a compliment she hands out one of the cards she insisted on having printed up with 'Margaret Heath, Dressmaker' and my telephone number. Mrs. Coulson gave me my next couple of orders."

Mr. Coulson had been a favored underling of Father's at the Niagara Power Company, and Father often said how clever and diligent and loyal Mr. Coulson was, which to my mind did little to offset the fact that he was pockmarked and stout, to use the polite word, and very nearly bald though he was ten years Father's junior. Father had hired him as a clerk, promoted him to floor manager and then to director of operations.

Mrs. Coulson, with her long neck, full bosom, and extraordinary height, is possibly the most daunting woman I know. Isabel and I were always a little awestruck when she came to the house, and then delighted to be sent upstairs with one of her coats. Though she never hesitated to scold children who were not her own, we would bury our faces and fingers in plush velvet, shearling trim, rosewater-scented mink, and then, once we had worked up the nerve, slip the garment over our own paltry frames and admire the transformation in the wardrobe mirror. "She's the last woman on earth to need another dress," I say.

"Mr. Coulson was appointed company director after your father was let go, and I suppose they think it's the least they can do."

"We're taking charity, then?"

Mother's lips become a thin line, her gaze lingering until my hand flits to a stray lock of hair. "I've been busy and Isabel's been alone too much," she says, "but that's where you come in."

"Should I go up now?"

"After breakfast you can take her a tray, just a biscuit and some tea." She glances at the clock. "What on earth is keeping your father?"

From the lower landing she calls up the stairs, and a few minutes later Father comes into the kitchen in the frock coat and starched collar of a working gentleman. "Bess," he says, clapping me on the back. "At last, you return."

The frock coat and cheerful greeting give me hope that some good news has come his way. But the business day began at least an hour ago, and he moves through the kitchen as though he has all the time in the world. "Yes," I say. "I'm finally home."

"And the festivities last night, how'd it all turn out?"

"The dining hall was beautiful, knee deep in roses and peonies," Mother says.

"If I'm not mistaken, you were in a play?" Father says.

I pause a moment, thinking of the picture Mother has set. "It went really well," I say.

"Jolly good." He lifts the cloth from the basket.

Before heading upstairs, Mother pours his tea and sets the pot on the table so I can help myself. She no longer has the time to ask about my plans for the day and then sit listening as though foraging for wild rhubarb were the most interesting activity in the world, to cram a year's worth of mothering into a few short months as Isabel and I used to tease.

Father is a small man, with large ears, a slender face, and a narrow chin. His eyebrows are bushy and separated by a crevice that deepens when he shifts his attention to some unshared thought. It can happen during a meal, a game of crokinole, or even midsentence as he speaks. Today, as he spreads butter on biscuits and stirs sugar into tea, his focus stays with me, but the crevice remains.

I bite into a biscuit, and while it is edible, I am struck by its heaviness and again bemoan that Bride has been let go.

"Your mother's victory biscuits," Father says. "She's saving the white flour for the boys overseas." Then he moves on to inquiring about my grades, about my progress in geometry and algebra and my lack of the same in harp, which I took up to escape sitting alongside Sister Louisa at the piano explaining, yet again, my failure to master Bach's "Minuet in G." Unruffled, he asks about the daughters of several of his former business associates. I nod and smile and say, "She'll win the prize for elocution next year" or "She's off to Boston for a holiday," as Mother would expect me to. He even brings up the tea dress I made for Isabel's trousseau.

"The dress turned out wonderfully," I say, even though it is balled in a corner of my trunk, wrinkled and out of sight.

"Jolly good."

I am at a loss for words. I cannot mention the power company, a topic once guaranteed to trigger a lengthy response. And his colleagues and associates might be precarious terrain. And though it is what I most want to know, I am afraid to ask where he is headed, dressed as he is.

He picks up yesterday's *Evening Review* from beside his plate and flips it open. "That Beck," he says. "He's at it again."

Most of Father's colleagues in the hydroelectric industry have nothing but loathing for Sir Adam Beck, and it is easy to understand why. He had given up politics and become the chairman of the Hydro-Electric Power Commission, set up by the premier to build the transmission lines that would carry Niagara's power all over Ontario but also to keep a watchful eye on the power companies, like Father's onetime employer.

Even so, Father admires him. We have had a Conservative government in Ontario for the last ten years, and Father insists it was Beck's campaign— that Niagara's water power should belong to the people of Canada—that got them in. Before Beck, nearly every bit of the electricity made by the powerhouses on the Canadian side of the river was shipped off to the United States. More than once I had watched as Father lifted whatever tumbler was nearby and said, "Here's to Beck. Without him, there'd be no Hydro-Electric Power Commission, no transmission lines, not much in the way of industry in Ontario."

"What's he up to?" I say, hopeful that, as in the old days, Father will have plenty to impart.

"He hasn't given up on building a powerhouse at Queenston." He swallows the last of his tea and wipes his mustache free of biscuit crumbs.

"He'll get his way. And you know what else? Any powerhouse he builds will dwarf the rest of them."

"But isn't he supposed to stick with transmission lines?" I say, certain I had once heard Father thank his lucky stars Beck's mandate had not included the generation of electricity.

Father lifts an open palm in my direction, halting me. "Beck made sure all the newspapers covered it when word got out our powerhouses were charging more in Canada than in the U.S. And then he kicked up a fuss about the powerhouses siphoning off more water from the river than their charters set out."

"The newspapers had a heyday," I say, remembering.

"He's been at it for a while, making sure everyone thinks the private power companies are as unscrupulous as they come. He'll get his mandate changed. Clever old Beck, he'll have it put to a vote. People love him. He's taken on the stuffed shirts and brought them cheap electricity, and you're too young to remember the coal famine, but plenty of voters do and plenty of them think it's Beck who'll keep them from ever again shivering in the dark." With that he gathers his top hat and portfolio from the bench in the entrance hall, says, "I'm off," and disappears out the front door.

From the upstairs hallway, I call past Isabel's partially open door, "I've brought biscuits and tea."

"Bess!" she says, and I push the door fully open with my hip.

Isabel was flirtatious and charming in the way only the prettiest girls dared to be, the sort of girl it would be easy to dislike. But she was one of the most popular to have graduated from the academy, maybe the only girl ever to have simultaneously held the office of president for both the Athletic Association and the Gamma Kappa fraternity. Her marks were short of excellent, only because she could too often be found in the cozy little clubroom of the Gamma Kappa, chattering over a game of mah-jongg or sneaking off to short-sheet the bed of an unsuspecting dorm mate.

But as I look at her now, she seems an altogether different person from the sister I know. Her complexion, once as smooth and pale as fresh cream, has lost the hint of ginger that keeps pallor in check. And her hair lies uncombed on her pillow, without the luster that comes with proper care. Worst of all, the bones of her cheeks and shoulders jut at sharp angles from beneath her scant flesh.

She pushes herself to sitting, struggling with the pillow behind her back. "Thank God you're home," she says. "I've missed you so much."

I set the tray on the foot of her bed and straighten the pillow myself. "You're so thin."

"Never mind about that," she says.

"You have to eat." I hand her the plate with the biscuit on it.

"Please, Bess. Don't make a fuss." She sets the plate on a small table beside her bed. "Mother's nagging is enough."

My fingers bristle, momentarily poised to return the plate to her lap, but I only say, "I've missed you, too. No one ever tells me anything except you."

"Oh, Bess," she says, "I wish I had better news."

"What's going on?"

She unclasps her bracelet, a series of ten linked oval plaques, each delicately embossed with tiny stars and edged with gilded cord, then re-clasps it around her thin wrist. Father had given it to her as a graduation gift two years ago. We were in the academy parlor, waiting for a slice of cake, when he pulled a small felt pouch from his pocket and showed the bracelet to Mother, Isabel, and me. He made much of the fact that it was hammered and chipped from a sheet of aluminum a half century ago, back when aluminum was as valuable as gold. As he handed her the bracelet, he said it was only recently that the scientists had figured out how to use electricity to make large quantities of aluminum from bauxite, a plentiful ore remarkably like dirt. It did little to convince the three of us of the bracelet's worth. His excitement waned momentarily, as he seemed to consider for the first time that Isabel might associate aluminum with the inner workings of an automobile. "Keep it in your jewelry box," he said, patting her hand, but she fastened the bracelet around her wrist and said, "I'll wear it every day."

The bracelet clatters dully as Isabel's hand flops onto the bed. "There isn't going to be an aluminum smelter in Niagara Falls," she says.

I had often heard father rhapsodizing in the academy parlor on Sunday afternoons about incomparable aluminum—beautiful to the eye, whiter than silver, indestructible by contact with air, strong, elastic, and so light that the imagination almost refuses to think of it as a metal. He said aluminum would turn Niagara Falls, with its never-ending stream of hydroelectricity, into an industrial power.

"Father and Mr. O'Reilly and Mr. Woodruff and God only knows who else bet their fortunes on the smelter," she says. "Everyone says Father prompted all the fuss."

"Their fortunes?"

"A couple of them had been promised orders from the Ministry of Militia and Defense if they sank a bit of cash into retooling their factories. But Father insisted the war wouldn't last. He made promises, said the smelter was a done deal, a sure bet."

I sit down on the edge of the bed. "But he wouldn't have said it if it wasn't true."

"He thought it was. A bunch of bigwigs from Toronto wanted the smelter, and Father was in on the discussions because his powerhouse was supposed to supply the electricity."

"They backed out?"

She nods, lets out a huff. "Yep, once all but the final documents were signed. And by then Father and his so-called pals had paid top dollar for land around the site and dumped loads of cash into everything from machinery for aluminum cookware to mail-order homes for the workers."

"Why'd the financiers back out?" My shoulders inch up.

"They said they couldn't make aluminum as cheaply as it's made at Shawinigan Falls. It's rubbish, though. With the war, it's easier to make money churning out explosives and artillery shells."

"There's nothing left?"

"Nothing," she says. "And it's a whole lot easier for everyone to blame Father for their troubles than to admit their own greed. No one's got time for him anymore, no one except Mr. Coulson. And I'll bet he's pleased as punch to have Father's job."

"Mr. Coulson is devoted to Father."

"I know. I know," she says, waving away my words. "Even so, he's as ambitious as they come. And Mrs. Coulson, too. She hasn't got the time of day for anyone with a smidgen less clout than Mr. Coulson."

"She used to bring us ribbons and paper dolls."

"Father was Mr. Coulson's boss."

Not quite ready to adopt Isabel's view, I pick at a thread on the coverlet. "She still gives Mother the time of day."

"Then she must figure Father isn't down and out for good."

"But if she thinks he'll get his job back . . ."

"There's no chance. Mr. Cruickshank had him sacked. That much I know. He must have gotten wind of the aluminum scheme."

"So?"

"Near as I can tell, he decided he didn't want his son involved with a bankrupt family, and the break would be a whole lot cleaner if he had Father sacked. At any rate, he could hardly keep Father on, not when he's on the outs with a half dozen of Niagara Power's customers." Her gaze falls to the coverlet.

"Did Boyce tell you that?"

"When he broke off our engagement, he just stood there, a great cringing coward, hardly looking up from his feet."

"I'm sorry," I say, tucking my heels beneath me so that I am sitting cross-legged on the bed.

"Don't be." She shakes her head. "He's spineless. He never could stand up to his father. I don't know why I ever thought that he would."

"We'll figure something out."

She raises her fingers to her temples, closes her eyes. "It gets worse," she says. "Father disappears every day and only comes back after midnight."

"He went out this morning, in his frock coat."

"He goes to one of the hotels. I'm almost sure. He's drinking too much. I've heard him late at night, stumbling up the stairs."

"What?" My voice suggests shock, yet somehow it feels I have only been reminded of what I already knew, at least since the evening before, when I first glimpsed Mother in the dining hall, twisting the program in her hands. She sat alone, an aisle on one side and on the other three empty seats, a gap Mr. and Mrs. Huntington had chosen to leave. Father had lost his job and his fortune, and convinced a handful of his colleagues to gamble away theirs. Even so, there was something more that had caused folks to turn their backs on a woman as respected as Mother, something truly appalling, like a husband whiling away the days with his nose in a pint, particularly with so many young men suffering overseas.

"Last week I told him I could smell the whiskey on him," Isabel says. "He said I sounded like a prohibitionist, and I said if prohibition meant keeping fathers sober, then, war or no war, maybe I was. He left after that, some excuse about getting to the post office before the mail was picked up. He's drinking, and Mother knows it and just pretends everything will be fine as long as she manages five dresses a week."

"We could help with the sewing," I say.

She folds her arms. "We'll earn enough for biscuits and tea, and if we work our fingers to the bone, maybe a ham at Christmastime."

"Mother used to do all right as a dressmaker."

"Father was working as a clerk," she says, "and they lived behind the slaughterhouse, and smelled blood and entrails all day long. They didn't have two daughters to support."

Dr. Galveston prescribed sunshine and rest and positive thoughts for Isabel, and so far I have only set her worrying whether there will be a ham at Christmastime. "Let's talk about something else."

"I've said my news—Father drinks, Mother sews."

"Just try, Isabel."

She sighs, says, "Tell me about Loretto."

There is a pause while I search for some scrap of safe news. "A young man helped Mother and me with my trunk last night. We took the trolley."

"Father didn't show up."

"I'd guess he was a couple of years older than I am," I say, refusing a return to the topic of Father. "He was camping at the whirlpool."

"You met him on the trolley?" she says, eyeing me skeptically. "What does he do?"

"He was wearing a workingman's clothes, but they were tidy, and plenty of gentlemen wouldn't have bothered to help."

She huffs, a clipped bit of laughter. "A shopgirl could do better if she played her cards right."

It is the sort of sentiment I expect from Mother, not from Isabel, who is almost always delighted with any whiff of romance. "No one else offered to help," I say.

"I'm surprised Mother didn't decide the two of you should carry the trunk yourselves."

"He carried the trunk on his shoulder, like it was nothing at all."

And then for a moment she is her old self, speaking with the impish grin that says "I am in cahoots with you." "Remember the heart from the birthday cake set?" she says. "You were promised true love."

I found the heart at Isabel's last birthday party, hidden inside a forkful of cake I had placed in my mouth. I slid my tongue over the metal, hoping for the heart, the token we all wanted most. But when I felt the hollow place where the two lobes met, I thought I had ended up with the thimble, which meant spinsterhood. I was pleased when I took the heart from my mouth, even more so when Kit picked a tiny, silver wishbone from her slice of cake. The wishbone, along with her good luck, confirmed the prophetic ability of the birthday cake set, even if Isabel was laughing and holding up the spinster's thimble, unperturbed. By then she was engaged to Boyce Cruickshank and the tokens meant nothing at all.

The heart is in a square tin in the bottom of my trunk, alongside a mishmash of programs—the Feast of the Nativity of Our Lady, Loretto Day, a Christmas pageant—also, a geometry examination on which I scored one hundred percent, several bits of embroidery I completed as a child, and the ribbon I was given for the prize for sewing. I do not know why I keep the heart. It is not useful or particularly pretty, and I know it is nonsensical and superstitious to believe in a birthday cake set. And it seems entirely wrong to hope for a bit of magic when an implication of the magic is a sister's spinsterhood.

I would like the conversation to linger on the heart and true love, but the thimble and spinsterhood are an easy leap away, so I say, "I bet we could find him. I've seen him before, one Saturday outing at the river."

"Bess," she says. "The Boyce Cruickshanks of the world might be out of the question, but you're pretty and clever and kind. You don't have to settle, not entirely."

"It's not like I'm marrying him, and besides, Father had nothing when Mother met him."

Again, that huff. "Case in point."

I want to tell her she is acting like Mother, but she appears fragile against the starched-white linens and the solid wood of the headboard, not at all herself. "I'll open the window," I say.

As I struggle with the window sash, I notice, just beyond the pane, small pieces of biscuit sitting on the windowsill. The birds left the crumbs behind, their bellies already full. I turn to her, my eyes surely saying what I know.

"If you tell Mother," she says, "I'll have to mention your crush."

"You're not well." I hand her the plate, roughly, so that the biscuit nearly slides onto her lap.

Suddenly she is weeping, tears silently streaming down her cheeks, unhindered by an attempt to wipe them away. "You're right," she says. "I'm not well."

What has become of my sister? Where is the girl who once taped a handy list of possible offenses to the confessional wall at the academy, the girl who let me borrow her rose chiffon gown even though she had not yet worn it herself, the girl who took so long to say good night that she regularly fell asleep in my bed? "I won't tell, but you have to eat the biscuit."

She places a small piece into her mouth and chews until it can be nothing more than a watery pulp. With great concentration, she swallows. I watch her throat constrict, also the barely perceptible heave that follows, convincing me she will be sick. Once half the biscuit is gone, I say, "That's enough."

She hands me what remains, and I place it on the windowsill with yesterday's crumbs.

Mother is in the spare bedroom, which I suppose I should call a sewing room now. The bed is gone, replaced by bolts of fabric, a dressmaker's mannequin, and a sewing machine. She is on her knees, pinning a craft-paper pattern of her own making to a length of pale gray silk. I piece together the forms, the almost rectangle of a skirt, the convex cap of a sleeve tapering to the wrist, the four pieces of a bodice, the smaller forms of the waistband, neckline facing, and cuffs.

On her feet, she lifts a length of the same silk from the back of a chair and says, "Take a look." She loosely gathers the fabric and sweeps it back and forth, causing it to catch and reflect light as a swaying skirt might. She holds up a delicate tulle, a coil of rouleau, and another of soutache, all of the same luminous gray. The end result of her handiwork will be quietly elegant, refined in a way that will set it apart from the flounced and sequined frocks at the party where the gown will first appear.

"Mrs. Coulson's third order," she says. "It's for a party at the Clifton House. The Chamberlains' eldest girl is coming out."

"Are we invited?" Even as the words leave my mouth, I know I should not have asked. The Chamberlains are acquaintances, unfamiliar enough to dodge any obligation others might feel.

She shakes her head and says, "But I'll have two gowns there: Mrs. Coulson's, and Mrs. Atwell is wearing one, too."

"I can pull out basting threads or sew on buttons or run up the seams," I say, "until I prove myself."

"You proved yourself with the tea dress. I unpacked your trunk this morning. Such a pretty thing deserves better than the corner of a trunk. You can press it later." She returns to her knees, smooths the craft-paper cuff over the silk, and begins to pin it into place. "I won't let you cut. Not yet. The fabric is too expensive and I haven't got time for another trip to Toronto. I'll look after the fitting. You can hand me the pins and chalk, and learn as much as you can."

So I am to work for the first time in my life. I can almost feel a needle between my fingers, basting together bodice seams, each stitch exactly the same length as the one before. There is serenity in sewing, maybe something like what I found sitting in my window seat.

"But Isabel takes priority," she says, looking up from the silk.

"She's sleeping." At least her cheek was on the pillow and her eyes were lightly shut when I tiptoed from her room. I let her think she had me convinced, even though her breathing had not slowed. She is not the type to be a burden, not now. Not ever.

"How did she seem?" Mother says.

"She didn't eat much, a biscuit and a few sips of tea."

Mother lets out a sigh, and it nearly causes me to run down the hallway and gather the crumbs from the windowsill and tell Isabel she must eat them no matter what, but surely it would be better to entice her with something other than the biscuit crumbs. "Are the strawberries by the back fence ready to be picked?" I say.

"I've been meaning to check."

At first blush, Mother's garden seems as immaculate as always. Intricate blooms of columbine nod in midmorning sun. Coneflowers stand erect, their central cores thrust forward, bristling with seeds. But all except the hardiest spires of foxglove and delphinium lay toppled, stalks collapsed under the weight of their own flowers. Peonies droop, their heavy blooms, unsupported by stakes, decaying on the ground. Beneath the garden's canopy of foliage, purslane spreads its weedy tendrils. Fronds of yarrow and tapered blades of crabgrass poke through once orderly beds of hosta and cranesbill. Instinctively, my fingers seek the base of a clump of crabgrass and gently ease the roots from the soil. As I reach for another, I see Mother has made a decision. Beauty is superfluous, beyond what we need to live. The weeds fall from my fingertips.

The strawberry crop is meager, half-choked by a tangle of silver-lace vine. As a child, I had been given the task of carefully untwisting the vine from the strawberry bushes. Today the work is tedious, though it had seemed pleasant enough back when a summer morning was only something to fritter away. I pinch off an offending tendril and let it fall to the garden floor, where it will rot in the shade.

Once I have gathered a small bowl of strawberries, I walk past the house into the front yard. Here, too, the gardens are unkempt, although slightly less so than in the back, as if Mother had not given up the pretense of order in the front quite so early on.

When I notice the faint rumble of the Niagara River tumbling through the gorge, I move closer, to the front of our property, and listen to the Whirlpool Rapids far below. I stand with my eyes shut, imagining great waves of surging green crashing and toppling to masses of frothy white. When I open my eyes, the fellow who carried my trunk is passing along River Road, likely returning from his camp at the whirlpool. He tips his cap, and I quickly turn away, embarrassed at the thought of myself a moment earlier, listening to the river.

As I reach for the screen door, I look over my shoulder intending to wave but, too late, see only his back. Three fair-size fish hang from a line slung over his shoulder. His bedroll swings back and forth in time with his gait. When he is far enough away that I can no longer tell his collar from his cap, I see him look back toward Glenview. I wave, and it seems he nods, though I cannot say for sure.

I decide then and there I will supervise Isabel's convalescence outdoors. She will sit on the veranda, and I will read to her from the collection of books Sister Ignatius piled in my arms. I will speak to Mother about moving the chaise longue to the veranda and bring down a wool blanket from the cedar-lined chest. Isabel will eat strawberries and tomatoes and cucumbers straight from the garden, and sip lemonade. But with Mother's commitment to sparing food for the troops, had she found time to plant the vegetable patch this year?

At any rate, my vigil will begin tomorrow. The fellow with the river eyes will not pass by again, not today.

4

Coaxing Isabel into the garden has remained a difficult task for the two weeks since my return. Always, the sun is too hot or the air too thick with humidity or the flies too bothersome. This morning, she says the day is too bright. The sun has in fact washed much of the color from the sky, leaving it a cloudless, faded blue, and I will have to squint away the light reflecting from the page as I read. But still I insist we move outdoors. I will not begin reading until we do. And Mother, well aware of Dr. Galveston's prescription for sunshine, says, "Out with the both of you." Then she is off to Toronto by steamboat in search of yard goods, leaving me alone with Isabel. Once, a day on our own would have meant frivolity, an adventure plotted by Isabel that I would have anticipated for a week. Would she fluster a hack driver by speaking to him in a language she was making up on the spot? Would she have made arrangements for us to meet up with a couple of the older brothers we had met in the academy parlor?

Instead she slouches on the chaise I dragged out to the veranda and complains when I place a dish of raspberries in her lap. Such has been the case for anything other than her beloved strawberries, and they were finished a week ago. When she finally swallows a berry, I seat myself in the wicker rocking chair and open *A Tale of Two Cities*.

Yesterday we finished *The Hound of the Baskervilles*. I loved it, at least until Holmes proved there was no supernatural black hound. I disliked that science trumped superstition in the end, that the common folk with their unfounded beliefs were made to look like fools. "You've gone soft in the head, believing in the miraculous," Isabel said.

"I've always believed in miracles."

"So, same as God, you believe in magic black dogs?"

I slid a hand along the wicker arm of my chair. "Sister Leocrita would call that blasphemy."

"Since when have you bothered about Sister Leocrita? Wasn't she the one who told you your bits of hovering tin were nothing more than tired eyes?"

"Make fun of me all you want. I know what I've seen."

She is silent throughout the first two chapters of *A Tale of Two Cities,* which is usual enough with her tendency to nod off. Hoping another paragraph or two will do the trick, I begin the third:

A wonderful fact to reflect upon, that every human creature is constituted to be that profound secret and mystery to every other.

If she slept, I could finish the buttonholes Mother left out for me. I glance in her direction. "Go on," she says.

A solemn consideration, when I enter a great city by night, that every one of those darkly clustered houses encloses its own secret; that every room in every one of them encloses its own secret; that every beating heart in the hundreds of thousands of breasts there, is, in some of its imaginings, a secret to the heart nearest it!

"It sounds like Dickens has figured out a thing or two," she says.

I shrug. The words strike me as grim, nothing it will do Isabel a bit of good to debate.

"All humans are mysteries to one another," she says.

"I'm not so sure."

"Do you think you know me?" She flicks a fallen leaf from the chaise.

"Yes," I say. But the lighthearted sister I once knew seems almost entirely gone, replaced by the infuriating girl sitting with me now.

"You don't."

"I want to," I say, closing the book. "Tell me something I don't know."

"Keep reading," she says.

And I do, though lounging on the veranda has begun to seem indulgent with Mother bent over the sewing machine and the notices in every newspaper discouraging idleness. There are bandages to be rolled, socks and scarves and wristlets to be knit, flannel shirts and pillowcases to be sewn.

A short while later I glimpse a figure approaching on River Road. I raise the book from my knees, so I only have to lift my eyes slightly to keep watch. Once I make out a tall fellow with a bedroll and a flat cap, I stumble through a few more paragraphs, losing my spot on the page several times.

Since my vigil began, it is the second time I have spotted him on River Road. The first time, he tipped his cap when he was just opposite the house and I gingerly lifted my palm to him, all the while continuing to read in a steady voice. Isabel's eyes remained downcast, on her fingers tracing the velvet piping of the chaise, and I thought I had fooled her.

But just now as I peek over the top of the book, her gaze meets mine. "Go ahead," she says. "Wave to your drudge."

I slam the book closed and stand, waving boldly overhead, more so once I remember that Mother has gone to Toronto and that Father left the house in a frock coat, the wrinkled one he was wearing the day before. A while back Mother would have told him he looked unkempt and pressed the coat. She said nothing this morning, and it made me think she does not care to impress the company he keeps. Still, I have seen the thin line her lips become when he appears at the breakfast table only after she has had to call up the stairs a half dozen times. I bet she listens late at night, same as I do, for his key in the lock, for the subsequent stumble up the stairs.

To my dismay and delight, my wave is returned, and he crosses River

Road and heads toward the slope leading to the high ground of our property. When he stops at the front walk of a small house along the way, my spirits sink. A squat mistress rises from the vegetable patch and shuffles over to him. She waits there, folding her arms, shaking her head, gesticulating her refusal, until she reaches into the pocket of her apron and exchanges a handful of coins for a fish he unties from his line. As he turns to continue up the slope, Isabel says, "He's a fishmonger, for God's sake."

When he cannot possibly be headed anywhere but Glenview, I walk to the front gate and open it.

"She wanted the pike," he says, jutting his chin toward the woman below, "but it's for you." He holds out a long, spotted fish, and I reach for it, hesitantly. I have never held a fish. "Do you know how to gut it?"

"You could show me," I say.

Because it seems I should already know his name, I do not ask it and introduce him to Isabel as the fellow who helped Mother and me with the trunk. She says, "Hello," but does not offer her hand. It is awkwardly silent for a moment, until he says to me, "Where's the water pump?"

We leave her on the veranda and walk around to the back of the house. He selects a flat piece of wood from the woodpile as we go. At the pump he lays the fish on the wood and says, "First, it needs to be scaled. Hang on to it by the tail."

I grasp the fish. "Like this?"

He nods and holds out a knife with a bone handle. I take it, my fingertips grazing his knuckles. "The blade needs to snag the free edge of the scales."

"Tail to head, then?" I say.

"Right."

My eyes on the pike, I try to make short work of the task. "In dressmaking we call it against the nap."

From his silence, I take it he has not understood.

"Think of velvet," I say. "Run a hand over its surface, with the nap and it's silky smooth, against the nap and it's less so."

"Can't say I've had a whole lot of experience with velvet."

"Well, your fingers would leave a trail," I say, thinking about the ordinariness of velvet in my life. I clear the scales collected on the knife blade on the edge of the wood.

While I pump, he rinses the fish, his forearms extending beyond his turned-up shirtsleeves. I have always considered myself somewhat squeamish, maybe because I was expected to be. But once he shows me where to insert the knife, I slit open the belly and pull the innards from the fish easily enough. As instructed, I lift the gill covers and pull them away, and cut along each side of the dorsal fin and lift it upward along with the root bones. My cheeks grow hot under his gaze.

"Can you cook?" he says.

Until recently my experience in the kitchen was limited to the pie and bread Bride used to let me help with. But to admit it might give the impression that I am lazy and spoiled, and I am neither, not anymore. "I don't know about fish."

"Have you got forcemeat?" he says.

"Yes."

"Stuff it into the gut and sew the opening closed. I used to smear it with egg and roll it in bread crumbs, but a rye flour paste and then a bit of cornmeal works, too, if you're conserving."

"My mother's got us down to white bread once a week," I say, though I sometimes wonder if her diligence has just as much to do with necessity as it does with the war.

"We'd better get used to it." He glances away, shakes his head so solemnly that I know he is thinking of Ypres, Canada's first and only battle to date. The line had been held, but massive artillery bombardments and a poison the newspapers called chlorine gas meant that in forty-eight hours one in three Canadian soldiers was a casualty. At the outset, not quite a year ago, there had been singing and cheering in the streets, declarations that the war would be over with by Christmastime. Ypres put an end to that.

"Do you like raspberries?" I say.

"Yep."

In the kitchen I tip a bowl of raspberries over a small brown paper sack and guide the fruit through the opening. I stand at the window a moment, my hips pressed against the wooden lip of the counter, contentedly watching him. He rinses the wood on which the fish was cleaned and then rounds the corner, likely headed toward the woodpile. A moment later I whirl around, startled to hear him call my name from just outside the kitchen door. "Bess," he says, "have you got a newspaper, for the guts?"

"You know my name."

"I heard your mother say it."

"I don't know yours," I say, stepping from the kitchen into the backyard.

"Tom," he says. "Thomas Cole."

While he scrapes up the innards, I wait idly, holding the berries, mouthing the name Tom, thinking I will not call him Thomas, although the few Thomases I know all go by the more formal name. This Thomas, who sleeps by the whirlpool, and catches fish and thinks enough of me to bring me one, called himself Tom. He rinses his hands clean, and I give him the brown paper sack.

"I could bring you a fish tomorrow?" he says.

Tomorrow Mother will be home and not at all pleased with a fish offered as a gift, even if it means more beef and bacon for the troops. "I can pay you with berries." I hold out the sack.

"I don't want to be paid."

"The cherries are almost ready, and soon there'll be gooseberries. I could make a pie."

"I like fishing," he says. "I catch more than I can eat."

"We're going to have loads of cherries this year."

"Suit yourself," he says, finally taking the berries from me.

No sooner have Isabel and I settled down to reading once again than an automobile turns from River Road onto Buttrey Street. It is not Father, and he drives one of the few automobiles in Silvertown. The neighboring men walk the several blocks between their homes and the International Silver Company, and their wives either shop nearby on Erie Avenue or go by electric trolley to Centre Street, where they can barter in Italian. "Are you expecting someone?" I say.

"It's the Atwells. I recognize the Runabout." She rolls her eyes at the mention of the automobile. "They ought to get rid of it. No one drives anything with a tiller anymore." But the Atwells are not wasteful or showy, and there is the war. "I'd die of embarrassment," she says.

"Shut up, Isabel." I am sick of telling myself that Boyce Cruickshank is to blame for her mood, that he is the person I ought to be angry with.

After the Runabout comes to a halt, Kit hops down from the bench seat. "I'm learning to drive," she says. Edward, her older brother, who failed matriculation at the University of Toronto, despite the best tutors and references, waves a large hand and grins.

They have spent the fortnight since the end of the term at a cousin's cottage on Stoney Lake. I notice the subtle changes—the lightly bronzed skin, the insect bites on her wrist, the fingernails not quite so chewed to the quick as they were during final exams, the splashes of near white in her flaxen hair—and wonder if she sees how different I am. I badly want to tell her, but what can I say? I have learned to gut a fish and to flawlessly pleat a blouse. I have become adept at ignoring the crumbs left on the windowsill and putting Father from my mind, though, like Isabel, he is utterly changed. No longer does he prattle on about the chemistry of aluminum or the ease with which falling water is made into electricity. There is no talk of a future in which Niagara Falls spearheads Canada's economy. And gone are the claps on the back, the eyes welled with pride for even the smallest feats: an unremarkable square of needlepoint, a mediocre pie, a middling bit of prose. Instead he is absent, hiding from Mother, Isabel, and me.

After the requisite chitchat on the veranda, I say to Kit, "Come help me with the tea," and we go inside, leaving Edward in my rocking chair and Isabel on the chaise. In the privacy of the kitchen, my mind stumbles from Father's late nights to Isabel's poor appetite to Mother's dressmaking, and then to Tom and my trunk and the pike. Yet I am unable to begin. "How was Stoney Lake?" I finally say.

"Restful. Quiet. Boring, in a pleasant way. All the days were the same, nothing to make one different from the next. Edward was good company, though. He always is. The time flew by."

What if Dickens is right? What if I can exist only inside my own head? Spurred on by the bleakness of the thought, I say, "These two weeks have been the longest of my life."

Her shoulders slump. "Is everything still awful?"

"So much has happened."

"For instance?"

"For instance, this morning, I picked raspberries, made biscuits, fin-ished twenty-three buttonholes—there are still seven more—combed Isabel's hair, pleaded with her to eat a handful of raspberries, read to her, and gutted a fish."

"She's so thin. Too thin."

"She doesn't eat," I say, throwing up my palms.

"Boyce Cruickshank?"

I shake my head. "I don't know. She's hardly mentioned him."

"So much has gone wrong and all at once."

"There's something she isn't telling me," I say. "Mother says it's only that she's used to having her own way. But you've seen her. She's half-starved. She isn't the same. She never laughs." I feel a lump rise in my throat, and I know I must stop. Another word and my voice will break, setting loose a flood. Kit must know it, too, because she stoops to fiddle with the hem of her skirt, and she is not the sort to care whether it has come fully loose, let alone whether there is a stray thread.

When I return from fetching a handkerchief and blowing my nose, she says, "I can't believe you gutted a fish."

It is my chance to tell her about Tom, but is there anything to say? He and I have spoken politely, only about practical things—scaling a fish, westerly winds pushing water over the falls. I learned his name just this morning. And I know little other than that he spends a great deal of time on the river and can easily shoulder the weight of a trunk. We have simply exchanged a fish for some berries as neighbors might, and only after I stood and waved from the veranda, giving him little choice other than to make the climb to Glenview. But I come back to one thought, as I have all afternoon: He said he would bring me a second fish. "I met a fellow on the trolley," I say. "He brought me a pike."

"What?"

"He helped Mother and me with my trunk when I left the academy. He was heading to his camp at the whirlpool."

"You're interested?"

I do my best to hide a smile. "I don't know."

"And the pike?" I had anticipated excitement, speculation, maybe even a bit of scheming about how the three of us might meet. She is listening closely, yet I cannot help but think that she seems more put out than anything else.

"He caught six or seven fish this morning and gave me one."

"Is he a student?"

"I expect he's through with school."

"Some sort of naturalist, then?"

I set a stack of saucers on a tray. "I don't think so."

"Bess, does he sell fish?" She is clever enough to question what a fellow who catches a half dozen fish at a time does with his haul. She watches me, dubious.

"Maybe. Sometimes."

"If he's wasting his days loafing, he should enlist. Even Edward's talking about it, and he's about run off his feet with two of Father's clerks already overseas."

"Let's join the others," I say.

On the veranda I pour the tea without making a mess, which is more difficult than it sounds, given that Isabel's head is thrown back in laughter, apparently in response to the story Edward is telling, a story both of us have heard many times. It involves a hunting excursion, a ruined boot, and a bullet-grazed foot. Then, as we sit chatting, she gobbles up three rye flour gingersnaps and pours herself a second cup of tea. Still, I am most flabbergasted when the conversation turns to dressmaking and she praises the gown Mother is making for Mrs. Atwell. "Gorgeous," she says. "And you should see the tea dress Bess made me. We'll have all the ladies in town clamoring at our door."

A moment later, when Edward is out of earshot fetching the hat he forgot in the Runabout, Kit says, "He's doing a first-rate job running the furniture store," which is not surprising news. He is too patient to rush a decision, too well-mannered to offend, too decent to have anything but his customers' best interests at heart.

"Has he got a sweetheart?" Isabel asks.

"Not yet," Kit says. "He'd make a great catch."

As he crosses the garden, returning in his Panama hat, it occurs to me that he is handsome, not like Tom, certainly not like Boyce Cruickshank, and I wonder if Isabel, with her gaze trained on him, is thinking the same thought. Maybe she is through with boys like Boyce Cruickshank, boys teeming with wit and charm. Maybe Edward's simplicity has its own appeal. His lack of shrewdness might matter a whole lot less to her than it would if he were not already financially set.

I have known Edward since I can remember and have spent many a summer day with him happily shepherding Kit and me around Queen Victoria Park or Goat Island or Chippawa Creek, excursions we would never have been allowed to make on our own. And to put it bluntly, Isabel could outsmart him at every turn. So much worse, though, he seems remarkably immune to her. And I do not know that she can manage another blow, not so soon, not now.

After Edward has cranked the Runabout, and he and Kit leave, I wait for Isabel to return to her sullen self. But instead she suggests we pick raspberries to serve for dessert with the biscuits I made earlier. As we walk toward the fence in the far corner of the yard where the raspberries grow, she says, "I know I've been a great curmudgeon."

"Or worse."

She stops and turns toward me, taking both my hands in hers. "You are the kindest sister in the world and deserve better than me."

"I want you to eat."

"Tonight I will eat your pike."

In the warm glow of late afternoon sun, it seems it is the old Isabel arranging herself on a spread shawl and picking the raspberries within easy reach. I want the shadows to remain long and the sun to remain low. I want the day to remain golden and muted and rich. I want time to slow, but the raspberries must be picked and the pike has got to be stuffed and there are potatoes to peel. Mother is due home in just over an hour.

When I catch the murmur of Isabel's voice, I prick up my ears. "Edward is kind of sweet, don't you think?"

"As sweet as they come."

"He's got a nice build."

"He spends entire weekends chopping wood."

"Really?" she says. "That's the sort of thing I'd rather not know." She winks then, the way she used to, inclusively, like you are her very best friend.

A s the screen door closes behind Mother, she drops two large bundles onto the floor. "At last," she says, setting her hat on the hall table. She stands still for a moment. "Is that fish I smell?"

"Stuffed pike," I say.

"Pike?"

"The fellow who helped with the trunk came by with it."

She eyes me carefully, then picks up the bundles and signals for me to follow her up the stairs. "How much did you pay?" Her voice is restrained, careful not to chide good intentions but anxious nevertheless.

"I gave him some raspberries."

She turns to face me in the hallway and stands stock-still, searching my face. I do not look away. "Well done," she says, at last. "You have no idea how nice it is to come home starved and find supper under way."

I curtsy, lifting imaginary skirts. "Supper will be served in a half hour."

She unties the string from one of the bundles, spreads the wrappings, and shakes open a folded length of sheer, cream-colored fabric. "Silk georgette," she says. "It's for the bodice of Miss O'Leary's wedding gown. There is a lighter-weight georgette for the skirt, also silk lining, and organza to support the beadwork." She slides a box the size of a small loaf from the middle of the stacked fabric and holds it out to me. "Take a look."

I lift the lid and unfold tissue paper. The pool of smooth, creamy beads glistens and then glitters as I run a finger through it. Some are shaped like rice, others like tears. There are spheres of three sizes, the largest like a pea, the smallest, a quarter the size.

"The entire bodice will be beaded, the neckline and a band around the hips most heavily," she says. "I've worked out a pattern, all flowers and vines."

She produces a wrinkled sheet of paper on which tear- and rice-shape beads radiate from spheres, forming an assortment of flowers, each amid a tangle of gracefully curved vine shaped from more of the rice-shape beads linked end to end. "Oh, Mother," I say.

"It's more than a month's work."

"I can follow the pattern exactly."

"I'll need your help," she says, refolding the georgette. "I'll just go see Isabel a minute, and then I'll be down to set the table."

"She said she'd have supper with us, and the table is set," I say.

Mother hesitates, the georgette motionless in her hands. She smiles and says, "It's your lovely pike."

I shrug and smile back.

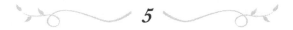

5

Tightrope walking

Eight consecutive evenings, from seven o'clock until half past nine, I have poked my needle through the organza of Miss O'Leary's wedding gown, wrong side to right, and strung a bead onto the thread, then poked my needle back though the organza and secured the thread with a knot. The pattern committed to memory, I beaded diligently, and Mother said my work was at least as good as her own. But tonight, rather than contentedly beading alongside her, I toil behind my closed bedroom door. "The light is better," I said.

I work, untroubled by the tear-shape petals lying slightly askew or the curved vines severed by eighth-inch gaps. Nor am I careful to pull the slack from the thread before making a knot. Without the ambition of perfection, the work is mindless, an empty passage of time. My only satisfaction will come later, when Mother examines the evening's progress.

Yesterday, as I carefully knotted the final bead of the evening into place, Mother's foot came off the treadle and she looked up from her work. "Tomorrow you can tell the young man who brings the fish we don't need any more," she said.

"I don't see why I should, not when we're being told to save the bacon and beef for the troops."

"I think you do." She gave me a few seconds to respond, and, when I did not, her foot settled back on the treadle. "Good night," she said over the rhythmic whir of the sewing machine.

T he first pike Tom brought was flaky and moist, not a bit dry, the way Mother said poorly cooked pike tends to be. He had come again the next day with a half dozen fish strung on his line. As I crossed the yard to the gate, I glanced over my shoulder and saw Mother at the window of the sewing room.

"Fine day," he said.

"Yes, so still."

His eyes flitted to the window twice as we stood there, at the gate, pretending to inspect the fish on his line. "Your mother is watching."

"I know," I said and felt my cheeks grow hot.

After an awkward gap, he said, "The pike turn out okay?"

"Delicious. My mother and Isabel thought so, too."

"I've only got sturgeon today." He nudged a fish. "This one's about four pounds, a good size for baking."

"I have your raspberries." I lifted a brown paper sack.

"You don't owe me anything."

"I picked them for you," I said.

He left, and I stood at the gate for a long while thinking that my imagination had run amok, that I was a silly girl with my head in the clouds. What did I want from him? Maybe only the chance to dream, a brief pause in the hard work life had become. Even so, the moment he became a shadowy figure disappearing in the distance, I began to await his return, hardly able to bear the idea of an entire day until then.

At suppertime, I watched on tenterhooks as Mother tasted her first forkful of the sturgeon. "Just lovely," she said. I had half-expected her disapproval to have made its way to the fish.

Another day, it rained and I was afraid he would not come. When he arrived at the gate, I called him to the veranda. I could hardly be criticized. I was wearing a white embroidered dress I had borrowed from Isabel and would have been scandalous soaked to the bone. "Was my mother watching?"

"I didn't see her."

"Have a seat, then," I said, "until the rain lets up." The rain was coming down in sheets, leaving the veranda a small, private room curtained from the world. "You're soaked." I wanted to offer him a towel but did not think I should risk going inside.

"This one's the best of the lot," he said, tapping a pike.

Once I finished describing how I had cooked the fish from the day before, we sat for several more minutes, each of us at a loss for words, until he finally said, "What do you think the average fellow sees when he looks at the falls?"

"I'm not sure," I said. "Loveliness?"

"Way back, people talked about its 'awful grandeur' and 'frightful beauty.'"

"Oh."

"Do you think people still see it?" He wiped a droplet of rain from his cheek.

"The majesty?"

"Sometimes it seems like the river is being made into a measly thing."

"I'm not sure I understand," I said.

He smoothes his palms over his thighs. "It started way back, when a ladder was dropped over the gorge wall so that Governor Simcoe's wife could get a better look. After that there were the covered stairs and the incline railways."

"And the bridges went up," I said.

"The river's been bound up with cables and concrete and steel, like a turkey at Christmastime."

It was the most I had ever heard him say, and his seeming idea that the river ought to be left alone took me by surprise. It was contrary to anything I had ever heard, particularly from Father, who surely thought the river was ours to use as we saw fit. "Go on," I said, curious, though I was not a bit sure I agreed with him.

He spoke next of the parade of stunters who came to Niagara, of Blondin on his tightrope leading the way. He said onlookers crowded the riverbanks and gawked into the gorge from above. Men swam in the river and navigated it in boats, sometimes without getting themselves killed. "And pretty soon there were barrels in the rapids and the whirlpool. And then, when that wasn't enough, the stunters got into their barrels above the falls."

"Annie Taylor," I said, naming the first to survive the plunge. I had seen the old schoolmarm more than once, in a shabby skirt at the top of Clifton Hill, hawking the autographed postcards that commemorated her feat.

"It's more than just the bridges and the stunters."

"How so?" I asked, wondering if the rain had let up enough that its drumming no longer kept our voices from Mother's ears.

"Way back all the water from the Great Lakes got to the Atlantic by going over the falls," he said. "Not anymore, though. The Erie and Welland canals take a bunch of it. At Chicago water is siphoned off to float the city's sewage to the Mississippi. A half dozen syndicates are clamoring for canals, all draining away water before it reaches the Niagara. They all want a shorter route to the Atlantic, with Georgian Bay hooked up with the Ottawa River, and five hundred miles cut out of the trip."

"There's an awful lot of water going over the brink."

"Someone's got to say, 'enough is enough.' The river's being bled dry." His fingers curled into his palms. "First it was just the gristmills on the rim of the gorge. An eyesore but harmless enough. But then the power companies came and dug their canals and tunnels, and started siphoning off water to spin their turbines and make electricity."

"My father worked for the Niagara Power Company," I said, because it seemed unfair to let him go on without knowing. A crack of thunder caused me to jump, and the most wonderful smile, a little lopsided, came to his face. We both laughed, and I said, "Angels bowling," and thought the thunder was a stroke of luck, a perfect chance to steer the conversation away from the power companies.

Still, when he next spoke he said that the Toronto Power Company, the last of the power companies to build on the Canadian side, was the worst of the bunch, that they built their powerhouse right on the river-bed, where the upper river's wildest rapids used to be. "Metal rods were sent down to gauge the river's depth," he said, "and when they came up bent, they just dumped rock and more rock, until the river was held back."

"A Mr. Lennox designed the powerhouse," I said in another attempt to shift the conversation. "It's the prettiest of the lot, with its Indiana limestone and colonnade." He looked at me queerly, and I knew he considered the aesthetics of a powerhouse unworthy of second thought.

"The tunnel for the tailrace is underneath the river," he said, "blasted straight through to the cliff face behind the falls. Mounds of rubble were shoved through the opening, just dumped into the cavern it'd taken the river hundreds of years to gnaw out."

I straightened myself on the chaise, trying to summon the nerve to point out that he was condemning what was until recently Father's livelihood.

"It's the power companies that brought Carborundum and Oneida and the like to Niagara," he said. "They were grateful for the cheap electricity, also for a fast-moving river to wash away whatever mess they made."

Finally, I said, "What about progress? What about mothers lessening their load with electric ranges and the streets being lit with electric light?" He fell silent, and I brought up the recipe I meant to try for the pike but was unable to set things at ease.

"I should get going," he said and stood up to leave.

Then yesterday I was in the sewing room, listening to Mother's instructions for making gooseberry jam. Through the window I spotted Tom a ways off on River Road and figured I had only a few more minutes to wait. I recited back the instructions and went to the kitchen as quickly as I dared. Midway through picking the best of the cherries from the colander, I slipped one into my mouth. I slid my tongue over its surface and let it drop to the cherries in the brown paper sack. Then I went out to the veranda, only to wait and wonder what was taking him so long. When I wandered into the yard to look, I saw him plucking daisies and black-eyed Susans from the field beneath the bluff. After gathering a small bouquet, he began the trek up the slope. I watched him glance up at Glenview and then drop the bouquet to the ground.

"Fine day," he said at the gate.

"It is."

"I've got sturgeon and pike."

"I've finally got cherries."

"Um," he said, holding out his line.

"I think I'll try another sturgeon."

"Your mother is at the window again."

I turned around, and there she was, hands on her hips, not even attempting to hide. I glared, and she folded her arms.

E ight consecutive days, he came with fish. I boiled pike with salt and vinegar, and served it with hollandaise sauce as is recommended in *Mrs. Beeton's All-About Cookery*. Her recipe for crimped and fried pike was less successful. The cornmeal blackened well before the fish flesh had become opaque. Given the chance, I should like to try again with a slower fire. For variety, I twice chose a sturgeon. My first effort was delicious— sturgeon baked in fat, lemon, and finely chopped herbs—even though I had not quite followed the recipe. It called for wine, and I had omitted it; the cache usually in the sideboard was no longer there. I followed her recipe for sturgeon cutlets exactly but did not like the result nearly so well.

Admittedly, much of the care I took in the kitchen was in anticipation of the few minutes Tom and I would spend at the gate. I usually managed to say how I had prepared the fish from the day before and liked the idea of him thinking I was a capable cook.

Eight consecutive days, he left with a small brown paper sack in his hand.

Eight consecutive days, I slipped my hand into my pocket and touched the rosary nestled there while I asked for Mother to announce another trip to Toronto so that I could bake him a pie. It was safe enough to predict Father would not be home to wonder about the sweetness wafting through the house, to expect a pie for dessert.

Today, shortly before noon, he arrived at the gate. I had not waved from the veranda as I usually did, and he did not say "Fine day," as he had every day except the day it rained. He stood silent, watching and waiting, until I said, "We don't need any more fish."

"I could bring a hare, already skinned and trussed?"

"No, thank you."

"Your mother?"

"I'm sorry," I said.

He looked down and scuffed the earth with the toe of his boot, a small cloud of dust settling on the leather. "We're saying good-bye, then?"

I nodded, even though I had consoled myself with pledges of defiance all through the night.

"That night I carried your trunk . . ."

"Yes."

"I knew it would come to this." He lifted his face.

"And you brought me a fish anyway?"

"When you waved from the veranda, I figured you for a girl with a little more pluck."

His accusation of cowardice smarted, and I blurted out, "I figured you for a gentleman."

"I hoped I could learn," he said and turned away.

Though sheer, silk georgette has the weight to hang pleasingly draped and the strength not to tear. Because it is supple, it follows curves beautifully but cannot hold heavy beadwork in place. To bead the neckline of a silk georgette gown, you must first knot the beads to a fabric rigid enough for support, yet sheer enough to disappear when sewn into place. Organza perfectly fits the bill.

Tonight I have beaded for less than two hours, yet the beads knotted into place on the organza outnumber any other evening's work. With such cavalier methods, I have made short work of the task. Still, time has trudged along and I cannot bear to thread another bead. And now, what am I to do? Should I sit with needle poised and wait for Mother to come into the room all smiles and compliments until she sees what I have done? Do I flop down onto my bed and weep, hoping she has the good sense to leave me alone? It seems a cruel trick that time contracts when you want to savor it and expands insatiably when you do not.

I set my work on the needlepoint seat of my chair, unfasten the buttons at the nape of my neck, and pull my dress over my head. Mother will not come. It is easier for her to cut and baste and sew pretty things, and tell herself she is doing all that she can for the family. I lay my dress over the back of the chair.

A s my eyes open in the morning, I realize I have not dreamed a single dream. I push myself to sitting and swing my legs over the side of the bed. The beadwork is as I left it, folded on the seat of my chair, but my dress is no longer draped over its back. I open the doors of the wardrobe and find my dress properly hung.

When I next glance at the beadwork, I see each askew bead has been put right. Closer examination makes plain the extent of the rework. Each knot was severed and each bead slid from the thread. Only then, and with great precision, had Mother poked her needle through the organza, wrong side to right, and strung a bead onto the thread. Only then had she poked her needle back through the organza and secured the thread with a knot. She had worked half the night to make sure I knew she would stand for no nonsense from me.

Beadwork in hand, I move my chair to the window and sit down to watch. Beyond the garden, beyond the bluff on which Glenview sits, beyond Mother's jurisdiction, is River Road, a scenic stretch of macadam used by the tourists and the locals traveling to and from the Queenston docks, and also by a certain fellow who has no idea a quiet battle has begun in the Glenview house.

The Reporter, June 30, 1848

NEAR TRAGEDY ON ELLET'S BRIDGE

Workmen constructing the first bridge to span the Niagara Gorge skirted disaster last Wednesday when a wind squall flipped one of the workers' footbridges upside down. The damaged structure wafted backward and forward like the broken web of a spider, while four helpless men dangled above the raging Niagara waters in constant expectation of a headlong plunge. Fellow workman Fergus Cole—the same Fergus Cole who fearlessly cleared the riverbed the day the falls stood still—leapt to their aid. In the face of pelting rain and gusting wind, he swung a ladder under his arm and climbed into an iron basket that had been rigged up to a cable for transporting supplies across the gorge. He then hollered at the dazed onlookers to ferry him to the stranded men. Upon reaching the wreck, he balanced the ladder between the basket and the overturned footbridge, careful to place the burden of each man's weight, as they made their way across the ladder, on the basket rather than on the ruined footbridge. All were brought back to firm ground, uninjured in person but well nigh scared to death.

"We've a true hero in our midst," remarked Clifford Lawson, one of the rescued men. "I owe my life to Fergus Cole."

6

Annie Taylor and her barrel

Isabel often wore a nightdress until noon, even as we sat on the veranda. It suited me just fine because I have few dresses of my own and it meant I usually had her wardrobe full of dresses to myself, and I wanted to look my best when Tom came to the gate. Sometimes I worried that the fussiness of her wardrobe would put him off. And because she was curvaceous in all the right places before becoming ill and I am not, her dresses mostly fit me too loosely through the bust and hips.

Still, after months of solemn Loretto black, I was pleased by what I glimpsed in the mirror.

But a few days ago Isabel began wearing dresses again, sometimes the very dress I was hoping to wear. When I suggested to Mother that I would like to sew a dress for myself, she said, "What about all your socks?" The Red Cross package I sent for had finally arrived, and Isabel and I now spend our afternoons knitting socks on the veranda, at least until she gets to the tricky part of the heel and throws down her needles in a huff.

"I'll find the time."

"Can't you borrow one of Isabel's? Miss O'Leary's wedding is just over a fortnight away."

"When I finish the beading, then?"

She lifted her foot from the treadle, just long enough to rotate the cuff she was stitching. "With a few nips and tucks, one of Isabel's will do."

"Which one?"

"Leave me be," she said, glancing up from her work, giving me a clear view of the darkness around her eyes.

Breakfast has moved from the dining room to the kitchen. It is easier to clean up, and Father, with his increasingly late evenings, seldom manages to get out of bed early enough to join us. As I lift the teapot, and Isabel removes the cloth from the perpetual biscuits, Mother, all smiles, announces Edward is coming by this afternoon to pick up the remnants of a gown she made for Mrs. Atwell. Her milliner needs them for a matching hat. "Bess, you should put on the tea dress you made for Isabel," Mother says.

"I'm to pretty myself up for Edward Atwell, then?"

Mother sighs deeply.

"He's staying for tea?" Isabel says.

"He might."

"But I'd like to wear the tea dress," Isabel says.

"You just heard me say Bess could wear it."

"Go ahead," I say. "I couldn't care less."

Mother's hand, alongside her plate, curls into a fist.

After breakfast she calls me upstairs, where I assume she will assign me some menial task—ripping out a seam, basting stays into place. But instead she opens the doors of Isabel's wardrobe, selects two dresses, and holds them out to me. "Try these on," she says. "Then come and show me in the sewing room."

The first, which Isabel had not worn in years, is light peach with Juliet sleeves and a princess waistline trimmed in white cotton lace. If it were an inch or two longer, the hem of the skirt would fall fashionably, just above the ankle, but as is, the three-quarter length is better suited to a child.

In the sewing room, I flick the peach cotton of the skirt and say, "You've got to be kidding." Mother appraises me for a moment, her head cocked, her lips pursed. She smoothes her fingers over the sleeve, an unexpected melancholy palpable in the lightness of her touch, in the way her hand drops to her side. "You've grown up," she says.

The second dress is entirely white with intricate lace inserts, embroidered panels, and cutwork. As I slip it over my shoulders, I cannot help but think what a lot I have yet to master with needle and thread.

Mother lifts my arms from my sides and guides me in a slow rotation. She frowns, seemingly unimpressed by the skillfulness of the embroidery and the neatness with which the ground fabric is cut away from the design. "It's really beautiful," I say, and then, as it occurs to me the work is her own, I wish I could take back the words.

I follow her to Isabel's bedroom where she pulls open the drawer housing Isabel's underclothes. "It's time you wore a corset."

"It's only tea," I say, feigning a bit of resistance.

"Try it on." She hands me a bundle of pale pink.

Stays run the length of the side seams; also over the ribs, front and back; and alongside the hooks and eyes of the front opening, and the grommets of the back opening through which the lace is pulled. In my camisole and drawers, I fasten hooks and eyes from just beneath my sternum to well below my hips. I have heard of the fainting and know the complaints, also the rhetoric of the suffragettes, yet a corset is a rite of passage, which places me a step closer to making decisions for myself. As Mother begins to tighten the laces, the irony in such thinking strikes me, and then, with the final tug, any notion linking a corset with independence seems entirely foolish.

"Are you comfortable?" she asks.

In the mirror, I glimpse the extra fullness across the bust, the soft draping of the bodice to my narrowed waist, the gently undulating curve of my hips and say, "Comfortable enough."

She pinches the extra fullness from the sides of the cutwork dress, takes it up with a line of pins. "It won't take but a minute," she says, but I know it is not true. The seams to be opened up and restitched are part of an underbodice veiled by the cutwork.

In the kitchen just past noon Mother says I ought to bake Scotch shortbread or macaroons. The biscuit tins are empty, and Edward might want a cookie with his tea. She tells me not to change from the cutwork dress while I bake, in case he arrives. "It's just Edward," I say, Edward with whom Kit and I have climbed in the crab apple trees and rolled down the steep slope of the bluff, my hair strewn with twigs and dry grass, my cheeks ruddy with heat and dirt. And what about the war? Are we suddenly baking with white flour and sugar and butter again? But then it hits me, he is not *just Edward* anymore. Not to Mother. Not to Isabel.

Isabel comes into the kitchen, wearing the tea dress, and says how lovely I look. I feel as transformed as a girl can be by a corset, a perfectly made dress, and painstakingly upswept hair, but Isabel outshines me as the sun does the moon. Even now, though her skin is still slightly sallow, especially when she first rises for the day, and her jawline and cheekbones too angular, her beauty easily tops my own diluted version of it.

Way back, the afternoon Isabel tried on the tea dress so that I could mark the hem, what had struck me most was how well-suited it was to a figure as nearly perfect as hers. I had admired my handiwork, the way the filmy layers clung ever so slightly to her curves. But thin as she is, the bodice gapes at the neckline yet somehow fits too snugly across the bust. Maybe I am learning more than I think, as I hand Mother pins and chalk, and listen to her speak of puckers and pulls, and the proper hang of a skirt. Maybe it was only inexperience that led me to think the dress fit as it should.

Isabel and I decide on macaroons because they bake in a cool oven and the embers from the morning's round of biscuits will do. Also, Mother will not veto a custard for tomorrow, not when the set-aside egg yolks would otherwise go to waste. I grind almonds in a porcelain mortar while Isabel measures the castor sugar and separates the whites from three eggs.

"You know what Mary Egan told me a while back?" she says. "She said Mr. Cruickshank was going around telling everyone Boyce and I were never engaged. He admits we courted, but only for a short while. He's saying Boyce broke up with me ages before he did."

"He thought he could make his son look like less of a cad," I say.

"Sometimes I think I imagined the whole thing." She forces breath from her nose, making a rough, huffing sound, likely meant to be dismissive but coming off as full of doubt.

"Oh, Isabel," I say. "He gave you a ring." I remember the night. I had woken to the ping of a pebble on the window of my room at the academy. I opened the shutters, and there were Isabel and Boyce down below.

"We're engaged," Isabel called up.

"What?" I said, half-asleep.

"Your sister has promised to marry me," Boyce called back.

"You'll be my maid of honor, won't you, Bess?"

"You're wet," I said. The two of them were standing arm in arm, laughing like a couple of hyenas, soaked to the bone.

"It's just mist," she said. "He proposed at the falls."

"I was on my knee in a puddle," Boyce said. "The tourists got a good show."

There was a sharp rap on my door, and I turned to see a wimpleless Sister Bede bustling into my room. "Quiet," she said, reaching to close the shutters. "And back to bed."

"Sister Bede," Isabel called up. "Congratulate me. I'm engaged."

Kit had woken up in the bed across from my own and was propped on her elbows, snickering into her sheets.

"Gracious me," Sister Bede said, leaning from the window. "Isabel's down there."

"And Boyce," I called out, "the luckiest fellow in the world."

"That I am," he called back to peals of laughter from Isabel.

"Hush. You'll have all the girls up any minute. Mother Febronie, too," Sister Bede said. "I'm closing the shutters."

"Wait. Please," I said to Sister Bede and turned back to the window. "Yes," I called down. "I'll be your maid of honor. I'd like to, very much, more than anything." No doubt there would be a flock of bridesmaids, but she had singled out me.

Isabel smoothes a length of wafer paper over a baking sheet and says, "When Boyce broke off our engagement, I reminded him about the ring, that he'd made a promise. He stammered out some nonsense about the ring being a token of affection. Not a promise."

"Then why did he take it back?"

"I threw it at him," she says. "It chipped his tooth."

"He loved you. He was with you at my window that night, saying he was the luckiest fellow in the world."

"Never mind," she says, waving her hand. "Water under the bridge."

When we hear the Runabout, Isabel unties the strings of her apron and hangs it in the pantry, and Mother signals for me to do the same. All this for Edward, who is unlikely to notice a thing and who would only find it embarrassing on the off chance that he did. "Hurry up," Mother says. I walk to the pantry slowly, all the while contemplating wiping the flour from my hands on my pretty dress.

"Edward," Isabel says in the yard. "What a treat." Her outstretched hand squeezes his left, which hangs witlessly at his side.

As I watch him take in the length of me, heat flares in my cheeks. "Heading out?" he asks.

"No," I say, "just playing dress up."

"Oh."

"You're too used to us in black," Isabel says.

His expression remains unchanged, vaguely blank. He has entirely missed the reference to the wool crepe of the academy. In his defense, it has been two years since Isabel graduated. Still, only a month ago he visited his six younger sisters in the Loretto parlor, all of us in somber black.

"You remember our Loretto dresses?" I say.

"Of course." He nods recognition, at long last.

"Sit down for a bit," Mother says, nudging the wicker rocker toward him. Once he is seated in the rocker, and Isabel and I in less comfortable chairs, Mother excuses herself and goes into the house.

A moment later Isabel, in the role of attentive hostess, says she has left the kettle boiling and would he like a cup of tea? She is on her feet and through the screen door before he has a chance to refuse, leaving just the two of us.

"Well," I say.

"Well."

I smile, just barely, like a child from behind her mother's legs, and he glances away. We sit quietly, unable to look each other squarely in the face, until he says, "I hear they took another floater out of the whirlpool yesterday."

Like most children in Niagara Falls, Edward and I grew up trading stories about the bodies pulled out of the river and the dreadful men who undertook the task. They were bleary-eyed and lecherous, and would tell you to throw yourself over the brink if you asked. It meant a bottle of rye whiskey as payment, a little wet on their tongues. For generations there had been at least one on the river, waiting to spy a bit of yellow-pink, a bit of flesh, bobbing in a pool. If only the floater could be gotten to and pulled in before the river whisked it away.

I have long since outgrown such talk; still, the familiar terrain is a relief and I say, "The summer months always mean a rash of suicides."

Then we are back to averted eyes and bashful smiles until he jumps up from the rocker, saying he forgot something in the Runabout.

As he lopes toward the automobile, I sit as straight as a pin, take several large breaths, and wonder about our new awkwardness. Is it only that we are both used to having Kit around? Or is it because Mother fussed with my hair? Or has he noticed the corset? He is well-mannered and I like him well enough, but Kit will head the family business for good reason. Right there, alongside the sisterly fondness I feel for him, is pity. And it is the more defining sentiment of the two.

On his return he hands me a square envelope. "An invitation," he says. "We'd like your family to have dinner with ours."

"Fine," I say, though I have had supper at the Atwells' more times than I can count and never once been given a formal invitation. "I'll give it to Mother."

Rather than set the envelope aside, I head indoors with it, pleased at a chance to escape. I meet Isabel in the hallway with a dish of macaroons. "We're invited to dinner at the Atwells'," I say, untucking the flap of the envelope and sliding a card from the opening.

She is delighted, and as her sister I ought to be, too. But what if the invitation has more to do with kindliness and our reduced circumstances than anything else? And then, there is Father, who used to be the life of any party, the first to tell a joke, the first to turn on the Victrola and whisk his wife around the room, the first to forget that Isabel and I were not in bed. He continues to leave Glenview midmorning and return late at night, once I am tucked beneath the coverlet, listening for his key in the lock.

"Can you get the rest of the tea things?" Isabel says.

"Sure."

"Take your time," she says, winking, her irresistible wink.

I do take my time, not only because I was asked to by Isabel but because Mother is hurrying me along. As I walk toward the pantry with a canister of sugar, she says, "I'll put it away." And as I line up the teaspoons on the tray, she says, "He won't notice." When I slop a bit of milk from the creamer and set down the tray to wipe up the mess, she says, "Honestly, Bess."

When I finally get back to the veranda, Edward is standing, stammering out some engagement he forgot, and Isabel is sitting with her dress hiked nearly to her knees. Her middle and ring fingers are hooked around her gaping neckline, exposing the lace trim of her camisole.

"You came for the fabric," I say, pivoting away quickly and again slopping milk. Feeling quite as unsettled as it seems Edward does, I set the tray on a table in the hallway and dash up the stairs to the sewing room. I find Mrs. Atwell's fabric quickly but flop down onto Mother's sewing bench. Am I catching my breath? Am I giving Isabel her chance? One thing for certain, my imagination had not run wild. She had in fact laughed too heartily as he droned on about shooting himself in the foot. She was pursuing him.

Peering through the small gap between the window casing and the draperies, I watch Edward retreat from Isabel until his backside is just several inches from the Runabout. The pace with which she approaches slows but does not altogether stop until she is close enough to tend his disheveled collar, which she offhandedly does. She wraps her arms around her waist and rocks from side to side, like a sulking child. A few seconds later he is stepping aside, clearing the way to the passenger seat of the Runabout. They are off in no time, Edward looking straight ahead, Isabel laughing with an arm reached around her head, holding her hair in place.

I envy Isabel. I envy her nerve, her get-up-and-go, her readiness to shape her world.

I only watch for Tom. For over a week. From the veranda, from the yard, from the window of the sewing room. Once while watching at the gate I saw a lone figure in the distance on River Road, tall and broad-shouldered like him, and wearing a flat cap and neckcloth as he does. I hurried into the house and sat on my hands in a chair. When I was certain he had passed, I ventured into the yard and gawked after the figure, by then too far gone to say whether it was in fact Tom, Tom who had quite rightly accused me of lacking pluck.

When I step away from the window, Mother is in the doorway of the sewing room, hands on her hips, looking tired and cross. "Where on earth are they off to?"

They had turned left, downriver, at River Road, which ruled out the falls as a destination and set the glen with its secluded woods as the more likely spot. Though the distress such a suggestion would bring Mother is tempting, I will not turn in Isabel. "The falls, I guess."

Mother shakes her head, too tired for more questions.

To my relief and, I admit, disappointment, the Runabout is back within ten minutes. Isabel climbs down from the automobile and stands at the gate, saying, "What fun" and "Maybe next visit we'll have more time," while I cross the yard with Mrs. Atwell's bundled fabric and hand it to him.

"I almost forgot," he says, tipping the package to his brow.

. . .

Mother paces the kitchen at half past five on the Sunday afternoon of the Atwell dinner. "Where is he?" she says. Isabel and I say nothing, just stand in our finery, our hands folded behind our backs pressed against the wall, waiting for Father.

Though Miss O'Leary's wedding gown is still incomplete and Mother had already spent the better part of a morning altering the cutwork dress, she fussed again, nipping and tucking one of Isabel's dinner dresses to snugly fit my newly induced curves. Isabel had worn the dress twice, first to a dinner at the Clifton House in honor of the visiting Duke and Duchess of Connaught and then to a concert put on by the Mendelssohn Choir at the Massey Music Hall in Toronto. None of the Atwells have yet glimpsed the soft rust of the featherweight silk, the crossover bodice, the narrow tiered skirt trimmed in wide bands of ecru lace, or the décolletage Mother has made just prim enough by moving a rosette.

"I'll kill him," Mother says, continuing to pace.

I am not enjoying Mother's agitation in the least, not when it is matched by Isabel's and my own. Polite excuses will be made, Father's absence explained away. Even so, I will know he has become capable of ditching the three of us for a pint of ale.

Isabel steps forward. "We'll go without him. We'll say he's ill."

Mother looks up from the linoleum. "Will we take the trolley, then?"

"No," Isabel says. "Edward will pick us up."

"Bess, can you telephone?" Mother asks.

The switchboard operator puts me through, and one of the Atwell girls—I am never sure which—answers. As I wait for Kit to come on the line, I hear an automobile and glimpse Father's Cadillac climbing the bluff on Buttrey Street.

"Where are you?" Kit asks.

"We're running late is all," I say. "We're leaving now."

"I'll tell Mother."

"Kit?" I lean my forehead against the wall.

"Yes."

"I'm wearing a corset," I say. "Don't laugh."

"I might."

"Don't."

"Hurry up," she says.

Father comes into the entrance hall in a tweed lounge jacket, double-breasted waistcoat, and white trousers. Mother looks him up and down, then steps toward him and takes the walking stick and Panama hat tucked under his arm. "You haven't forgotten?" she says.

"Ladies," he says, bowing slightly to Isabel and me. "Shall we be off to the Atwells'?"

Mother smoothes the shoulder seams of his jacket. "I think," she says, "with such pretty daughters to escort, you should put on a suit."

He turns to Isabel and me. "Excuse me a minute. I've been told to change."

As he makes his way toward the staircase, Mother says, "You're most handsome in the one with the jacket edged in silk grosgrain."

"Then it's the suit I'll wear," he calls from the stairs, and it occurs to me that Mother might be just as able as Isabel to shape her world.

"Get his top hat," Mother says to Isabel, "the one with the moleskin band."

Mother shifts her attention to me. "Turn." Her index finger draws a semicircle in the air. As I shuffle my feet in a slow circle, she says, "Stand up straight."

"I can't slouch in this contraption."

"All the more reason to wear it," she says.

She gathers the tin of walnut toffee Isabel and I made and, from the table in the entrance hall, her handbag and hat. As she places her hat on her head, she lets go a great sigh. "I'm so fond of the Atwells," she says, "and Edward's turned out to be such a gentleman."

"Except that Kit got his share of the brains," I say. The words are cruel, the worst she has heard from me in a long while. Still, she only presses her lips closed.

As Father comes down the stairs, Mother watches him closely. I watch, too, trying to figure out just what she is looking for, to see what she does. "You haven't changed your collar," she says.

"Enough." He snatches his top hat from Isabel.

•   •   •

At the Atwells' there are anchovy fingers, foie gras toast, and deviled chickens' livers to start. Each entrée is fussy: chicken and béchamel jellied and then turned from timbale molds; baked tomatoes stuffed with ham, Parmesan, parsley, and bread crumbs; a mold with an outer layer of asparagus spears and sliced tongue, an in-between layer of quenelle, and an interior of roughly diced sweetbread; and, my favorite, pilau of mutton, a dish Mrs. Atwell tells us is Indian. It is chock-full of the ordinary—mutton, onions, and cloves—and also the exotic—nuts called pistachios, and spices called cumin and cardamom—all of which she has saved since before the war.

"The missus starved us last week," Mr. Atwell says. "Not a speck of beef, no milk, no butter, not a single egg, not an ounce of white flour. She said, 'If we're to feast on Sunday, we'll do our bit by making up for it now.'"

The table around which we sit is finely laid with linen and cut crystal, silverware and Limoges china. The youngest Atwells are gathered around a smaller table, shuttled into the dining room for the meal but just as beautifully laid. Mr. and Mrs. Atwell are at each end of the main table. After weeks of Father arriving long after supper has been cleared away, I am pleased to be placed next to him. But Edward is seated on my opposite side and Isabel far off, catercorner to him.

"The mutton is lovely," I say to Edward, trying to ignore my uneasiness with the seating arrangement.

"Quite."

"You're lucky to have such a daring mother in the kitchen."

He nods.

"I'm learning to cook."

He stabs a bit of asparagus and mutters a few words.

I lean toward him. "I didn't hear?"

This time his words are intelligible. "I'd like a wife who can cook."

I focus my attention on my plate. Is he attempting to flirt? I steal a sideways glance. He is shoveling mutton onto his fork, his eyes on the meat, his cheeks lifted in a grin, pleased as punch with himself. I turn to the opposite end of the table, cock my head, and, for the remainder of dinner, feign great interest in all Mr. Atwell and Father have to say.

"I hear one of your clerks was shipped off to the Petawawa camp," Father says.

"Istvan Szabo," Mr. Atwell says.

I knit my brow, and Father, noticing, says to me, "He was circulating an enemy rag."

Mr. Atwell sets down his fork. "A cousin of his in Winnipeg publishes the *Canadian Hungarian,* which no one in the Department of Justice even bothered to translate. Istvan handed out the half dozen copies his cousin mailed him to the Hungarian families in Niagara Falls."

"It isn't an easy job, figuring out who's a threat, with all the foreigners we've got living here, half of them from enemy countries," Father says. "Over Fallsview way the streets are full of them."

"I sent a character reference off to the director of internment operations. Istvan's got a wife and three boys to support." Mr. Atwell pushes himself ever so slightly away from the table, away from Father. "This unfettered patriotism, ever since Ypres, it makes me ashamed."

Father's head bobs from side to side, neither a shake nor a nod.

When dinner finally ends, I manage to drag Kit out to the veranda, though she wanted to stay inside, playing crokinole with Edward and Isabel. We sit on the stairs, I with the stays of the corset digging into my thighs. "Edward said something strange at dinner," I say. "He said he'd like a wife who can cook."

She shrugs.

"I'd just finished saying I was learning to cook."

"He thinks a lot of you," she says.

I keep my gaze on her, though it seems she would rather I not, as though she were an ant caught under a magnifying lens in the sun. As I wait for her to say more, Mother comes to the front door and says Kit and I ought to join Isabel and Edward in the drawing room. "In a minute," I say.

Once she is gone from the doorway, I turn back to Kit and say, "I like Edward. I like him a lot, but not like that." I peer through the screen door, making sure the coast is clear. "It's Isabel who's got her eye on him."

"That's obvious enough," Kit says, getting to her feet, "but Edward isn't interested in her, not a bit. He's interested in you."

In my panic I nearly step on Kit's heels as I follow her indoors. My mind flits to the possibility of a conversation between Mother and Mrs. Atwell. Mother would have promoted Isabel; she is older and a graduate and her trousseau is very nearly complete. Had Edward put his foot down? Had Kit held undue sway?

In the entrance hall she stops abruptly. "You'd better pay attention, Bess. He'd be good to you," she says.

"You'd never compromise."

"Compromise? He's kind. He's good. He's financially set. You won't get another chance, not like this." She reaches for my hand, but I snatch it away.

I am short of breath in the corset I should never have worn, in the contraption I will never wear again. It was pride that caused me to put it on, and more than likely my newfound curves are at least a little responsible for Edward's sudden interest in me. A fondness for pretty things, vanity itself, is surely a snare.

I look up from the crokinole board when Father steps into the drawing room from the smoking room with a decanter of amber liquid in his hand. Mrs. Atwell folds her arms, and Mr. Atwell signals his helplessness to her with a shrug. Then I miss my shot.

I watch, disheartened, as Father becomes loquacious, his gestures more sweeping, as though it were the old days. I watch my poised mother, perched on the arm of the chair where he sits, his hand at rest on the scrimshaw eagle crowning his walking stick. It makes a pretty picture, if one does not look too closely, if one avoids the flat-bottomed glass tipped to his lips, nearly drained a fourth time, if one ignores the slight tremor at the corner of Mother's mouth. "Best be off," she says, rising from the arm of the chair.

"So soon," Mrs. Atwell says, quickly on her feet.

Leaning over the crokinole board, Edward takes a shot, knocking one of my disks from the board. "Well done," Kit says.

He and Kit lag behind Isabel and me by twenty-five points, yet I fling my disk carelessly, eager to abandon the game. But no sooner has my disk bounced from a peg and skidded across the board into the gutter than Father says, too harshly, "Let them finish," and Mother obediently reseats herself on the arm of the chair. I suppose she has judged the situation and decided it better to risk another ounce of rye whiskey than to have her daughters and the Atwells witness a spat.

O n River Road, Father drives too quickly and Mother clutches her hat to her head, her jaw set as she refuses to ask him to slow down. The sun is low, setting beyond the rail yards and roundhouse to the west of the Lower Steel Arch Bridge. Shadows are deep and colors gold-tinged, vivid versions of their earlier washed-out selves. Father's lips part, and quiet words intended for Mother's ears are delivered by rushing air to Isabel and me in the backseat. "Why wasn't Isabel seated beside Edward?" he says.

"Shush."

"I'll say what I please."

"And do as you please, too, it seems."

He snorts exaggerated laughter, his head falling backward.

"The Atwells are prohibitionists," she says, "and you're well aware of it."

"How it is, then, that there was a decanter of rye whiskey sitting out?"

"You know as well as I do that it wasn't meant to leave the smoking room."

"A little hypocritical, I'd say." He takes the corner onto Buttrey Street too quickly. In unison Mother and I grip the doors adjacent to each of us, and Isabel's hand lands protectively on my ribs.

Neither speaks another word until the Cadillac is parked at Glenview and the engine turned off. "What a lovely evening," Mother says to Isabel and me.

"I think it went rather badly," I say, glaring.

"Bess," Isabel says ever so quietly, laying a warning hand on my thigh.

In a momentary lapse of manners, Father steps toward the house but then remembers Mother still seated, waiting to be escorted from the Cadillac.

He opens the automobile door and takes her hand as she reaches a foot to solid earth.

7

I walk River Road, uncertain why I stoop to pick up a number of the stones in my path and slip them into my pocket. I tread southward, upriver, until I reach the Lower Steel Arch Bridge. Then I turn and retrace my steps.

Just opposite Glenview, I rest, leaning against a tree, gazing up at the house. What might Tom see as he passes by on River Road, that is, if he even bothers to look? Faded glory? The eaves could use a fresh coat of paint, several of the supporting brackets show signs of rot, and a pane of the pediment window is cracked. I know these flaws exist yet can see no evidence from the road. Maybe he sees grandeur. Glenview does loom large, even more so because of its position atop the bluff. The skirting homes could almost be the shanties of a manor, a flock of goslings seeking shelter under the wing of mother goose.

I remember the day Isabel and I were first shown the house. Mother held our hands as she led us from one empty room to the next, describing where the furniture would be placed, the wallpaper she would hang. She spent a good deal of time in each of the bedrooms that would become ours, pointing out the loftiness of the ceilings, the grace of the plaster moldings, the quarter-cut oak of the floors, the view of the gorge, and then joined in when Isabel and I galloped each room, marveling at the breadth.

Might Tom look up at Glenview and decide he was a fool to have ever handed over the best of his sturgeon and pike? Such thinking seems an acquiescence to Mother, and I suppose in our quiet battle she has gained the upper hand. There is, after all, a hole in my day that used to be filled by a minute or two at the gate, a hole that is becoming clogged with self-reproach. Before I snapped back, accusing him of lacking gentlemanliness, he had said only that he had figured me for a girl with a little pluck. And is a bit of courage so wrong a thing for him to want from me when any friendship between the two of us demands it on my part?

I take a stone from my pocket and place it on the side of the road. I place another, and another, until I have spelled out the word *Hello* with gray, jagged stones. He will come upon the stones as he passes by on his way to his fishing camp at the whirlpool, today or tomorrow or the day after that. I stand back surveying my work, and unsure he will know the message is for him, I add just beneath it his name, *Tom*.

All day I am anxious. Mother would be furious if she were to come upon the stones. She would say I had disobeyed her, and while I could argue that she only said for me to tell Tom not to bring any more fish, we would both know I understood what she meant. I was to see no more of him. His credentials were not up to snuff. I would never have the courage, but here is what I would like to say to her: Jesus collected the less fortunate, even the destitute, and called them his friends. He would say Mother was wrong.

In the evening the sky is particularly red and strewn with strands of flat, orange-pink cloud, and I pray for the courage to say to Mother that I will go down to River Road, that from there I will take in the setting sun.

As I stand in the doorway of the sewing room saying what I had planned, my heart does not race, my voice does not tremble, my palms do not grow damp. And Mother busily waves me away without a second thought.

The stones have not been knocked about the roadside by a careless passerby but stacked in a neat pyramid. I squeeze a handful of the stones, then study the indentations and chalky white residue on my palm, but cannot read whether it was Tom who shaped the monument. I restack the stones, but a foot or so closer to the edge of the gorge, on trampled grass rather than hard-packed dirt.

The following afternoon I am on River Road again, returning from the shops with a roasting chicken and a concoction of rice, rye, and whole wheat flours recommended for wartime in the newspaper. As I approach the spot in front of Glenview, I squint to see the stone pyramid, but the struggling grass appears unmarred except by a fallen branch. A few steps farther on, I speed up, almost sure the side of the road has been somehow altered.

The stones I come upon are much prettier than those I gathered, each seemingly selected for some particular quality. One is pale pink, another prettily speckled, the next translucent and white. All the stones are worn smooth, their contours rounded by the water and grit of the river over time. They are laid on the ground to form the word *Bess*.

I gather the stones quickly and run up the steep rise of Buttrey Street, panting and sweating, and thinking all the while of what I will next leave for him.

As I had hoped, Mother is not in the sewing room. I take six small beads meant for Miss O'Leary's wedding gown from the box sitting on the windowsill and clutch them in my fist as I dash from the house.

But on River Road, my choice seems poorly thought out. He had left me a bit of his world, and I intended to leave him a bit of my own, but I can hardly expect him to find six small beads amid packed dirt and broken stone. I walk in slow circles on the trampled grass until I find a half walnut shell. I make a small basin in the roadside using a stone and set the shell into it, upright. In the sunshine, the bead-filled shell glistens, and surely he will be looking. He will find it.

•   •   •

It is well past midnight as I lie awake in bed. I do not toss and turn, my body one minute too warm and the next chilled. I lie contentedly, even blissfully awake, thinking of what I will next leave.

In response to the beads, he leaves two pieces of flat shale with an assortment of pressed ferns sandwiched between. I consult Mother's guide to flora, looking for some secret meaning in the names of the ferns. The first one I identify is lady fern, which seems a compliment of sorts, even more so when I discover the second to be called maidenhair. But the next is narrow-leaf spleenwort and the one after that common polypody. Still, the ferns were fed by his river, cut from the shady depths of his gorge.

In return I leave a swatch of green-blue charmeuse, the color and luster of the fabric much like sunshine on the river. Does he ponder my leavings the way I do his? Does he understand how the swatch of fabric implies the meeting of our worlds?

I find a feather at our roadside spot, held upright there by a ring of supporting stones. The shaft of the feather in one hand, I pull the flattened mesh of the vane through my fingers, mulling over the gift. Herons are known to wade in the shallows of the Niagara, and the feather is in fact oversize and gray-blue. Does he somehow know the great blue heron is a bird I adore? Vast wings spread in flight, lengthy legs angled behind, elongated neck held in an S-curve, the heron seems otherworldly or maybe from an earlier time.

Even so, the feather disappoints me. I thought he would hint his understanding of the message underlying the charmeuse. I decide to be more blatant and pull threads from the frayed edge of the charmeuse and braid them together with a lock of hair snipped from my head.

He leaves a wooden container, rather like a pencil box, with a sliding panel. When I open it, a small cinnamon-colored butterfly flutters from the box, escaping its confines. In this I find meaning, also the courage to leave him a note.

I compose as I lie in bed, but in the morning, fountain pen put to paper, I am not satisfied. Rather than go down for breakfast, I work on the note, which causes Mother to rap on my door and me to hurl myself into bed and claim a headache.

The content of the note settled, I copy it onto stationery and, after three attempts, am finally happy with my penmanship. I hold the stationery an arm's length away, trying to see what he might. My name, along with "Glenview," appears in embossed type at the bottom of the page, which would be disastrous if it ended up in the wrong hands, but, more important, he might be unnerved by it. I copy the words onto plain paper.

The final product is simple, laughable, considering the effort.

> Dear Tom,
>
> Perhaps we might spend an afternoon together. On Thursday, Mother will go to Toronto to purchase yard goods.
>
> Bess

I tuck the note between two rocks and return to Glenview but twice make excuses and head back to River Road. Both times, I slide the note from the rocks and reread it, though I know the content by heart. Then, with just enough of a corner protruding, I replace the note between the rocks.

A day later, I glimpse a bit of white between the same two rocks. From a few steps closer, I know by the tattered edge of the paper that it has been exchanged for my note. I snatch quickly, and, paper trembling in my hands, I read.

> Dear Bess,
>
> Thursday, then. 1 o'clock at the Canadian end of the Lower Steel Arch Bridge.
>
> Tom

Did he struggle with the reply? Has he an outing in mind? Does he lie awake with my note pressed to his heart?

Will Thursday ever arrive?

The Reporter, June 14, 1850

THE COLLAPSE OF TABLE ROCK

Up until Monday evening, Table Rock, a large dolostone platform jutting out over the gorge, was the favored vantage point from which to view the falls. Dismayed locals flocked to the site when shortly after 7:00 P.M. a mass two hundred feet long, sixty feet wide, and one hundred feet thick broke off and collapsed into the gorge. The crash was heard as far away as Bender Hill.

Local hackman Eugene Waverly was washing his carriage on the rock at the time it broke away. He fled with moments to spare, but his carriage plunged into the gorge, splintering to smithereens. When asked to comment, he said, "Suppose I should've heeded Mr. Cole."

Town resident Fergus Cole flat out refused to set foot on the rock and had been shooing tourists away for a month. To those who lent an ear, he explained that the rock was set down in layers with a dolostone cap and soft shale beneath. The shale was riddled with water-filled cracks and fissures, always expanding and contracting at nature's whim. Mr. Cole was adamant the shale was flaking away and on more than one occasion pointed to the talus beneath the overhang as proof. "What's holding up all that dolostone?" he would say. "I'll tell you what: less today than yesterday."

The collapse of Table Rock confirmed Mr. Cole's prophetic ability when it comes to the Niagara River and Gorge.

8

Tom waves as I approach at exactly one o'clock on Thursday afternoon. Last night I slept poorly, my mind endlessly looping, becoming more and more irrational as each hour passed. What if Isabel had been playing a practical joke and left the ferns and pretty stones? What if I waited for no one at the bridge? By daylight it was unimaginable, but in that place between sleep and wakefulness where the mind churns without the clarity of daylight, even the most unlikely can seem possible. So, I am both relieved and highly anxious to see him waiting at the foot of the bridge.

He is dressed as always, in a flat cap, and matching waistcoat and jacket. Only the absence of his usual neckcloth hints at today being different from all the rest. I had stood in front of the wardrobe mirror at least an hour, one dress after another held up to my collarbones and eventually dismissed. Too long; I might stumble. Too tailored; a certain status is implied. Too low a neckline; I have little to flaunt. I settled on a light pink dress with a small turned-down collar and a sash set just higher than the natural level of the waist.

His eyes flit from my tidy hair to my ankles and then back to my face. He smiles, his handsome lopsided smile, and I think I have chosen well.

"I have tickets for the Great Gorge Route," he says.

The Great Gorge Route has been called the most delightful electric trolley ride in the world, yet I have never completed the circuit that most every visitor to Niagara Falls has. "I've wanted to go for years," I say.

"You've never been?"

I have ridden the trolley on the Canadian side, where the tracks stretch atop the gorge from the falls to Queenston Heights, and then descend to the base of the escarpment and the wharf where the Toronto steamboats dock. The tracks cross the river there, at the suspension bridge linking Queenston and Lewiston, New York. The portion of the circuit along the American side of the river is at the base of the gorge wall, just above river level. "I haven't crossed to the American side," I say. "My mother says it's dangerous, and I've never been able to change her mind."

Years ago, just opposite where Tom and I stand, an avalanche of ice fell to the river-level tracks during spring thaw, killing the conductor and eight passengers. Another time two passengers were injured when a pair of trolleys collided head-on. And just several weeks back, Mother slapped the *Evening Review* down on the table in front of me as though her point was now irrefutably made. The headline read TROLLEY CAR ACCIDENT AT QUEENSTON. It seemed rain had interrupted the Sunday school picnic of a Toronto church at Queenston Heights and the group's homeward journey began with an overloaded trolley car. Thirteen people were killed and dozens more injured when wet brakes failed while descending the escarpment. Ironically, calamity struck on a portion of track that Mother had always considered safe. She routinely used it on her way to the Toronto steamboats at the Queenston wharf. Just this morning, she had stood in the back garden, dressed for traveling in a serge bolero and skirt. "Maybe I should postpone the trip," she said, gazing at a lone, wispy bit of cloud. "Do you think it might rain?" She had been anticipating the journey for a week, ever since the unremittingly loyal Mr. Coulson had given Mrs. Coulson carte blanche to order as many dresses as she pleased.

"I know the river," Tom says. "I can tell when it isn't safe." He speaks quietly, with humility, as though he is uncomfortable with making such a claim. Still, there is a confidence. So far as he is concerned, the claim is a statement of fact.

As I stand at the Lower Steel Arch Bridge, a trolley ride in his company so close to the river seems as thrilling an afternoon as I have ever spent, but no sooner have I said "I'm not afraid" than I imagine Mother climbing onto a trolley as she returns from Toronto. I imagine her relief at setting down packages, heavy with silk and wool and trim. I imagine her rubbing a strained forearm as her gaze drifts to me, also on the trolley, seated alongside Tom.

"What is it?" he says.

"My mother will be coming home from Toronto."

"I thought of that," he says. "We'll head downriver first, crossing at Queenston."

He and I are usually alone in the scenarios I play out in my head, but I like the idea of an outing in the company of others. A walk in some lonely place would seem furtive, an admission of wrongdoing, and there is enough stealth in avoiding Mother.

"It'll be my first time seeing the rapids up close," I say.

"You haven't hiked in the glen?"

"Only midway, never to the river."

"It'll be like nothing you've ever seen, not as wild as in the spring, but fierce enough." He touches my elbow. "Let's go," he says.

With the war keeping the tourists away, the trolley is less than a quarter full, just a few families with small children held back from the open sides of the car and a handful of young couples, mostly honeymooning soldiers and war brides, judging by the uniforms and the intimacy.

Once we are settled and traveling north through the pleasant, wooded country atop the almost vertical walls of the gorge, Tom pokes his chin in the direction of one of the uniformed men. "He'll be off soon enough."

"Suppose so."

"I wasn't raised to think much of wars," he says, "but I can't see myself holding out much longer, not with the chlorine gas at Ypres and now all the rot about the *Lusitania.*"

The newspapers are back to carrying stories about the ocean liner that sank in eighteen minutes, killing more than half of the two thousand civilians aboard. They say that, from the outset, ships like the *Lusitania* were deemed unfit for war—too much coal, too easy targets, too large crews to put at risk. "It sounds like the Germans knew it wasn't a warship and torpedoed it anyway," I say.

"That Schwieger fellow who gave the order . . . I can't just wait around, hoping he gets what he deserves."

I have seen the posters addressed "To the Women of Canada," instructing them to think about the Germans invading their homes, imploring them to "help and send a man to enlist," but now that I have my first chance, it seems too personal a decision for me to attempt to tip the scales either way. "The only good news about the whole mess is that it might help convince Woodrow Wilson it's high time the Americans joined the Allies," I say.

After that we are quiet and solemn, and I try my best to concentrate on the views of the rapids far below. The panorama is splendid, yet I look to his hands, folded in his lap. They are large, like the rest of him, and entirely masculine, just sinew and sturdy bone in a jacket of bronzed, chapped skin. I lift my gaze to the side of his face. In profile, his nose is not entirely straight but slightly curved at the bridge. His hair is thick and a little unruly, and I suppose he could use a haircut, but there is something appealing about a man who does not fuss, though all men ought to be clean-shaven, which he certainly is. His lashes are thick and dark, accentuating the paleness of his eyes. Soft lines radiate from the outside corners, causing me to wonder for a moment if he is more than a few years older than I. But on closer inspection, I see the lines are only streaks of pale from squinting into sunshine.

He turns and catches me studying him but does not seem to mind. "Was it much of a hike for you to the bridge?" I say.

He shakes his head. "I've got a room at the Windsor Hotel."

The Windsor Hotel is three-story and square, featureless except for the swirls of wrought iron enclosing a narrow, second-floor veranda, and an ungainly fire escape. It is home to foreigners and drifters and whoever else does not much mind living above a saloon.

"There's not much to it, but it's comfortable enough," he says. "I'm at the end of the hall, so I don't hear anyone else."

A rented room at the Windsor Hotel? What had I expected? The truth is I had not much considered an existence beyond the fictitious one where we steal away from Mother and he takes me by the hand and pulls me in close.

We reach the whirlpool, a swirling basin of water some sixty acres in extent at the foot of the gorge, and wait as passengers disembark and others step onto the running boards of the trolley and slide along the seats. As we set off, I say, "You're on your own?" breaking the quiet.

"I have been for six years," he says, "since I was sixteen."

"What about your parents?"

He shakes his head. "It isn't something I much like talking about." But there is nothing harsh in his voice, nothing callous to suggest case closed.

"I'll have no choice but to think the worst if you leave it at that."

"They're dead, is all." My hand flits to his arm, lingers a moment, before I pull it back to my lap. His shoulders inch up. The palms of his hands slide over his thighs. "My mother died when I was born and then afterward, my father. A broken heart, they say. My grandparents took me in."

"I'm sorry."

"I never felt I missed out." He looks me square in the face. "Any kid would've been lucky to have what I did."

"And six years ago?"

"Six years ago, in the winter, the three of us came down with influenza. My grandmother held on for a couple of months, until she'd buried my grandfather and seen me through the worst of it." He turns away. "It's okay now, mostly, but it was a lot."

He lives at the Windsor Hotel because he has grit. If I had a sliver of it, I would admit to my life not being quite as it must seem. "I'm not going back to Loretto in the fall."

He nods, as though he already knows. "I figured out who your father is. Sometimes he comes into the hotel, quite a lot lately."

"You know him?"

"I work in the saloon a couple of nights a week."

I nod, trying to keep my face from changing while I wonder what working in a saloon means about his own fondness for drink.

"I heard him talking about Glenview, and that's when I figured it out," he says.

A handful of times I have cringed in silence as Father publicly reeled off the most impressive accomplishments of the fellow who built Glenview. I look at Tom and say, "I suppose he was going on about how the fellow who built Glenview also built Town Hall and the transept of Christ Church Anglican on Zimmerman Avenue."

He nods.

"It's true."

"I didn't doubt it."

"There's more you should know." I put a hand on the seat in front of us, steadying myself. "I might live in a big house, but these days my mother and I sew dresses to keep our family afloat."

He nods, again as though he already knows. But how can he? I am bewildered for the second it takes me to realize that men are inclined to gloat, particularly after swallowing a mouthful of drink, particularly when someone as proud as Father is down on his luck. "I like him," he says. "All the boys at work do."

And then, without considering whether I want the answer I suspect I will get, I say, "How much does he drink?"

"I counted eight ounces of rye whiskey the other night and he still wasn't slurring his words."

"A lot, then?"

"I'm no prohibitionist."

"Too much?" I say.

"Too much."

I feel no new sorrow. Nor has coming clean steered my thoughts away from the bleakness of the Windsor Hotel.

At the Niagara Glen, he says we will get off for a bit, until the next trolley comes along, in fifteen minutes or so. We step from the trolley and cross the flats. As we peer into a less steep section of the gorge that the locals refer to as the glen, he says, "When I was a kid I thought it was where the fairies lived, in the woods."

"Your own enchanted forest," I say.

He smiles. "There are arches and boulders as big as houses, some with potholes worn right through the middle by the river way back, when it was higher than it is now. The ferns are waist deep in places, growing as thick as I've ever seen."

I try to focus on his words, but there is the bristle hair of his forearm tickling the smooth skin of my own, and now I am wondering whether he will kiss me when we part, also whether I want him to.

Back on the trolley, I move over a smidgen because I need to keep my wits about me and I can feel the heat of his thigh through my skirt. A fellow sitting behind us says, "It's pretty enough but a calamity, really, all the energy still running to waste, all that water tumbling over the brink."

Tom's face hardens, and I am reminded of the day we sat on the veranda, partitioned from the world by a curtain of rain. He had spoken of all the affronts the river had suffered, of man's efforts to truss up the river like a turkey at Christmastime. Afterward I had skimmed the Book of Genesis, looking for a verse I was sure I had read before: "And God blessed them, and God said unto them, Be fruitful, and multiply, and replenish the earth, and subdue it." It had bothered me then that Tom's sentiment seemed in opposition to Father's, let alone God's. And it bothers me still. "Have you heard about the powerhouse Beck wants?" I say. "My father says as long as Beck's involved it will be the biggest powerhouse around."

"Do you know about the Boundary Waters Treaty?"

"Yes." Over the years I had heard Father grumble about the treaty that limited the water diverted from the river for hydroelectricity to about a quarter of the natural flow. "Sheer idiocy," he would say. "You can't tell me we shouldn't be allowed a little more when the river's high in the spring. And who cares how much is going over the brink in the middle of the night?"

"Near as I can figure," Tom says, "with the powerhouses already on the river taking what they're allowed, there's not enough left for the hundred thousand horsepower Beck is talking about."

"My father says Beck's a genius at having things turn out his way."

"Beck's a self-promoting industrialist who doesn't give two hoots about destroying the river." Tom blows out though closed lips, then catches himself—fortunately—and shifts to a softer tone. "I just hope the Boundary Waters Treaty isn't as easy to ignore as the Burton Act."

The Burton Act, the first piece of legislation meant to preserve Niagara Falls, was quietly swept aside a half dozen years ago in favor of the more lenient Boundary Waters Treaty. "History isn't on your side," I say.

Once we have crossed to the American side, the railbed descends to just a few feet above the water, and he says, "My grandfather used to say we were going back in time when we went into the gorge."

I cock my head, perplexed.

"Look at the bands in the wall. We're heading down to the oldest layers."

My gaze moves across strata of gray, pale beige, pink-brown, some jagged, others worn smooth. At the base of the walls, the river writhes and bucks in response to the narrowed gorge. "Just wait," he says. "At the Whirlpool Rapids, the waves are thirty feet high. It's where Captain Webb died."

It is part of the lore the locals gather as children: Captain Matthew Webb coming to Niagara to swim the rapids some thirty years ago, fresh from being the first to conquer the English Channel. It took four days for his body to surface, and when it did there was a three-inch gash in his temple. Like that of the Maid of the Mist and her canoe, like that of Blondin and his tightrope, like that of Annie Taylor and her barrel, it is a story I have heard more times than I can count. "He was a fool," I say.

"My grandfather told him that."

"Your grandfather knew Captain Webb?"

"He showed up one morning, asking my grandfather for his opinion on swimming the rapids. My grandfather told him drowning takes a few minutes, that he wouldn't last long enough for that."

"Why your grandfather?"

"Everyone knew he was the fellow to talk to about the river," he says.

I am sitting very still, thinking hard, because I am on the cusp of dredging up some bit of lore, something the children in Niagara Falls are told as they are tucked into beds. It is a story Father had handed down to me, something about a fellow—a giant with shoulders that filled a doorway and hands the size of pie plates when he spread his fingers wide—who had come to Niagara Falls from the north and lived out his days in a cabin overlooking the gorge, always an eye on the river, always predictions being made, always the predictions coming true.

"Was he a giant?" I blurt it out.

"That's what some folks say."

"He came from the north."

"His name was Fergus, and he'd been logging in the wilderness."

"He walked all the way here." I can almost hear Father, stretched out on his back, me in the crook of his arm, spinning the tale of Fergus Cole: After growing tired of salt pork and molasses, baked beans and tea, bunkhouses smelling of tar paper, tobacco, and drying socks, he started walking south, and kept walking until he hit Toronto. He stayed for only a few months before the squalor and the din of city life pushed him around the western curve of Lake Ontario and onward to the mouth of the Niagara. He walked alongside the river, over the plains beneath the escarpment, and then up the escarpment itself. The last leg of his journey ought to have been easy going; there was a decent road. But he left it and made his way through the forest thick with pine, spruce, cedar, and oak along the rim of the gorge, not stopping until he reached the Horseshoe and American falls.

"My father used to tell me about Fergus. I know about the tar paper and the drying socks."

"Tar paper?" He laughs.

"I know about the day the falls stood still. He told me about that," I say, picturing Father's giant dragging the last of the stragglers by the scruffs of their necks from the muddy bed of the upper river.

"It was the first of his predictions," Tom says. "The first of his rescues."

"Father always says it was the river's way of letting the town know Fergus Cole had arrived."

"I can't believe you know all this stuff." It is plain to see he is pleased.

"Everyone does."

Then, as we round Whirlpool Point, he points toward the Lower

Steel Arch Bridge and says, "That's where Ellet built his bridge, the first to cross the gorge."

"Wasn't he the fellow who hung an iron basket from a cable strung across the gorge?"

"He charged tourists a dollar for a ride. Fergus worked on the bridge as a carpenter for a bit. It made him furious, people dangling in a basket meant for moving workmen and supplies."

From the trolley car I have a clear view of the river's boiling fury. It is easy to imagine the tourists suspended up above, daring to look down, peeking between gloved fingers, laughing to show their nerve. As I scan the height of the gorge walls, the story of Father's giant using the basket and a ladder to reach a group of stranded workmen comes to me. "There was a wind squall. It was your grandfather who rescued the men."

"He quit after that," Tom says. "He said the squall was a warning."

"Is that what you think?"

He is quiet a moment, then shrugs. "No one should mock the river."

"I think it would have been God that sent the wind, not the river."

"Maybe either way is one and the same."

I am thinking of Father, wondering if he knows it is the grandson of Fergus Cole pouring his drinks at the Windsor Hotel. "Fergus taught you about the river, then?" I say.

He nods. "We lived in a cabin at Colt's Point. The gorge was right there. It's what we did: hike down to the river, set a few snares, catch a few fish. Once we pulled a fawn from the forebay of a powerhouse, and my grandmother let me keep it in the summer kitchen right the winter through."

"I remember my father saying the constables were always on your doorstep, asking for help."

"They'd show up if a tourist or a boy or a fisherman was late," he says, smiling at the thought of it. "Fergus always took me along. I don't remember not knowing about eddies and undercurrents and standing waves."

"What about your grandmother?"

"Sadie."

And then I cajole and prod and piece together the details he gives me. Sadie was a woman who knew that groundnut root would pass for yam once it was peeled and boiled. She knew it could be ground into flour to make a fine loaf. She cured Fergus of the warts that had plagued him since his days felling trees in wet socks. A drop of orange-red sap from bloodroot smeared between the toes twice a day. The minute Tom sniffled, she handed him a cup of pine needle tea. The minute he coughed, it was a tincture of honey and boiled white pine bark.

"I'm sorry I won't meet them," I say and hear the implication, that I would have been introduced had they still been alive. And while I spoke the words sincerely, the seriousness of the idea gives me pause. I want to take back my words.

He turns to me and says, "Fergus had just barely gotten the news the Burton Act was passed when he died. Sadie paid a boy, and he brought the newspaper every day. She'd flip through the pages, and then one day she said the act had been passed. By then I was on the mend and sitting up in the bed she'd set up beside his. When she was gone he said, 'It's good news. There'll be something left for my great-grandchildren.' It was the most he'd said in a week, and he had a fit of coughing. Then Sadie was back, stroking his forehead and telling him to take a deep breath. They were his last words."

I fidget with a button, face straight ahead, the best I can do to give him a bit of privacy, and try to ignore the way his voice cracked, his halted breath. And then a moment later, almost certain it is not usual for him to speak so openly, I am wondering if he might be thinking of me as someone he has been waiting for and feeling uneasy about my part in fostering the idea if I am right.

We are a short ways from the Lower Steel Arch Bridge when he leans from the trolley and tilts his face upward, scanning the wall of the gorge. "It's cooled off," he says. "I don't like being in the gorge when the temperature drops."

"It's still pleasant enough."

"Bess," he says, shifting his weight to his feet, "we'd better get off."

"Here?"

"We can follow the tracks to the rim and catch the next trolley up top."

The railbed is several yards across with a few feet clearance between the track and the gorge wall and, on the opposite side, a steeply sloping riverbank.

"We'd better hurry," he says, grasping my upper arm and steering me toward the open side of the car while several fellow passengers turn their heads to watch.

"You want me to jump?" I am poised at the opening, the brush alongside the track rushing by my feet, when I first hear what begins as a low rumble and ends seconds later as a resounding crash. A cloud of gray dust rises from the railbed a dozen yards ahead. Passengers scream and leap from the sides of the car as the trolley slows to a stop. My initial instinct is to join them. But a greater instinct wins out and I remain beside Tom, his hand firmly on my arm. A moment later he is telling me to stay put and leaping from the trolley and then running up alongside it. "It's safe," he yells. "You're all safe."

Passengers turn to him. He nods. "No more rock will fall."

"I've sprained my ankle," a woman says and flops onto the grass beside the track.

"You nearly trampled me to death," another woman says to a man with his hand on her elbow in a proprietary way.

"I'll sue," a second man says.

"Have you got a crowbar?" Tom hollers up to the conductor. "It isn't much of a slide. We can clear it ourselves."

"We'd better wait for the authorities," says the man who said he would sue.

"You can wait all you like," another man says.

Tom makes his way back to me. "Are you okay for a bit?"

"I'm fine."

Then he is off. He takes the crowbar from the conductor as he passes and a moment later is tipping fallen rocks into the river. Soon enough, a handful of men follow him and begin helping out.

I wait in the trolley, watching, noticing the way the men defer to him. Which rock should be moved next? Should the rubble at the base of the wall be left to shore it up? They see his comfort with the work, his certainty that the wall above will hold. And he is easily the strongest among them, the one to whom the crowbar is passed each time a particularly large rock is exposed.

When I am nearly to the fallen rock, he hands off the crowbar and lopes toward me. "What is it?" he says.

"How did you know?"

"Know what?"

"You knew we were in for a slide," I say.

"I was pretty sure." He slips his hands into the pockets of his trousers.

"But how?"

"There were crevices but no scrub. Crevices without enough soil for a bit of scrub are new and need to be watched. And the temperature dropped."

"And water in cracks expands and contracts."

Then he speaks almost shyly, as though he is not sure I want to hear: "There's something more, too. There are moments, usually on the river. It's nothing I know how to explain."

I watch him, filling with wonder. I have heard Father argue that intuition is entirely rational. There is no mystery, no magic, nothing astonishing as far as he is concerned. A woman knows her child is ill, even before laying her palm on his forehead, only because he slept late and called out in the night and ate poorly the evening before. It does not matter one iota that she cannot articulate the clues. Father would say, "We do not always know what we know."

But I am not so quick to rule out mystery and magic. I like the astonishing and do not doubt that it exists. What is God, after all, if not mystery and magic, and astonishing? I have little inclination to scoff at Tom's bit of mystery. From my window seat at the academy, I saw prayers in the rising mist.

I want to hear more, but men are glancing over, waiting, uncertain what to do next. I nod so he will know I have understood.

"I should get to work," he says.

As I make my way back to the trolley, I am determined to contribute in some small way. When I reach the woman with the sprain, I tear a strip of fabric from the hem of my underskirt and bind her swollen ankle with it. As I help her to her feet, she says, "You make a handsome pair," and I smile.

Once the woman is hobbling about, her arm looped through that of a fellow in a uniform who seems to be her husband, I occupy several children with a game of I Spy, my attention often shifting to Tom. A girl of about twelve cups her hand around my ear and whispers, "Is he your beau?"

I cup my hand around her ear and whisper back, "Yes."

I will feel Tom's lips on mine today. I know it for sure. I know it because if he does not lean toward me, offering his mouth, I will lean toward him, offering mine, the Windsor Hotel pushed from my thoughts.

9

The legend of the Maid of the Mist

I have been made an offer of marriage. As the proposal was stammered out, I had the strangest sensation, as though I were watching one of those scenes in a play that causes the audience to snicker in their seats. A young actor announces he is heartbroken or, alternately, deeply in love. In either case, friends and relations of the lovesick fellow express condolences or congratulations, whichever is appropriate. All the while their minds are searching for some tidbit of missed information that will let them in on just who the coveted female is.

What a dreadful episode, Edward proposing to me.

Not five minutes ago, he went down on bended knee, and took my hand in his, at which point I became momentarily dumb, my tongue thick and dry. I was sitting on the chaise on the veranda, uncomfortable though I had forgone a corset. The dress was Mother's, made acceptable enough by the addition of a ruffle of itchy tulle at the neckline. Isabel had been called inside, ostensibly to help prepare tea, but had been gone twenty minutes or more when Edward dropped to his knee.

I was half-listening to him ramble on about how well wicker furniture was selling in spite of the war when next thing I knew he was on his knee, his head bowed, unable to meet my eye. "Will you marry me?" he said.

Silence ensued while I tried to regain the use of my tongue. "Edward?"

He cleared his throat and, a little louder, said, "Will you marry me?"

"Are you serious?"

He looked at me. Seriously.

"But I'm only seventeen," I said. Until I turned eighteen, marriage was impossible, unless my father gave his consent.

"I've already asked and your father has agreed."

"Oh."

He looked up. "Kit said not to expect an answer right away."

"I'm so surprised. And flattered, but, Edward, I . . ."

"I could help you, your family," he said.

My hand flew to my hip. "Did Kit tell you that?"

"Are you angry?"

"Did she put you up to this?"

"No," he said.

Suddenly Isabel and Mother were on the veranda with the tea.

Isabel's eyes went to Edward, kneeling beside the chaise.

"A button fell off his shirt," I said.

As she peered under the chaise, I said, "I think it rolled through a crack."

"I have a box of spare buttons upstairs," Mother said, although she could see just as well as Isabel that no button was missing from his shirt.

He stood up from kneeling, and I waited for him to say, "Button? What button? Did a button fall off my shirt?" But for once his eyes glinted comprehension. "There are plenty of buttons at home," he said. He tipped his Panama hat to Mother and Isabel, and then to me. "I'll be off." Rude or not, he meant to escape before tea was served.

I stood up from the chaise and stepped toward him, already heading for the Runabout. Isabel and Mother remained on the veranda, Mother's arm firmly looped through Isabel's. When we were midway to the automobile, Mother and Isabel called out their good-byes and disappeared into the house, likely to tend to some newly urgent housekeeping task.

At the Runabout, he said, "I'll be in touch." He leaned toward me and delivered a dry, papery kiss to my cheek.

I sit on the chaise, forehead in my hands, elbows on my knees. Edward has never kissed me before, and I wonder what, if anything, invited the kiss. Was it because I did not reject his proposal flat out? Or because we conspired about the lost button? Was it that he had read too much into my tidy hair and itchy dress? While logic says the kiss would have come, invited or not, I am riddled with guilt.

As a first kiss, Edward's effort would have been a great disappointment, a kick in the teeth really, given the imaginings of my girlhood and the secrets whispered in the Loretto corridors. But because it was not the first, it merely provided proof that nothing more than friendship exists between Edward and me.

When Tom kissed me at the close of our afternoon circuiting the gorge, I did not purse my lips. They fell slightly open, entirely receptive to the warm breath and wet of his mouth. The kiss lasted only seconds; we were barely hidden in the shadows of the Lower Steel Arch Bridge. Still, I have imagined that kiss a thousand times since. I have imagined his tongue against mine. Afterward, when we stood looking at each other, my flesh was taut, my skin goose-pimpled, my breath noticeably short, at least until the Coulsons passed by in their Oldsmobile, came to a halt, and insisted I climb into the backseat.

Before I even had the door pulled shut, Mrs. Coulson twisted around to face me. "Good gracious, Bess," she said. "Who on earth was that?"

I was trembling under her piercing gaze, hardly able to breathe. "He used to bring us fish."

"His hand was on your arm."

I stared down at my knees, thanked God that, when we pulled into Glenview, Mother would not yet be back from Toronto or Father from the Windsor Hotel.

"What about your family?" she said, an angry knot of lines appearing on her brow. "A good connection is what you need." Mr. Coulson patted her arm, as though to calm her, but she shrugged off his hand. Her voice grew louder. "People gossip, Bess. And there you are, fueling the flames. And that layabout. You were raised better than that." She was silent as we turned onto Buttrey Street except for the occasional sigh.

At Glenview I said, "I wasn't doing anything indecent at all," and willed the tears not to come as I scrambled from the automobile.

Then, it was "You stay away from the likes of him," quietly hurled from her lips.

T he screen door claps the wood of the jamb, and I look at Mother, standing there, watching, probably mulling over how best to approach me, particularly if Mrs. Coulson has called, which she very likely has. "Bess?" she says. "May I sit with you?"

I shift to the tall end of the chaise, and she sits at the foot.

"Well?" she says.

"He proposed."

"It's wonderful," she says. "He's kind and generous. And most of all, he adores you."

I throw my palms open. "I'm only seventeen."

She lays a hand on my thigh. "You're a woman. You've shown all of us that this summer," she says.

"Then I should decide whom I'll marry." I mean to thump the chaise with my fist but only let it flop down beside me.

"It is your decision, Bess."

"But I don't love him," I say. I am absolutely sure of it, given Tom, given our kiss.

I am delivered a long, possibly rehearsed lecture, the net of which is that there are two kinds of love. One that is slow in coming and builds with shared kindnesses. And another that is all-consuming, blind, little more than lust. "The first can last a lifetime," she says. "The second is founded on nothing and cannot."

I find myself wondering into which camp she and Father fall. They married young and speak fondly of their early days, of the winter Mother's shoe soles wore through and Father stuffed newspaper into the toes of his boots and gave them to her. But lately she has begun to sigh deeply when his back is turned. Does she regret marrying him? I will not ask. To do so might lend a bit of credence to her words.

"That fellow who brought the fish," she says and waits, eyes narrowed, head cocked.

"I was out walking on River Road."

"He has nothing to offer you."

"I don't want anything from him." I smooth damp palms over my skirt, anxious that she somehow knows just how badly I want a second kiss.

"You'll want a roof over your head, the odd pretty dress, sugar for your tea . . ."

"And Edward can give me all that so I should marry him?" I stand up from the chaise, walk to the far corner of the veranda, and stand with my back to her.

"He is a gentleman. He'll devote himself to you."

I turn toward her. "I know. I know he would, but still."

"As for the fellow who brought the fish," she says, and I shrink under her steady gaze. "He brought you to some dark corner of the Lower Steel Arch Bridge. Your reputation was the furthest thing from his mind. He isn't a gentleman, not in the least."

"Mrs. Coulson is a busybody." Brave words from a girl of seventeen with a month's worth of daydreams under scrutiny and withering.

"He behaved improperly."

Not feeling altogether well, I sit back down on the chaise and say, "Edward should marry Isabel."

"He wants to marry you." She brushes my cheek with the back of her hand.

"What about love growing over time and all that?"

Her gaze leaves mine. "Edward has made up his mind."

"And so have I," I say, though my head is a muddled, murky pool. "And I won't marry him."

I begin to cry, and she takes me into her arms. My cheek against her breast, she rocks me back and forth, cooing, "You'll decide for yourself" and "I only want what's best," though I have already said I will not marry Edward.

She rubs the place that aches between my shoulder blades and smoothes my hair. I sniffle and bawl, needing that embrace like a child, like a child taking those first few steps toward the safety net of outstretched arms.

If she insisted, or argued even a little bit, I think I might be able to stop the tears, the second guessing. But, wrapped in my mother's love, I cannot. With each heave of my shoulders, with each gasp for breath, her words gain a smidgen of credibility.

Eventually, I am able to say, "Isabel would hate me if I married Edward."

She is silent a moment, her hand motionless on my back. Then she gently guides me to sitting upright and tilts my chin so that she can see my face. "Take your time deciding," she says and wipes my cheeks and nose with her handkerchief. "Isabel will see the upside in having Edward as a brother-in-law."

She is beautiful just now, her forehead smooth, her eyes bright, brimming with hope.

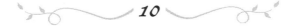

10

The August night is sweltering and my four-poster bed seems entirely too small. Shift and turn as I might, every square inch of linen is wrinkled and damp, and I find no reprieve from the warmth my body has set down. Away from Mother and her comforting words, Edward's proposal seems a warren of trapdoors, regardless of what I decide. I pray for guidance, but my mind only drifts from pleas for good judgment and clarity to Tom's warm mouth on my own. And somehow I am depraved enough to wonder, Is it a sign? Surely God could nudge that kiss from my prayers.

By the time there is enough light to make out the straw-colored vines of the paper covering my walls, I am determined to find Tom, in the glen, at the whirlpool, or even at the Windsor Hotel. I am determined to keep my head clear, my mind sharp, much as Mother would, rather than a stew of bristle hair against skin and forearms rippling with strength each time the crowbar is passed. I will ask about ambition and schooling and intentions, and rye whiskey drunk at the Windsor Hotel or any other place, questions a father not as negligent as my own would surely ask. And if Tom minds? Well, then, mind he must. At least I will know. I dress quickly, straining to hear any stirrings in my parents' bedroom, and tiptoe downstairs, careful to avoid the creaky third step.

I am on River Road before the birdsong has ended or the dew dried from the grass. Facing south and then north, I squint into the distance, but the road is empty.

At the Wintergreen Flats overlooking the glen, I stop for a moment and survey the woods far below, but the leafy canopy easily blocks any glimpse of him. I descend the stairway of some seventy steps, the only way to reach the winding pathways of the talus slope. Overhead the uppermost layers of the flats protrude beyond the cliff wall forming a natural amphitheater and, to the north, a spectacular promontory. I stand gazing upward at the river's handiwork.

There are giant boulders strewn about the woods, some precariously poised, others with great basins or even curiously round hollows carved all the way through. Smaller fragments of sheared rock are only partially covered with earth, yet the scenery is sylvan, pretty, too, a paradise of wildflowers and ferns. Each time a pathway intersects mine, I select the route with the steepest descent, thinking it will lead me most quickly to the river and to Tom.

The thunder of the Niagara tells me the rapids are near long before I am able to glimpse the froth and spray through the woods. I can see only a few feet in any one direction, and my spirit wanes, my search seeming futile, even dangerous, the scheme of a naïve girl expecting providence to intervene. But I continue along the path, humming in an attempt to keep my imagination in check, until I come to a spot where a glut of boulders between the pathway and the riverbank has kept the vegetation down. I pick my way across the boulders, scaling their sides, descending their slopes, striding the crevices in between, until I come to a thin stream of river severed from the main flow by a boulder. The boulder would provide the perfect vantage point from which to view a good chunk of the shore, yet I once read in the newspaper about a group of tourists who were marooned on a boulder that became an island when the river unexpectedly rose. Also, at its farthest reach, the boulder is lashed by rushing water, much of it curling backward and forming an angry standing wave as it smashes headlong into the current surging downstream.

Regardless, I remove my stockings and shoes and hike up my skirts. The stream is deceptive, possibly because of its juxtaposition with the Niagara. Midway to the boulder, the current tugs my shins, threatening to sweep my feet from beneath me and deliver me to the river proper, from which even Captain Webb could not escape.

Once on the boulder, I need only a moment to scan the empty shoreline and then a further moment to take in the majesty of the gorge wall. So as not to lose my nerve, I keep the river at my back.

My return to the pathway is without mishap, and, elated by my daring, I continue on, in a southern direction, toward the whirlpool, though the pathway narrows and then becomes altogether difficult to pick out. It is likely the route Tom follows as he makes his way between glen and whirlpool, also other fishermen and the most adventuresome of the tourists. There is evidence, too, of deer, tidy brown pellets that fortunately do not stick to my shoes.

Earlier I arranged my hair hastily, with little thought given to a scramble in the woods. Now slim branches pull long strands from their clips. My right forearm is scraped in two places, and a thin line of red appears on the back of my hand. My skirt is caked in dust, which will likely shake loose. But in several spots the dirt is ground in. I will have to tell Mother I went into the glen to walk and to think. I will say that I became lost, that I panicked and stumbled in my rush.

The stone beach of the whirlpool could not be a more welcome sight, except that the lone gentleman catching his breakfast on the far shore is not Tom. Disheartened, but anxious to take up the most efficient route to the Windsor Hotel, I make my way across the beach to what looks like a trailhead of sorts. Years ago the whirlpool was accessible from the rim of the gorge by means of an incline railway, and likely the break in the leafy canopy above the trailhead marks the remains of the tracks. With luck the old ties will serve as footholds while I climb the bank leading out of the gorge.

My hunch is correct, and soon enough I am clambering up a still solid set of tracks. I move quickly, not stopping to smooth my hair or skirt, or wipe the dirt from my hands. When a small fox rustles the underbrush, I am startled and my hands fly to my chest. My gaze settles on a rough path of trampled ferns leading away from the tracks. Twenty feet from where I stand, the path ends at a weather-beaten chest. I notice the set of initials carved into the lid: "T. C." And it is of no surprise to me that Thomas Cole would not have a middle name, also that he would know about the old tracks and have a secret place to stash his gear.

As I open the lid and prop it against a beech tree, I am expecting to find camping equipment, or maybe fishing line, lures, and bait. But the interior is filled with heavy rope, straps and belts, and a folded canvas tarpaulin, none of which immediately makes sense. I lift the tarpaulin. It is heavier than I expected, and I hold it by the corners, allowing its contents to spill out. A large, many-pronged hook lands in the underbrush, and I make the connection between it and an object I heard described many years ago.

At the academy, when I was still in the little school, a girl called Mary Morse, whose father was the local undertaker, told me about grappling hooks. "Like a fishhook," she said, "except big." The sister supervising our dorm had nodded off, and the cane with which she struck the floor to silence us had slipped to her feet. Mary wriggled to the edge of her bed closest to mine and asked whether I was awake. She went on to tell me about a body—she called it a floater—her father had recently nailed shut inside a pine coffin. She said it had been in the river at least a week. No one could say exactly how long, but great gobs of flesh were missing; the skin was too rotten to withstand the tug of the grappling hook dragging it to shore. The picture I conjured was terrifying and nearly complete—a stark white body, folded at the waist; a V being dragged through the river; arms, legs, and a mass of hair trailing behind.

"Your father has one?" A grappling hook seemed the right sort of paraphernalia for a man who regularly shaved corpses and forced eyelids shut.

"The man who pulls out the floaters does," she said. "He brings them to the back door. Mother says he can't come in."

"Why not?"

"Mother says he's the worst sort, waiting at the river day and night, hoping someone will throw himself over the falls, just so he can get drunk as a skunk."

I muddled up my face.

"Father pays a bottle of rye whiskey for a floater," she said, "and the town pays him fifteen dollars to bury it."

I sink to the forest floor as images fill my head: hands easing free a grappling hook jammed between a pair of ribs; a naked breast tattered by an errant toss; a bulky tarpaulin slung over a shoulder, the juices from within soaking through to the jacket beneath.

So this is something Tom does.

Isabel had said a shopgirl could do better, and all we had known then was that Tom rode the trolley and wore the clothes of a workingman. Kit had guessed at his livelihood, becoming ever more dubious, even when he appeared something as harmless as a fisherman. Mother had not wanted him coming to the door back when he only seemed a regular fellow, nice enough to help with a trunk. Had they known then what I do now, their distaste would have been tenfold, a revulsion that matches my own.

Tom is one of those men, bleary-eyed and lecherous, waiting at the whirlpool for a floater to turn up. Never mind the rotting flesh, the smashed skulls, the severed limbs. Snag the floater. Haul it in. Cart the bloated, sloppy, stinking mess all the way to Morse and Son, and use the back door. Collect the bottle of rye whiskey. Knock back a swig, and then another. And another after that, because who wants to remember a pair of eye sockets nibbled empty by the fish?

Dickens is correct: Every human creature is a profound secret and mystery to every other. It seems the saddest thing in the world to know he is right. And I want to cry, to drum my fists upon the earth, but more than that, I want to be rid of this place.

I resume my climb up the track, one heavy foot in front of the other. When I reach for my rosary, I find my pocket is empty. The rosary is in my bedroom, forgotten, hidden beneath my underclothes.

I do not look up from the ties and know I am out of the gorge only when the tracks come to an end. Forsaking the whirlpool, the gorge, the river below, I step onto River Road. Chin still tucked to my chest, I stride toward home.

But when I arrive, there is no solace to be had, only red-faced Mother, continuing to bellow even as she sees me cross the yard, her words tangled and hardly making sense, also Father, his shirtfront dribbled with the rye whiskey–stinking vomit pooled on the veranda steps.

There is still the offer from Edward. Good, kind, sober, set-for-life Edward, who can save me, my family, from the wrecks our lives have become.

11

Collapse of Table Rock

I throw myself onto my bed without bothering to remove my soiled dress and cry facedown into the coverlet for a solid half hour, trying all the while to dispel from my thoughts an ugly image of Tom heaving a grappling hook. Will Mother come and put her arms around me like she did yesterday? It is nearly ten o'clock, and surely she has noticed I have not yet had my biscuit and tea. Maybe she thinks I am lingering in bed after a sleepless night. Maybe she thinks the odds of me accepting Edward's proposal go up with each hour of rest I am allowed. Or maybe she has no time for my nonsense, not with Isabel and Father and the five perfect dresses she must produce every week.

When knuckles rap my door, I do not respond, but the door creaks open anyway, as I had hoped, and then there is a hand on my back.

"Bess?" It is Isabel.

I sniffle, and she presses her handkerchief into my palm and then strokes my hair, which only makes the sniffling worse.

"Tell me," she says.

But what is there to tell? Father drinks. Mother sews and sews, her foot on the treadle having become a vice of sorts. Isabel already knows. She knows, too, that her own body is still bitterly thin, that she eats only enough to keep Dr. Galveston away, only enough to appease those counting the spoonfuls entering her mouth. And I will not tell about the bloated bodies the river gives up, or the grappling hook Tom uses to haul them to shore, or the bottle of rye whiskey with which payment is made. But I want her to stay with me. I want to prolong the gentle tug of her fingertips in my hair. "I could go on for hours," I say.

"Is it Edward? Mother told me he proposed."

"I won't marry him if you say I shouldn't."

"He'd make a fine husband. And, Bess, don't worry about me. It's easy to see that it's you he wants. I never stood a chance."

I sniffle and uselessly wipe the wet from my cheeks. "He must be blind."

"I don't think so," she says. "I think he sees remarkably well."

"Should I marry him?"

"If it's what you want."

"I've given up," I say.

She shifts, moving closer, and rests a cheek between my shoulder blades. We lie still a long while, until the rise and fall of my back is in perfect unison with each breath she takes. I am in that place just before slumber when she speaks. "Me too," she says.

In early afternoon, I telephone the Atwells' and Edward picks up. "Hello," he says.

"Hello," I say back, but he is silent and stumped, until I say, "It's Bess."

"Oh. Yes, Bess."

"I'm calling to accept." The line goes quiet for a second time, and I think I will have to lay out exactly what I mean by "I'm calling to accept." But then he says, "I'd like to come over. I have a gift," and I see it is only that I have short-circuited the bit of ceremony he had planned.

"Yes, come," I say. "I should have waited to tell you."

Then I hear muffled voices, as though his hand is over the mouthpiece of the telephone. I make out "It's Bess" and "She's said *yes,*" before a round of dampened shouts and claps and shushes begins.

Suddenly Kit is on the line. "Hurray," she says, as though she has forgiven that I called Edward a compromise.

I manage only a quiet thank-you before Edward is back, saying, "I'll be there lickety-split."

And so it is done. I am to be his wife. How different the coming year will be from what I had just months ago assumed. I will not attend chapel in black wool each morning or listen each evening for the bell signaling lights out. I will not be able to say with much accuracy just what I will be doing at any given hour. And yet I feel tranquil, much as I did sitting in my window seat, gazing at the mist. Though different, maybe my days will again be comforting in their predictability.

After hanging up the telephone, I climb the stairs to the sewing room. Mother would have heard my footsteps stop at the doorway; still, she remains focused on turning a velvet collar right side out. Once she completes the finicky work of making the points precise by poking a crochet hook into each from the inside, I clear my throat.

She takes in my soiled, rumpled dress, and I wait to be scolded, but she only inhales a deep breath and says, "Can you press these for me?" and holds out the velvet collar and a pair of matching cuffs. "I don't want the pile crushed, so just put a piece of damp muslin on top of the stove and pass them through the steam."

"I've said yes to Edward. Just now, on the telephone."

Her fingers let go of the collar and cuffs, which drop first onto her lap and then onto the floor as she stands. "How wonderful, Bess."

"He's on his way over," I say. "He said he has a gift for me."

"You'll have to call Father, then."

"At the Windsor Hotel?"

She nods, unfazed by the mention of the hotel, then takes me by the hand and leads me into the bedroom she and Father share. She lifts a small box from his chest of drawers and hands it to me. "Look inside," she says.

I open the lid and find a pair of cuff links, each with a sapphire set in a mother-of-pearl disk ringed with gold.

"You can give them to Edward," she says. "A woman I used to sew for gave them to Father when we got married." When my fingers hesitate just short of picking one up, she says, "Your father won't mind. He insists on that awful aluminum pair."

In the sewing room she wraps a length of grosgrain ribbon around the box holding the cuff links and ties it in a knot. She cuts the ends of the ribbon on an angle and tells me to sew a couple of beads onto it. "Quickly," she says, leaving the sewing room. "You need to change."

She is back in a moment, with the fine, cutwork dress I wore the day I found Isabel on the chaise with her tea dress hiked nearly to her knees. The pale pink corset I pledged never again to wear is tucked under Mother's arm.

I submit to the corset, to the brush she tugs through my hair, to her suggestion that I drag my teeth across my lips until they flare red, also to the telephone call to the Windsor Hotel.

"May I speak to Mr. Heath?" I say into the din carried across the line.

"Speak up, darlin'," says a male voice, mercifully not Tom's.

"Mr. Heath, please."

"Hang on," the voice says, and then, a whole lot louder, "Heath-ee, it's for you."

"Hello," Father says, a moment later. "Who's calling?" He sounds somewhat stricken, satisfyingly so.

"It's Bess," I say.

"What is it?" His anxiety has risen a notch.

"I have news."

"Tell it, then."

"I'm going to marry Edward," I say, and then think to add, "Edward Atwell."

"Ah, Bess," he says. "Things just have a way of working themselves out."

"He'll be here any minute."

"Splendid," he says. "I'm coming home."

After we say good-bye, but before the line is cut, I hear my jolly father announce a round of rye whiskey, on him. I stand in the hallway a moment, imagining him leaning up against the bar, talking of grand schemes and his daughters, both Loretto girls, while the men around him nod and swallow the round that he bought. Once he leaves, the men huddle together. "I wonder if his missus will still be making pretty frocks," they say. And "Loretto girls! His youngest hasn't finished and already he's packing her off."

E dward crosses the yard with a small, silver box shaped like a heart as I wait on the veranda, my own prettily decorated box held behind my skirt. I hold it out to him when he nudges his box toward me, and he makes a great fuss over the few beads sewn onto the grosgrain. "I like that you bothered, for me," he says.

But the beads were for Mother, sewn into place because I am trying to be good, to do what I am told.

He unties the grosgrain, carefully, and coils it into a tidy cylinder, then lifts the lid of the box. He insists on wearing the cuff links then and there, and holds up one wrist after the other while I replace his plain, silver pair. It strikes me as intimate, this ritual between man and woman, husband and wife. He kisses me then, quickly, awkwardly, which is my fault because I inadvertently turn my head.

As I open the heart-shaped box, I am prepared to feign enthusiasm equal to his, no matter the contents. But inside is the most exquisite choker I have ever seen. The centerpiece is made from small diamonds and seed pearls arranged in swirl upon swirl around a large central pearl. More pearls, strings of them in neat rows, form a band an inch wide, which extends right around to the clasp at the back. "Oh, Edward," I say.

"With the war it wasn't the easiest thing to find. Kit and I went to Toronto, to Birks-Ellis."

"It's beautiful."

"I want you to be happy," he says.

"I know," I say, my voice breaking.

He sets the coiled grosgrain on the chaise and faces me, placing a hand on each side of my waist. I lift my arms to his shoulders, my fingers holding the choker at the nape of his neck, and he responds by gingerly sliding his hands upward along my ribs. I feel something then. I am almost sure my breath grows short, as it did in the shadows of the Lower Steel Arch Bridge.

Soon enough Father is on the veranda, clapping Edward's back and shaking his hand. "We're delighted," he says, "to unite our families, to welcome you to ours." Then he cups my chin in the palms of his hands and leans in close enough that I can smell rye whiskey and tobacco on his breath. "Well done," he says. Then his arms are around me, and he rocks me back and forth, muttering in my ear, "Bess. Bess. My sweet Bess," with a distinct slur.

Over his shoulder, I glimpse Mother on the far side of the screen door, watching, sizing up. She steps onto the veranda. "Edward," she says, "we're so very pleased."

After seeing Edward off, I take my time crossing the yard to the veranda, watching as Mother puts her hands on her hips, then reconsiders the posture and brings them together at her waist. Father drops to the chaise and sets his elbows on his knees and his forehead against his palms. When I am within earshot, I hear her say, "Please, just stop, at least until the wedding," and I know she thinks he might cause me to lose Edward, but I know he cannot. She pulls open the screen door. "I'll put on some coffee."

I am set to follow her indoors when Father says, "Hang on a moment, Bess," and reaches into the inside pocket of his jacket. He pulls out a sealed envelope. "A fellow who works at the hotel asked me to deliver his congratulations."

Working to keep my voice steady, my face unchanged, I say, "Who?" though I know that boasts of my engagement accompanied the round of rye whiskey Father bought, that Tom poured the round. "Edward's a fine lad," Father would have said, loudly enough for all to hear. "And well-positioned, too."

Father hands me the envelope. "Tom Cole. He said he carried your trunk, and I wouldn't doubt it. He's as strong as an ox, never even bothers with a dolly when he changes the keg."

"It was the night I came home from Loretto," I say, moving my hands behind my back so he will not notice the envelope trembling.

"He's Fergus Cole's grandson. You remember—the giant, the fellow who saved half the town the day the falls stood still, and then a handful of men when they were knocked from Ellet's bridge. He had the nasty task of dealing with the floaters, too."

I sit on the edge of my bed, smoothing the envelope over my thighs. The decent thing to do would be to toss the envelope into the oven, reducing its contents to ash. How could there be anything important inside when there is nothing of consequence he can say? Still, I slide a fingertip under the corner of the flap.

The handwriting is different from the careful script of the note he left on River Road, tucked between the rocks. It is sharp, hurried, and the paper on which it is written looks as though it were scrunched into a ball and then pressed flat as an afterthought. When I read "Bess," it is his voice I hear: low, soft, the rumble of the Niagara from far away.

> Bess,
>
> Is it true? It must be. But why? I don't understand. I thought you felt like I did. Two days ago you let me kiss you. No, more than that—you kissed me back. Was I only your entertainment for an afternoon? I want to think differently but I cannot.
>
> Tom

It was right to read the note, to see the harm I have done. My head in the clouds, I added yet another wretched episode to his already miserable life, and no one deserves that. It sets more firmly my resolve to do right by Edward, to be a good wife. I fold the note in quarters, slip it into a sachet of lavender, and return the sachet to its place, alongside my rosary, beneath the underclothes in my chest of drawers.

A while later I venture into the hallway and meet Mother coming from her bedroom with a coffeepot and an empty cup. She mouths the word *quiet* and with a quick tilt of her head signals for me to follow.

I take the coffeepot and cup from Mother in the kitchen and set them on the counter. I shake soap flakes into the sink and wait for her to say whatever it is, and become anxious when she does not. When she finally speaks, she says, "Father told me about the envelope."

"I burned it." What else can I say? To tell her a smidgen of what it said would mean to explain about the roadside stones and ferns and notes, an afternoon circuiting the gorge, a misbegotten kiss.

"You're finished with that nonsense, then?"

"Yes."

"Good," she says.

12

My eyes open to weak morning light, and I see Mother standing over me, saying words I cannot immediately make out. I lie there, looking up at her stricken face, eventually sorting out what she has said. "Have you seen Isabel?"

But I have been asleep and Isabel was not in my dreams. "No," I say, shielding my eyes from the brightness of the window, from the day I am not yet awake enough to meet.

"What about last night? Did you look in on her after we got home?"

She is looking at me intently, her eyes pleading. She wants me to say yes, and I do.

"Thank goodness." She pats the coverlet draping my hip, and only then do I understand the question she asked.

She hurries into the hallway and calls down the stairs, "She was here last night. Bess checked when we got home."

"I'll take a look outside," Father calls up from below.

The kitchen door bangs shut, and Mother's footsteps move from room to room and then down the staircase.

The evening before, Mother, Father, and I went to the Clifton House as the Atwells' guests. Isabel had surprised the three of us by climbing into bed a few minutes before we were set to leave. "A headache," she said.

"Get up," Mother said. "I just pressed that dress."

"It's your sister's engagement party," Father said.

"I'm not going."

"Suit yourself," Mother said and marched off with Father on her heels.

"I'm sorry, Bess," Isabel said.

"Why aren't you coming?"

"My headache." From her wrist, she unclasped the aluminum bracelet Father had given her as a graduation gift.

Mother called me from the bottom of the stairs. "Really?" I said to Isabel.

She pressed the chain of delicate, oval plaques into my palm and said, "Wear it so I'll be there in spirit."

She pulled me into her arms and held me until Father called up, "Right this minute, Bess," and I wriggled loose. The moment I was in the Cadillac, sitting behind Mother in a hat she had overhauled with a bit of tulle and a few rosettes, and Father in his best frock coat, I forgot all about Isabel.

We pulled into the circular drive at the Clifton House, and instantly a doorman appeared, tipping his hat to Father and opening doors for Mother and me. The Atwells met us on the veranda, and Edward put his hand on my elbow and the two of us led the way to the table with the best view of the falls. Father declined an aperitif, and it seemed we all relaxed a little after that. We sipped iced tea and said the falls were stunning and glorious and magnificent. I quoted a line about our cataract from the *Life and Letters of Harriet Beecher Stowe,* one of the books Sister Ignatius had given me. "Oh, it is lovelier than it is great; it is like the Mind that made it: great, but so veiled in beauty that we gaze without terror."

Mrs. Atwell's face lit up. "It's always lovely to hear from Mrs. Stowe," she said.

We moved inside to the dining room, and for a moment I stood taken aback. Despite the war, the scene was the same as always—chandeliers, and tables laid with silver, and gentlemen handsome in their frock coats, and women head to toe in embroidered taffeta, velvet ribbon, flouncing, and lace.

I was wearing the pearl choker, and everyone said how well it suited me, how the pearls made my complexion glow. There were toasts and more toasts, and Kit's eyes welled with tears as she said she had wished I were her sister ever since we were little girls. It made our spat the evening of the pilau of mutton feel like aeons ago. Old acquaintances came up to our table and offered congratulations and best wishes to Edward and me, also to Father and Mother, who accepted graciously, as though they had forgotten the slights our family has endured.

Eventually the talk turned to setting a date, which caused me to twist the serviette on my lap. I said, "I'd like to wait until I'm eighteen, which isn't until the new year," but then Edward said, "I'm enlisting with the next battalion raised in Niagara Falls and might be overseas by then."

Kit and Mr. Atwell turned toward Mrs. Atwell. I watched the knuckles of her clasped hands go white. "Sooner rather than later, then," she finally said.

"Bess, you could finish up at Loretto while I'm gone," Edward said. Faces turned in my direction, awaiting my response, and because Father's eyes were among those trained on me, I finally understood what it seemed everyone else already did. When I was Edward's wife, Loretto was not out of the question. The expense would be his.

"I'm not sure," I said, but I had grown used to the idea that I would not return to Loretto and graduate with the girls I had known since I was a child. I had convinced myself I did not much care. Harp and elocution were for the frivolous. And I was not interested in crocheting pretty doilies and tatting snowflakes to hang on a Christmas tree, not anymore.

I never once thought of Isabel, not the whole evening through, and now that she has stomped off, it seems I should have gone to her room, afterward, and described everything she missed. Instead I went straight to my bed, leaving her to wonder whether the Clifton House had changed, whether the women were as chic as always, whether the filbert tartlets were still divine, whether with my good fortune I had completely forgotten her.

I find Mother in the kitchen, rolling out biscuits in her dressing gown. In one fell swoop she unties her apron and tosses it to me. "I'm going to look for her," she says, stepping around me and taking the stairs to the second-floor bedrooms two at a time.

I sink my fingers into the concoction of mixed flours on the counter, then run my palms over a disk of partially rolled dough. I ought to tell, to explain that I was half-asleep, that I was not at all clear about what I was being asked. I sprinkle a bit of flour over the dough and roll the pin across its surface. Surely Isabel is simply out of sight behind the peonies or walking on River Road or sitting in a sunny spot, away from the breeze, wondering if we have missed her yet.

On her way out the front door, Mother calls into the kitchen, "Forget the biscuits. Come and help."

By midday I have looked in the fruit cellar and attic, opened each wardrobe, and lifted the skirt of each bed. I have stood upstairs and downstairs in the empty house, pleading with Isabel to give up the game, telling her I am sorry if she is angry, that she can wear my pearl choker any time she likes as long as she shows herself. I have peered up each tree and behind each shrub and knocked on the doors of a dozen neighbors I have never before met.

Out of breath, I climb the bluff a final time. Mother and Father halt their clipped exchange on the veranda and turn to face me. They wait, as still as pillars, as wanting as starved dogs. "I didn't look in on Isabel last night," I say. "I should never have said that I did."

Mother eyes me warily, and I do not glance away until tears spill onto her cheeks. Father's arms are around her then, until she throws them off, saying, "For God's sake, call the police."

Constable Peters arrives on foot nearly two hours later and has little to say other than that with the war he is short of men and that young women are subject to bouts of hysteria, which generally pass. "Young, employed girls seldom have the disease," he says, "but indolent girls are prone to it." He has seen it time and again, the irregular muscle action, the laughter interrupted by cries.

"You aren't describing Isabel," Mother says. "She isn't ill."

"You said she doesn't eat."

"She's missing, not ill."

"Hysteria usually comes at a certain time of the month," he says.

"Look," Father says, stepping closer to Constable Peters, who does not back away. "You will take her description, and canvass the neighborhood or organize a search party, whatever it is you usually do."

"There's a war on, sir. I'm short of men."

"The war is an excuse."

"Has she recently lost a beau?"

"You can go," Father says, his voice steady and cold.

Mother and Father stand in the doorway as Constable Peters makes his way down the bluff. "Maybe we should go around to some of her friends," Mother says.

Isabel was forever passing notes in study hall, forever being caught. And more times than I can count, her whispers were interrupted by the slap of the presiding sister's palm against a tabletop. Still, she was well-liked by the sisters, who seemed to welcome a bit of fun. By the girls, she was adored. They linked their arms with hers as she strolled the academy grounds and arranged themselves in the dining hall only once she had selected a seat. Mother had mentioned visitors in the spring, but the visits dwindled and then, before I had come home, altogether stopped. Even so, I jot down the name of each of the local girls from Isabel's graduating class: Mary Egan, Grace Swan, Maeve O'Neill, Vivian Spence.

Father waits in the Cadillac while Mother puts on her hat. The last pin slid from her lips, she says, "Stay put," and quickly embraces me.

The Cadillac descends Buttrey Street, turns onto River Road, and disappears. I stand a long while—fingering Isabel's aluminum bracelet, gazing after the automobile—until the telephone rings, startling me.

"Hello," I say.

"It's Mrs. Coulson. It's Bess, isn't it?"

"It is," I say, struck by her composure. It is our first contact since the episode in the Oldsmobile. "I'm afraid Mother's out."

"Well, it's you I ought to be congratulating at any rate."

For a moment I am clueless. "Oh," I say and then remembering myself, "Thank you. Thank you very much."

"I ran into Mrs. Woodruff, and she said you were absolutely beaming at the Clifton House."

"How kind of her. And very nice of you to call," I say, wanting to free up the line.

"I'm just so pleased; Mr. Coulson, too," she says. "The Atwells are a lovely family, and Edward is well-positioned."

"I'll tell my mother you called."

"Just a moment, Bess. About the other day, our little chat." No doubt she is patting herself on the back, chalking up my engagement to her bit of spat advice. "I hope I didn't cause much of a fuss with your mother?"

"None whatsoever," I say. No chance will I mention the lecture I was delivered on the veranda, the tears that followed it, certain proof, in her eyes, of yet another notch in her belt.

"Tell your father congratulations from Mr. Coulson, too."

Once I am off the line, I move out to the veranda, my gaze sweeping the yard, the bluff, River Road. But Isabel is nowhere to be seen. Eventually I sink to the chaise and pull my feet up alongside me.

When I next glance toward the river, a lone figure is sprinting up the bluff. Before I am on my feet, I know it is Tom. Soaking wet and hatless, he bounds up the steps of the veranda, saying, "Are you alone?"

"Yes."

"You should come with me."

Although he is out of breath from the climb, there is firmness in his voice, an almost irresistible certainty. Still, I am equally certain I should not follow him. It is a test. "I won't."

"Just come." He grasps my upper arm.

Shaking loose his grip, I say, "I'm staying here. I'm waiting for Isabel."

He inhales, long and slow. His fingers splay, then curl into loose fists.

"It's Isabel?" I say.

"Yes."

FALLS

August 1915–January 1916

13

Isabel seems peaceful, lying there on the stone beach, her wet hair smoothed from her face and fanned about her head. Her skin is too white, tinged with blue, not unlike watery milk. The tea dress I made for her is torn from breast to hem but carefully arranged to cover her flesh. The cotton is laden with water and clings to her frame, to the bony shoulders, protruding collarbones, and wasted thighs, to the swollen breasts and the exaggerated roundness of her belly. Her eyelids have been shut.

It is her, yet it is not. She is so very alive, so utterly unlike the body laid out before me, and it is not possible for her to have become nothing at all.

I drop to my knees and then onto Isabel, sobbing, kissing her cold skin, her wet hair. Tom stands quietly aside, at the fringe of the woods abutting the whirlpool's stone beach. He speaks to a group of boys who have made their way down the bank, sends them off to a fishing hole farther downriver, not that I care in the least what sort of spectacle I have become.

Why did I not guess it? It should have been so easy, with her morning pallor and unwillingness to eat, and the tea dress that fit the day it was hemmed but before long was too large for her shrunken frame except across her swelling breasts. And there was our conversation the final time she came to the academy. She had said, "I need a favor from his father and Boyce is afraid to ask," and then, "I'll convince Boyce. It'll just take a bit of work."

She had given herself to Boyce Cruickshank. And exacted a promise from him: He would talk to his father about ours. To lie on her back for him must have seemed a small price. And maybe Boyce Cruickshank had followed through. Maybe he just did not hold as much sway as she had thought.

Isabel is gone. It seems a mantra of sorts, the words echoing in my head. Never again will she throw her head back in laughter. Never again will she wink her own special wink. Never again will she lie with her cheek resting between my shoulder blades. Then a fresh, chilling thought flies into my head: She wanted to die. She chose to inflict death. But *inflict* implies something unwelcome, and it must have looked otherwise to her, at least in the beginning. As she waded into the upper river, was she thinking of the fiancé who turned his back, the mother who seldom takes her foot from the treadle, the father who drinks? Or was it me, rushing off to the Clifton House? From the place in the river where she first knew there was no turning back, was there a moment when she did not want to die? Or was she thinking only of the belly swelling beneath her skirts?

When I have emptied myself of tears, I lie on my side on the stone beach, facing her body, shivering though the day is warm. Tom leaves the edge of the woods and sits next to me. When my shivers turn to quakes, he lies down, his chest against my back, the tops of his thighs against the undersides of mine, an arm over my arm, my hand lost in his. "She's still with you," he says.

I survey her skin but am unable to locate the spot where the grappling hook bit into her flesh. It seems that only her dress was snagged and that the cotton held for a while, until it tore clear through to the hem. Remembering him soaking wet and hatless on the veranda, I say, "You went into the whirlpool?"

"I had her through the worst of it when the dress ripped."

The river is wild here, at an elbow where the flow turns ninety degrees. A good portion of the river, attempting to proceed along its original course, is forced back upon itself by the gorge wall, and then whirled round and round, endlessly so. The whirlpool is where a stunter called Maud Willard circled in her barrel, like the driftwood held prisoner there now, until long after she had run out of air.

Isabel was guided from the whirlpool by expert hands, hands that knew when to slacken the rope and when to coax her toward an eddy that would float her away from the main current to the beach. But he lost her, and, unable to toss the hook another time, unable to risk marring her flesh, he threw himself into the whirlpool after her, swimming with all his might. The revulsion I had felt as I held his tarpaulin by the corners and watched a grappling hook fall to the underbrush was entirely wrong.

"I don't want my parents to know she was with child," I say.

His chest rises and falls against my back before he speaks. "I can take her to Morse and Son and have her body prepared there, before it's brought around to your house. It's what usually happens with the bodies the river gives up. You'll need to bring new clothes." As an afterthought, he says, "Something with a full skirt."

"I knew Mr. Morse's daughter at the academy. She was always gossiping about so-and-so's disfigurement or so-and-so's underclothes."

"The bodies from the river are easy money for him. The city pays for the burial when one isn't claimed. I'll warn him: If word gets out, I'll take the bodies to Patterson's."

"You're paid for the bodies?"

"Three dollars," he says.

"Mary Morse called them floaters."

"I never have."

A long while later, when the sun slides behind the bank and the beach is cast in shadow, he says, "You should think about getting home." I ask him to stay with me, at least to River Road, but he says no, that he will follow, I suppose so I will not see Isabel wrapped in the tarpaulin.

The trudge up the old incline railway ties leading out of the gorge is long, and I am weeping again and tripping on my skirt and not bothering with the mucus coming from my nose. Then I am running, scrambling over ties, panting, my heartbeat echoing in my ears, hurrying to be home.

But what will I say to Mother and Father when I am there? That she is dead, drowned in the river? They will ask where she was found, and I will say in the whirlpool, and then they will know. The river gives up those who plummet from the brink in one of two places, an eddy at the *Maid of the Mist* landing or the whirlpool. I catch myself thinking that Isabel will know what to say to Mother and Father. And for a long moment I cannot grasp that I cannot ask her advice.

As the screen door closes behind me, Father and Mother rush into the entrance hall, and I can almost hear their silent pleas: Say she is well. Say she is well and I will never take another drink. Say she is well and I will be a perfect mother, a mother who has all the time in the world. As I hesitate, as they take in my eyes, surely swollen and red, hope falls away and Mother says, "We'll sit in the kitchen and you'll tell us what you know."

Mother sobs, great, heaving sobs, her face in her hands, and Father begins to pace, asking questions. "Who found her body?" "Where, exactly?" "How did you come to know?" I answer vaguely, referring to Tom only as a fisherman who somehow knew where Isabel lived.

"Was she disfigured?" Father asks. Mother looks up, waiting.

"Her dress was torn," I say.

She stands. "I want to see her."

"She's at Morse and Son. They'll bring her here once she's prepared," I say. "It's what they do with the bodies from the river. I'm supposed to bring a dress."

Mother collapses back into her chair, and I wonder if it was a mistake, letting someone other than her tend to Isabel. Father goes to her and wraps his arms around her head, cradling it against his waist. I kneel at her feet, my cheek on her knees. Her fingers are in my hair, comforting, soothing both of us. The awfulness of it is as much as I can bear, another ounce and I think I should be crushed, yet I know it is worse for Mother.

In the doorway of Isabel's bedroom, Mother stumbles, and I grip her forearm and the sobbing begins anew. We cling to each other a long while, until I say, "They're waiting for the dress."

I have no idea what is usual, but it seems right that Isabel should be properly clothed. I select a pale blue gown with a fleur-de-lis motif, high collar, and gathered skirt, as well as undergarments and stockings. From the tin where she kept her hairpins, ribbons, and combs, I lift a length of velvet of the same blue as the dress. I hold up each selection and wait for Mother to nod, but she only shrugs and lifts her palms. "You decide," she says.

The three of us drive to Morse and Son, Father thumping his fists against the steering wheel several times as we go. Because Mother has chucked her hat to her feet and clawed at her hair and given in to reckless weeping by the time we arrive, Father stays put with her in the Cadillac, behind a black carriage with glass windows and velvet drapery, and a pair of horses with black plumes on their heads. All the way here I had been calming myself with assurances of Mr. Morse having the grace to conceal the roundness of Isabel's belly. Still, when Father says, "You okay going in on your own, Bess?" I am relieved.

A bell tinkles as I step through the vestibule into a parlor like any other, except that the air is heavily perfumed. I hear muffled footsteps coming up carpeted stairs, and a moment later Mr. Morse is dabbing his forehead with a handkerchief and looking more ordinary than I had expected an undertaker would. I suppose Isabel is in the basement, with the formaldehyde and tubes. I expect it is where he works, in a smock, with the black suit he is wearing underneath, an ear cocked to the bell. He takes my hand in one of his and places the other on top. His palms are damp but not clammy, as though they have been freshly washed. "My deepest sympathies," he says.

As I hand over the package of Isabel's things, I catch myself sizing him up, the way Mother would. He seems as unlike a gossip as anyone can—tired, somber, glum, as though, given the choice, he would prefer not talking at all. Still, I linger, wondering how I might exact some bit of reassurance from him. But then he says, "Tom talked to me, and I gave him my word."

A t Glenview there is no supper, just a mother staring into space and a father pacing, relentlessly. "There is cold chicken," I say, but Mother only shrugs, and Father turns to retrace his path. I climb the stairs.

I lie on my bed, wondering. Had Isabel gone to the falls with the intention of killing herself? She knew the legends, the stories the hack drivers churn out for the tourists in their carriages—the accidents, the suicides, the botched stunts. It would have been easy for death to slither into her mind as she stood at the brink. Even Mrs. Stowe had written about the lure of the falls, the sudden impulse that seized her when she gazed too long. I take *Life and Letters of Harriet Beecher Stowe* from the secretary and easily enough find the passage. "I felt as if I could have *gone over* with the waters; it would be so beautiful a death; there would be no fear in it." Though she does not say it, it seems Mrs. Stowe had the wherewithal for careful deliberation, even at the brink. It seems her more rational mind prevailed. In a calmer, clearer moment, would Isabel have made a different choice? Was she able to wonder, to think about the possibility of the hopelessness she surely felt letting up in a day or a month or a year? Had she been lucid enough to understand the finality of what she was about to do?

If she had told me she was pregnant, if I had guessed it, might her burden have been lightened enough for her to bear? I ought to have been a better sister, one she felt she could tell. At the very least, I should have pieced together the facts. But no, I rushed off to the Clifton House, rather than staying home and taking her into my arms and making her believe all could be put right. Mother and Father would have come around.

Was my acceptance of Edward's proposal the final straw? She had told me I could marry him with an earnestness that could not have been feigned. But still the words we spoke, as we lay huddled with her cheek resting between my shoulder blades, come to me. I said, "I've given up," and she said, "Me too."

I understand so little of her death, though a single fact is more than clear: She chose certain death. She chose the falls.

Mrs. Stowe's book hurled across the room, I slam a fist into my bed. Then I am standing, uselessly kicking my mattress and pulling up sheets and wanting my pillow to burst as I thwack it against the headboard. Exhausted, I slump down onto my knees, close my eyes, and fold my hands in prayer. I want to pray that Isabel remained firm in her desire to die even as she met the brink of the falls. I want to pray that there was no moment of doubt when she struggled in vain, the shore beyond her reach.

But history cannot be altered, even by God. And if there was a chance, I should not be asking for anything as easy as peace of mind for Isabel. I should be asking for today to be rolled back to yesterday or the day before or the day before that. I should be asking for a second chance.

Instead I think of Sister Leocrita, who taught Christian doctrine, saying that suicide violates our duty to God, that the length of our time on earth is up to Him. And I wonder why, then, does He give to some the will and the capacity to take their lives? Is it possible God is not nearly as benevolent and omnipotent as I have always thought? Would He not have wanted happiness for Isabel if He were good? Would He not have made it so if He were all-powerful? But she threw herself from the brink of the falls, and there is one conclusion to be drawn: When it comes to goodness or power, maybe even both, God does not meet the grade.

I make a solemn promise or, more accurately, a threat. If Isabel is weeping and gnashing her teeth, then for me God is dead. I glance around my room, but despite my blasphemy, nothing has changed, and it is more worrisome than comforting.

If Isabel could read my thoughts just now, she would laugh. She often claimed a sore throat or headache as Mother bustled about her room Sunday morning, pulling back bedclothes, opening drapes, and imploring her to get up. And at Morrison Street Methodist, until Mother put on her sternest face and gave out a quick thwack, Isabel's hymnbook was upside down. Was she right to scoff?

Standing in front of the wardrobe mirror, I seek some trace of Isabel in my reflection, but there is only my untidy hair, loose tendrils hanging limp, without her soft curls. Some have said she and I are similar around the eyes, and I have glimpsed the likeness in the odd photograph, also once when she was reading quietly across the table from me in study hall. But I see nothing now, only myself, exposed, defenseless, as naked as I have ever been though I am fully clothed. Just when it seems she is entirely gone from me, the reflection of her aluminum bracelet on my wrist catches my eye.

As I smooth my thumb from one oval plaque to the next, I wonder if the bracelet should be brought to her at Morse and Son. But then her words, as she fastened it around my wrist, come to me: "Wear it so I'll be there in spirit." Lips to the bracelet, I say, "Isabel," and know that she meant for me to wear it always and be reminded of her, that she loved me, even as she set out for the falls.

14

The clip-clop of hooves on Buttrey Street wakes me, and as the sound gives way to whinnies and blusters beneath my window, I know Isabel's body has arrived. My gaze drifts from the ceiling, falls to the somber, black dress pressed and hung over the back of my chair while I slept. Has Mother managed to compose the announcement, too? Maybe she is already copying it onto sheets of black-edged paper to be circulated around Niagara Falls. I climb out of bed, quickly, thinking I should get up and help, but then flop back down again. There is no need to rush; the announcement will bring only old news. The plumed horses clip-clopped all the way from Main and Ferry. They stopped at Glenview. Everyone knows.

From the staircase I see Mother sitting on the edge of a straight-backed chair, her attention given over to the carpet beneath her feet. Father is wearing his black suit and holding open the screen door while the casket and a pair of claw-footed stands are transported into the house by a couple of Mr. Morse's sons, judging by their looks. Mr. Morse stands aside, directing—lilies here, casket there, ferns at either end. Then he opens the lid.

Isabel lies on a bed of pink satin, her hands at her waist, one clasping the opposite wrist. Her nails are filed as they seldom were and painted to mimic their natural color. Her eyes are shut, her hair set in a soft halo of perfect curls. Her cheeks are smooth, lightly rouged. Her lips are tinted pink and tightly closed, unnaturally so.

"They sew the mouth shut," Mother says. With that she begins to tremble and an otherworldly sound escapes, deep and hollow from her lips. "It's not Isabel," she says.

"No," I say. "Isabel is gone."

The first to arrive is a woman called Mrs. Calaguiro. I've seen her before, picking grapes from the vine-clad arbor of a house at the base of the bluff. She holds out a pot and lifts the lid. *"Farfalle,"* she says.

Before she relinquishes the pot, she wraps a sturdy arm around my neck and pulls me into her bosom. *"Dio ti benedica,"* she says. She kisses my hair twice and rocks me back and forth, and I let her because she is soft and scented with garlic. She shakes her head when I lift my palm, directing her to the casket. I expect that there is a rosary deep within her apron pocket, that she will pray, uselessly, for Isabel tonight.

Then Reverend Tiplin from Morrison Street Methodist is on the veranda and, a moment later, through the door, though I have not yet invited him in. He stands, head bowed over the casket, his voice sure and so loud I can only conclude he is speaking for the benefit of Mother, Father, and me rather than Isabel.

Father, I commend the soul of Isabel Heath into your hands,
With boundless confidence,
For you are our Father.
Do with her what you will.
Whatever you may do, we thank you.
We accept all.
Amen.

In meek objection I open my eyes midway through the prayer and find Mother's open as well, her focus shifted from the carpet, severe on the reverend's back.

After a few moments of one-sided talk about shepherds and lambs and surrender, the reverend finally seems to notice her hard gaze. Yet he blathers on about God's infinite knowledge, about His wondrous plan for each of us. And just when it seems he will never stop, just when I begin to suspect he is rattling on because he is afraid of what Mother might say, she interrupts. "We want a private ceremony at the graveside," she says, "only us and the Atwells."

"No service at the church?"

She shakes her head.

The reverend speaks slowly, tentatively. "Your friends will want a chance to grieve."

She shrugs away their need.

The Coulsons are the next to step into the drawing room, and for once I am not left agog. No, Mrs. Coulson's eyes are red-rimmed, and her cheeks and lips without the hint of color I had assumed was their natural state. Her hair is unornamented, as are her wrists and ears. There is no décolletage, not so much as a locket to lure the eye there. When Father stands to take Mr. Coulson's offered hand, Mr. Coulson only shakes his head, and then I see, for the first time, two grown men embrace.

Soon enough the house is filled with women, Mrs. Forsythe, Mrs. Cummings, Mrs. Hall, Mrs. Woodruff, each bustling about with a tea towel flung over her shoulder, making coffee, arranging chairs, setting out the steady stream of food that arrives at the door. Before settling down to work, each stood alongside the casket a moment, shaking her head, saying how lovely Isabel looks, Mrs. Forsythe daring to pat Isabel's hair. "She looks thinner than I remember," Mrs. Coulson whispers to Mrs. Hall. Mrs. Coulson turns to me and says, "Was she ill?" and in doing so undoes any bit of goodwill her stricken face had aroused. By now they have all heard the whispered truth, that so-and-so said so-and-so's son had been sent away from the whirlpool the afternoon before. Yet another suicide had turned up.

Midmorning, Mother is accepting condolences, albeit with a barely perceptible nod. But by noontime, she is slipping her hand from beneath any hand placed atop her own on the arm of the chair. And by mid-afternoon she has laughed twice, a short, derisive huff each time, once in response to Mrs. Westover, who said, "She's in a better place," and then just after Mr. Hall mistakenly referred to Isabel using my name.

I had wondered if Mother refused a church service out of fear that with our reduced standing no one would come. But she seems not a bit surprised by the mounds of food accumulating on the countertops. As I watch her glare into yet another sorrowful face, I see the extent to which she holds the pie bakers, the dish driers, the matchers of cups and saucers responsible for appearing on our doorstep only now. To accept a jellied salad or a ham, to offer an opportunity for prayer is to forgive the smirks, the whispers, the flippant remarks, the turned backs our family has suffered. And Mother will not allow righteousness to be as easy as that. When she finally shuts herself in her bedroom, I breathe a sigh of relief.

I keep an eye on Father, and he does not sneak off, thank goodness, even for a minute, to some private stash of rye whiskey. Rather, with Mother gone, he takes charge, thanking those who come for their kindness, their prayers, their offering of pork loin stuffed with onion and sage. "We'll manage," he says. And I wonder about the awkwardness that does not seem to exist with these people who had judged him so harshly just yesterday.

Much of the congregation from Morrison Street Methodist, Mother's garden society, also her bridge club, crowd into the drawing room. Father's business associates step through the doorway with their wives and shift their hats to their waists, as do other less familiar men, maybe his compatriots from the Windsor Hotel. Most of the men leave their women at Glenview and stay only a short while; there is no liquor set out, and they can hardly busy themselves scraping dishes and slicing loaves. The local girls from Isabel's graduating class come, too, my classmates, as well. Each weeps and sniffles, and Mary Egan collapses, her knees buckling with shame. The sisters from Loretto step into the front entranceway, and I walk among them with their carefully selected words, their clumsy embraces, their prayers. I want to be soothed by those who come, but, like Mother, I am not.

Edward arrives with the entire Atwell clan and is tender and sweet, and holds my hand and tells me that he is glad he knew Isabel, that he will always help me remember her. And I wish I did not want to pull my hand away and I wish I was not displeased when Father asks the Atwells to join us at the cemetery in the morning and I wish I did not feel compelled to whisper, "I'd like some time alone," when his family is leaving and he offers to stay.

When all has quieted downstairs, I lift the pearl choker Edward gave me from its heart-shaped box and slip it into the pocket of my skirt. If I am to wear Isabel's aluminum bracelet and be reminded of her, it seems she ought to have with her a memento of me. From the staircase, I can see the drawing room is empty, though there is the sound of teacups clinking in the kitchen sink.

I struggle with the clasp of the choker, with fastening it, blindly, at the back of Isabel's neck. Once I have straightened her collar, hiding what I have done, I lean in close. "Show me," I say. I am not so daft as to expect the lights to suddenly dim or the floor to tremble beneath my feet. But I want something, a fullness, a scrap of certainty, a breeze like a warm embrace, something to help me believe that this lifeless body is not Isabel, that she is somewhere else. I wait. No comfort comes. I lay a hand on her cheek and recoil at the cold rigidity beneath my fingertips.

O n River Road I put one foot in front of the other and count my steps and recite Portia's mercy soliloquy and hum, anything to drown out the voice inside my head that says I must not take another step. And I wonder if maybe Isabel had done the same as she walked toward the upper river, toward the brink of the falls.

An automobile pulls up beside me. "Bess?" It is Mr. Forsythe, who has likely just picked up his wife at Glenview.

"Hello," I say.

"Where're you headed?"

"Just walking."

"We'll take you home," Mrs. Forsythe says, from the passenger seat.

"I'd like to walk." I turn my body toward Glenview and take an appeasing step.

"You're sure?" Mr. Forsythe calls out.

When the automobile is out of sight, I resume my march in the direction opposite Glenview. At the whirlpool Tom had said, "She's still with you," and I had not asked what he meant. And the afternoon we rode the trolley in the gorge he said that it was the crevices without scrub that told him we were in for a rockslide but also that there was something more. We had not finished the conversation because the men clearing the fallen rocks were watching and waiting for Tom to say what should be done next. And now Isabel is gone and I am doubtful there is anything he can say that will let me believe otherwise. Still, I cling to a flimsy bit of solace, a lifeline of sorts, pretending that he can.

I stand for a moment outside the Windsor Hotel, willing Tom to look from his window and see me in the darkness below. On the second and third stories of the front façade alone, there are ten windows spaced well enough apart that each must belong to a separate room. I remember Tom saying he seldom heard the other tenants, that his room was at the end of the hall. But the hall on which floor? And does his room face the street or the lot to the rear? As I peek through a main-floor window, I see that the saloon is full, that the staircase leading to the second and third floors is clear across the room. I can ask the barman exactly where Tom's room is, or make my way from door to door, testing my luck. Either way I will have to cross the saloon. Either way someone is bound to tilt a pint of ale in my direction. "What on earth? It's the Heath girl and still in mourning dress." But what does it matter? My sister is dead.

Tom opens the door of his room wearing trousers and a singlet, and I put myself in his arms even before the door is shut. My tears wet the front of his singlet, and I wait for the peace I felt as we lay on the stone beach, and then weep further because it does not come. Despite the size of him, I feel as unprotected as I ever have.

He moves me to a metal-framed bed, unmade in the corner of the room. Along the opposite wall there is a washstand and wrinkled towel, a single chair, a fishing rod and tackle box, a canvas bag that appears to be crammed with rope, a propped tintype of a large, heavily bearded man, who must be Fergus, and a tall, sinewy woman, who must be Sadie. He takes a small, knitted coverlet from the back of the chair and wraps it around my shoulders. "You're shivering," he says. Then he says something about grief slowing the circulation, or so Sadie thought, but I am hardly listening.

"You said Isabel was still with me," I say, "and I want to know what you meant."

He positions a chair across from me, sits down, and looks me in the face. "Okay," he says. "When Fergus died, I put a hair on the edge of a glass. If he was really watching over me, as Sadie said he was, then he'd make the hair fall into the glass. A draft would've been enough. But the hair stayed put, and Sadie told me I couldn't demand proof. She said he was out there, to keep my eyes open, that one day I'd know."

"And?" I say, impatient, yet certain I will be let down.

"I can feel him. I can feel him with me. Especially on the river. Sometimes it feels just like it did when I was a kid."

"What is it you feel?"

He shrugs. "I don't know. Maybe a sort of warmth."

"Like being loved?"

He nods. "I guess."

At one time the explanation would have been enough. I had felt God, felt His love, the nearness of Him, and been certain, as certain as Tom is of Fergus. But just now I need more. "Does he speak to you? Have you heard him speak?"

"Sometimes I wake up in the middle of the night," he says, "and I just know I should go to one of the powerhouses. I'll find a deer half-drowned in the forebay, or somebody's dog. Why is that? And why can I say when the wind will change? And why was I watching the whirlpool yesterday and the gorge wall the day of the slide?"

"You watch, closely," I say. "Fergus taught you how to watch."

"I'm not so sure that's it," he says.

I sit on his bed, avoiding his eyes, wondering how it could be that I had lapped up his words like an eager child the day of the slide; how it could be that I had so readily embraced his bit of magic, never doubting that it was anything but real. It seems I have crossed over to Father's way of thinking. Intuition can be explained. Tom wakes up in the middle of the night because he heard a pack of barking dogs, because it registered in his subconscious a deer was being chased. As for his prediction of the slide, there were signs: the sudden drop in temperature, a cliff face full of crevices without the slightest bit of scrub.

Eventually he clears his throat. "Someday you'll know," he says and taps an oval plaque of Isabel's bracelet. And I want to believe him but cannot.

I say, "Lie down with me," and lower myself onto my side.

We lie still a long while, like before, his chest against my back, the tops of his thighs against the undersides of mine. At least it seems a long while, but time has become indistinct. When he next speaks, he says, "Was it busy downstairs?"

"Yes."

"I take it, then, that you're no longer marrying someone called Edward Atwell?"

"No," I say. "I'm not." My shoulders heave, and Tom strokes my hair. Not for a moment has Edward deserved the likes of me, the way I have bandied about his heart.

Mother and Father and Reverend Tiplin wait beside Isabel's casket at Fairview Cemetery. It might look as though I am waiting, too, but I am not. I am only standing alongside them, staring at the hole into which Isabel, along with the pearl choker I fastened around her neck, will be lowered. By the light of day, I regret the choker, my first blunder in an evening full of errors, but what am I to do? The casket had already been shuttled from Glenview to the hearse when I woke. The choker and whatever remained of Isabel were gone from the house.

On Ash Wednesdays she and I would kneel in the academy chapel, and Father O'Laughlin would daub a bit of ash on our foreheads and say, "Remember, man, thou art dust and unto dust thou shalt return." The point, he said, was to make us think of our own mortality. Only when we truly understood the fragility of our earthly existence could we begin to seek true spirituality. The message was lost on me, on Isabel, sisters who had sidestepped privation, despair, sisters who had no experience with death. Now, with Isabel gone and mortality all too real, Father O'Laughlin might think me a prime candidate. But a quest seems impossible, even with the vast emptiness in my gut, my heart, my head, the blank page waiting to be filled up where Isabel used to be.

The loam of the hole is hard-packed, threaded with spindly roots, many crisp and white, newly severed by the leading edge of a spade. There are worms, too, teased from darkness by the rain overnight, desperately burrowing now that the sun is out. Reverend Tiplin snaps shut his pocket watch, and Mother squints in the direction of the main gates. "What could be keeping them?" she says.

The Atwells' absence attests to the vigor of the grapevine in Niagara Falls. It is easy enough to figure out that someone in the saloon had used his bit of gossip to mollify his wife, to make up for the rye whiskey on his breath, the lateness of the hour. "You'll never guess who showed up at the Windsor," he might have said. "The Heath girl, that's who, the one who didn't jump. She went upstairs, wearing black. It was Fergus Cole's grandson she was visiting with, for the better part of an hour, had the nerve to ask what room was his." How many wives had lain awake planning and fussing? Just whom to telephone first?

It was foolish not to consider what would come about, needlessly cruel not to have explained myself to Edward first. Had I waited a day or two, and called off the engagement before I went to the hotel, my parents would have been spared an extra dose of humiliation, at least until after we had buried Isabel. And maybe Kit, who once loved me, though she loves Edward more, would not despise me so much as she surely does just now. Maybe I would have managed to keep my only friend.

"The Atwells won't come," I say.

Mother turns her tired eyes to me. "It's that ne'er-do-well with the fish?"

I stare at my feet, at the August-yellow grass trampled beneath, and I nod.

As I look up she crumples against Father, defeated.

15

These weeks following Isabel's death, I am mostly confined to Glenview, to the dusty, still rooms, to a silence seldom broken by anything other than my feet on the hardwood floors of an empty house. There is no longer the drone of the sewing machine, unless it is my foot on the treadle. Nor are there the noises of a kitchen where meals are prepared and afterward dishes washed up. Mother seldom emerges from her room, and when she does it is to wander aimlessly, quietly. Twice each day Father brings her tea, and slices of the loaves and salty ham—prosciutto, I was told—that Mrs. Calaguiro or one of her entourage bring to the door. Mostly he sits with the newspaper spread before him, sometimes stuck on the same page for the better part of an hour, sometimes startling when I speak. Late in the afternoon, he leaves Glenview, returning before the sun sets to join me in the dining room for a meal of thick soup—minestrone, Mrs. Calaguiro said—or whatever the women at the base of the bluff have guessed we might like. We have lapsed back into only occasional visits from Loretto girls and garden society friends, possibly because I am awkward and Mother is unfriendly and Father is seldom home, possibly because the crowded drawing room at Isabel's visitation had more to do with the good manners of well-bred men and women than anything else. Tom says Father no longer goes to the Windsor, and I have watched closely and have seen nothing to make me think he has moved on to another hotel. I believe he is out walking, thinking, planning how to best salvage what is left of our family. I am almost certain I am right; depending on the day's weather, the cuffs of his trousers are caked with dust or splattered with mud.

The mornings when it seems entirely impossible to throw back the curtains and squint into sunshine, those are the mornings when it is most important to get out of bed. I force myself to rise quickly, and wash and dress in somber black. I have come to think of mourning clothes as a blessing of sorts, one less decision to make, one less decision to weigh on the coverlet that must be pushed aside in order to get out of bed.

To pretend it is personal fortitude that enables me to face each day would be entirely false. I am lured by the contentment, delight, even bliss I feel each time I meet Tom in the woods of the glen.

At first I told Father I was going for a walk, or returning loaf tins and such, but he seemed not to hear, so now I just leave and no one questions where I go daily between the hours of eleven and three. I meet Tom at the base of the stairs descending into the glen, and he takes my hand. At first, he led me to the river, stopping only when we reached a limestone boulder flat enough for sitting and with footholds enough to climb. More recently, though, we have been taking our time getting to the river, often settling for a while at a quieter place, a sun-dappled spot where the violet anemones are in bloom or a patch of undergrowth where the ferns grow exceptionally thick. He has kissed me and put his hands on my ribs, atop the black wool, and then slid them upward along my sides until the heels of his palms were at my breasts. He has apologized more times than I can say and dropped his hands from where I want them to be.

"I'm sorry," he says.

"I don't mind."

"It's just that . . ."

"I'm fine," I say, "really, I am."

I have crawled on top of him when he is lying on his back in the glen, and felt the hardness between his legs and seen his embarrassment.

"I'm sorry," he says.

"I don't mind," I say, staying put.

I have opened my mouth to his and said, "Unbutton my dress," when I feared he would not, and slipped the straps of my camisole from my shoulders when his fingers hesitated too long. "I just want to look," he has said, and I have wanted his hands on my bare skin and told him it was so, though soon it was not enough. I wanted more and drew him closer and thought it was ecstasy when his mouth finally reached my breasts. I have hiked my skirts and petticoat and sat straddling him, a knee on either side of his hips as he lay on his back. I have moved with him, rhythmically, and waited for pleasure to overcome grief or at least push a good piece of it aside. I have watched his face change from contorted to serene and felt his body move from rigid to spent, all the while his trousers remaining buttoned and my bloomers in place. "I'm sorry," he says.

Once we went to the whirlpool. Rather than settling on the wooded slope, Tom stopped only when we had reached the stone beach, which had little in the way of privacy. I was baffled until he said, "I thought maybe Isabel would seem closer here." He sat me down on a flattish rock and then retreated a few steps. I stared at frothy white. I stared at rushing green. I stared at a massive standing wave, and then at the hollow near its base. Did he think if I stared long enough I would eventually conjure Isabel? Would he ever guess that mostly my mind was occupied with just how long I had been sitting on the rock and whether there was still time for the glen? When it seemed I had sat still long enough, I swiveled toward him and shrugged.

"Maybe some other time," he said.

"Maybe."

"Sometimes geese fly in circles, squawking away, when one of their flock dies," he said. "I've seen a couple of them keep at it until they're lost."

Without him, nothing mattered very much at all, and so I did my best to take in what he said, to step beyond the invisible wall that seemed to be keeping me separate from the world. "You think I'm erratic," I said, knowing he was right.

I had badgered him, asking time and again whether Isabel had drowned in the upper rapids, whether she had survived the plunge from the brink, whether she had been flailing in the lower river when she drew her last breath. I had wanted to pinpoint every detail of her final moments. How else was I to run through the story in my head, again and again, always hopeful of a changed ending?

I had recounted as much as I could of the hours leading up to her death. What she wore. What she said. Her cheek between my shoulder blades. The bit of sleep I had noticed in the corner of her eye. I had told him more than once, and he had commented on how much I was able to recall. He said I saw her final hours through a magnifying glass. Even so, I had wept mercilessly because I could not remember into which teacup I had poured her tea the day she went to the brink of the falls.

I had insisted we walk a half dozen blocks out of our way so that we might avoid Mary Egan's house, rather than risk some memory of Mary and Isabel at the academy, linked arm in arm. At Table Rock, I turned my back on the falls. And though Tom had been waiting for the new lures to arrive, I would not set foot in Clark's Hardware, not when Isabel had once delighted me by handing Mr. Clark a few dimes in exchange for a packet of Chinese crackers after Father had said, "Absolutely not."

I had gone over a dozen times the ways Isabel could be with me still, the ways I could have intervened, the ways I had not.

Sitting on the rock at the whirlpool, I began yet again. "I should have known."

"She wasn't showing much," he said.

"The tea dress I made all of a sudden didn't fit."

He held his open palm toward me, telling me to stop. "You were a good sister."

"I left her alone and went to the Clifton House."

"She wouldn't want you blaming yourself."

"We could have managed. We could have gone to Toronto. They say there's plenty of work with the war."

"You can manage now, too. I can help you, Bess."

He took my hand and helped me up from the rock. "Grief isn't something to get over," he said. "It stays with you, always, just not so raw."

At three o'clock we part on River Road, he to his shift at the Windsor Hotel and I to Glenview, to the half dozen, partially made dresses it seems Mother will not complete. His hands and mouth upon me, I have felt such bliss that afterward, in the sewing room, it seems traitorous to Isabel. Threading a needle, I have questioned whether the happiness is even real. In my grief, have I mistaken oblivion for bliss?

Other times the hours with Tom seem a cruel joke, a scrap, a taste, just enough to fill me afterward with dread. I have not yet lost everything. There is something more to be taken away.

I wonder, too, if I am wanton, whether other women feel desire as I do. I look to the evidence—the well-thought-of girls who disappear for a half year, only to return slightly more full through the hips; the hurried marriages, the babies who arrive before nine months' time; the tired mothers with ten or more children pawing at their skirts; the forbidding scriptures; the edict that says a young woman should not find herself alone in the company of a young man. I can only conclude that I am not alone, that it is natural for physical intimacy to hold lovers in its grip. And it occurs to me that maybe it was not as large a sacrifice as I had once assumed when Isabel gave herself to Boyce. We are designed to want more, to fill the earth.

I think about Tom's hesitation, wonder if he feels Fergus's eye on him. Tom told me once that, with her high cheekbones and shiny black hair, Sadie was often taken for a half-breed, an assumption never confirmed by the missionaries who raised her. She spent a good chunk of her teenage years posing for the tourists in buckskin outside one of the curio shops selling beaded change purses and moccasins, and bark painted with turtles and geese. At eighteen she batted away the hand of the shop owner, who had come to think it his right to cop a feel whenever he pleased. For resisting, she was beaten with a broomstick until Fergus, just passing by, felled the owner with a single slug. She lost her livelihood and, with it, the bit of floor at the back of the shop where she curled up each night. Fergus could hardly believe his good luck when she asked if he might consider giving her room and board in return for cooking and cleaning. She could read to him, too, if he cared about that sort of thing. She had been taught by a missionary and had three books, if he would not mind heading into the curio shop and gathering them up. Back at the cabin overlooking the gorge, Fergus slept on the floor for the month until they were wed. And when Tom was a boy, Sadie told him Fergus was the first gentleman she had ever met. It was years later when Tom finally understood Fergus had not taken advantage, even if she had figured it was the price of room and board.

These are my thoughts as I lift a navy blue skirt in the sewing room and find the chalk markings above its unfinished hem that tell me Mother gave Mrs. Woodruff her final fitting before Isabel disappeared. I am determined to finish the dresses, to keep them moving along from bolt of uncut fabric to beautifully pressed gown. Several times I have gone to Mother's room and found her fully dressed on the edge of a perfectly made bed. Her hair is tidily pinned up and her cheeks lightly rouged. Only the handful of seconds it takes for her to leave her thoughts and turn toward the doorway hint all is not well. I ask whether a cuff is to be pleated or gathered, whether the opalescent buttons are for the rust chiffon or the mauve taffeta. She answers my questions thoroughly, patiently, and says, "Thank you, Bess." And I am making progress, although I have cried over a shoulder seam that puckered and a lapel I stitched three times before it lay flat.

I cannot wait much longer for her to return to the sewing room, for Father to implement the plan he is surely working out as he walks. Eventually the few dollars Mother set aside while dressmaking will be used up. Eventually no more prosciutto and minestrone will be brought to the door. Eventually winter will come and there will be nothing for coal. Eventually Mr. Morse will demand what he is due, as will the Municipal Electric Light and Power Company and the City Water Works.

I asked Tom's advice a while back, and he said I could likely find work as a clerk in an office even though I cannot take shorthand or type. Even in Niagara Falls the businesses are having to make do with so many men overseas. He went on to say he would do his bit, too, and sign on with the next battalion recruited in Niagara Falls. It was the conversation we had circumnavigated time and again but never quite broached. Tears welled in my eyes at the thought of a parting and spilled onto my cheeks at the idea of losing him. "There are sacrifices being made all over the world," he said. Of course I was proud, but mostly I was afraid and, in the end, altogether sorry we had spoken of work.

I wonder if I could take in sewing, even hire myself out as a dressmaker after I have had the chance to fill in what I do not know. I have never conceived a design from its beginnings, never turned a customer's vague notion of a "smart coat" into a sketch of a fitted, velvet affair with neck, cuffs, and hem trimmed in wide bands of krimmer fur. Nor have I accompanied Mother to Toronto, to the Spadina Avenue shops full of the finest silks and wools, and even if I was able to find them, I do not have the faintest idea what a yard of charmeuse should cost, much less what a gown cut from it is worth.

When I have finished hemming Mrs. Woodruff's navy skirt, I push needle into pincushion and flip through the *Niagara Falls City Directory* until I find the handful of entries listed under "Dressmaking." If Mrs. Goddard or Miss Percy knew the extent of my work in sewing her gown, I could ask for a reference letter. If the tea dress I made for Isabel had not been torn and then incinerated at Morse and Son, I could have shown it alongside the letter. Still, there must be a way, and, because surely Mother knows what it is, I head up the stairs to her bedroom.

Once she notices me in the doorway I say, "I need to find work and I'm thinking about dressmaking."

"Oh, Bess." She sits down on the coverlet she was smoothing over the bed.

"It seems to come to me easily enough. I know I have more to learn."

Mother picks up yesterday's *Evening Review* from the bedside table and flips through pages until she finds what she wants—a recipe for "Canada war cake." "No butter, no milk, no eggs," she says. "I just wonder how long it'll be before no one will wear anything but the plainest ready-made frock."

I want to say there will always be women too vain to give up pretty frocks and use the women at the Clifton House as proof, but I have no wish to bring up the night we lost Isabel. "But you were run off your feet with dressmaking."

Sadness comes to her eyes, and I wonder if it is the realization that I must go elsewhere to learn what she is not rousing herself to teach me at home.

"I could apprentice with someone else," I say, "just until you're feeling better."

She pats the bed beside her, and I sit down. "There are employers who will keep a girl busy pulling out basting threads and sewing on buttons and running up seams, and then let her go before she's got enough experience to demand a fair wage. But you ought to be worth ten dollars a week to the right dressmaker, maybe even fifteen."

What I know is a pound of butter costs twenty-five cents, also a dozen eggs. A large loaf is ten cents and sugar, fifty cents for ten pounds. My weekly visit to the grocers on Bridge Street is the sum total of my experience in household economics; still, fifteen dollars a week seems an extraordinary amount, as does even ten. With a bit of luck there might be a bit left over for a victory bond.

"I'll write a letter," she says.

It all seems quite possible, that I will work, that I will be paid. She sees my hopefulness, and it seems to annoy her, after all I have done. "A reference from Mrs. Atwell would have helped," she says, and I feel a familiar pang. My recklessness has caused suffering, and, worse still, the fellow who has borne the brunt of it is entirely good.

The afternoon of Isabel's burial, I spoke with Edward on the telephone and asked him to meet me so I could explain. "There's only one explanation for what you've done," he said. "You aren't the girl I thought you were. You've made a fool of me and disgraced your family. And haven't your parents had enough heartache without you parading around like a harlot, even though you were engaged, and all within days of your sister throwing herself over the falls?" When it became obvious I was weeping, he relented. "All right," he said. "I'll bring the cuff links."

But then I told him that I could not return the pearl choker, that it was buried with Isabel, and the telephone line went dead. When I called back and Kit finally answered, she said, "How dare you be so hateful to my brother? Don't you ever call here again."

I wrote letters to each of them, letters filled with regret, and sent them through the post. And I thought a long while about what penance I could make, but the only thing that seemed adequate was to give up Tom. But it seemed foolish to throw away what I had already hurt my parents and Kit and Edward to get. It seemed impossible. I had not gone to the Windsor Hotel on a whim. I could not have done otherwise.

In the morning I go to Mother's room with a pot of tea as an excuse. Really I am wondering about the letter she promised the day before. And sure enough it is there, a sheet of notepaper folded in thirds on the table beside her bed. "Forget Mrs. Langley and Mrs. Cavell," she says. "From what I've seen neither one of them can teach you a thing. Mrs. Hoffmann is good. Start with her." I read the letter in the hallway, the moment I close her door.

To whom it may concern,

My daughter, Elizabeth Heath, apprenticed as a dressmaker with me for a period of several months. Prior to the apprenticeship she had shown a natural ability in sewing and won the Prize for Sewing at Loretto Academy. She has proven herself diligent and capable. Her skills include pattern layout, basting, construction, finishing, and detailing, such as embroidery and beadwork.

I realize it is unorthodox for an applicant's mother to provide a letter of recommendation. Thus, I propose a weeklong trial period, after which wages will be owed only if you are satisfied with her work. I believe you will decide her skill merits ten dollars a week, with an increase due once she has gained your confidence and begins cutting and fitting.

Yours truly,
Mrs. M. Heath, Dressmaker

Mrs. Hoffmann answers her door, looking somewhat put out until she takes in the delicate cutwork of the dress I changed into after Father saw me in black and said no one would want to take on a girl who might mope and weep. But it seems I had not chosen wisely. The frock is exceptional, the sort of finery a paying customer would wear. "Mrs. Hoffmann?" I say.

"Yez."

"I'm looking for work." I hold out the letter from Mother.

Mrs. Hoffmann's false smile collapses, and she says, "I have no verk."

I flap the letter slightly, hoping to remind her of its presence.

"Who made duh drez?" she says.

I gather a fold of skirt in my hand. "My mother, Margaret Heath," I say. "She taught me. It says so here." I flap the letter again.

"Fine drez."

"My mother sent me," I say, "because you're the best dressmaker in Niagara Falls."

She exhales a short huff of air from her mouth. "Still, I have no verk."

Maybe Mother was right about the war and thrift and ready-made frocks.

"Try Mizez Androovz," Mrs. Hoffmann says.

"Andrews?" I say, remembering the name listed in the city directory, and Mrs. Hoffmann nods.

After I knock a second time, Mrs. Andrews comes to the door looking quite severe, with her silver hair pulled back into a tight knot and reading glasses perched on the end of her nose. I have interrupted; in one hand she holds a small tool used to rip apart seams and, in the other, a collar. "May I help you?" she says.

"I'm Elizabeth Heath and I'm looking for work."

"Can you sew?"

"My mother taught me. I have a letter from her."

Instead of taking the letter, she hands me the collar. "Look at it," she says, and I do, noticing the poor workmanship straightaway.

"Well?" she says.

Hoping it is a critique she wants, I say, "The seams aren't graded. They aren't understitched, and the corners of the stiffening layer haven't been clipped. And, I can't say for sure, but given the rest of the work, I doubt the undercollar was properly trimmed."

"Come inside," she says. "I let the girl who made it go."

We stand in the hallway while she reads Mother's letter. "Why don't you sew for her?" she says.

"She isn't taking any more work."

Mrs. Andrews is pensive a moment, and I expect she is wondering why a woman well-off enough to give up her livelihood ever worked as a dressmaker. Or maybe she is sizing up my cutwork dress, my Loretto girl ways, and thinking me too refined for a working girl. "I cannot train someone," she says, "and then have her flitting off."

"I want to work," I say and then hang my head. "I need to work."

"You'll sew here, where I can keep an eye on you," she says. "I don't pay carfare and I won't promise an increase, even if you take on cutting and fitting. Your mother has a lot of nerve suggesting it. You can tell her that."

I want to gush, to leap, to run and tell Tom. But Mrs. Andrews has no time for foolishness, and I am no longer a child.

"You'll start tomorrow. I'm up to my knees in work. Half of Mrs. Hoffmann's customers are coming to me."

I am perplexed, and she sees it in my face. "Mrs. Hoffmann's a German," she says.

16

CITY OF TORONTO ARCHIVES, FONDS 1244, ITEM 973

I t is mid-October as I pin my hat in the front entranceway, a final act before departing the stillness of Glenview and heading off to the bustle of Mrs. Andrews's sewing room. Father appears on the stairs, and I say, "You're up early."

"I'm off to Buffalo," he says. "I've got an appointment with Mr. Mc-Micking."

My grandfather had worked in Mr. McMicking's Buffalo tannery as a laborer, also Father as an errand boy. I know the story well—how Mr. McMicking was the first to see Father's potential, how he convinced Father to attend business college, how he footed the bill. "The tannery owner?" I say.

He nods, and I fill with trepidation. Surely Father is not considering a position in the Buffalo tannery where he worked as a boy. He cannot mean for us to restart our lives away from Niagara Falls.

"Buffalo?"

"A war ought to be good business for a tannery," he says.

"Oh."

"Well, I'm off," he says, crossing the threshold of the front door. "Wish me luck."

I stand silent, dismayed, as a gush of cold air hits me. Eventually the briskness of the weather sinks in and I make an about-face, heading up the stairs to find a cardigan somber enough for mourning yet warm enough for the day.

I pause at Isabel's wardrobe, fingering the clothes still hanging there, a tailored wool suit Mother made for her trousseau, a sea green chiffon gown. The spring before, Isabel had worn the gown to the pageant marking Mother Febronie's silver jubilee and was easily the most beautiful woman in the dining hall, also the most envied on Boyce Cruickshank's arm. Leaning into the wardrobe, I spread my arms wide, embracing the clothing hanging there. But there is nothing of substance, just silk and wool and linen, all limp, lifeless, easily crumpled.

On River Road I walk quickly, as I do each morning, and wait for fresh air and sunshine to clear away the rain cloud that accumulates in my head each night. This morning I will sew welt pockets and loop buttonholes, the sort of finicky work that causes Mrs. Andrews to pat my shoulder and say, "Not bad for a girl as coddled as you." Still, the cloud is stubborn, foreboding.

I spend the better part of two hours stitching a welt pocket, ripping it out, and then restitching it, all the while wondering if a move to Buffalo is the comeuppance that has seemed just around the corner, inevitable, every time my thoughts linger on poor Edward. Mrs. Andrews says, "What is it, Bess?" and my worries shift. With all the fuss over a single welt pocket, is she regretting increasing my wages to twelve dollars a week on only my fourth day?

"Nothing much." I cannot say that my family might be pulling up stakes, not when she hired me just weeks ago.

"Too many late nights."

"I suppose so," I say, glancing up at the wall clock and wishing away the final half hour remaining before noon. Tom and I will meet in the corner of the athletic field at Victoria Avenue and Bridge Street, and share a picnic lunch as we have each day since I began working for Mrs. Andrews, and I will tell him about Mr. McMicking and Buffalo.

In the athletic field, he does not dismiss my worries, as he sometimes does. He does not say that nothing has been decided, that things have a way of working themselves out. He becomes still midway through spreading the picnic blanket and says, "Buffalo?" and I twist Isabel's aluminum bracelet around my wrist and say that Mr. McMicking thinks the world of Father, that he paid Father's tuition at business college, that he gave me an entire set of sterling silver flatware, just for being born. After a long silence Tom gets back to spreading the picnic blanket, and, once I have unpacked a lunch of hard-boiled eggs and apples, and the lemon squares he especially likes, he motions for me to sit and squats at my knees. He takes my hands in his, looks me firmly in the eyes. "Will you marry me?" he says.

I have imagined waking in his arms each morning and sharing his pillow each night. I have dared to dream the question he just asked, dared to whisper "yes" into my sheets, into the upturned collar of my coat, into the air as I sew. And now I whisper, "Yes," for real, to him, and then I say it louder and again and again. I push myself to my knees and throw my arms around his neck and lean into him until he topples over. I am on top of him and I do not care a bit that we are conspicuous in the athletic field. We are engaged.

We laugh and kiss, and he calls me Mrs. Cole. "We'll get married in January, as soon as you're eighteen," he says, which makes perfect sense since we would need Father's consent otherwise. But even a few months is a long time away, or so I have consoled myself when I am thinking about Tom going off to Belgium or France.

"What if you're gone?" There has been more talk of a battalion being raised in Niagara Falls, and Tom has said more than once he will sign up. Of course he is courageous and has a mind of his own; still, there are recruitment posters and parades, and clergy preaching duty, and women wearing badges embroidered with the words "Knit or Fight" and pinning men on the streets with feathers to show their cowardice. There is instant respect and honor the moment a fellow signs up, respect and honor for the soldier, also for his family. And the message—that you are a yellow-bellied shirker and an oddity if you do not enlist—very often seems too loud, too harsh. And even if all the nonsense has had as little impact on Tom as I expect, there is the possibility that he will not come back.

"Everyone says the recruiting won't happen until late in the year, and I've heard we'll be trained here, at Camp Niagara, instead of being shipped off to Valcartier," Tom says.

I smile as brightly as I can, as brightly as a newly engaged woman should, and, yes, I am happy, but still, I cannot return to the elation of moments ago.

He walks me back to Mrs. Andrews's, as he does each day, and says good-bye to me in front of her house. It seems peculiar that I will spend the afternoon as I spend every other, coaxing form from a length of silk or wool. It hardly seems possible that so momentous a change is inconsequential to everyone else.

Because I feel I might burst if I do not, I tell Mrs. Andrews that Tom proposed, that we will be married before he goes overseas. She says, "You're hardly old enough to wipe your own nose," but then she is out the door and halfway down the street, calling out for Tom to stop, with me on her heels. When he finally glances over his shoulder, she embraces me and says, "Go on and celebrate with your young man."

And so we end up in the glen, unexpectedly, and we lie wrapped in the picnic blanket, my cheek against his chest. We talk about children and someday a small house with a view of the river, and a garden bursting with tomatoes and cucumbers, also a cherry tree, and maybe a couple of chickens, enough to keep us in eggs, and a cow for milking. He will trap and fish and show me the book where Sadie kept her recipes for tinctures and groundnut root. And making do, living by our wits, sounds decidedly less dull than trying to remember the correct placement of an oyster fork when shellfish is served.

We talk, too, about finding me an inexpensive room, on the off chance that my parents pick up and move to Buffalo before we are wed.

Ideally, I would board with a family at the north end of Crysler or St. Clair Avenue, midway between the Windsor Hotel and Mrs. Andrews. "Or better yet," he says, "Mrs. Andrews might let you stay with her."

Her house has four bedrooms: one where she sleeps, a utilitarian affair with a narrow bed and plain wardrobe, nothing as extravagant as a rug or shelf of books. Another where she sews, with hanging patterns, bolts of fabric, spools of grosgrain and roleau and embroidery floss. Tacked to the window casing is a curious collection of postcards—the Great Wall of China, the Taj Mahal, the Hanging Gardens of Babylon. From time to time I have caught her gazing and once ventured to ask, but she only waved away the question as though she had not the faintest idea about the significance of the cards. The doors of the other two bedrooms are kept shut with rolled-up mats along the bottom edges to block any draft. She had meant to fill the rooms with children, she once said, but her Everett had been killed in a rail yard accident before they were even married a year. "She's been alone a long time," I say to Tom. "She likes it that way."

"Come on, Bess. She asked you to stay for supper twice last week and at least once the week before."

"What if my father doesn't come home and say we're moving to Buffalo?" I ask, suddenly anxious about our plans not working out.

"Nothing will change, other than you staying put at Glenview until you're eighteen."

It all seems so effortless, as though each piece of the puzzle will drop into place, as though our future will be quite the same way it is in our talk; still, as I lie in his arms, I am unable to shake a sort of fearfulness that has seemed to follow me about for the months since Isabel's death.

I have come to believe that for me grief feels remarkably like fear. There is the same constricted breath, the same muscular tension, the same agitation, the same need to swallow. At the outset, I supposed I was afraid because I had lost Isabel and was beginning to grasp that she was never coming back. Since, though, I have come to realize there is something more, and it has turned my world on its ear, making it disquieting at times, more uncertain than ever before. With the first glimpse of Isabel, lifeless on the stone beach, came a wariness, a wariness that grew heavy and thickened to doubt. And then, one day doubt solidified to conviction and I knew there was no mystery, no magic, nothing of the sort. I knew there was no eye on the sparrow. I knew there was no God.

"You're quiet," Tom says.

"I'm thinking about Isabel."

He pulls the picnic blanket around us a little more tightly.

"It's more than just Isabel," I say.

"Tell me."

He stays silent, his palm on the nape of my neck, while I think how to put it. Finally I say, "Every day, one way or another, there are moments when it feels like I'm met head-on by meaninglessness."

Tom has never once set foot in a church and has certainly not bought into any run-of-the-mill view of God; still, I am not surprised when he says, "But there's meaning in everything. In dew. And wind. Even in the birds squawking at dawn."

"The birds squawking?" I say.

"They're calling their mates, and telling the other birds which branch is theirs."

"So?"

"If the birds couldn't find their mates, pretty soon we'd have no birds."

I shrug.

"Knock out a creature, and a long line of other ones lose their prey."

"And that's proof there's something more than . . ." I wave my palms through the air.

"That kind of complexity doesn't happen by chance."

What I saw was a deep respect for nature, tinged with awe, not unlike my own for God, back before Isabel had thrown herself from the brink of the falls.

Father arrives home from Buffalo well after sunset and, without removing his frock coat, takes the stairs two at a time. "Come on up, Bess. I have news."

"Well?" Mother says, as he crosses the threshold of their room.

"Everything's set. The first of November I start as head foreman, and Mr. McMicking let it slip that the missus has been at him to step back from running the place and his son isn't any more interested in leather than in widgets. You ought to see it. He's expanded into the buildings on either side, and he's got an order backlog that's long enough to see him through to the spring."

"I knew he'd still have a soft spot for you." She takes his hand, and the smile I have not seen in weeks comes to her face.

He sits down on the edge of their bed. "It isn't aluminum."

"It's enough," she says. "In the morning, you can telephone Mr. Brimley and ask him to come out and let you know what Glenview is worth." And I wonder if Mother is so suddenly well that she will have Glenview gleaming by the time Mr. Brimley arrives.

Father speaks to her and she to him, without glancing in my direction. Why had he even bothered to call me upstairs? In their minds I am still a child, relegated to the sidelines, content to observe while my lot is cast. And so when I speak, their faces do not change. "I have a job here," I say, "and a beau. A fiancé, actually. And I'll board here, in Niagara Falls, maybe with Mrs. Andrews, until I'm eighteen, and then I'm marrying Tom Cole."

"What?" Father says.

"That fishmonger?" Mother says.

"Fergus Cole's grandson? He's a bartender at the Windsor, for God's sake," Father says.

They wear shock and distaste on their faces, and I see there will be coldness toward both Tom and me, but there will be no lasting rift. I am their only child, their last hope. And Tom and I are a package now. My job is to make sure they see it that way. "He's the most honorable man I've ever met."

"You're being rash," Mother says.

"You married Father when you were eighteen," I say, "and I won't need consent." Now the upturned corners of her lips drop and her mouth forms a straight line. Very likely she is remembering her own resolve at eighteen, a resolve that was no doubt formidable. Almost certainly, she knows there is nothing that can be done, that I will marry Tom.

17

Today I become Mrs. Tom Cole. At ten o'clock. I know it the moment I wake in my bedroom at Mrs. Andrews's house. I know it before I remember it is my birthday, so trivial in comparison, except that, at eighteen, I am suddenly seen as fit to decide whom I will wed. I throw back the coverlet and feel the hardwood cold beneath my feet. From the window I see the day is as I had hoped, bright with a high blue sky and beneath it newly fallen snow, white and pristine.

Mrs. Andrews must have been listening for water gurgling in the drain, because the minute I am back from my bath, she arrives carrying a tray with toast, tea, and a precious orange. While I eat she combs my hair and expertly loops and pins locks of it into place, all the while complaining about how unruly it is. For a moment I feel wistful. It should be Kit and Isabel buttoning me into my dress, dabbing a bit of rouge onto my cheeks. Oh, Mrs. Andrews is doing a fine job. It is not that. Brashness and all, she could not be any kinder, even if I were her daughter, rather than a substitute landed on her doorstep already fully grown. It just seems I should be giggling, whispering, remembering with girls I have known my entire life. As I clasp Isabel's bracelet around my wrist, it occurs to me if she were here, alive, fastening the bracelet, I would not be marrying Tom at all. It was her death that led me back to him. A final parting gift.

Last week Mrs. Andrews gave Tom and me what amounted to a first-rate trousseau. For him there was a canvas fishing vest with a dozen buttoned pockets, two of which were lined with rubber. She said she had seen something like it in a shop window in Toronto and had stopped then and there to sketch what she saw. For me there were two pretty housedresses, the practical sort I do not own. The week before she had asked me to model each while she pinned and marked the final adjustments and claimed the dresses were for a Mrs. Fenwick, who she said was built like me, rather like a boy. There were stacks of pillowcases and sheets with delicately crocheted or embroidered trim, and tablecloths and serviettes with bands of fine drawnwork, and intricately patterned quilts, also tea towels and aprons with rows of cross-stitch. It seemed a lifetime's work, work begun by Mrs. Andrews as a young girl with dreams of her own. "You're sure?" I said.

"I was going to give it to the Daughters of Rebekah," she said, "but I hardly thought a pack of orphans would appreciate the workmanship."

The wedding dress I have made for myself might best be described as charming or sweet. It is not a bit showy, not like the gown I beaded for Miss O'Leary. An overblouse of fine cotton tulle prettily drapes the fitted bodice. Three-quarter-length faux sleeves fall open at the shoulder, romantically so. The skirt is layered, long, filmy tiers of tulle. And the embroidery bordering the neckline and hem is my finest yet, but the fabric is inexpensive, suitable for kitchen sheers. I cannot help but think the dress exactly right, a sort of metaphor for the honest life Tom and I will live.

We will be married at Town Hall. Mrs. Andrews will witness, also a fellow from the Windsor Hotel called Sean Garvey. Mother and Father made the trip from Buffalo yesterday and will head back after the ceremony. Tom and I met them at the train station, and it all started off really rather well, with Father shaking Tom's hand warmly, and Mother saying he has made a habit of telling everyone I was marrying Fergus Cole's grandson. But then on the walk from the station to Mrs. Andrews's we came upon a group of women crowded around the Hydro Circus, the caravan that travels from community to community promoting the advantages of electric appliances on behalf of Sir Adam Beck and his Hydro-Electric Power Commission. Father said, "That Beck, he's certainly figured out how to make sure we'll always need more electricity."

I thought there might be an argument. Father's admiration of Beck was easily matched by Tom's disdain. The earliest of the power companies took water from the Niagara just upriver from the falls, then whisked it through penstocks to turbines and returned it to the lower river just beneath the brink. The falls themselves were diminished, but the lower river was left intact. But if Beck's powerhouse were to be built at Queenston, more water would be siphoned off, and this time it would be diverted around the falls, and also the rapids and whirlpool of the lower river.

"If he gets his way, there'll be nothing left to go over the falls," Tom said.

I waited on tenterhooks. How many times had I heard Father comment on the water still running to waste over the brink? "Maybe so," he said, "but all that water would rise again as power and light."

Tom jutted his chin toward the caravan. "He's pumping up demand, telling people like Bess and I we're not keeping up if we haven't got an electric dust collector."

"It's called progress," Father said.

"That's enough from the both of you," Mother said, and then after a moment, "Tom, it's 'telling people like Bess and me' not 'Bess and I.'"

"Mother!" I said.

Mrs. Andrews hosted a supper for the five of us—roast beef, braised parsnips, and, for dessert, apple tart. Afterward she made herself scarce, and Mother and Father presented Tom and me with a bank draft for three hundred dollars. I found myself wondering, unkindly, if the generosity of the gift might be their way of telling me that they were doing just fine, that I had been mistaken not to follow them to Buffalo.

It was the first I had seen of them since late autumn, since the near silence of the weeks spent packing up Glenview. While Father busied himself with finding suitable accommodation in Buffalo and then selling the many possessions that would not fit into the three rooms he had leased, Mother and I sorted out Isabel's room. I had proposed the task before, but Mother had been unwilling. My own uneasiness became obvious once we began. To disturb Isabel's things seemed to risk erasing some telltale detail of her life. Was there significance in the position of the dresses in her wardrobe? Had the book on her bedside table meant anything? What about the pages flanking the embroidered bit of ribbon she used to mark her page?

I made discoveries, too, that caused me to wonder whether I had really known her at all. There was the spinster's thimble from the birthday cake, for instance, tucked into a handkerchief, hidden in the back corner of a drawer. At her birthday party she had held it aloft, laughing and unperturbed, already engaged. And yet, she had been unable to toss the cheap bit of metal into the wastebasket.

There was a newspaper clipping, too, about the Victor Home for Women in Toronto, where pregnant girls and unwed mothers were given shelter and sent to a laundry each day to learn the trade that would set them on the path to self-sufficiency. Penciled into the margin in Isabel's untidy hand was "341 Jarvis Street." I sat on her bed, the clipping bunched in my fist, unable to imagine her thinking the Victor Home enough of a possibility to have sought the address.

Most of her clothes, even the ones I did not think I would use, went into the several trunks I would take to Mrs. Andrews's house. It was easier than giving them away and certainly better than deciding a chemise, showing signs of wear, was to be pitched. Mother would sigh, holding up a dress. I would nod, remembering Isabel off to a concert or a luncheon in the mint dupioni or ivory lace. We both wept as Mother tucked the wedding gown she had painstakingly beaded for Isabel into one of my trunks. By the time we finished with the house, none of us had an ounce of energy to spend on a wrenching good-bye. They waved from the railcar window—Father had sold the Cadillac to Mr. Coulson—and I waved back. Though I felt melancholy afterward, the dominant emotion was relief.

"Husband." I try out the word I have wanted to say ever since we left Town Hall. I waited, until now, until we were behind the closed door of his room at the Windsor Hotel. In all honesty, the spot falls far short of my ideal for a wedding night, but when Mother asked a month ago, I smilingly said, "Tom's room at the Windsor Hotel, of course," and afterward could hardly have suggested to him that we splurge. But more than that, twice he had teased me about my spend-thrift ways, once when I said I was tired of pike and suggested he bring less fish to Mrs. Andrews, and a second time when I paid twenty-five cents for the lemons I needed to make his beloved lemon squares.

He kisses the nape of my neck and says, "You'll tell me, won't you, when you hear me make a mistake?"

I am baffled for the second it takes me to grasp that he is talking about the grammar errors Mother is so fond of pointing out. "If you want me to. You hardly ever do."

"I want you to be proud." With that his mouth moves lower, kissing each vertebra of my spine as he unbuttons my dress. When I am standing in only my bloomers and stockings, my dress circling my feet, he picks me up in his arms and lays me on his narrow bed. "Wife," he says, lying down beside me.

Then his hands are on me, loosening my hair, sliding over my skin. I lift my hips, and he pushes my bloomers to my thighs and then sits up a minute to slip them past my feet. Lying on his bed in nothing but my stockings and garters, I watch him look at me, at the way his eyes linger, the way he swallows, the way his chest rises and falls. He enters me still wearing his best shirt, and I feel a sharp pain.

It is all over more quickly than I would have guessed and I suppose, truth be told, a disappointment. When he lifts himself from me, I can still feel his warmth inside me, between my legs. Then he is grinning and stroking my hair and saying that next time will be slower, that next time will be for me.

He enters me a second time, after much of the touching and kissing that had been confined to the glen. I bend my knees and place my feet flat on the bed, alongside his thighs, and raise my hips, pushing against his weight as it somehow feels I should. After a bit of awkwardness we fall into a rhythm, and soon I am breathless, and then moaning and trembling, and then, at last, still.

Today I became the wife of a soldier. At ten o'clock. The forms with which he would enlist were in his breast pocket, over his heart, even as we were pronounced husband and wife.

I was the one who asked him to wait until the afternoon to hand them in, until I was his wife. He had laughed and said, "No one is going to drag me off the minute I sign up, if that's what you think," but I said, "Please, Tom, just to be sure," and he said, "All right, Bess. All right."

We went directly from Town Hall to the recruiting office, I still in my gown, Tom still in his suit. He signed the forms and said, "Grandson," when the officer asked if he was related to Fergus Cole.

"Remarkable fellow, your grandfather."

"He was," Tom said, sliding the forms along the desktop to me. I wrote out my name. And it was done, as easy as that.

I know he did not worry, even for a moment, that I might withhold my consent, that as his wife I could. And I did not consider, even for a moment, that I could refuse to sign, that as his wife it was within my rights. I did not think it, not for a moment, even though his leaving is what I fear most.

He will cross a vast ocean I have never seen and fight in a land I do not know, where already so many have been lost. He will leave me, his train disappearing from view as I stand waving, bereft, already waiting for him to come home.

Book
TWO

LOWER RIVER

January 1919–August 1923

18

For nearly three years I have waited for this day, the day Tom will at long last return. More times than I can count, I have imagined the crush of his embrace as he lifts me and my feet leave the railway station platform. I have imagined him picking up Jesse, too, and swinging him in a full circle while he shrieks his delight. But in reality, Tom is a stranger to Jesse, as is Jesse to Tom.

It was early summer, the year we were married, when Tom's battalion left Camp Niagara, where they had been training and camping out, and by then Jesse hardly showed, only a slight rise between my hips where it used to be flat. He was born in the autumn, and even after six hours of pushing and thinking I would die if the contractions did not let up, I gasped at my first glimpse of him. He was more blue than pink, and his small mouth was struggling for breath beneath a thin, slick veil. Dr. Galveston said it was nothing, only a caul, a portion of the amniotic membrane, and lifted it from Jesse's face. Some said it was a sign of good luck. Others said it meant Jesse would have second sight. Mrs. Andrews said she mentioned it to the Polish butcher, and he said in his country werewolves came into the world with cauls. I paid little attention to the nonsense, but then a letter from Tom arrived.

November 2, 1916

My Dear Bess,

My company has set up camp about seven miles back from the front. We're mostly fixing up a heavily shelled road, easy work, so don't worry about me.

You have made me into a father and I just about split in two with happiness when I got the news. I only wish I were there to hold my son and you, too. I read your letter over and over, and when I shut my eyes I can picture you cradling our Jesse.

I was born with a caul. Fergus, too. Did I ever tell you that? I bet by now someone has told you being born with a caul means Jesse will never drown. Sailors used to buy them for good luck, and sometimes bits of them were dried out and put in a locket around a child's neck. When I told the others about Jesse, one of the boys, who's always got his nose in a book, quoted Dickens. "I was born with a caul, which was advertised for sale, in the newspapers, at the low price of fifteen guineas." He said it's from *David Copperfield*, but I'll bet you already knew that. I remember asking Sadie about cauls and why mine wasn't saved. She said amulets were a lot of bunk. She said the stripping of the amniotic sac from a child in birth was like a snake going through a tight spot to scrap off its old skin. For her their only use was in figuring out the health of the child. A firm caul and the child was well, a limp one and the child was not. But you have told me that Jesse is pink and fat, that he nurses well.

I guess by the time I meet our son he'll be old enough to learn all about the river. Until then, daydreams will have to do.

Thank Mrs. Andrews for me. It makes me feel a whole lot better to know she is watching over you and Jesse.

I miss you every day, and now I will miss Jesse, too.

All my love to both of you,

Tom

After I folded the letter, I sat for a while, as I usually did, with it held in my hands. I wondered if he was still out of the trenches, which since he was an infantryman of the Third Division were his fate. He was still alive. I would feel it if he were not. For a moment I questioned whether I ought to have kept a bit of the caul and sent it to him; a talisman tucked into his pocket could bring no harm. But then Sadie's snake analogy came to me. And its implication—that saving a caul at birth is akin to bringing into the world of the living the dead skin of a snake—made me glad it had disappeared along with the rest of the afterbirth.

This morning, after dressing, I compared my reflection in the mirror with the photograph of me on our wedding day. I wanted to know just how much the intervening years showed on my face, to see what Tom might. I suppose I am thinner, maybe not so fresh-faced as I was at eighteen or even as twenty-one-year-old girls used to be, before their beaus and husbands and fathers left, before they waited and grieved and picked up the slack at home. Still, the differences hardly show. There is no hint that I have given birth and become a wage earner and managed on my own; that the larder has never been empty, or the bank account, though Mrs. Andrews hardly charges Jesse and me full freight for room and board. It is not plain to see I can now cook a tasty meal with just a handful of potatoes and a few chicken bones, all the while a child balanced on my hip, or that I can copy any dress from a magazine, that when there is no picture, I draw one myself, often improving upon the design a woman has in her head. The wonderment that sometimes fills me as I watch our son is not obvious, or the ever-present ache called motherhood. I cannot find evidence of the wretched days that followed the news of Passchendaele, the most deadly of the battles in which Tom fought. The intervening years show only slightly, in the thinness of my cheeks, the jawline that is no longer round. Tom will not see the more sweeping changes. Or maybe I am entirely wrong and I have not changed at all. Maybe he knew I would make out all right before I knew it myself. Maybe he knew, even as he held my gaze from the window of his train departing for the war.

The railway station is imposing: redbrick and stone with Gothic windows and massive wood-paneled doors, an expense the city's forefathers insisted upon, a first impression for the tourists coming to Niagara Falls. Though the interior of the station is warm and spacious, Jesse and I quickly pass through to the wooden-plank platform out back. While the Spanish flu has let up since its arrival in earnest four months ago, it is still upon us. And with so many soldiers coming home from overseas, there is renewed fear: Might they bring with them more of the contagion that has caused so many to die? Surely it is best to wait in the frosty air beneath the wide, overhanging eaves. Mrs. Andrews said that if I had a scrap of sense I would stay home, that it would be entirely my fault if the household began hacking up blood, but I could not bear to let Tom arrive even a tiny bit hopeful and then not find us waiting. I could not postpone by even twenty minutes the moment when he would meet Jesse.

The town has changed while Tom has been away. There is no doubt of that. If I were parachuted to Table Rock, at the brink of the falls, I would see within seconds that all was not as it once was. I would be nearly alone rather than surrounded by a gawking horde proclaiming the falls wondrous, a marvel, a sight well worth the trip. If anyone did happen to be close by, odds are it would be a woman, and more likely than not she would be striding purposefully toward some place of employment, some position that had until recently been considered unsuitable for the weaker sex, some position that she would in all likelihood have to give up with the men coming home. She might be wearing a gauze mask over her mouth and nose, as had just about everyone during October and November, when every day the newspaper reported yet another victim of the Spanish flu, when it was commonplace to hear stories of four women sitting down to a game of bridge in the evening only to be, all four, coughing up blood by midnight and then gulping their final breaths by dawn.

The scarcity of tourists and men seems of little significance when considered alongside Sir Adam Beck's mammoth undertaking here. Two years ago he had the possibility of a powerhouse at Queenston put to a vote and I agonized over how to mark my ballot, but not because what was best for Niagara Falls, or even all of Canada, was unclear in my mind. As things stand, we need more coal to heat our homes, to cook our meals, to light our rooms so that we might extend a December day beyond five o'clock in the afternoon, and there is a limited supply. To argue differently would be to claim ignorance of lit rooms inexplicably flickering to blackness, machinery suddenly grinding to a halt, windows frosting over when the coal wagon fails to make the rounds. And such occurrences have become regular events.

One afternoon a while before the vote, I was walking through Queen Victoria Park, just opposite the falls. The mist was thick, raining down, and I was doing my best to keep myself dry. But then a moment later I was at the brink, standing there until I was soaked through. I remembered Tom saying if the power companies had their way, Niagara Falls would be reduced to a heap of spent coal. But as I stood there, it seemed he was entirely wrong. What I saw was water and more water, never-ending water tumbling over the brink. It was not a bit like coal. Coal clawed from the earth would never be replaced.

I thought of Isabel, too, swept over the brink, hurled to the plunge pool far below. I knew from Tom it could have been worse: a bloated body trapped behind the falls for days or months, on occasion forevermore. Or worse still, a mangled corpse pummeled by careening water upon the rocks at the base of the falls. Plenty of folks said, "Best not gaze too long," and there were tales of those who had not heeded the bit of advice and, unable to resist, waded into the treacherous current of the upper river. And for a long moment, I stood there at the brink, shivering and afraid, thinking a whole lot less water suited me just fine.

And while the wartime shortage of men had meant nearly any fellow left behind could choose where he worked, I knew even as I cast my ballot that one day the munitions factories would close, some permanently, others for extended periods while they were retooled. Unemployment and the unrest that comes with it would skyrocket as ever more men were shipped home. It would be the same the country over, from Victoria to St. John's, unemployment everywhere, everywhere except Niagara Falls. And while I knew the Hydro-Electric Power Commission would never be Tom's first choice, it was comforting to think of employment there as a safety net of sorts.

I wrote to Tom before the vote to say as gently as I could that it seemed to me the bounty of the river might be twofold. There was the beauty of it, also its usefulness. I carried the letter in my handbag for a week before mailing it, hesitating each time I passed the post office. Might the letter distract him? Might it cause him a sleepless night? In the end, I sent it. I could not stand that the post might find its way to his company at the front without a letter from me, and it seemed entirely wrong to substitute a different letter, one that did not mention the vote.

His reply came back two weeks before the ballot.

December 15, 1916

My Dear Bess,

I got your parcel with the sweater and heating coils yesterday, and then today your letter and the bits you clipped from the newspaper. The sweater fits perfectly and is just right to wear under my uniform. I can see that with the heating coils I'll soon be the most popular fellow in the company.

You should vote however you think you should, but here's my opinion on what Beck's proposed.

Remember way back, the afternoon we spent riding the electric trolley in the gorge? We talked about the Boundary Waters Treaty. I'd done some calculations showing that with the powerhouses already on the river taking the water they were allowed, there wasn't enough left even for the hundred thousand horsepower Beck was talking about back then. He spent the last ten years blowing the whistle every time one of the private companies took an ounce more water than it was allowed. But now that it suits him, he's all set to chuck the treaty out the door.

You said that the power companies have been told to ignore the limits in their charters, that they've been told to develop electricity to the max to help out with the war. It's Beck's doing. He's wrapping himself in the flag, using the war as an excuse to take as much of the river as he wants.

You wrote about blackouts as some sort of justification, but can't you see that demand has been upped by the war, that it will drop once the war is done? It's why Beck's Hydro Circus makes the rounds. He knows that with his powerhouse he'll be generating way more electricity than we can use, that he's got to push up the demand.

I have been to the whirlpool twice when there wasn't a whirlpool at all. Both times the wind was unusual, from the east and strong, and there wasn't much water flowing into the river from Lake Erie. At both shores of the falls the riverbed was dry. There wasn't any mist. No thunder either.

The water in the river was down, enough so that there weren't any standing waves. The Niagara wasn't all that different from any other river in the world, definitely not something that would cause a man walking by to stop, and maybe fill with wonder for a bit and be lifted up from the drudgery of his day. With Beck's powerhouse, the river will be drained as never before, and those two times when there wasn't a whirlpool at all, I saw what lies ahead with the river swallowed up by tunnels and canals.

Again, I miss you every day. Last night I fell asleep thinking about some Christmas when I'd take you and Jesse out searching for a tree.

The merriest Christmas possible to both of you.

All my love,

Tom

I thought for a long while about the river and the falls and awestruck passersby, and a few days after reading the letter, I even said to Father, "What about the wonder so many feel at the brink?"

"What about it?" he answered back. "We were given the river, also the ingenuity to harness it."

Despite Father's dismissal, despite the many arguments in favor of the project, I agonized over the ballot; marking it as I knew I would seemed traitorous to Tom.

The people of Ontario gave their approval, overwhelmingly, and just as Father had predicted, Beck's initial concept of a powerhouse producing one hundred thousand horsepower had grown. He promised a scheme that would eclipse any hydroelectric powerhouse already built in Niagara Falls and be larger than any even contemplated elsewhere in the world.

Construction began the spring of 1917, and ever since the landscape of Niagara Falls has been marred. It started with a narrow belt of cleared earth that was soon enough hollowed out to a partially dug canal lined on either side with excavated rock waiting to be hauled away. And then, with the summertime heat, came a new scar, a scar that now seems as permanent as the canal. Quickly and quietly, Beck's Hydro-Electric Power Commission bought the Ontario Power Company and laid a third conduit from the intake gates at Dufferin Islands to the powerhouse. Left as it was in an open ditch, the conduit was an eyesore. Yet I was thankful for the slapdash construction. When I wrote to Tom, I was able to say it really did seem the Hydro-Electric Power Commission was being truthful in saying the new conduit was temporary, an emergency measure made necessary by wartime manufacturing. Slapdash or not, there was sorrow and anger in his reply.

September 15, 1917

My Dear Bess,

There's more misery over here, but I won't write about it, not today. I got your letter just now, and the mailman is waiting for me to finish up with mine.

I guess I shouldn't have expected much better from Beck. The new conduit will be buried one day, but not until everyone has long forgotten he once promised it would be temporary. The water siphoned off from the river has never been cut. No one's ever said, "Let's just take what we need." The power companies on the Canadian side are already making more than we can use. Ask your father. He'll tell you we're shipping the extra to the U.S.

We are out of the trenches for a few days' rest so expect a longer letter soon.

Give Jesse a kiss for me.

All my love to you both,

Tom

After reading the letter, I sat thinking about my last months at Glenview, the months after Hilde and Bride had been let go. There were hours lugging coal from the basement, loading it into the stove, coaxing it to the right heat. And then there was the soot, the ashes, the scorched biscuits, the hours in an endlessly heated kitchen on a summer's day, all to be erased by the magic of a waterfall.

Mrs. Andrews and I had grown into a habit of reading each other bits from the newspaper. Not long after the armistice, it was a piece arguing Canada was changed forevermore by the war. I read, both of us nodding our agreement with the claim that our country had outgrown the nest of the British Empire and become a nation in its own right on the battlefields of Belgium and France. Our troops had proven themselves, fighting valiantly at the Somme, Vimy Ridge, and Passchendaele, and like everyone else at home, Mrs. Andrews and I had heard stories of the Allies leaking it to the Huns that they would be meeting up with the Canadians at such and such a battle, even when it was not true. "Puts the fear of God in them," Tom had written, "the idea of coming face-to-face with a man who'd once spent his days chopping down the wilderness and wrestling grizzly bears to the ground."

When I got to the bit about the outrage the entire country felt when Canada was not offered a seat at the Paris Peace Conference at the end of the war, Mrs. Andrews said, "The Brits couldn't bring themselves to cut the apron strings, even with Canada all grown up." According to the essay, Prime Minister Borden saw his chance and pounced, arguing vehemently, playing his trump card—the fact that we had lost a far greater chunk of our population than the United States. In the end Britain relented. The United States finally gave in. And Canada sent a delegation to the talks.

Finished with the essay, I set down the newspaper and began threading my sewing machine. "That's it?" Mrs. Andrews said, flicking the newspaper hard enough to send it careering to the floor. "All this talk of nationhood, but what about French and English Canada hating each other like never before?"

She had a point, and I nodded, my face growing hot as I remembered a comment I had made about French Canada not pulling its weight when it came to sending men overseas. I had used the term *shirking Frenchie frogs,* and it had caused Mrs. Andrews to lift her foot from the treadle of her sewing machine. Enough days had passed since Vimy Ridge to lessen the odds of a dreaded telegram; still, I was agitated to the point of having bitten the inside of a cheek raw. "I suppose you'd march off to fight for some country your ancestors didn't come from," she said, "especially if that country spoke a language that wasn't your own and you were told by the higher-ups they had no intention of setting up a company of men you could exchange a few words with. You'd be taking orders in a new language, too, the one all the officers spoke."

The sentiment seemed dangerous, a way of thinking that could undermine Borden's efforts to steamroll ahead with an act allowing the conscription of men countrywide, and a new wave of men to replace those fallen at Vimy Ridge was the surest bet of Tom ever coming home. I shrugged, and she said, *"Faut se mettre dans la peau de quelqu'un,"* before returning her foot to the treadle.

I remembered her maiden name then—Lambert—written on the backside of an old photograph, and I knew the correct pronunciation was *lambair,* rather than as I had assumed. Even so, I got up from my sewing machine and stood over her with my hands on my hips. "If you had someone over there, you wouldn't think any differently than the rest of us." Then I strode off, slamming the door as I went.

I was facedown on my bed, weeping into a wet pillow, when Mrs. Andrews put her hand on my back. "He's fine, Bess," she said. "I know he is." Her kindness made me bawl all the harder. I was tired and ashamed and sick to death of the war, wreaking havoc from four thousand miles away.

Conscription became the issue on which Borden's reelection hinged, and, never mind that French Canada teetered on the brink of mutiny, he was doing whatever he could to make sure it went his way. He gave the vote to the overseas soldiers, who could only see conscription as boosting their odds, and mandated that their votes could be scattered among the electoral districts as he saw fit. He abolished the notion that all women were unfit for the broils and excitements of a federal election and replaced it with legislation that gave those with husbands or sons or brothers fighting in the war the right to vote. As final assurance, conscientious objectors and immigrants from enemy countries were told they no longer had a say.

I could see his methods were suspect, but to my mind the end—the landslide victory he won—justified the means. After I cast my ballot, my heart was light. It took at least half the walk back to Mrs. Andrews's house to work out the reason why: At long last I had made Tom's future more certain, if only by a single vote.

His letters arrived in fits and starts, though seldom did more than a fortnight pass without some news from him. But then in the autumn of 1917, the newspaper confirmed the rumors we had been hearing for weeks and his correspondence altogether stopped. Our boys had moved on to Passchendaele.

The battlefield of Passchendaele was a dreary wasteland, a swampy marsh of mud and water even without the rain that had not let up all fall. There was no relic of civilization, only shell holes and charred trees and decomposing bodies, or so said Mrs. Mitchell at the post office one Thursday afternoon. She had heard it from a cousin, who was back from the front by way of Wandsworth Hospital in London, where he had a piece of shrapnel the size of peach pit wrenched from his eye and caught an earful from an Aussie fresh from Passchendaele. "The boys use duckboards— something like ladders but laid on the ground—to keep themselves from drowning in the mud," she said. "If a fellow takes a hit and goes off balance, well, that's pretty much it. He'll get swallowed up."

Hearsay abounded; the worst of it, too disheartening to be allowed in the newspapers, arrived in Niagara Falls via some route just as circuitous as Mrs. Mitchell's. Plenty of it reported the near annihilation of the British, Australian, and New Zealand divisions our boys were meant to replace. And there was a retired colonel in Queenston who insisted the high ground of the town of Passchendaele was in no way worth the bloodbath capturing it would mean.

Still, on a Monday in early November the *Evening Review* headline read OUR BOYS TAKE PASSCHENDAELE. The account that followed trumpeted the victory of the Third and Fourth divisions, which had captured the town of Passchendaele and hung on to it by the skin of their teeth, and the First and Second divisions, which had come to their aid, finally forcing the Germans ringing the area into retreat.

Other versions came quick on the heels, littering the glory of the newspaper account like an ash bin emptied onto newly fallen snow. Our dead were three deep in places, many sunk too deep in the mud to ever be found. As for how many Canadian soldiers were lost, there were the oldtimers who endlessly plotted the war on the maps laid out in the rear of Clark's Hardware, and a few had made extrapolations using the list of casualties from the newspaper and estimated it at fifteen thousand or more. I made the mistake of speaking to milky-eyed Mr. Chapman one afternoon while waiting for Mr. Clark to package up another round of heating coils for Tom. Once I had confirmed that, yes, Tom was in fact an infantryman in the Third Division, he shook his head. His calculations pointed to as many as four-fifths of the fellows in Tom's boots having fallen by the time the reinforcements arrived. As I stood there, numb, he misjudged me for someone eager for more. "Near as I can figure Passchendaele cost the Allies half a million in casualties, including upwards of a hundred thousand dead. With the five miles the boys pushed back the front, works out to three inches for every man lost."

All this, and not a word from Tom for forty-one days, twenty-nine since the headline in the *Evening Review.*

Home from Clark's Hardware, I put Jesse in his high chair and set a dish of cold macaroni from the supper before on the tray. When I noticed my hands shaking, I lifted the teapot from the cupboard, thinking a cup of chamomile might calm my nerves. It was then that I saw the boy who delivered the telegrams pause at the far end of the front walk. He flipped through the papers in his hands, looked up at the house and then down again. I closed my eyes, pressed my face against my palms, and with every ounce of will I could muster wished away the boy and the telegram addressed to me.

When I looked up again, he had wandered on, to some other address, some other widowed wife, some other fatherless child. I touched my fingertips to the teapot and circled them twice around the lid. Then I lifted that teapot and hurled it with all my might. I moved on, to a wool skirt for Miss Bingley, pressed for a final time earlier in the day and folded on the ironing board, and tried, unsuccessfully, to tear it from the waistband clear through to the hem. Jesse watched from his high chair, eyes wide, a spoon clenched in his tiny fist. When he threw that spoon toward the cupboard beneath which the rubble of the teapot lay, I was immediately upon him. "How dare you!" I spat the words, my arm jerking upward in preparation. Then Mrs. Andrews was there, her fingers tightly wrapping my raised arm, her body pushing mine from the kitchen as Jesse began to wail.

Once I regained my composure, which took the better part of the afternoon, even with the rocking chair Mrs. Andrews insisted upon, even with the milky tea she brought, even with the wool blanket she smoothed over my thighs, I told her about the boy pausing at the end of the walk, but her jaw was firmly set and did not change.

"Your father will be arriving on the ten o'clock tomorrow," she said. "He'll be taking you back to Buffalo for two weeks."

She laid a hand firmly on the wool blanket and did not shift her gaze from mine, even as tears welled in my eyes at the idea of having to explain myself to Mother and Father, even as it occurred to me there was nothing left to tell. "Jesse?"

"It's just a bit of a holiday, for the both of you." She smiled then, her eyes as soft as I had ever seen them, the backs of her fingers stroking my cheek with a tenderness I had guessed at but never seen.

I thought then of Mrs. Doherty, with her six children and livelihood of folding boxes and husband already shot full of holes. "I'm so ashamed."

"It's dances and pretty dresses that girls your age ought to be worrying about," Mrs. Andrews said.

Waiting for Father at the train station with Jesse good as gold on my knees, I thought about my raised arm, whether given another moment I would have followed through. The odd passerby noticed my wet cheeks and smiled kindheartedly, lingeringly, and a gentleman with a cane even patted my arm. The kindnesses were not the standard fare from before the war, the usual "Sorry for your troubles, miss." No, those concerned folk assumed the boy at the end of the walk had not ambled on after checking Mrs. Andrews's address against that of the telegram in his hands.

The three rooms Mother and Father let in Buffalo were on Jewett Avenue, an address that implied the prestigious neighborhood of Parkside, though they were in fact a good mile from Delaware Park. The bedroom, parlor, and dining room, where they ate whatever Mother rustled up on a hot plate, were crowded with the best pieces from Glenview: three bureaus; a four-poster bed; two chesterfields; a club chair; a mahogany table with matching china cabinet and sideboard, crammed with the usual silver and crystal but also with books. With six carpets, all overlapping, and Mother's cleverness for decorating, the rooms appeared studiously disheveled, pleasingly so.

By the time Father, Jesse, and I arrived, the dining room table had been pushed into a corner and two cots set up in its place. On the train there had been no mention of the episode behind my visit, only delight that he and Mother would have Jesse and me to themselves. Mother followed suit, though she smoothed my hair, put a hand on my shoulder, stroked my forearm, every chance she got. I told myself the tenderness was only concern over my fragile state, but with each touch there came an awful moment when it seemed she was convinced of my widowhood.

The first evening Father talked about an order the tannery had been given for ammunition pouches, fifty thousand of them all told, and the expansion he had had the good sense to undertake in just the nick of time. Mother said, "It's all working out wonderfully well," and I thought better than to ask why, then, was she wearing the same lovely dress she had had on when she last came to Niagara Falls, why then, had Father decided on a trolley rather than a hack from the train station to Jewett Avenue when there was a fair-size valise to be carried, also Jesse, who was sound asleep.

Two days later I woke to Mother scrubbing away at handkerchiefs and stockings and underclothes a few feet from my cot. "Rise and shine," she said, with enough vigor to make it clear she did not consider languor a cure for losing heart. "Your father's long gone, and Jesse got up an hour ago."

"You don't send the laundry out?" I said, once I was awake enough to be sure of what I was seeing.

"It's only a few things."

"But where do you hang the clothes to dry?" Bewildered as I was, the question had somehow risen to the top of the list.

"I've attached a few lines to the underside of the dining table." She looked up from the laundry tub and smiled as though I ought to be impressed with her ingenuity.

I shifted to sitting on the cot. "I thought Father was as good as running the tannery?"

"He's earning plenty," she said, "more than enough."

I nudged the laundry tub with my toe and turned up my palms.

She handed me a basket of wrung-out bloomers and camisoles, and a tin of clothespins. "Would you mind?" she said, pointing toward the table. "It's his latest mania. Saving."

"Mania?" I said, no less confused than a minute earlier.

"First it was aluminum. Then it was rye whiskey, and now it's saving up enough to buy the tannery." She tossed another pair of bloomers into the basket beside me. "He doesn't have it in him to do anything halfway. Never has."

I knew what she meant. Always, it had struck me that he loved her, and not in an everyday sort of way but with a rapt, enviable intensity. Even so, he was not giving her enough money to run the household.

"I prefer penny-pinching to rye whiskey," she said, clearing a stray lock from her forehead with the back of her hand.

In the evening Father came through the doorway with Sir Charles Lyell's *Travels in North America* in his hand. "I'm sending it over to Tom," he said. "There's a chapter where he uses the distance between the edge of the escarpment and the falls, and the rate they're eroding back to calculate the age of the Niagara Gorge."

I knew the book. Kit had complained bitterly when Mother Febronie pitched a copy that had snuck its way onto the shelves of the library at the academy. If Lyell were right, the date of creation set by Saint Bede using the Bible as a guide was entirely wrong.

I slipped my arms around Father's neck and glimpsed an approving smile come to Mother's lips. "He'll love it," I said, squeezing him like I had not since I was a child. A book was an extravagance, something my penny-pinching father would surely not have bought if he thought Tom had drowned in the mud.

It was the next morning when Mrs. Andrews called, breathlessly hollering into the telephone that a whole slew of letters from Tom had arrived, that she had opened all of them, that the most recent was dated November 17. "He survived Passchendaele," she said, her voice beginning to crack. And then it was some nonsense about someone at her door. She would make me wait until she had pulled herself together to hear another word.

There are plenty of fellows who will not step onto the railway station platform at Niagara Falls today, plenty of fellows who had not survived Ypres and the Somme, Vimy Ridge and Passchendaele: Fred and George Anderson, whom I knew from Morrison Street Methodist; Walter Canfield and Frank Romea, who worked for Father at the Niagara Power Company; James Muir and Clement Swan and Thomas Wood, who visited their sisters at the academy; Gordon Dobbie, who delivered the flowers from his father's shop; William Hewson, who courted Isabel for a while; 124 others, including Edward Atwell, who was once my betrothed.

His death was reported in the *Evening Review.* "Killed in action," it said. I cried balled up on my bed until Mrs. Andrews brought me a cup of tea with brandy and said that Jesse was waiting in the hall, but in another five minutes she was sending him in and that it was not right for a child to see his mother carrying on so.

I sent a heartfelt condolence to Kit and did not receive a reply. I thought about dropping in on her at one of the Erie Avenue shops she now ran on her family's behalf and had very nearly worked up the nerve when I saw her, lounging on a blanket in Queen Victoria Park, listening to the Niagara Falls Citizens Band. She was leaning against a fellow fifteen years her senior and tall with a hollow chest and a dusting of freckles and sparse, tan hair. Surely he was Leslie Scott, her husband, who had been sent home from the war early with chlorine gas–damaged lungs and then come to Niagara Falls from Toronto as the Hydro-Electric Power Commission's chief hydraulic engineer. Midconcert I caught her eye. There was a moment of recognition, and then pursed lips and her hard gaze lingering too long before shifting from mine. Edward was not going to come home from the war and marry a pretty girl and set to work on a brood of his own. He was not coming home, not at all, and there was no hope of me becoming a mere hiccup along the way to a full life.

Boyce Cruickshank had survived the war; at least his name had not appeared in the death notices of *The Buffalo Evening News,* which my parents watched as closely as I did those of the *Evening Review.* We knew he had enlisted early on with the American Expeditionary Forces because Father had seen him in uniform a short while after the United States finally joined the Allies and began shipping ten thousand men a day to France.

"Your father ran into Boyce the other day," Mother had said.

"Boyce Cruickshank?" As far as I knew it was the first they had seen of him since he left Isabel high and dry.

"He said Boyce cut clear across the street to speak to him. He's got more backbone than his father. I'll give him that."

"Was he rude?" The more senior Mr. Cruickshank had looked the other way when he met Mother on the street and turned his back when he came upon Father at the bank.

"He hung his head and said he was sorry, that he had been a great disappointment to Isabel, that she deserved better. Apparently he was wearing a soldier's uniform."

Amid influenza and the ballot for the power commission, amid worry and grief over men too far away or ruined or altogether lost, there has been pleasure, often short-lived, sometimes persisting for an hour or a day or a week. There is Jesse, who is happy, who claps his hands in delight when I step into a room. At two years old he is clever enough to know limestone from shale, agile enough to have scaled a handful of the boulders in the glen, spirited enough to have thrown himself into a pool at Dufferin Islands, certain that he could swim, which turned out to be right.

There is the work that has kept the two of us afloat, the needle between my fingers like a tiny magic wand. There are the dresses that cause women to marvel, the really special ones that cause me to marvel as well. I have a handful of clients who are my very own, rather than Mrs. Andrews's with me as assistant. It began one morning with Mrs. Andrews answering the door and me in the sewing room, my foot stock-still on the treadle once I recognized Mrs. Coulson's precise enunciation, almost British though she was born in Niagara Falls. "I've heard you've taken on Bess Cole as an apprentice," she said. Of course Mrs. Coulson knew, her ear all but pressed to the ground. Of course she had come. She needed to see for herself what had become of the girl who had discarded the bit of advice hurled at her in the backseat of an Oldsmobile and married the likes of Tom Cole.

"I have." I could picture Mrs. Andrews—her spectacles perched low on her nose, her chin indiscreetly inching upward as she took in Mrs. Coulson's full height.

"I'm an old friend, a benefactor, some might say."

"How so?"

"I'm not sure it's any of your business."

"You brought it up."

"I was wondering whether I might order a skirt," Mrs. Coulson said. "I'd want Bess to do more than run up the seams."

"Why not just say you'd rather her make the skirt than me?"

Mrs. Coulson cleared her throat. "All right," she said. "I'd rather Bess made the skirt."

Was I wrong about her? Was it possible Mrs. Coulson was extending the favor she had shown Mother to me? To have a client of my own would be a streak of good luck. And that it was Mrs. Coulson, who had the height and curves to be the perfect model for a perfect dress, also the social connections to bring news of my old world at a time when the cocoon of just Mrs. Andrews, Jesse, and me was sometimes too snug, at least partially offset my dislike of her busybody ways.

I made the skirt, a straightforward affair, six panels, a yoke. She was pleased and ordered a blouse, no pleats, no ruffles, nothing for me to mess up. That was before I showed her a design I had come up with for an evening gown. She settled on pale blue-green silk for the main body and an ivory shadow lace for the neckline and sleeves. After that more women came to the door, saying, "I heard you sew for Mrs. Coulson."

With Mrs. Coulson ordering an evening gown or a dinner dress nearly every month, it seemed there was no shortage of funds in the Coulson household, and it was hardly a surprise. Mr. Coulson had been hired away from the Niagara Power Company for what everyone said was a top-brass position with the Hydro-Electric Power Commission. And then, a few days after the Armistice, Mrs. Coulson confirmed he was in fact senior enough to hire anyone he pleased. I was fitting her for a velvet evening coat and had just finished adjusting the bodice darts to fit her ample bust when she said, "You should send Tom to see Mr. Coulson about work once he's home."

It had occurred to me that Mr. Coulson might have the clout to add another man to the payroll, and I had thought how simple it would be to ask Mrs. Coulson to put in a word on Tom's behalf, even if it meant handing her on a silver platter the opportunity to gloat. Until that moment in the fitting room, though, I had always reminded myself that the Hydro-Electric Power Commission was not for Tom, at least not until necessity made it so, and pressed my lips shut until the notion passed. "He'll need to find something," I said, aiming for just enough enthusiasm to keep the Hydro-Electric Power Commission as an option. "I'll tell him when he gets home."

"Mr. Coulson would keep an eye on him," she said. "He'd make sure he was treated well."

I ran a bit of chalk along the length of a newly marked dart. "I really appreciate it, both Mr. Coulson's help and all the orders you send my way."

"Your father was always looking out for Mr. Coulson, and Mr. Coulson doesn't forget very much." She glanced in the mirror, sliding her hands from ribs to hips.

I remembered Isabel saying Mr. Coulson was as ambitious as they come, and Mrs. Coulson, too, and the thought sent me back to her tirade in the Oldsmobile. She was a woman used to doling out orders, a woman used to having everything work out just as she had planned. She turned, suddenly, to admire her profile, causing me to stick myself with a pin.

Mother knew I was sewing for Mrs. Coulson and was always wanting to hear about whatever pretty frock I had on the go for her. Given the dearth of new frocks in Mother's life, I tended to gloss over the imported lace, mohair soutache, and underskirts cut from the finest of silks. I kept Mr. Coulson's workplace advancement to myself. Doing otherwise would have seemed rather like pouring salt into an open wound. Even so, it appeared news traveled to Buffalo, and one Sunday telephone call, Mother said, "You might mention to Mrs. Coulson that Tom will be looking for work once he's home."

"I can't see Tom working for the Hydro," I said, though I still clung to Mrs. Coulson's offer to help.

"He might not have a choice."

"As far as I know, conscription ended with the war." My tone was unfair. She was only saying the obvious. I had thought the same thought.

"I meant it might be the only work to be had," she said.

"We could get by on what I make." It was not true, not unless the three of us stayed on with Mrs. Andrews for the rest of our days.

"I admire Tom's attachment to the river, Bess. I really do. But I'm all for give-and-take, and there's an awful lot of water tumbling over the brink."

"I'm to drag him off to the Hydro, then?"

"You won't need to drag him anywhere. You only need to pave the way."

Married soldiers are being shipped home in advance of the others, and so the gathering on the platform is mostly women and children, none quite as young as Jesse. We are the lucky ones, and it seems immensely wrong of me to be waiting on the platform feeling nearly as much anxiety as joy. Our dreams have come true. The train pulling into the station, its windows full of cap-waving, cap-tossing soldiers, is about to deliver our men, the ones who have come home.

I see Tom before he sees me and watch as he disembarks in a khaki tunic and puttees, like the others, except that his cap is solemnly upon his head, causing him to look subdued among the melee of soldiers lifting children, embracing wives, clapping backs. "Tom," I call out, raising my arm. He stands three or four inches taller than the rest of the crowd, and somehow the size of him takes me by surprise. I can see even from a distance that he is thin, that his hair has been shorn, likely to rid him of lice before his return. I lift Jesse so that he might see his father approach, so that his father might see him. Then Tom's arms are around the both of us, pulling us close. Jesse wriggles an arm free and wraps it around Tom's neck. "Daddy," he says.

When Tom loosens his embrace, I pull back slightly, but he keeps his face buried in my scarf, and I hear a gasp and feel his chest heave. Sobbing is distinct from weeping, and he is sobbing. The other fellows, with wet cheeks and smiles, they are weeping, joyfully, even the one who hobbled off the train, the leg of one pant tucked up beneath his thigh.

A length of muslin painted with the words "Welcome Home" is strung across Mrs. Andrews's kitchen cupboards. There is a ham stuck with cloves ready for the oven and peeled potatoes ready for the pot, also the lemon squares he used to love, set on a plate. And a month ago, Mrs. Andrews insisted on giving Jesse, for no additional rent, the spare room next to the larger one he and I had shared while Tom was away. "It's unnatural," she said, "a two-and-a-half-year-old sharing his mother's bed." I scrubbed both rooms floor to ceiling, cut new liners for the drawers, and replaced the lavender in the sachet I keep with my underclothes. Our bed is made up with freshly laundered sheets, the best from my trousseau. But as I stand with Tom sobbing into my scarf, the efforts seem misguided, a foolish attempt at merriment. At least I had the good sense to put Mother and Father off when they proposed coming to welcome Tom home.

When he finally lets go, he says, "It was awful over there."

I wipe away the tear clinging to his chin. "I know, Tom. I know."

"You don't," he says, "and it's a blessing."

I remember another letter, different from the rest, late last summer, a short while after the newspapers were full of the good news of Amiens.

August 24, 1918

My Dear Bess,

I am sorry I've taken so long to write, but I have been putting it off, waiting for my mood to change. I am not sick in any way, but I am feeling beaten down—by the smell, the smashed men twitching like squashed, charred insects, the upright corpses mistaken for living men, the landscape of barren earth without so much as a blade of grass. I am feeling alone, lost, and I can't figure out how to feel like myself again.

I decided to write anyway because you will know I was at Amiens, and I do not want you worrying about me.

I'll end now with love to you and Jesse.

Tom

He takes off his cap, and I want him to toss it into the air without a second thought to it being trampled or lost beneath the planks of the platform. But he only shoves it into the pocket of his tunic, as though he does not quite believe he is through with the war.

19

Building Niagara's Toronto powerhouse

I lie on my side, cheek in hand, elbow propped on a pillow, watching Tom sleep as I have most mornings for the six weeks since his return. He is still handsome, though not so youthful as before the war. There are dusky hollows beneath his eyes and, on his chin, stubble that did not used to appear overnight. At the uppermost edge of his cheekbone, there is a small, ragged scar where a bit of shrapnel missed his eye. His hair has yet to grow long enough for waves, and, having met only winter sun, it is dark in color, more like earth than like beach. I cannot see the river on him the way I once thought I could, in the feral locks, in the underside of a chin bronzed by reflected light, in the green of his eyes. The color has seemed muted, diluted by the bleak wasteland of a battlefield.

Again he slept only fitfully, calling out *no,* sweating profusely with tangled linens wrapped about his legs. Three times, I woke him and saw relief flood his face as his eyes fluttered open to discover my hands on his shoulders, shaking him from the nightmares he mostly keeps to himself. The fourth time, it was early morning, and in the dim light I could see his eyes, open but wide with fear. His mouth was twisted with effort, and his hands were reaching, desperately. When he was truly awake I asked what he had seen. "A hand," he said, "a hand in the mud. A soldier was being swallowed up by it. Only the hand was left."

"It was a dream. It's gone." I stroked his cheek.

"At Passchendaele I was told to keep advancing. I was told I'd only imagined the fingers were reaching for help. 'Might even belong to a Hun,' is what my officer said."

A short while later the three of us are eating toast in the kitchen. I lift the coffeepot in Tom's direction. "More?" He nods, and I fill his raised mug. As I push myself back from the table to tend to the bacon sizzling on the stove, Jesse breaks the quiet. "Daddy, play outside?"

It is the question he asks most mornings. And Tom usually says yes and they put on their coats and boots, and Jesse marches in the snow and calls it quicksand. Every now and then he topples over and hollers until he is saved. I have watched through the kitchen window and seen Tom leaning against the pump, aloof. Yesterday I saw him startle, caught off guard, when Jesse aimed a stick and shrieked that Tom was a Hun.

"What about setting a snare or two?" I say. "I could make a rabbit stew." He used to take such pleasure in the river, and Foster's Flats, the lowermost terrace of the glen, was once his preferred spot for snaring small game. I have thought an outing there might help, an idea that has grown as the days pass with Tom never setting out for the rapids, whirlpool, or falls. I remember, too, an early letter from overseas: "I guess by the time I meet our son he'll be old enough to learn all about the river. Until then, daydreams will have to do."

"I told Mrs. Andrews I'd bring in some wood," Tom says. It is how he spends his days—mending a latch, straightening the woodpile, sanding and staining the windowsills. But soon there will be nothing left of the tasks Mrs. Andrews and I had put off for so long.

"Jesse should be taught how to trap," I say.

"All right. All right. I'll show him how it's done."

For a moment I feel the beginnings of hope, a warm ember set to spark. He will make his way to the river, and, better yet, Jesse will accompany him. It is not the first time I have chucked prudence aside and let myself think he was turning a corner of sorts. But then he says, "There used to be rabbits just to the west of the rail yards," and hope fizzles to ash.

As I lift a strip of bacon from the pan and wait for the fat to drip away, it seems to me the odor is slightly off. I hold the pan out to Tom. "It smells like it should," he says. Then he and Jesse devour nearly a half pound. But the idea of putting a forkful into my mouth is so unpleasant that I let two strips grow cold on my plate. With Jesse, I lost my taste for bacon early, months before my belly swelled.

My immediate reaction is disbelief. Our intimacy has been sporadic at best, with only three instances since his return, and the first was an abysmal failure, with Tom pumping and pumping until I felt rubbed raw and then, when I was very nearly at my wits' end, rolling away from me onto his back and saying, "I'm sorry, Bess." Even so, disbelief shifts to panic as I calculate that my period is late. Yes, I want a playmate for Jesse, a baby for Tom to know from birth, another child to love. Eventually. But not just now. We have not yet figured out how to be a family of three, and, as a baby, Jesse took every ounce of stamina I could muster and then some. And I can only imagine what Mrs. Andrews will say. At first it was just me and a wardrobe full of clothes. Then came the baby, who howled in the night and peed on her favorite carpet and cut a ragged triangle from the sheers hanging in the dining room. And now, there is Tom, who sometimes calls out in the night and flinches if a door swings shut too abruptly and leaves whiskers in the sink and eats enough so that a roasting chicken no longer does for two meals. Oh, she would never put us out the door, but it hardly seems right to stay. Even with a family of three, the bustle of the house has become a strain by the end of the day. When it was just the two of us, she sat in the kitchen in the evenings playing solitaire or cro-cheting lace collars and cuffs. But she has begun heading up to her bed-room ever earlier and quietly closing the door. I count out nine months and tell myself I have got until the fall to coax Tom from his stupor, to figure out how we will manage with a second child.

Tom heads out to the shed after breakfast, likely to dig up a few snares. As I wipe the table and tuck in the chairs, it occurs to me the timing of Jesse's arrival had seemed far from idyllic at first, with Tom away. Yet I have no doubt it was Jesse's tiny hand in my own that forced me to keep my chin up and my eyes mostly dry. And there was comfort in holding him in my arms, in feeling Tom was with me though he was not. So maybe there is reason to be pleased. Maybe a second child will be the magic that turns the three of us into a family. Surely Tom will rise to the occasion. Surely he will place his hands on my belly and marvel at the tiny heel kicking beneath. I lift my sweater from the peg at the back door.

I am in the shed doorway with my sweater pulled tight around my waist when Tom turns toward me, his arms full of snares. He juts his chin in my direction. "What's the smile about?" he says.

"I think I'm pregnant."

"Oh."

"The bacon seemed off. It's what happened with Jesse." I wrap my sweater tighter still around my waist.

"You're sure?"

"I'm late, too."

"Wow," he says. He smiles, but it is not the same lopsided smile I had imagined a thousand times while he was overseas, and he hangs on to the snares, rather than returning them to the crate and putting his arms around me.

"I know it's a shock."

He sighs and says, "What about money, Bess?"

"We'll manage."

"I need to look for work."

A week earlier Mother and Father had come to welcome Tom home, and knowing Mother would relish a visit with Mrs. Coulson, I had sched-uled a fitting—a jacket and skirt cut from charcoal gray wool crepe—to coincide. While I marked the hem, the talk turned to the Queenston-Chippawa power project, and Mrs. Coulson told Mother and me how Mr. Coulson was run off his feet trying to make sure all the men the Hydro had hired were put to good use. And then she said, "I'm sure Bess has told you I've been after her to send Tom along to Mr. Coulson," and I marveled at her audacity. She would see to it Tom worked at the Hydro, as she had decided was best, even if it meant prompting Mother to harp at me as well.

Both women turned to me, waiting, Mother's lifted eyebrows questioning that I had withheld this bit of news from her. "Well?" Mother said.

"He's barely home."

"Best send him to Mr. Coulson while he still needs men," Mother said.

"He isn't adjusted to being back. He's still restless at night." I wouldn't say more than that, not within earshot of Mrs. Coulson. At any rate, Mother knew my worries. I had had to explain why I put off their visit by more than a month and ended up saying more than I thought I would—the calling out in the night, the failed intimacy, the way Jesse was overlooked. But she had been dismissive. "Remember the trouble your father had over all that aluminum business? He was over it the minute he set foot in the tannery."

"There's nothing like a good day's work to tire a fellow out," Mrs. Coulson said.

I did my best to appear sidetracked by a particularly stubborn pin. "I'm just not sure the Hydro is for Tom, even once he's rested up," I finally said. Immediately I was regretful. Might my apparent indifference have cost Tom his only chance for work? And what was more, I had seen nothing to hint his allegiance to the river had even survived the war, nothing to hint he had not altogether forgotten the writhing, bucking water, shattering to mist and spray and thunder at the brink of the falls.

"Not sure?" Mrs. Coulson said, a furrow coming to her brow.

Another stubborn pin was more than Mother could endure, and she said, "Tom isn't much for progress. He wants all the water left going over the falls," causing me to cringe.

"There's plenty of water," Mrs. Coulson said. "Plenty of water and almost no work. Has Tom made the rounds?"

I shook my head.

"He should," Mrs. Coulson said. "There isn't any other work. He should see for himself."

I could see she was put out. I nodded, a little sheepishly, and Mrs. Coulson relented, shifting the conversation to the plans of the Great War Veterans' Association for a cenotaph. "You should come out to a meeting, Bess," she said. I had been lonely for ages, and with Tom home I was no longer able to bolster myself with thoughts of *Once the war ends . . . , Once Tom's back . . .* Being in the company of other women, especially women with husbands just home from overseas, seemed like an evening well spent. But Mrs. Coulson did not mention a date or a place, and it seemed she would have if the invitation were sincere. I supposed there was the problem of how she would introduce me. Her dressmaker? Daughter of the disgraced Mr. and Mrs. Heath? Wife of a layabout?

I take a snare from the bundle in Tom's arms and fiddle with the lock. Should I mention the Hydro? Might Mother and Mrs. Coulson, with their pronouncements of work as a cure, be right? "What you need is to rest up a little longer," I finally say. "We've got the money from my parents." I had hoped to one day put the three hundred dollars toward a home of our own, a home that has surely become all the more pressing now that we are to be a family of four.

Eventually Tom and Jesse set out for the rail yards, and I stand at the front door, watching as they wade through drifted snow, Jesse with his small, mittened hand held in Tom's. But when the wind gusts and snow swirls around their legs, Tom reaches to turn up the collar of his coat and in doing so drops Jesse's hand. My last glimpse, as they round the corner, is of Jesse padding behind, his forgotten hand held aloft, straining for Tom's.

With the war and then the Spanish flu and now Tom, I feel more than ever that I lack whatever it is that brings others serenity. For ages, since well before Tom's return, I have found myself thinking longingly of my Loretto days: wake-up bell, morning chapel, breakfast, classes, lunch, sewing, more classes, recreation, supper, music practice, study hall, evening prayers, lights out. Always the same. It occurred to me that by following the rules, by behaving in a certain way, we had strewn our daily life with rituals, rituals that had given me peace.

With Tom still away, I had gone to Morrison Street Methodist in search of that peace. The Order of Service, and the words of the Creed and the Lord's Prayer and the Benediction, remained unchanged from week to week. There was the same odor of old hymnals, the sun warming the third pew each Sunday at ten o'clock. I suppose there was comfort in the predictability of it all. And sometimes I was encouraged by the reading of a particular scripture or roused by the beauty of the stained glass. I attended regularly enough that when I missed, I would be stopped on Bridge Street or Erie Avenue. "Are you well, Bess?" one or another of the Methodists would say. Still, I was not soothed in the way I had hoped, and it seemed as unlikely as ever there was a being up there, keeping watch. Soon enough I was mouthing the words to the Creed—I believe in God, the Father Almighty, maker of heaven and earth—rather than speaking them aloud. Eventually church without belief seemed a foolhardy pursuit, and Sunday mornings again became lazy breakfasts and walks in the woods of the glen with Jesse.

After Morrison Street Methodist, I began to wonder if what I really needed was to pray, if with all the hymns and scripture readings and homilies, the time left over for quiet reflection had been inadequate. And I wanted to pray for Tom at the front. I remembered a feeling of warmth and love coming to me in the academy chapel, a feeling of being a part of something much greater than myself. I remembered moments of consolation, certainty that the way things turned out was anything but sheer luck.

Every evening for three months, I sat cross-legged on my bed before turning in, hands folded in prayer, and resolved to stay on track this time. But always it was the same, my mind drifting to Tom overseas, to Jesse in his bed, to whether Isabel's child might have resembled him in some way, to a frock I had yet to complete, even to a grocery list. I tried to remember mist dappled with bits of shimmering silver, making its way heavenward. But in the end all that seemed certain was that I had not made the future any more sure.

Maybe I need to take my cue from Jesse, who simply offers his hand again and again, who seems entirely oblivious to any difference between this father and the daddy I promised for so long. When I asked Mrs. Andrews what she thought, she only lifted a shoulder, as though she had not noticed a thing. But she knows that Tom has not yet felt the full weight of Jesse tugging at his heartstrings, that certain doors are flung shut even to me. It is why she shoos Tom and me out the door in the evening, why she is bleary-eyed from sewing for Mrs. Usher and Mrs. Cox and all three Leonard girls, while I sew for only Miss Bingley and Mrs. Coulson. It is why I hear her shushing Jesse most mornings as she leads him past our closed bedroom door, why she made me a nightdress of sheer silk, causing me to sneak into bed earlier in the week and lay there shivering, cold silk against my breasts, far too self-conscious to coax Tom to the middle of the bed. Admittedly, it was almost a relief, not to persuade, not to hope, not to feign pleasure, not to stroke his hair afterward. But I am afraid that I might lack the fortitude to reach for him again.

One evening a while back, when Mrs. Andrews was insistent that I needed a bit of fresh air, Tom and I left the house. With Tom leading the way, we headed west on Bridge Street, in the direction opposite the river, which hardly came as a surprise. We ended up at Fairview Cemetery, and I followed him under the arch at the entranceway and along the rutted path to his family plot, where both Fergus and Sadie were buried. As he brushed the snow from their headstones, he looked so broken that I was unnerved. I said, "Tell me, Tom. I think it might help to tell."

"It's just that . . ." He looked away from me, to the trampled snow at his feet. "I lost my nerve over there. I felt really alone, more than I ever have, and then my nerves went."

I remembered the letter. "I am feeling alone, lost, and I can't figure out how to feel like myself again."

"I'd lie awake, in the trench, staring up at nothing, thinking up ways to get away from the front." He said more, of how he hoped for a blighty, a generous bit of shrapnel in the thigh, a wound just serious enough to mean his removal from the battlefield. "I thought about shooting myself in the foot. But shooting yourself was a capital offense, and even if other fellows said it was true, I wasn't sure a sandbag between my boot and the gun would stop the powder marks. And then there was the chance of gangrene setting in."

"I wouldn't think much of a man who wasn't fazed by war."

"I thought about claiming shell shock. But I'd heard the troops sent to Queens Square Hospital in London were treated with jolts of current, not enough to kill a man, just enough to deaden his mind before sending him back." He laughed then, a short, mocking huff. "I wouldn't have had to fake much." After a particularly long night of shelling, he said he had caught himself stuttering. But Queens Square Hospital in mind, he had simply pressed his lips shut. And when he trembled and tea slopped over the rim of the cup clenched in his hands, he emptied it into the slick beneath the duckboards.

"Tom," I said, stooping so that I might meet his down-turned gaze. "Thinking about how to save yourself isn't a crime. Plenty of the fellows were doing more than just daydreaming about it. Why else would the rules about self-inflicted wounds even exist? Why else would anyone even know about sandbags and powder marks?"

"Sadie used to say I had the eyes of a hawk," he said. "I could pick out a mole in a thicket or spy a grouse too far off for anyone else to see."

"You've always noticed what others don't."

He lifted a shoulder, dismissively. "Even when I was running across no-man's-land, I could pick out the nose of a rifle in the sandbags or figure out the range of a machine gun in a pillbox. Not at Amiens though. By the time I got to Amiens, I couldn't make sense of anything."

In my mind's eye, Tom runs through smoke, kicked-up dust, barbed wire, a deafening cacophony of exploding shells. It was the sort of image I had pushed away during the years he was gone. "No one should have to endure what you did, Tom."

"Let me tell you something," he said, folding his arms over his ribs. "At Amiens I couldn't make out where the bullets were coming from. At first I thought I only had to stay quiet, to pay attention, that, like every other time, what to do would come to me. I waited until I couldn't wait anymore. Then I climbed out of the trench and hightailed it toward the enemy line. They called the fellows who didn't shirkers and degenerates, and shot by firing squad. One morning we were made to roll out and fall in at dawn. They sat a kid called Bobby Marshall on a crate in front of us. He was handcuffed to a post behind his back. They pinned a round piece of white paper over his heart. We were made to watch. That's why I ran."

"It's all over now." My fingers grazed the sleeve of his coat.

"The fellow in front of me took a bullet in the head."

"You came back."

He touched Fergus's headstone. Then he took my hand and led me home and said nothing more.

I stand at the window long after Jesse and Tom have disappeared, watching whirlwinds of snow flit from hemlock to oak, then dither a moment before moving on. What can I do to help him regain his old self? When Isabel died, like Tom, I had lost any sense of sure-footedness in the world. Yet my fear was certainly only a sliver of what he had known at the front. And by the time I had completely given up on God, Tom was there beside me—my solace, my antidote to an out-of-kilter world.

When I went to him at the Windsor Hotel, he had said he could feel Fergus with him, especially on the river. It was the place where our realities differed. Even in death, Fergus had remained close to him, while for me Isabel was gone, a precious memory, a sister who was no longer able to love me as she once had.

It hits me now that while my own feelings about the river are at least somewhat ambivalent, it is of the utmost importance to him. He once went to the river. He watched. He listened. It fed his sense of awe and wonder and mystery, some notion of order in the world. And now he has spent too much time away from the place he loved most, too much time away from all that kept Fergus close. I know it with a certainty that is like a cold slap. I must take him by the hand, or the scruff of the neck if it comes to that, and help him find what is lost.

Niagara Falls Review, September 21, 1888

FERGUS COLE PULLS DAREDEVIL FROM THE WHIRLPOOL

More than a thousand spectators turned out to witness twenty-year-old Youngstown native Walter Campbell navigate the whirlpool rapids in a small rowboat on Saturday afternoon. Luckily for him, Fergus Cole was in their midst.

Mr. Campbell set out from the *Maid of the Mist* landing wearing red trunks and a suit constructed of sixteen pieces of one-inch-thick cork. At the outset he rode the heavy swells, standing upright in the boat like a Venetian gondolier, using his single oar as a rudder. On meeting the first breakers of the rapids, he lost his oar and dropped to his knees, holding fast to the sides of the boat as it pitched wildly in the water. Just opposite Buttrey's elevator, a vicious wave lifted him high on its crest, capsized his boat, and smashed it to pieces. He was swept into the whirlpool where five years earlier Captain Matthew Webb met his untimely death.

On the shore Mr. Cole was ready with a coil of rope lashed to a pine log. He hurled the makeshift device out over the whirlpool, some estimating the magnificent throw at more than fifty feet. It met the water short of Mr. Campbell, but as Mr. Cole had surely planned, the current whisked it within easy reach. Once landed, Mr. Campbell lay flat on his stomach a minute or two before getting to his feet and swallowing a mouthful of the rye whiskey offered him.

Asked to comment, Mr. Cole had this to say: "Another couple of seconds and he would've been flung to the spot where the water leaving the whirlpool is sucked under the incoming flow. I've watched logs hit that spot. I've seen them disappear."

Mr. Campbell has been offered a thousand dollars for a four-week appearance at the old Wonderland in Buffalo, New York.

20

CITY OF TORONTO ARCHIVES, FONDS 1868, ITEM 176

Two days later, ready to act on my plan, Jesse and I lean over the limestone wall and peer into the gorge just downriver from the brink of the falls. The landscape below is otherworldly—a massive clot of white-blue ice extending from shore to shore, frozen mounds of accumulated spray nearly sixty feet in height, sections of cliff face transformed by stalactites of ice as thick as the trunk of any tree. Yet there are children sledding on the hillocks, adults milling about, a path crossing the ice from shore to shore, also shanties with hand-painted signs advertising beef tea and sandwiches, coffee and cake.

He asks where the river is, and I tell him it is still there, just underneath all the ice. "It's why this is called the ice bridge."

"Let's go see."

"Only if Daddy goes with us," I say. "Not without Daddy."

"Please." He tugs the sleeve of my coat.

"Guess what," I say.

"What?"

"On Sunday mornings lots of boys get up early and hurry across the ice. They all want to be the first to get to the other side."

"Me too," he says, his gaze back on the ice bridge.

"Maybe," I say. "Guess what else."

"What?"

"When Daddy was little, he would get up really early with Great-grandpa Fergus and be the first across."

"I go with Daddy."

Jesse talks nonstop about the ice bridge for three days, about being the first across. Then at breakfast Thursday morning Tom finally says, "We'll see," rather than "When you're older" or "Maybe next year," and Jesse throws his arms around Tom's neck as though he has already agreed. And it seems that Jesse knows better than I, because the next thing out of Tom's mouth is "We'll go on Sunday."

Eventually Jesse untangles himself and Tom returns to stoking the fire.

"Where does all that ice come from, anyway?" I ask, wanting Tom to go on, as he once would have, as though there is nothing quite so fascinating in all the world as the river.

"Lake Erie," he says.

"We didn't get much of a bridge last year."

"If it stays below freezing more than six weeks, the ice is too thick and stays put until spring."

"What's best, thickness-wise?"

"Ten inches or so," he says and goes back to nudging the logs.

"Then what?" I get up from the table, where I have been finishing buttonholes, and stand facing him with my back to the stove.

"Why so interested?"

"Because I got used to you telling me about the river and now I miss it."

He smiles at me then, his lopsided smile. "All right," he says. "If it warms up and the wind is strong, the ice'll get ripped off the shore and pushed out into the lake. In the upper river, blocks of it are mashed into a soup of ice and slush. That's what goes over the brink and gets slammed into the ice that the eddies have collected on either side of the gorge. Some of it sticks, and pretty soon you've got a solid bridge of ice linking Canada and the U.S."

While he speaks, the stove's heat radiates through to my bones. I tell myself I am putting too much weight on a single outing. I warn myself to stop. But it does not matter a bit. I will dust and sew and scrub the knees of trousers, and hum while I work, ticking off the hours until Sunday.

S unday morning is bitterly cold. I can hear it in the rattling windows and feel it in the kitchen not yet warmed by the stove. Jesse, Tom, and I eat oatmeal, because it will stick to our ribs, and sip hot cocoa because it is a special day.

At the falls the trees and lampposts and limestone wall are shrouded in a layer of frozen mist. Branches bend under the weight. Brittle ice snaps and clatters to the ground. In biting cold and gusting wind, mist has turned to sleet. It is not at all the scene I had imagined for Tom's return to the river. Still, he stops in his tracks. He listens. He swallows. His gaze sweeps the gorge, lingers on the spot several hundred feet downriver where the Niagara emerges from beneath the ice bridge.

We make our way down the steep road leading to the wooden landing used for the *Maid of the Mist* steamboats in the summertime. Jesse is between Tom and me, tugging our arms, leading the charge.

"I hear the new conduit's still running full steam," Tom says, looking toward the powerhouse at the foot of the falls. It continues to be fed by the conduit Beck had once called temporary.

"It's true," I say. "Father says no one will be telling the powerhouses to cut off the factories that have switched from munitions to silverware and ladies' shoes. There's pent-up demand."

He shakes his head at the sham of it, and I take it as a good sign, Tom irked on the river's behalf.

The path across the ice bridge is empty but well-trodden and easy for us to follow as it snakes its way around hillocks and between fissures. Jesse plods forward, doggedly, and Tom matches his pace. I walk a step or two behind, close enough to listen, far away enough to make it seem they are out on their own, father and son. Tom points to the Bridal Veil Falls wedged between the Horseshoe and American falls. "There's a cave behind the water," he says to Jesse. "I'll show you in the spring." Jesse smiles up at Tom.

Midway across the ice, I glance back, toward the Canadian shore. There are no challengers, only a lone couple taking in the view from the *Maid of the Mist* landing, not yet out on the ice, and a group of boys with a sled making their way down the bank.

As Jesse climbs up onto the boat landing on the American side, Tom and I clap and yell, "Hooray." I slip my hand into Tom's pocket and lace my gloved fingers with his. I put my lips almost against his ear. "Someday he'll bring his own son."

We pick our way back, not on the path but by way of a route chosen by Jesse while Tom knelt beside him, pointing out the fissures too wide to be traversed. They scale the handful of hillocks we come to and slide down the opposite sides on their seats. I do not join in; my warmest coat is also my best. And then there is the child I am carrying to think of as well. Never mind though. I am happy just to watch.

Eventually Tom whisks Jesse back to the main path and begins to hurry him along. The sleet, driven nearly horizontal by the wind now, feels like pins and needles on my skin, and I say, "I could use a cup of beef tea." But the morning crowd, just beginning to wend its way over the ice, is smaller than usual, and it seems the shanty keepers have had the good sense to stay put in their cozy beds. When we finally come to a shanty with a thin line of blue smoke seeping from the stovepipe stuck through its roof, I hesitate. But Tom only says, "This wind," and gathers Jesse into his arms and picks up the pace.

I want to dig my heels in. Yes, money is tight, but not so tight that we cannot afford a celebratory cup of tea on a freezing day. Still, I want the day to be exactly right, and to insist on tea when Tom is already striding away, his hand firmly tugging my arm, can only lead to one of us feeling put out.

By the time we reach the Canadian shore, I am out of breath from the pace but relieved to be somewhat sheltered from the wind. Tom sets Jesse on the landing and looks over his shoulder to the ice. And then I hear what Tom already has: a faint rumble growing louder. Then there is a loud bang, almost like the shot of a gun. "Stay put," he says, with such forcefulness that I reach for Jesse and pull him against my coat. "Get off the ice," he yells, leaping over a newly formed fissure between the landing and the ice bridge.

I watch as I might a play, captivated, but at the same time keenly aware that the drama before me is not the product of actors and sets. The ice bridge has broken free from the moorings anchoring it to shore and become a slow-moving mass. "Let go," Jesse says. I loosen my grip, but as he darts toward the ice, I yank him back by the collar of his coat.

The fissure between the landing and the bridge has grown to a foot-wide gap of water and slush. Tom is near the center of the mass gesturing toward the Canadian shore, his voice lost in the wind. My gaze flits to the wide, dark channel of water formed at the opposite bank, and I see what he already knows.

As men, women, and children flee, he stoops to help a woman kneeling on the ice, pounding her fists. He unstraps her ice creepers, which had become twisted sideways on her boots, hauls her up by the arm, and all but drags her ungainly body toward the shore. Alarms sound on each side of the river, and onlookers begin to gather at the rim of the gorge. Men arrive with coils of rope and spread out along the banks. The landing becomes crowded with those who have escaped the ice, also with gawkers from above. I am ruthless in keeping the position Jesse and I hold.

By the time Tom and the woman reach the gap between the floating ice and the landing, it is six feet in width. I know that she will not make the leap, also that he will not leave her on the ice. I imagine myself on the mass, giving the woman a mighty shove. Then in one fell swoop he gathers her in his arms and hurtles the gap for the both of them.

Fear gives way to pride, and I remember the trolley ride in the gorge, the way we all deferred to him. But then, after glancing over his shoulder toward Jesse and me, he again jumps the gap and is back on the floating ice.

Leaping fissures and rounding hillocks, he races toward a young couple and two teenage boys, the lone group still out on the ice. As he makes his way toward them, a massive chunk of ice breaks off the tail end and the ice floe picks up speed.

"It's got to be moving at least five miles an hour," says a voice from behind.

"More like ten."

They agree on one point: The floe is heading toward the Whirlpool Rapids, where it will be smashed to smithereens.

Once Tom reaches the group, he points toward the Canadian shore, but the group heads off in the opposite direction with the man leading the way. Tom follows a few steps and then grabs the man by the shoulder. The man pushes his hand away, shakes his head no. As Tom takes a single step backward, in our direction, one of the boys, the shorter one, does the same. The taller boy looks from Tom to the man, trying to decide. When the woman takes the man's hand, the boy sides with the couple and the three rush off. From the landing, it is obvious they have made a poor choice. The channel on the American side is twenty feet wide. Yet I hardly care. Tom is heading for the Canadian shore.

He races a step or two ahead of the shorter boy, the one who chose to go with him, and slows to look over his shoulder only when the ice splits in two. The new fissure runs parallel to the shores and puts to an end any hope of the threesome undoing their mistake. Tom crosses the ice on a diagonal, heading toward the footing of the Upper Steel Arch Bridge, where the gap is at its narrowest, nine or ten feet.

New fissures are forming at an alarming rate. Smaller cakes of ice break away and pick up speed in the current. The threesome's cake is no more than ten paces across, as it passes under the bridge and disappears from view.

Tom turns often now, his pace slower as he urges the boy to jump from one cake to the next. The bridge looms near, and my gaze is fixed on Tom, willing him not to miss his chance. His leap is graceful and ample, and I can see from the beginning that he will safely reach the bank. But even as the crowd cheers his success, the boy stops in his tracks, on the far side of the channel.

In my arms, Jesse has not buried his face against my shoulder as might be expected. Rather he watches, cheering on Tom with the crowd, yelling "Jump" to the boy as though he would attempt the feat himself.

"Who's that fellow, anyway?" Again, it is the voice from behind.

"Don't know."

"I used to see him on the river. I think he fished the floaters out a while back."

If the boy leaps, Tom might follow him into the channel. If he does not, Tom might attempt a return to the ice. I want Tom to look our way and be reminded of all he has to lose. But no, his gaze is locked on the boy.

Tom's arms fly up in front, palms facing the boy. Stay put.

A moment later he is snatching a coiled rope from one of the men on the bank and then running along the shoreline, scrambling over the rocky fragments of the talus slope, avoiding boulders too large to leap, keeping pace with the ice cake floating the boy down the river. When the cake is swung from the main current toward shore by an eddy, I know Tom was as sure of the position of the eddy as I am of the position of the maple tree in Mrs. Andrews's backyard. He tosses the rope, which the boy catches and ties around his waist. He leaps into the river, and Tom pulls him to shore and up onto the bank. He strips the boy of his coat and wraps him in his own.

The cheers of the crowd lining the rim, crammed onto the landing, dotting the riverbanks reverberate in the gorge. I stand, mute, caught somewhere between awe and an as yet unidentified emotion, which rises like bile in my throat. How could Tom be so reckless? How could he have forgotten Jesse and me, waiting on pins and needles for three years? How could he not think of us, watching, dreading that his cake of ice might overturn?

"Daddy," Jesse says, wriggling from my arms to the landing.

"Stop."

He squeezes between the throng of legs, calling out, "Daddy, Daddy, Daddy," as he goes. I grab the sleeve of his coat and stay on his heels as the crowd parts. Almost everyone is headed in the opposite direction, likely hoping to be out of the gorge in time to catch a glimpse of the threesome farther downriver, floating their way to certain death.

Jesse keeps up his "Daddy, Daddy" chant as we pick our way along the riverbank, and soon men are tipping their caps. "He's your husband? Quite a daredevil you got yourself." Women are smiling. "Bet you're awfully proud." A man with a notepad and a pencil says, "Mind if I ask a few questions?" Though I have not yet answered, he falls in line with Jesse and me. "His name, for instance?"

The man keeps pace with us with us, his pencil poised. "Tom Cole," I say.

"Local fellow?"

"Yes."

"Born and raised here?"

"Yes."

"Canadian side?"

"Yes."

He taps his temple with the end of this pencil. "Any relation to Fergus Cole?"

"Grandson."

"Beauty," he says, shaking his head. "Occupation?"

"He only just got back from overseas."

He lets out a soft whistle. "A real hero, then."

When we meet Tom, he scoops up Jesse and hugs the both of us at the same time, and I cling to him and he to me, until it is impossible to think he had forgotten us on the riverbank and my anger seems irrational. Eventually a man holds out Tom's returned coat, and Tom lets go of me and sets Jesse on the ground.

The man with the notepad and pencil introduces himself as Cecil Randal from the *Evening Review* and asks Tom for his version of the events. In the story he tells, there is no mention that the woman was in his arms when he leapt the gap, or of the way the boy slowed him down. As for the man who led the others astray, Tom just says, "It was hard to tell what was right out there on the ice." I knew from the start Tom would not boast, but it strikes me now that he is entirely oblivious to the fact he has earned the right. I find myself leaning closer, my hand seeking his.

"Any guess as to why the bridge broke up?" Mr. Randal asks. "It's always been safe until the spring thaw."

"It's the wind," Tom says. "It's blowing hard from the west, pushing the water to the end of the lake where the river is."

"Like tea pooling at the side of a cup when you blow?"

"Pretty much," Tom says, putting an arm around me.

"Too much water in the river, then?"

"There wasn't space enough for all of it under the bridge. The water level went up and snapped the bridge from the banks." Tom's free hand moves to Jesse's shoulder.

"We've had wind like this before?"

"The ice keeping the bridge in place couldn't have been as solid as it usually is. Maybe it's the river bobbing up or down every time one of the power companies closes or opens an intake gate."

"You're saying, with the power companies, the bridge isn't safe anymore?" I bite my lip. It is a question that could end up with Tom quoted in the newspaper, and then trouble for the power companies.

"It's just a guess," Tom says. "I haven't been out on the ice much for a while."

Mr. Randal scribbles, indecipherably, then looks up from his notepad. "Any chance the others made it to shore?"

Tom looks away.

Mr. Randal closes his notepad. "Off the record, what are the odds?"

"I'd like to get my family home. We're cold and tired and wet."

River Road is swarming with spectators. Some point at Tom. Some stare, not quite sure. Some call out: "You're the one who was on the ice." "Never seen anybody jump like that." "Hope that kid appreciates what you done for him." "Heard he promised you a thousand bucks."

There are more somberly spoken words, too. Workmen dropped ropes to the threesome from the Lower Steel Arch Bridge. The boy managed to grab hold of one but was dangling forty feet above the river when his strength gave out. The man caught a makeshift line made from three coils of insulated telephone wire, but it came apart as he was tying it around his wife's waist. They were on their knees, praying in each other's arms, some said, when their bit of ice overturned.

Just past the Upper Steel Arch Bridge we leave River Road, preferring to walk home on less traveled streets. When Jesse is out of earshot up ahead, I ask the question I have been unable to shake: "What if you didn't clear the channel?"

"If I wasn't going to make it, I wouldn't have jumped."

"And then what?"

"I'd have waited for the eddy, the one that pushed the boy toward the shore."

"You were sure?" My pace slows, and Tom follows suit.

"I was," he says.

"But the river's unpredictable. You've said so yourself."

"Not today. I knew something was up, even when the three of us were still out on the bridge."

This much I can swallow. I was out of breath from keeping up by the time we reached the shore. He felt a tremor, heard a rumbling, noticed the sleet being driven horizontal in the wind. It is not a stretch to think he knew the ice bridge would come unhinged. "The wind?" I say.

"There was more to it than that."

A few steps farther, I say, "Go on."

"I could see what had to be done. That's all."

"For example . . ." I halt a moment. "It's like pulling teeth with you."

He takes my upper arm, coaxes me along. "I knew how much time I had. I could feel it when the ice would split and knew where to be standing when it did. I knew where the eddies were. I saw the men with the rope."

Maybe he did know where the eddies were. Quite possibly the positions of the men with the ropes did register in his mind. Still, predicting when a cake of ice would split and knowing where to be standing when it did? It is difficult, even impossible, to accept. I had schemed to get him to the river. I had schemed with his best interests at heart. I had thought that with finding the river a sort of faith would come to Tom, a lessening of fear, but I am unprepared for this notion of invincibility.

When he puts his arm around my waist and pulls me close, I know he has read my thoughts. "I can't explain it," he says.

As we walk the falling snow softens from twinkling shards to downy flakes the size of a dime. Eventually we catch up with Jesse, who has stopped to tilt his face upward, toward the falling snow. Tom sweeps him up and sets him on his shoulders. But Jesse wants down. He wants to pretend we are on the ice. He leaps cracks and fissures, rescues Tom from a snowbank that is a bit of ice-choked river as far as he is concerned. Only then does he want Tom's shoulders, the glory due a hero, the dizzying heights of being held aloft.

Once Tom is off galloping with Jesse bouncing on his shoulders and hooting with delight, happiness wells inside of me like the spreading warmth of a hot drink. Despite the trials of the day, my scheme seems to have been a success. I catch up with Tom and elbow him in the ribs, hard. With Jesse still balanced on his shoulders, Tom knocks me into the piled snow at the side of the road. I stay put a moment, until he extends a hand. Then I throw a handful of snow in his face and say, "I wanted to push that woman with the ice creepers into the gap."

He laughs, and I laugh with him, and then he pulls me up and we walk home.

I wake in the nighttime and tell myself that it was only a dream, that no harm will come to Jesse. His bravado on the way home from the river was only a game. Eyes wide open, I look to the bureau and see the familiar outline of my comb, brush, and mirror. So how is it that the image from my dream, the one I want to leave behind, stays firmly put?

On a pristinely white sheet in a pool of dark blood, newborn Jesse lies between my naked legs. My thighs are smeared with afterbirth, and my pubic hair is wet. My arms have lost function, and I cannot lift the section of amnion covering his face. With each breath, he sucks the caul into his mouth, forming a taut, membranous basin over his parted lips. With each breath, the basin becomes more shallow and his skin more gray.

His eyes are open. Pleading.

21

Ice bridge

The following day the *Evening Review* ran a detailed account of the tragedy and the rescue, also a shorter article eulogizing the dead and an editorial saying the ice bridge should be made off limits, all on the front page. There was nothing about intake gates and weakened moorings, nothing implying that the power companies were at fault, and it was a relief. Mrs. Coulson was still after me to send Tom along to Mr. Coulson, and to have lost the chance of his assistance before I had even told Tom would have been a bitter pill. When I flipped to page two, I saw a fourth piece, by Cecil Randal:

NIAGARA'S OWN RIVERMAN

Tom Cole knows the Niagara River and Gorge like most folks know the backs of their hands. He can point out the exact locations of eddies and undercurrents and standing waves, but then he is the grandson of the late Fergus Cole, and his extraordinary knowledge of the river hardly comes as a surprise.

Fergus Cole arrived in Niagara Falls on March 30, 1848, the day the falls stood still. He made the first of his rescues that same day, and then went on to save the four workmen left dangling from Ellet's bridge, Walter Campbell when his boat splintered to bits in the whirlpool, and at least a dozen others—naïve tourists, careless fishermen, heedless boys. He predicted the fall of Table Rock, the demise of Captain Matthew Webb, and a handful of rockslides in the Niagara Gorge.

And now we have his grandson as our riverman. As a boy he was taught how to rescue dogs and waterfowl, how to clear a body from the river, how to pin down the exact location where one would turn up. He inherited his grandfather's ability to say where the fish were biting on any given day, also his knack for reading the river with an eerie accuracy. They say Tom Cole wakes in the morning knowing whether he will find a body in the river that day. They say he can forecast the weather just by listening to the roar of the falls and that he predicted a rockslide that nearly struck a trolley in the gorge. Yesterday he knew before anyone the ice bridge was breaking up, and then cleared the ice and masterfully rescued a boy when it seemed to everyone else the two of them were doomed.

Like his grandfather before him Tom Cole has a gift, and the citizens of Niagara Falls should heed what he says.

When he finished the article, Tom said, "A bit of an overstatement."

"I don't think so." I was bursting with pride. Oh, I would have preferred that the reference to the bodies be left out. Though I had seen firsthand the care he took with Isabel and knew better than anyone the nobility in the work, I was well aware of the lifted eyebrows the mention of the task usually aroused.

"I can't say where the fish are biting."

"Where on earth did Mr. Randal dig it all up?" I asked.

"I guess I've said quite a bit over the years at the Windsor. A couple of fellows there were always pestering me about stuff they'd heard."

Ever since "Niagara's Own Riverman," people approach Tom on the street, wanting to know whether it will rain a week from Sunday. They are planning a family picnic and thought it best to run it by him first. Men with fishing tackle stop if he is in the yard and want an opinion on their latest lure. A week ago I answered the telephone to find a frantic woman on the other end of the line. "He slipped," she said, between sobs. "My baby slipped out of my arms."

"I'll get Tom." Since the ice bridge he has recovered three bodies. I know because each time he has come home, shoulders slumped, and handed me the stipend from Morse and Son.

"He was crying and crying," the woman said. "He wouldn't stop."

Tom had told me of another infant, another mother too tired, too overwhelmed, too desperate to resist the lure of the falls. I covered the mouthpiece and called for Tom.

"I only meant to loosen the blanket," the woman said, her final words before the line went dead.

"A baby," I said to Tom. "She said he slipped out of her arms."

"I'll go." He reached for the packsack he kept by the back door.

Four months since the ice bridge, four months since Tom's nighttime terrors began to abate, a full three weeks since he last called out in his sleep, and still, I wake, eyes fluttering open, consciousness creeping in, panic rising as I take stock. I turn quickly, but he is there, on his side, his face toward me, unlined, his brow smooth like a child's. I search out the rise and fall of his chest, a practice once reserved for Jesse. Draped linen becomes taut and then slack as breath is exhaled. My anxiety is misplaced, even ludicrous. He is merely sleeping peacefully, as should any man who spent the day before splitting wood and tilling the earth for a vegetable patch. I am still not used to it, to his easy sleep.

His eyes open and I am caught watching and he smiles. He says, "I was dreaming about you," and pulls me to him, and I feel the hardness between his legs. His hands are innocent just now, one on the small of my back, atop my nightdress—flannel—and the other, propping his head. Still, desire comes. His hand moves from my back to my front, slides upward, over my ribs.

Which part of our returned intimacy have I most missed? Is it early on, when pleasure and anticipation are inseparable, when I ache for more but have no wish to alter in the slightest the stroking, the murmured endearments, the hands and mouth on my skin? Or is it later, when our bodies are entwined, moving together, when anticipation fades and the pleasure of the moment reigns? Or afterward, when we share a pillow, when there is a feeling of fullness, of completeness, that I have become whole?

At breakfast Tom is in high spirits, chuckling to himself because Jesse, still in his pajamas, is waiting at the back door, fishing rod in hand. It has become their routine, setting off for the river each morning, coming back in time for supper. Every few days I will catch him in the doorway, golden in the late afternoon sun, eyes glinting, filled with wonder and awe. "Jesse spent half the morning tossing twigs and stones into a pool, figuring out what floats," he will say, or "The standing wave off Thompson's Point was as wild as I've ever seen it" or, most notably of all, "I felt Fergus out there with us today."

Other days he comes in, and there is sorrow in his voice and I know he is again mourning the river, the river we have not yet lost.

Lake Erie sits a full three hundred feet above Lake Ontario, a drop nearly twice that of the falls, and the clever engineers of Beck's Hydro-Electric Power Commission have figured out how to put an end to the power and money still running to waste. More water will be diverted and much farther back from the brink, as far upriver as Chippawa. And it will be put back only once the river flattens out at Queenston Heights, the farthest reach of the gorge, twelve miles away. In between they are digging a canal and making their own waterfall, hidden inside the penstocks delivering the plunging river to the turbines of the powerhouse. The newspapers say the Queenston-Chippawa power project dwarfs any hydroelectric scheme yet undertaken in the world. They say it rivals the Panama Canal. They say eight thousand men toil day and night, blasting, shoveling, hauling away solid rock.

I have heard Tom's distress and said, "But only the other day you were saying how spectacular the standing wave off Thompson's Point was."

"Not for long. The river is changing. Remember the American channel all jammed up with ice."

Goat Island divides the Niagara River into two channels at the brink of the falls, and during spring thaw the American channel became so congested that in places the cliff face of the American Falls was bone dry. Tom said that the channel was shallower than the Canadian one, that with all the canals and powerhouses the river level had dropped, that there just was not enough water to carry the ice over the brink.

"Open any newspaper," he said. "You've seen the ads."

For weeks he has made a habit of pointing out the Hydro-Electric Power Commission advertisements telling us we ought to be using electric griddles and kettles and irons, and cranking up the electric heaters when a sweater would do. And then he stopped in at the Windsor Hotel to say hello the other day and struck up a conversation with a small group of men meeting there, among them a tour operator, a pair of lawyers, several merchants, and an alderman.

Afterward he stood, wild-eyed, nearly filling the doorway of the sewing room. "All of them are against the Queenston-Chippawa power project, or at least that there's no one keeping an eye on Beck," he said. "They say the Niagara Falls Park Commission's a joke, and they're right, considering it was set up to preserve the area around the falls."

"The commission's done wonders with Queen Victoria Park," I said. And they had. There were drinking fountains and restrooms and livery stables and picnic grounds with a tennis lawn, a ball field, and a bowling green. There was a decent road and no one stopping you to pay a toll.

"You know where they get their money?" He folded his arms, rocked back on his heels. "By selling the rights to siphon off water to the power companies."

I set down the collar I was understitching. "Before the commission, we had a bunch of hucksters charging the tourists a fee just to look at the falls, and burning down each other's property every chance they got."

"It gets worse," he said. "The chairman of the commission is Philip Ellis, and he used to head up the Toronto Hydro-Electric Power Commission. Some watchdog. He's a crony of Beck, for God's sake."

He unrolled a magazine he had kept clenched in his fist since coming home. "It's called *The Hydro Lamp,* and it's Beck's," he said, thwacking it against the frame of the door. "It's him behind the sales effort. He's got the Hydro Circus and Hydro stores and floats in parades, advertisements everywhere you look, and now he's got a magazine all about upping the demand for electricity."

"No need to raise your voice," I said, irked that I might never own an electric iron.

"As long as he keeps the blackouts coming, everyone will keep clapping him on the back for getting the Queenston-Chippawa project under way."

Mostly I admire Tom's allegiance to the river. Still, when I am tallying our unpaid bills and working out how many more gowns I need to take on in order to put aside even a dollar or two for a house of our own, or when Mother calls, always getting around to asking whether I have spoken to Tom about employment with the Hydro, there is a part of me that wishes he was just as pleased with the Queenston-Chippawa power project as nearly everyone else. The canal is only partially dug. The penstocks do not exist. Twice already I have dipped into the money my parents gave us as a wedding gift. And soon there will be another mouth to feed, another body to clothe, another round of bills from Dr. Galveston to pay.

And now, with breakfast finished and Tom laughing and saying to Jesse, "Maybe I'll put my pajamas back on. Maybe we can trick the fish into thinking we're not fishermen," it seems as good a time as any to pass along what I had promised Mrs. Coulson I would.

"There'll be no fishing in your pajamas," I say to Jesse, and then, when he is halfway up the stairs, I turn to Tom, still sitting at the table. "You know I've been sewing for Mrs. Coulson."

He nods.

"I've told you Mr. Coulson used to work for my father, that Father took him under his wing."

"Yes."

"It's why she comes to me," I say. I would never say to Tom that I sometimes wonder if she is trying to guard me from the ruin she feels is inevitable without her guiding hand.

He pushes his chair back from the table. "She comes to you because you're good."

"It's not why she came in the first place. She didn't even think I could sew; her first order was for a skirt I could have made when I was ten."

"I know all this, Bess. I know the Coulsons are indebted to your father, to your family."

"He's with the Hydro, top brass on the Queenston-Chippawa project." It is something more he would already know, as would anyone who picked up the *Evening Review* every now and then.

"He's offering me a job?" Tom says. "Is that what this is about?" He plunks his mug down on the table.

"I know it isn't ideal, but there's not much out there and there's the baby on the way." There is pleading in my voice, a whiny, breathless want, and so I pause, clear my throat. "We did talk about a place of our own, way back when we were first engaged."

"We talked about trapping and fishing and chickens in the yard, too." He folds his arms, tips his chair onto its hind legs.

"It's our old dream," I say, remembering—a small house with a view of the river and a garden to keep us in vegetables, a couple of chickens to keep us in eggs, a cow to keep us in milk. It is more than enough.

His face softens, and he tilts his chair back to upright.

"You'd be a foreman. You wouldn't start on the bottom rung."

"A foreman?" Bewilderment comes to his face.

"That's what Mrs. Coulson said. She's been after me to send you along to Mr. Coulson for ages, and then ever since the ice bridge, she's been badgering me nonstop."

"It doesn't make sense."

I shrug, smile.

His brow knits. His lips become a thin line. "I'll think about it," he finally says.

22

I walk beneath the maples of Fairview Cemetery, pausing at Sadie's and Fergus's headstones, laying a handful of daisies at the base of each, and then continue on. I am here for Isabel today, the fourth anniversary of her death.

From a ways off I see a bouquet propped against her headstone, and I remember Mother saying she and Father had stopped by the Sunday before. The day had been hot, and she had complained about the grass. "As dry and as bleached as straw," she said. "Thank goodness for the maples. Thank goodness Isabel has a bit of shade."

I pick up the bouquet—irises, pale yellow with dark yellow throats—and I am perplexed. The petals are fresh, despite the heat, despite the drought and the three days that have passed since Mother and Father were in town. Also, they are the dwarf variety, and I am sure I remember Mother saying the shortest of the irises come first, with the daffodils, the next with the tulips, and the tallest no later than July. But it is August, and the irises are less than a foot in length. Someone had bothered with a florist, and it was not Mother, even if she could somehow have managed to coax a few coins from Father. No. There is no Mason jar of water on the yellow grass, nothing to have kept the blooms from collapsing in the heat for three days.

What is more perplexing still is that irises were Isabel's favorite, and of the lot she preferred the dainty blooms and slender leaves of the dwarfs. She preferred pale yellow. I remember that.

Mother had provided the flowers for the May Day celebrations at the academy every year, and every year Isabel and I were chosen to help out. After all, it was our mother's garden that had been stripped bare, Glenview's flowers that we would twist into crowns, bind into bouquets, tie to the maypole around which we would later dance.

I remember Isabel at the far end of a long table in the academy dining hall, her fingers knotting a bit of twine around a simple bouquet. She works, spreading the stalks, fanning the pale yellow blooms. She holds up the bouquet to inspect it and sees me approach. "My very favorite," she says. "Like winter butter, except the throats. They're more like lemon drops."

I raise the bouquet, the one left behind on her grave, to my chin. "Who?" I say, a bloom brushing my bottom lip. Who would know the anniversary? Who would know she liked the pale yellow dwarfs? Mary Egan? Grace Swan? Maeve O'Neill? Vivian Spence? Each had come to view Isabel laid out in the drawing room. Each had said she would call again, and Mary Egan had, but only a few times. Mrs. Coulson? She had been hit hard by Isabel's death; still, I could hardly imagine her wandering in a cemetery, and irises would be an improbable guess. Kit Atwell? A warming thought, but only wishful thinking on my part.

I set the bouquet back against the headstone and gather my skirt, arranging myself on the yellow grass. At Fairview, more often than not, my thoughts linger on Isabel and I am able to lose myself in some memory: the time she balanced a penny atop every hymnal in the academy chapel, so that when we picked up the books to sing, the pennies clattered to the ground; the time she sent an anonymous valentine to Father O'Laughlin; the time she challenged Boyce to a game of one-on-one and whipped him eleven baskets to six. My most troubled moments come when I realize I have not thought of her for several days or more. It is then it seems that her life was inconsequential, that mine may be as well and everyone else's, too. We all matter so very little, not at all after a generation or two. And it is the same for all mankind; not even the greatest of men amount to anything that will survive the forward march of time. It is in these moments of despair I most miss the idea of God, the idea that life has meaning, the idea that we are something more than the products of the random variations and natural selection Charles Darwin put forth.

I wait, fingers quietly raking the grass, but today nothing comes. Mother has said that she often whispers a prayer, that she sometimes talks to Isabel as though she were still here. "About what?" I asked. "Whatever I need to sort out," she said.

"Isabel," I say, shredding the seeds from a stalk of grass with my fingernail. I want to tell her about Tom, that we are married, that I have found true love. I want to tell her about the Queenston-Chippawa power project, about the position Tom has not yet seen Mr. Coulson about. "Is it wrong to want my husband to work?" I want to ask. "Is it wrong, when there is a second child on the way?" "Is it wrong, when it is what eight thousand men do every day, when the project is steamrolling forward with or without Tom?"

Oh, how I want to put these questions to Isabel, to watch her mull them over, to hear her reply. What would I give for a single word? Any word. A sigh. A throat cleared.

But nothing has changed in four years. I live without Isabel. I weigh options and make decisions, and know Isabel cannot so much as hint what is best. Nor is there some other shepherd tending and guiding, nudging me onto the right path.

In the evening I telephone Mother and say, "I went to the cemetery today, and there was a bouquet on Isabel's grave."

"Maybe one of the girls from the academy?"

"It was irises, pale yellow dwarfs."

"Oh," Mother says and then moment later, "Could it have been Boyce?"

"Boyce?" I lean my forehead against the wall and hear Father, his voice muffled in the background, ask who is paying for the call.

"I wouldn't be surprised," Mother says, likely waving him away.

But if Boyce is remembering Isabel's favorites, and then finding dwarf irises in the summertime and making the trek to Niagara Falls, does it mean he loved her even as she was swept over the brink of the falls? Would he eventually have defied his father and made her his wife? Had she misjudged?

Surviving adversity was the furthest thing from my mind as I tramped the Loretto corridors from one predictable day to the next. Still, I can say with near certainty, if I had been asked to bet on one of us, it would have been Isabel. Even now it seems a sort of bullheadedness is chief among the traits necessary to prevail, a trait Isabel had in spades. I had marveled as she worked her magic, as Mother added my entire class to the wedding list though my own pleas had been turned down, and marveled again when Isabel brought about a letter-writing campaign, the net of which was the Duchess of Connaught and Princess Patricia standing in the academy cupola, taking in the view of the falls. Even Mother Febronie had acquiesced and hung the basketball hoop Isabel had not given up on despite two years of "It isn't seemly, Isabel, girls ruddy and hot, panting and out of breath."

"I should be getting Jesse into bed," I say to Mother before hanging up the telephone.

I remember Isabel and me in the central foyer at Loretto, looking at the painting of Saint Michael the Archangel hanging on the wall. Head cocked, she says, "It hints at womanly strength. That's why the sisters put it up."

In the portrait Saint Michael's sandaled foot firmly pins an enemy's head to the earth. His right arm is held high, brandishing a sword. His abdomen is muscled, his chest well defined, his thighs sculpted, his calves taut. "You're daft," I say.

"He's wearing a frock. It's proof enough for me."

His tunic is short and its bodice sheer, just a wash of blue, and I suppose it really could be described as an immodest dress. I consider his golden locks, his full lips, his rounded chin, his feathery wings. Beyond the muscled body, he is feminine, androgynous at least. "Maybe," I say.

"Women aren't so meek. The suffragettes know it. And the sisters, too."

I sit curled up beneath the telephone, elbows on my knees, palms cupping my chin. If only Isabel had tapped into the girl she had been and persevered, just for a bit. It is nothing new, me thinking that Isabel could have managed, that happiness was a hairbreadth away. After all, I have become a mother and a wage earner. I have survived, and she could have done the same. Yes, I have Tom, but she would have had me. And now, though it is devastating even to think it, there is the possibility she would have had Boyce.

23

Tom is in the kitchen washing up after breakfast when the telephone rings. I am in the sewing room, an ear cocked, wondering about the likelihood of Mr. Coulson calling so soon. It was only yesterday that Mrs. Coulson had been in for a fitting. As usual she inquired about Tom, and when I said, "No, he hasn't found anything, not yet," she said, "Bess, do you think he'd mind very much if Mr. Coulson gave him a call?"

I hear Tom say, "Hello," and "Yes, of course, I know who you are," and then after a long pause, "The newspaper lays it on pretty thick, but thanks anyway," and after a longer pause still, "Yes, it's a lot of money. I need a bit of time though. I want to talk it over with Bess."

Then he is on the stairs and, a moment later, in the doorway of the sewing room. I look up from the lapel I am turning right side out.

"It was Mr. Coulson," he says. "The Queenston-Chippawa power project still needs a foreman, and the job pays thirty-five dollars a week."

"Thirty-five dollars."

"It's a lot," he says. I hear uncertainty rather than delight.

"He's grateful to my father."

"There's more to it than that," he says.

And he is right. There are telephone calls when the river rises, stranding a fisherman on a rock, and more calls when migrating whistling swans, having settled on the upper river for rest, find themselves swept over the brink and then, moments later, maimed and exhausted below. When an empty rowboat turns up in the river, when a boy does not show up for a meal, when someone other than Tom spots a body, the telephone rings, and he and Jesse head out the door. Cecil Randal reports the rescued swans and fishermen in the *Evening Review,* and it makes sense that Mr. Coulson would see the articles and be just as impressed as everyone else. "Everyone loves a hero, Tom," I say.

He runs his fingers through his hair, momentarily clearing his forehead. "It could be that he thinks putting me on the payroll means less trouble for the power companies. You remember those men I met at the Windsor, the ones who are against Beck. I bumped into one of them the other day and we got to talking about the ice bridge and he was interested in the idea of the bridge being weakened by the intake gates and the river bobbing up and down all the time."

I swallow, working to keep the distress from my voice. "You said it was just a guess."

"It is," he says. "There isn't proof. I told him that. Still, word could have got around to Mr. Coulson. You said Mrs. Coulson's been badgering you nonstop. They'd both know folks around here take pretty much anything I say about the river as fact."

"Mr. Coulson was talking about hiring you way before the ice bridge broke up. Mrs. Coulson brought it up before you even got home," I say, becoming more and more certain Tom's imagination has run amok. "Maybe he is persistent, but I overheard the telephone call. He's a little awestruck, is all. Like everyone else."

Tom mutters something about thinking the offer over for a bit and then disappears down the hall. Before I have decided whether I should follow him, he is back in the doorway of the sewing room wearing his best waistcoat and a clean shirt. "You're going to see Mr. Coulson," I say, setting down my work, a lead-up to throwing my arms around his neck.

"I'm off to International Silver," he says, smoothing his waistcoat. "I thought I should see about my options."

In the nine months since his return, he has made the rounds more times than I can count—Cyanamid and Norton, Oneida and International Silver, American Can and Shredded Wheat—and always been told they were not hiring. I sit silent, hand on my hard mound of a belly. "You'll have a hard time matching thirty-five dollars a week," I finally say.

I am in the yard, hanging bed linens on the line, when Tom returns. The day is tranquil and warm, one of those unusually still autumn days when the temperature seems at odds with the brittle leaves drifting to the earth. The air, too, is strange, without the haze and humidity that almost always accompany such warmth.

"Can you believe this weather?" I say, though what I really want to know is where he stands on Mr. Coulson's offer.

"There's nothing," he says.

I nod and take a pillowcase from my basket.

He's halfway up the back stoop when I call out to him. "Tom." Mrs. Andrews never minds me skipping out for a few hours, not so long as my work gets done on time, and I need to say my piece before it is too late. "How about a picnic at the whirlpool? We won't have many more days like this."

Jesse and Tom are at the edge of the whirlpool, trousers cuffed to their knees. I lie stretched out on my side, comfortable despite my cumbersome belly and the stones carpeting the beach. Before spreading the blanket, Tom had put down a thick bed of leaves, as though I were the type to notice a pea under twenty mattresses and twenty feather beds.

I am glad we have come. Despite my belly, the descent was easy, with him holding my upper arm as though I were a china doll and pointing out each root and stone in my path. And he is in good spirits. My chance will come after lunch, once Jesse has fallen asleep.

From the edge of the whirlpool, Jesse calls out, "Mommy, watch," and drops a twig into an eddy. He drops another and another, and then Tom holds Jesse's hand still and asks him to guess what will happen to the next twig. They move to another eddy and repeat the process, then another and another, until Jesse can accurately point out the path a twig will take. It almost feels as though I have been transported back through time, as though I have been handed a chance to glimpse my husband as he was with Fergus, and I feel a rush of gratitude.

When I next glance toward the whirlpool, Tom is holding Jesse by the upper arms, lowering him knee deep into the water. Once his feet are settled, Jesse begins to plod against the current. Tom continues to hold his arms, and I know it is a lesson in gauging the power of the river. Still, I am alarmed. I press my lips closed to stop myself from calling out. Even so, as Jesse's feet are swept from beneath him and Tom lifts him from the water without missing a beat, I holler, "Tom!"

Father and son look in my direction. Jesse waves.

Eventually the three of us are settled on the blanket, and Jesse begins to rub his eyes, still chattering about the pike and muskie and walleye he will catch. I stroke his back until his eyelids droop and he curls up in the folds of my skirt.

"The two of you make a pretty scene," Tom says. His son like a cherub, his wife the picture of motherhood, one hand on her swollen belly and the other on her sleeping son's brow.

He sits, watching us, studying us, until I say, "I love you, Tom."

"I know. You love me even though you've worked yourself to the bone ever since you became my wife."

"Tom, I've worked myself to the bone ever since my father lost his fortune and his job."

"I want to provide for you and Jesse. The baby, too."

"You will," I say, smiling my confidence in him but all the while thinking his words are measured, surely a prelude to news I do not want to hear.

"The whirlpool's spectacular today."

"Yes."

"It won't always be," he says.

I think of Lord Kelvin, who came up with the absolute temperature scale and knew everything there was to know about magnetism and electricity, and his hope that the falls would one day exist only inside penstocks, hidden from view. "I do not hope our children's children will ever see Niagara's cataract," he had said. The sentiment had always struck me as brutally harsh. Yet just now I find myself swayed. "The Queenston-Chippawa project is happening whether or not you accept Mr. Coulson's offer," I say.

"I've told myself that a hundred times."

"And?"

"What'll I tell Jesse in twenty years when there isn't a whirlpool at all, not unless some big shot orders the intake gates shut every now and then so the tourists can get a look at the real thing?"

He picks up another pebble and tosses it into the whirlpool, and I do the same. I want him to consider that just possibly hydroelectricity is a good and wondrous thing. But more than that, I want him to put his family first, and I am through with waiting for the perfect moment, a moment that may never come. "There is lots you'll have to explain before you get to the whirlpool," I say. "For starters, you can tell Jesse why he's being raised in a house that isn't even our own. You can tell him why he can't invite friends over and why we say 'shush' a hundred times a day. You can tell him why his mother rarely has an afternoon just for him. Put us first, Tom. Put your family first."

Suddenly I feel a tightening in the underside of my belly, a radiating hardness. My hands move to the place.

"What?" he says.

"I'm not sure."

"Labor?"

"The baby isn't due for a month."

By the time we have woken Jesse and packed up the blanket, and gathered the fishing tackle and the several stones he wanted to keep, my belly has grown hard a second and third time.

Midway up the old incline railway tracks, the intensity of a contraction causes me to pause, my fingers curled into my palms. My lips part and then close as I consider the pointlessness of saying that I am afraid. Tom drops the fishing rods and blanket. He lifts Jesse from his shoulders and sets him on the ground. "Show me how fast you can run," he says. As Jesse sets off, Tom sweeps me up into his arms. He takes the railway ties several at a time, all the while calling out encouragement to Jesse.

I can see his face in profile, the slight curve at the bridge of his nose. His brow is furrowed, his lips pressed into a line. When my body tenses with another contraction and a small moan escapes, he says, "Relax, Bess. Just try to relax."

"I can't make it stop."

"I'll take the job," he says. "Everything will be okay."

Though we are still a good five minutes from River Road and then a further mile from Mrs. Andrews's house, I feel a fresh sort of calm. The child will be born, probably in our bed, and if I cannot hang on then elsewhere, maybe in the kitchen of some house along the way. The child will be fat and pink and nurse well from the start. We will find a house of our own, and I will sew curtains sheer enough to let the sun shine in. Jesse will scamper around, wild and fast, as noisy as he pleases. And Tom and I will make love early in the morning, before he sets off to work for the day.

24

The day after Francis was born, Tom called Mr. Coulson. Within fifteen minutes arrangements had been made for Tom to start at the Hydro-Electric Power Commission the next day. He had not mentioned the new baby, which would likely have meant a bit of grace. His sudden rush had not struck me as odd. It only seemed he had linked providing for his family, as he had said he would, with tiny Francis putting on a bit of weight.

He was born in our bed, with Tom just outside the door. By the time Dr. Galveston arrived, Mrs. Andrews had proven herself capable in midwifery. She left him only the placenta to deliver and the umbilical cord to cut, and told him he ought to be ashamed of himself when he charged us full price. There was no caul, which somehow felt a disappointment and a relief at the same time. With his early arrival, Francis was small and disturbingly thin. The skin on his cheeks was slack, and his eyes appeared large in fleshless sockets, causing him to look like a wise and elderly man. Small or not, his cry was piercing, and it seemed he meant to fill out lickety-split. But after a minute or two at each breast his strength would give way. He would catnap, no more than ten minutes, and then, hungry again, he would startle me from my stupor in the rocking chair. The intensity of his wails had surprised even Dr. Galveston. "Generally," he said, "the early ones sound more like bleating lambs." Surely it was a good sign.

We were still living with Mrs. Andrews, but with her own dress-making commitments as well as the work I had abandoned midstream, she was fully occupied and seldom able to help out. And Tom had begun setting off each morning to a not-yet-dug section of the hydroelectric canal. Though it meant I was left alone to manage a toddler with stamina enough to climb in and out of the gorge several times each week, and an infant who napped only for ten-minute intervals and hollered in between, I did not for a moment wish circumstances were otherwise. At long last, Tom was employed.

He came home from the canal happy and tired, and said his crew was the best of the lot. "I never have to tell any of them off," he said. "I just get down to work. They're all decent, not the sort to sit around while other men sweat." Mr. Coulson went to see Tom from time to time, at first with Tom's weekly foreman's report clutched in his hand. He would take Tom aside. "No one was late? No one is slacking off? No one is giving you any guff? It doesn't reflect badly on you to write it down." After six weeks the questioning let up. Tom's crew was managing to clear as much blasted rock as any crew on the canal.

He did his best in the evenings, cooking sausage and bacon and toast, or beef stew. He made a list before he went to work in the morning and stopped in at the market on the way home. After supper he and Jesse romped outdoors, seldom straying from the yard. They went to the river only twice in those first months, once for a body—I had begun to argue Jesse was not old enough but relented when I remembered Isabel's body laid out on the stone beach—and, a second time, when a boy's tackle box was found abandoned on a boulder near the Devil's Hole Rapids. In the nighttime Tom often got to Francis first, and lifted him from the cradle and placed him at my breast. He would watch, the corner of his mouth lifted, his face filled with wonder. His eyes would take on a sheen as he slid a finger into the curl of Francis's fist. "It's a miracle," he would say, and though I sometimes felt the truth in it and tried my best to cultivate the sentiment when I did, it was never quite enough to tilt me toward believing in the miraculous once the moment had passed.

Several times, in those first few months, Mother managed to cajole train fare from Father and came alone to Niagara Falls to stay for a few days. A hotel room out of the question, she would put her travel case under the narrow cot Mrs. Andrews had set up for her in a corner of the sewing room, and I would sigh a great sigh of relief as she got down to the business of putting things right. I expect, though, that Tom had not anticipated her visits in quite the same way.

No sooner had she joined Tom and me at supper one evening than she plopped a catalog onto the table. "Take a look," she said.

It took me a moment of flipping through pages to figure out the catalog was advertising a line of kits for homes put out by Sears, Roebuck and Company.

"Some of them are just lovely." She turned to a model called the Westly. "There's a balcony off the front bedroom, and it's got a center hall plan." I was only just beginning to wonder what Father would make of her fascination with the Westly and whether she even had the nerve to broach the topic of a catalog home with him when she said, "It's got three bedrooms, just perfect for you."

"For us?" I said.

She looked up and smiled. "You're saving." It was true; still, it would be a good while before we had enough for a down payment.

"It's more house than we'll ever need," Tom said.

"Oh, dream a little." She patted his hand. "You're spoiling your wife's fun."

"He isn't," I said, but already he was pushing back from the table and saying he was going out to the shed.

Mother took in my folded arms and with him still in earshot said, "Come on, Bess. You want a house with a center hall plan. I know you do."

And one morning she came into the kitchen while he was packing his lunch and told him he should think about wearing a collar to work, that if he dressed like a laborer it was what he would always be. "Mr. Coulson wants to help," she said. "You might as well make it easy for him."

Tom snapped his lunch pail closed and met Mother's gaze. Without a hint of malice, he said, "I prefer a neckcloth to a collar. It comes in handy when I'm using a pickax, which is most of the time."

Then Francis was awake and hollering upstairs, and Mother said she would go and left the two of us.

"I'm sorry," I said.

"She wants the best for you, is all."

"I can't believe her, spouting off, when she can't work up the nerve to ask my father for fifteen cents."

"It's got nothing to do with nerve, Bess. It's got to do with knowing your father, and knowing what's possible and what's not." He buttoned up his jacket.

I wondered whether he was right, also whether the same cleverness that kept her from badgering Father suggested that she keep pestering Tom, that one day the effort would be worthwhile. "Thirty-five dollars a week is more than enough for me. I don't care if you ever make a penny more."

I had meant to reassure, and he smiled, but then when it seemed he was about to speak, he pressed his lips closed.

"What?" I said.

"The first generators at the powerhouse will be switched on in a little over a year. Men are already getting laid off." He lifted his lunch pail from the countertop.

"Mr. Coulson's watching out for you," I said. "He's already said your crew is moving on to the forebay once you're through with the canal."

"And once the forebay's dug?"

"There are eight more generators scheduled for the powerhouse," I said. "It's all going to take a long time."

B y the time Francis was a year old we had almost saved enough for a down payment and I had begun looking in earnest for a house. It was during the house hunting that Mrs. Andrews called me into the parlor one evening. She sat down on the chesterfield across from the chair where she had gestured for me to sit and said, "There are things I'd like to do before I'm six feet under. I want to see my sister in San Francisco and then keeping going west. I want to stand on the Great Wall of China. I want to see the white marble of the Taj Mahal, maybe tick off a few more of the Seven Wonders of the World."

I must have looked doubtful, because she laughed and went on. "I inherited this house and have put away most of what I've made. I'm no spendthrift. And I have an uncle, a well-connected uncle, who put my savings in the Steel Company of Canada. With automobiles and then the war, I've done pretty well."

I sat with my hands folded in my lap, thinking of the postcard collection tacked to the window casing in the sewing room. "Your postcards," I said.

"Most of them were Everett's. He'd been collecting since before we were married, and then after he died people kept bringing them to me. He used to say we'd see all those places." She paused a moment, then patted her thighs and said, "Back to the reason I called you in here. You're a fine seamstress. And the new styles? Well, you're more comfortable with them than I'll ever be. You've got a head for numbers, too."

I nodded, uncertain. I knew she thought I was a capable seamstress, though it was not the sort of thing she ever said. And then to pay me a second compliment, she was not a bit herself.

"You know all the regulars, and I've been showing off your work. Half the customers you aren't already sewing for wish that you were. They just can't figure out how to say so." She pushed her glasses upward, to the bridge of her nose. "The news that I'm handing over the business to you will come as a relief."

"I don't know," I said. I had imagined I would continue to spend my mornings and afternoons alongside her, chatting away the hours, laughing at her commentary on Mrs. So-and-So's abysmal taste or ever-expanding rear end. It had occurred to me that someday I would like a business of my own, but that someday had always been in the far-off future, when Mrs. Andrews was tired, when she had taught me all that she could.

"What's not to know?"

It was true that I had become competent with needle and thread, and that over the years she had persisted in explaining the business side of dressmaking to me. Maybe she was right. Maybe there was no reason to be anything but pleased. "You have been so kind, from the start," I said. "You have given me so much. Tom and the boys, too."

She glanced away, but not before I noticed her eyes were damp. "I haven't given you anything," she said, "that you haven't given me." With that she stood up and turned away to adjust the position of a vase on the windowsill.

*   *   *

Tom's only requirement for our house was that it be an easy walk from the whirlpool and lower rapids. I wanted three bedrooms—one for Tom and me, and one for the boys, and one for sewing. I wanted a veranda, even if it was small, a place to lounge with a book and remember the days when I read to Isabel. I wanted a living room with a chesterfield where I could sit alongside Tom on winter evenings, our stocking feet extending beyond a blanket and resting on a hearth before a simmering fire. I wanted closets, those modern tiny rooms for housing linens and clothing and other bits best kept tucked away. I wanted an up-to-date bathroom, with a basin, toilet, and bath. I wanted electric light, so commonplace now that putting it on the list hardly made sense. But I had heard Tom say he preferred the soft glow of a kerosene lamp to the brightness of an electric bulb, and I needed to make sure I did not end up the only woman in town still scrubbing away soot.

The houses closest to the whirlpool and lower rapids, on River Road, were large, with wraparound verandas and leaded glass and three chimneys, the sorts of places we could not afford. That left only Silvertown. And because I did not much like the greedy view of myself apparent in my own long list, I agreed. We would live just beneath the bluff on which Glenview sits, a neighborhood where I was sure to catch the odd summertime whiff of the privies that still existed there though almost nowhere else in Niagara Falls.

I found a near perfect house on May Avenue and for a price we were able to pay, though there would not be a penny left for a rainy day, let alone furniture. The ceilings were lower than I had hoped and the rooms only moderate in size. The only real disappointment, though, was the stove, an antiquated wood-burning affair. The cast iron was freshly blackened, but that did little to disguise the fact that it would need to be polished again and again. In Mrs. Andrews's kitchen, I had grown used to enamel that wiped clean with just a cloth and become a competent cook, an accomplishment surely tied to the electric burners of her stove.

When Tom first saw the house, he looked around uneasily. "What'll we put in all the rooms?" he said.

"We'll have it furnished in a couple of years."

"It'll cost a fortune to heat."

"We'll manage."

As he became ever more quiet, it struck me that while our anxiety over such a large purchase was evenly matched, only mine was offset by glee. It was I who spun in the kitchen and threw my arms around his neck in the bedroom I wanted to share with him and I, again, who smoothed my palms over the oak of the mantelpiece. He began scrutinizing the walls, pressing his fingertips against them to test the give. He examined the wooden siding and cedar shingles of the exterior, looking for rot. When he said he wondered if he felt a bit of spring in the dining room floor, he returned to the cellar to take another look at the joists. He stayed down there a long while, long enough for me to know he was through with the joists. When he emerged, he said, "They're number one yellow pine, spaced sixteen inches apart."

"And?"

"It's good."

"Then there's no reason not to take it," I said.

$$25$$

Late afternoon I sit on the back stoop of our very own May Avenue house peeling apples for a pie. Jesse is busy kicking up the leaves trapped in the nook between the cellar door and the stoop. Francis is fully engaged by the fluttering leaves, and so I ignore the heaviness of the diaper drooping between his thighs.

I glance up the bluff and see Glenview's freshly painted eaves, also the pediment window that is no longer cracked. I do not know the people who live there, only that their name is Haversham and that their daughter gallops around the yard in lovely dresses much as Isabel and I had. Once when Mother was visiting, we went up to the house, ostensibly to leave a business card, though I suspect she had it in her head Mrs. Haversham would make a more suitable friend for me than any of the half dozen Italian neighbor women I have met. It would explain why Mother had washed and pressed her one decent dress the evening before and then badgered me into changing from my best housedress into a pretty frock that would have been just right had we been summoned up the bluff to tea before the hemlines had risen from ankle to calf. In the end, it had not mattered. A housekeeper answered the knocker, asked why we were calling, and, once I had handed over my business card, promptly shut the door.

But even if Mrs. Haversham had opened the door and mistaken me as someone belonging to her set, even if I were invited in, my isolation would have remained much as it is. I am stuck somewhere between my new life and my old, not truly fitting in with my Silvertown neighbors, who grow tomatoes in their front yards and collect dandelion greens from the side of the road and haggle with the ice cart driver though the price is set, not truly fitting in with society. After running into Lucy Simpson, whom I had been friendly with at Loretto, that much had become abundantly clear. She had astonished me by inviting me to a luncheon at her house. "You'll know everyone," she said.

I gathered she meant the guests had gone to Loretto and said, "Will Kit be there?"

"She isn't much for parties midafternoon. She prefers work. Poor Leslie, with half the town thinking he can't support his wife."

"Everyone knows he's with the Hydro, the chief hydraulic engineer," I said, a little bewildered to find myself irked on Kit's behalf.

"Well?"

"I'll have to see about arrangements for the boys," I said. It was an excuse.

"Come," Lucy said. "You can tell us all about your famous Tom Cole."

And then in the evening, Tom said, "You should go. You could use a friend." It was not anything I had not thought myself. Still, hearing it aloud made me feel pitiable, and I had no wish to be, and so I nipped and tucked and fussed over one of Isabel's old dresses and set off for a luncheon I did not much want to attend.

In Lucy Simpson's grand dining room, I told the boys' ages and said that, yes, of course I was afraid when Tom was out there on the ice bridge. There were more questions, about other rescues, and then finally about the bodies he pulls from the river. Lucy called them floaters and made a joke about the stink, and I knew there was no point trying to explain about the care he took. It bothered me, too, her tactlessness, the way it seemed she had entirely forgotten about Isabel, and I began making less of an effort to join in, which was hardly a chore. I had nothing to say about the latest ball at the Clifton House and I had not traveled to New York and I knew nothing about the fund-raising dilemmas of the Lundy's Lane Historical Society. Nor would my old classmates have wanted to hear that I had found a yard goods shop in Toronto that carried lace from Burano, Italy, for a fair price, even less so that Garner Brothers hardware had washboards on sale for sixty-five cents. It occurred to me, afterward, that Kit would have saved me from the banality, and it caused me to miss her very much.

I walked home by way of Erie Avenue and peered into each of the shops the Atwells owned, looking for her. But no matter that for once I had worked up the resolve to talk to her, even plead, if that was what it took, she was nowhere to be seen, even as I made a second pass, daring to step into each of the shops.

After a while Francis grows bored with the fluttering leaves and his squawks become insistent. I whisk him into the house and set him on the bench that substitutes for kitchen chairs. In the way of furnishings we have little more than the tablecloths and serviettes from the trousseau Mrs. Andrews had given us. One hand on his belly, I deftly unfold a clean diaper and slide it under his bottom. While I rinse and wring the old diaper, I balance him on a hip and glance around wistfully, thinking I should put the apples aside a moment and get the breakfast dishes cleaned up. And the floor needs to be swept. And the stove needs to be blackened yet again. When he rubs his eyes, I return to the stoop, hoping he will nurse. If I am lucky, he will drift off and the apples will be peeled and the dishes washed and the floor swept before Tom comes in from work. The stove will have to wait.

Six days a week I sew from early morning straight through to midafternoon. I am able to manage it only because a neighbor called Mrs. Mancuso looks after the boys. Under her watchful eye, Jesse has learned to differentiate basil from mint, and to say when a tomato is ready to be picked. He can turn the handle of a pasta machine and knows *fusilli* is like a corkscrew and *penne* like a tube. She coddles them, though. For instance, she shoos the boys out the door after lunch and clears the table herself, which means I am back to reminding Jesse to put his dirty dishes in the sink. And he does not see why he should eat beef stew for supper, not when Mrs. Mancuso made him meatballs for lunch after he turned up his nose at the macaroni she had first served. But there is never a fuss in the morning when we walk to her house, and the boys are returned to me midafternoon clean and well-fed. What is more, her house is only an empty lot over from our own.

When there is more sewing than I can manage, I save the handwork for the evenings. On occasion I have sat overcasting what seems a never-ending stream of buttonholes and thought I would like to take on less work. But we have agreed to the schedule of repayment set out in our mortgage contract, and the expense is large, mostly on account of my long list.

In the evening, I collect a blouse with cuffs to be hand-stitched from the sewing room and head for the kitchen, where I expect to find Francis contentedly toppling blocks, and Tom and Jesse playing dominoes or Chinese checkers, or whooping it up with Tom on his knees and Jesse on his back. But Tom is alone, sitting at the kitchen table, writing in a small notebook. "Where are the boys?" I say.

"The Mancuso girls were over, begging to take them for a walk." He closes the cover of the notebook.

I slide in beside him on the bench and poke my chin toward the notebook.

"It's nothing," he says.

I move a hand toward the notebook but stop short. "Nothing?"

"I'm tracking the river's height at a couple of spots."

"Some sort of record?"

He nods, and the nod seems sheepish, as though there is a good chance I will not approve. "It bothers me that I couldn't say for sure what happened to the ice bridge."

"You're tracking what the Queenston-Chippawa project is doing to the river? You've hooked up with those men you met at the Windsor way back?"

He places his hands flat on the table, spreads his fingers wide. "Bess, I'm a workingman, not the sort they'd ask to join their meetings."

"What's it for, then?"

"It's just for me," he says, tapping the notebook. "It's the least I can do."

He has never given me cause to doubt his word. I remind myself of it again and again, as I stitch the cuffs, as I kiss Jesse good night, as I pace the main floor with Francis in my arms and my lips against his downy hair.

Still, try as I might, the notebook is firmly lodged in my thoughts.

26

Queenston powerhouse under construction

My coat is the same one I wore my final winter at Loretto, seven years ago. Twice I have raised the hemline, but there is nothing to be done about the worn cuffs and unfashionably nipped-in waist. For the past several years I have put off wearing it until the snow flies and then packed it away at the first sign of a thaw. As a result, I have spent many a cold morning shivering in a sweater, thinking I really should get down to the business of sewing myself a decent coat.

The coat I am making is narrow at the midcalf hem, broad through the waist, broader still through the hips. My first thought was velvet, but my practical side overruled and I am using a chestnut wool, as soft as cashmere but not nearly so dear. I had not quite made up my mind about the fabric for the collar and cuffs, but then Tom showed up with a typeset invitation, and I knew I would cut them from silk. If I was to wear the coat in the company of Premier Drury and Sir Adam Beck, it needed to be more than just warm.

Tom brought the invitation home from work on a Tuesday. Mr. Coulson had hand-delivered it to him that afternoon and said management thought the workers ought to be represented at the official opening of the Queenston powerhouse. "We'd like to include everyone," he said to Tom, "but we can't, and you're the one we chose."

I was delighted, but as Tom spread the invitation on the kitchen table, he said, "I'm not so sure."

We get few invitations, certainly none as grand as the opening. There were to be speeches and pomp at the powerhouse, and then dinner and dancing in the ballroom of the Clifton House. I wanted to go. "I don't think Mr. Coulson would understand if you declined," I said. "It's an honor to be picked."

"I'd get mixed up about which fork to use." I had explained it to him once, about starting with the utensil farthest from the plate, and he had shrugged his shoulders but never since made a mistake.

I raised my eyebrows, waiting for the truth.

"I'd feel like a phony, celebrating."

I shifted my attention from the invitation to the saucer I was wiping dry. "You can accept or decline," I said, aiming for nonchalance. "I won't bother you about it either way."

"You've got your heart set on going."

"I wonder if Kit might be there with her husband." Foolish or not, I was hopeful. It had been four years since Edward was killed, four years since I had seen the hostility in her gaze as she sat listening to the Niagara Falls Citizens Band. What is more, I came upon her in the street a short while ago and as usual she glanced away, but afterward I was almost certain of a moment's hesitation before she did. Maybe enough time had passed.

"Let's go," he said. "I wouldn't mind shaking Drury's hand." Since he became premier, Drury's government has set out policies more sweeping than Ontario has ever seen for replanting forests and conserving water, and Tom very much approved. Still, I knew he had changed his mind on account of me.

I smiled. "I'll finally get going on a new coat."

"But I like your black one," he said.

We drive along River Road in the Packard Mr. Coulson sent for us. The walk from Silvertown to the powerhouse is four and a half miles, and Tom regularly makes it on foot. But today the road is muddy and rutted, and the slush along the sides is at least six inches deep. Had we walked, we would have been spotted with dirt long before we arrived.

I made Tom's overcoat as a Christmas gift the year before, and his suit has hardly been worn since our wedding day. The seams were ample, and I let out the trouser legs, also the waist of the jacket. His figure is as trim as ever, but a boxier sort of tailoring has come into style. I bought him a charcoal gray bowler with a small, speckled feather tucked into the band. He says he looks a fop in it, but he is wrong. Without trying, he is elegant. A quick shave and a comb through his hair. That is all it takes.

I had plenty of dresses to choose from and tried on one after another, remembering Isabel in the frock, heading off to a tea or in solemn procession at her graduation. When I got to my white concert dress, the memory was of me, hauling a trunk at Loretto, a section of skirt hiked up and tucked under the sash around my waist. A too long hemline is easy enough to fix, but women cast off the boning and lace collars and heavy skirts of the dresses ages ago, during the war, once they had learned to hoe potatoes and grind the noses of artillery shells.

There was no time for an entirely new frock, not if it was to have a bit of beadwork, but hidden away in my old trunk was the gown Isabel had meant to wear on her wedding day. Mother had put hours of work into beading the overskirt. I had never forgotten how lovely it was, with swirl upon swirl of seed pearls aligned end to end. It had always seemed such a waste.

So I am decked out in a midcalf-length chemise with an outer layer made from the overskirt of Isabel's wedding gown. The frock was a cinch to make with the beading already done. The underlayer is pale pink, a silk georgette that feels luxurious against my skin, even more so when I think of the low whistle Tom let out as he saw me coming down the stairs. "I'll have to make sure some rich fellow doesn't run off with you," he said. Because the dress easily stands on its own, I wear no jewelry other than Isabel's aluminum bracelet, which is always clasped around my wrist.

Two more of my designs will debut tonight at the Clifton House. Mrs. Harriman chose a chic suit of sea green, sequined French serge, which Mrs. Coulson had insisted on inspecting when I made the mistake of mentioning it. She had traced a finger along a lapel and let out a satisfied *humph*. "Lovely, but I prefer my own," she said. I decided against showing her my chemise. The beadwork is exceptional, and what is more she is curvaceous and the newer styles are more suited to women with the flat chest and narrow hips of a boy. At long last my figure is in style and my dress is perfect and Tom is handsome in his bowler and we are being driven in a Packard to the party of the year.

Before descending to the powerhouse at the river's edge, Tom leads me over a series of planks to the rim of the gorge. Nine immense troughs have been at least partially gouged into the cliff face. Only two have been laid with the giant pipes through which the water will fall. Solid walls exist for the southern end of the screen house at the top of the gorge. The northern end is a hodgepodge of girders and scaffolding roughly marking out what has yet to be built. And at the base of the gorge the massive building meant to house the turbines and generators is as ramshackle as its counterpart above. "It hardly seems ready," I say. I am not disappointed. The newspapers are correct; it will be another five years before all the generators are switched on, another five years of steady income for Tom.

Inside the powerhouse a crowd of men in bowlers and overcoats has gathered around a single enormous drum. There is no rope guarding it, yet the men maintain a gap of several feet between themselves and the gleaming generator, as though it were a shrine of sorts. I survey the crowd and find Leslie Scott. With my tendency to ask about him and to perk up my ears at the mention of his name, Tom has accused me of a schoolgirl crush. He chuckles as he says it, knowing full well I am only trying to glean what I can about Kit. She is not among the men at the powerhouse, which is hardly a surprise given it is four o'clock in the afternoon, not yet closing time for the businesses on Erie Avenue. The other wives, it seems, have mostly opted to stay home and make their entrances at the Clifton House, but I am glad I have come. There is excitement in the air, and Tom is holding my arm, and men nod in our direction, tentatively, as though their greetings might not be returned. Eventually one of the younger fellows comes over and introduces himself. "I'm Gerald Wolfrey," he says, "and everyone knows you're Tom Cole." A colleague of Mr. Wolfrey wanders over and joins our small circle, then another and another. I had not expected it, but even the administrators and engineers charged with overseeing the workers digging the forebay and canal are deferential to my riverman.

It is easy to pick out Sir Adam Beck, with his high starched collar, regal profile, and tired eyes. Surely it has been a grueling few months. True, his dream is finally more than blueprints and excavated dirt, but his wife died several months ago, and the mudslinging is at an all-time high. The cost overruns are staggering, and his pat answers—conditions that could not have been foreseen, results that could not have been anticipated, wartime inflation, and shortages of men—no longer seem to suffice. His daughter is at his side, looking defiant and bored, as though she had accompanied her father against her will. I cannot yet see what she has on underneath, but my coat is not out of place alongside hers. Premier Drury's suit is finely tailored, yet he looks every bit the farmer that he is, with his hair disheveled and his tie askew. Though he has been feuding with Beck in the newspapers, here they seem on friendly enough terms. I suppose it is only a premier's job to scold when the books have been so sloppily kept and budgets so easily ignored.

Beck moves to the podium, clears his throat, waits for the crowd to hush. Then he begins:

Dona naturae pro populo sunt. The gifts of nature are for the people.

> *These are the words I spoke to Premier Whitney back in 1905, the very words with which the Hydro-Electric Power*

Commission was born, the very words with which the triumph of public power over private greed began. No longer would private industry be allowed to gouge manufacturers and citizens alike when a publicly owned company could provide cheaper electricity more efficiently. And surely those words, spoken to Premier Whitney in 1905, are as fitting as ever when considering the Queenston-Chippawa power project. At long last the bounty of Niagara Falls truly belongs to the people.

He goes on to thank the citizens of Ontario for having had the foresight to vote for the hydroelectric generating station five years ago. He says they have rid themselves of coal embargos and blackouts, and will pay less for electricity than anyone else in the world. With their source of abundant, cheap power, they will brighten their homes and places of work, and lighten the burden of farm and household chores, and more cost-efficiently run the factories and thus ensure more jobs and lower prices, placing more goods than ever before within reach of the common man. He thanks the administrators and the laborers, but most particularly he thanks the engineers, whom he says designed the most efficient power plant yet built.

While the others in the room applaud, Tom's hands remain at his sides. I clap, tentatively, and wonder whether anyone else has noticed Sir Adam Beck's adeptness at recognizing others while, at the same time, patting himself on the back. And when Premier Drury speaks, he is just as shrewd. Though the room is filled with businessmen, his words focus on the contributions of the laborers, the men who elected his party. He had correctly guessed there would be reporters scribbling. He had expected the flashes of the newspaper cameras in the crowd.

At the close of his speech, he flicks a switch, and a sign behind him reading THE LARGEST HYDRO-ELECTRIC PLANT IN THE WORLD lights up. The crowd applauds on cue, and I strain to pick out a sudden mechanical whir. But the room was loud with conversation when we arrived and is louder now with whoops and applause. I scrutinize the generator, looking for some hint of activity, but nothing has changed. Tom leans toward me and says into my ear, "It's been on since last Wednesday."

But the crowd is filing from the room, seemingly satisfied. "You're sure?"

"The river dropped a half foot."

The Clifton House ballroom is as I remember, with polished hardwood, Corinthian columns, giant ferns, and tasseled chandeliers, yet it seems grander, too, maybe because I am no longer used to opulence. The first strains of a fox-trot fill the room, confirming the thought I had just begun to think: I do not belong at the Clifton House, not anymore. The only steps I know are from before the war, learned at Loretto, practiced in the cozy little clubroom of the Gamma Kappa fraternity, one hand on Kit's shoulder, the other on her waist. Fortunately the next song is an older one-step, and Tom's hand is reassuring on my arm.

As we make our way around the ballroom, the odd flask is pulled from a pocket, tipped against the rim of a half-full glass. It seems a badge of honor, so grandly is the liquor offered, so openly is it poured. The Ontario Temperance Act has surely failed in the eyes of the legislators, unless, as some suggest, the laws are deliberately lax, meant only to shush the debate for a while. Whatever the case, just now I would like nothing more than a splash of rye whiskey in my ginger ale.

The women in the ballroom are glittering in beads and sequins, diamonds and pearls. I point out my handiwork to Tom, and he says it is the best in the room. Only Marion Beck's dress is in the same league, and she is hiding it behind her crossly folded arms.

More men recognize Tom and lift their flasks in offering. He holds out his tumbler, then points to mine and I am poured a bit of rye. They want to hear about the ice bridge, and he tells the story as I have heard it told before, with modesty, as though anyone in the room would have done exactly as he did. And then they want to hear about Fergus and the workers knocked from Ellet's bridge and the fellows rescued from the riverbed the day the falls stood still. He is laughing and at ease, and they offer their flasks again. Their wives compliment my dress and ask where I got it. When I tell them I made it myself, several take down my details and tuck the scraps of paper into their tiny drawstring bags. Eventually Mrs. Harriman finds me in the crowd and asks me to call her by her first name and says, "You really are a marvel," and looks longingly at my frock. Mrs. Harriman, or rather Mabel, looks longingly at Tom as well. Mrs. Coulson only waves from across the room and then later, as she passes by, points to my dress, smirks, and says, "Best of the lot."

I am standing among a small gathering of women, keeping an eye out for Kit, when a woman called Mrs. Jenkins turns to me and says, "How did you and Tom meet?"

"I was on my way home from Loretto, on the electric trolley. I had a trunk with me and he offered to help."

"I'm a Loretto girl, too," she says, patting my arm now that we have been identified as kin of sorts. "Class of 1906." She waits, ear cocked, for me to say my class.

"I left in 1915." Then, before I am cornered into confessing that I did not graduate, I say, "I lived at Glenview, and my sister and I spent half the summer reading on the veranda, but really waiting for Tom to pass by on River Road."

"And it seems he did," says another woman, Mrs. Henderson, clasping tiny, lily-white hands together in feigned delight.

"He came by with a pike one day, and then he kept it up, coming every day, always with a fish."

"Just imagine," Mrs. Henderson says.

The rosy picture I have painted does not include Isabel convalescing on the veranda, half-starved, pregnant, and unwed. I wonder for a moment at my seeming desire to fit in.

I check over my shoulder for Tom, and there he is, looking in my direction, smiling his lopsided smile, raising his glass to me. I lift my own in return. And then I feel the light touch of a hand on my forearm, and I turn to see Kit. She stands silent, breezily elegant with her simple gray silk tunic and hastily pinned up flaxen locks. I cannot help but notice that her fingernails, while no longer chewed to the quick, are clipped as short as a man's.

"I was hoping you'd be here," I say.

"Leslie told me your husband was on the guest list."

We both laugh, nervously, and then we step away from the other women. "When I'm on Erie Avenue, I'm always looking into your shops."

"I saw you once," she says.

"I've wanted to go in and tell you I was sorry about Edward. I've promised myself a hundred times I'd call you the next day, but I never worked up the nerve."

She hugs her arms around her waist, as though she were cold.

"That time in Queen Victoria Park with the Niagara Falls Citizens Band," I say. "I'd remember that and it'd seem hopeless, speaking to you."

"I told myself Edward wouldn't have enlisted if you hadn't broken off with him. It didn't matter that it wasn't true. I wasn't in my right head."

"If I'd been thinking straight I wouldn't have gone to Tom without explaining myself to Edward first." Though her gaze is as intense as always, I do not shy away. "It just didn't register that I had no business burying a choker he'd given me."

We stand in awkward silence a moment or two, until she finally says, "I still have the note you sent after he was killed. It took me ages to open it, but when I did, I could see you knew how I felt. You'd spelled out my bewilderment; you know firsthand about someone becoming nothing at all. You understand."

"I don't understand, not really," I say.

"But that's exactly it. You didn't say he'd gone to a better place or died gloriously. You didn't give me some pat answer." Her gaze falls to the floor, and her shoulders creep up, her palms opening toward the ceiling. "It was wrong of me to miss Isabel's burial. I've been to her grave a dozen times, not that it makes up for anything."

"Did you leave irises?"

"No," she says, a rare flash of confusion coming to her face.

"Someone left irises."

She shrugs, and I ask about Edward. "Is he buried somewhere?"

"He's outside of Mons. Someday I'll go." She shakes her head. "But enough of that sort of talk. Just look at your frock. It's stunning. It really is, but then everyone says you're the best dressmaker in town."

I think better than to say that any credit should be shared with Mother, that she beaded the overskirt, for Isabel, for her wedding gown. "That shade of gray is lovely on you."

She gathers a bit of skirt in her hand. "I'm sure everyone here is deathly tired of it. You could make me a new one?"

"We could catch up properly."

"Let's have supper, with my Leslie and your Tom, the boys, too."

Our dining room is without a table and in our kitchen we sit on benches Tom rigged up, not that the old Kit would mind in the least. She was one of the few at Loretto who had not bothered with trinkets—a pair of bookends, a framed painting—to mark her room as her own. "We barely have a stick of furniture," I say.

"Throw a picnic blanket on the floor or come to our place first. That'll put you at ease. Furniture store or not, I'm not much for decorating."

We linger, though the waiters are ushering everyone to their tables. Eventually Leslie and Tom come, and there are handshakes all around, and Leslie says he knows a hundred wonderful stories about me, and Tom says, "I know at least as many about Kit." Then the two of us are wedged apart and escorted to our seats.

The guests are assigned to tables of eight for dinner, and I am alarmed to find my place card between Premier Drury's and Tom's. "I won't be able to swallow a bite," I say to Tom.

"He was a farmer a lot longer than he's been the premier."

As it turns out, Premier Drury is keenly interested in the grievances of the town's workers. And because I live in Silvertown, where the men walk to International Silver each morning, or travel by trolley to T. G. Bright, Norton, and Cyanamid, I often hear over the clothesline just how fed up the labor force is. Whether it is silver, wine, abrasives, fertilizer, or hydroelectricity, the workers want better wages and an eight-hour day. I tell him, too, that there is a hopelessness among the men that was not there a year or two ago, before the high unemployment made it so easy to replace anyone who suggested the workers organize. I do not suppose for a minute I have told him something he has not heard a hundred times before. But he is attentive and kind enough to say he is glad to find himself beside a sympathetic ear.

The Coulsons are at our table as well, Mrs. Coulson ignoring me, Mr. Coulson monopolizing Tom, so I am surprised, on my return from the powder room, to find Premier Drury in my seat, his arm draped over Tom's shoulder. Then I see the camera pointed at the two of them. A split second after the flash, Tom's eyes are on the camera and he is pulling out from under Premier Drury's arm. But it is too late.

T he picture, which appears on the front page of the *Evening Review* and page three of Toronto's *Globe,* shows Tom and the premier, mid-laugh, glasses raised. The headline in the *Evening Review* reads RIVERMAN CELEBRATES THE OPENING OF THE QUEENSTON POWERHOUSE WITH PREMIER DRURY. The *Globe* headline is innocuous enough: PREMIER DRURY TOASTS QUEENSTON POWERHOUSE. But the body of the article is not: "In his opening remarks Premier Drury praised the contributions of the laborers at great length. Niagara riverman Thomas Cole (of ice bridge tragedy fame) was among the workers enjoying the evening's festivities."

Tom thwacks the *Evening Review* with the back sides of his fingers. "Drury planned that photo. He thinks I've got clout with the working-man."

"It'll blow over."

"He's all for siphoning off half the river, and it looks like I am, too."

"I don't know what to say. I know that it matters. I know that it matters a whole lot to you." As far as he is concerned, it is all there in black and white; Tom Cole is a hypocrite.

27

Scow rescue

Francis is barking like a seal. It is what everyone says about the cough that accompanies croup, and now that I have heard it, the description seems exactly right. My heart is pounding, and I am pulling up his undershirt again and saying to Tom, "His lips don't look blue." Same as a moment ago, Francis's midriff is smooth, without the tugged-in valleys between the ribs that come with strangled breath. Still, I recall a hole cut through a girl's throat into her windpipe and a length of hollow wood jammed into the opening. It is only something I overheard as a child, a memory belonging to someone else. Yet I can imagine the low whistle of breath sucked through a tube.

"Maybe you should sing," Tom says. His voice is steady, barely above a whisper, soothing. Without saying so, he has told me that I must calm myself, that Francis, who is wild-eyed in my arms, needs me to be calm. It is a difference between Tom and me. He does not panic. He needs me to calm down, and he accomplishes it by giving me something to do.

I sit down at the kitchen table with Francis on my lap and begin to hum a nameless tune, which is easily drowned out by the barks. Tom places a basin of hot water on the table, and I put my face into the steam to see that it will not scald.

"It's like the mist at the falls," I say to Francis. He continues to bark and wail, and pulls back from the steam.

"I'm going to make a tent for you and Mommy," Tom says.

He drapes a tablecloth over Francis and me and the basin. A few minutes later the barking stops.

"Night air is supposed to help, too," I say, pushing the tent aside.

After Tom checks on Jesse, still soundly sleeping, we sit on the back stoop with Francis curled up in my arms, though he is heavy at three and a half. Tom's arm is around me, and the three of us are snug, wrapped in wool. The night is warm for March; still, the air has a nip to it that is surely good for the croup. Francis relaxes against me and drifts off, mumbling about sleeping in a tent.

When I notice Tom's gaze on the stars, I lift my chin. The night is clear, and the hour is well past when all but the most hardened night owls turn off their electric lights. The stars shine rather than twinkle. Bold, brazen, true.

How did I ever manage without Tom? Forget that he spends hours with his boys, more so than any man I know. Forget that he puts up with my parents, has even charmed them a little, that the last time they came to May Avenue for the weekend, Mother went as far as to say Jesse was becoming quite the gentleman, that he had a good role model in Tom. Forget the wages he brings home every week. Forget that with his aptitude for fixing what is broken, our house has become a refuge for cast-off lamps and broken piano stools and chairs missing their seats, each mended and polished and given its own special charm. Forget, too, our quiet tête-à-têtes, our whispered endearments, our lovemaking. How did I manage without a helpmate whose happiness is so intrinsically aligned with my own? Tonight there was great comfort in his gaze lifting to meet mine when the barking began, in knowing his fear and later his relief matched my own. Yes, sorrow, misfortune, or worry split in two is more easily borne. I say all of this aloud to Tom as we look up at the stars.

"It isn't the same for joy," he says, "when it's divided up."

I lean my temple against his shoulder to show him I have understood. Joy shared with another is so much larger than joy felt alone.

We sit a little longer, until the telephone rings, splintering the quiet. It happens every three or four weeks, our telephone ringing late in the night. Once it was a group of boys who had been making mischief at the whirlpool when they snagged a burlap sack with a rotting torso inside. Another time it was a drunkard, who was convinced he had seen fairies swimming in the plunge pool at the base of the falls. Sometimes a woman is on the line; her husband is late. Other times it is the police. And Tom always goes.

Through the screen door I hear him say, "Where, exactly?" and "How many are onboard?" and "Has anyone called the coast guard at Fort Niagara? They've got a lifeline gun."

He is back a moment later with his waders and the packsack he keeps by the kitchen door. "There's a boat grounded in the upper rapids," he says. "Two men are onboard."

I nod, though I do not want him to go, not tonight, not with the warmth between the two of us, not with the worry that will surely take its place.

He kisses me on the forehead and touches his fingertips to Francis's cheek. Then he lopes off with his waders and packsack of grappling hooks and rope.

He knows my fears. I have told him, once when we were lying together. He laughed when I first began and said that I had forgotten about the caul, that he could never drown. When he saw my seriousness, he pulled me close. "I'm careful, Bess. I know what the river can do."

I wish I could pray. I wish I thought it would do a bit of good.

I wait with sleeping Francis on the back stoop for what must be the better part of an hour. His brow is smooth and his lips pucker now and then as though he is nursing in his dreams. There is something wistful about this child sleeping in my arms when he mostly spends his days venturing ever farther away from me, or stamping his feet and saying, "I'm a big boy," when I hand him some toy Jesse long ago gave up. I do my best to focus on these thoughts, rather than on Tom, the river, and the ropes.

Maybe I will become pregnant again, now that Francis manages so much on his own, though the timing is hardly right. I am earning less than I was a year ago, when I could barely manage to fit in a new coat. High unemployment has led to thrift, and what is more, women's fashions have become a whole lot less painstaking to make. Waistlines have dropped and in some cases altogether disappeared. Fabrics are soft, pliable, comfortable to wear. Hemlines have stayed at the ankle or midcalf, out of the way. A dress is no longer a second skin, close-fitting when a figure is good, even more so when flesh must be cajoled into place. And then there is Mrs. Coulson, who has curtailed her orders since the opening of the powerhouse. She came the Monday afterward but left in a snit when I said, "It just isn't possible," to her demand that I piece together a dress for her with what was left of Isabel's wedding gown and the dress I had made from it for myself. Still, I am managing all right. Quite a few of the women who come to me are from households with buffer enough to ignore the economic woes. They still want a bit of glitz appliquéd to their formless frocks. And then there is Kit, who had never put much thought into clothes, suddenly needing a suit, a frock, a gown. I am glad for the work. I need it, but more than that, I am glad for the evenings together in my sewing room.

The last time she came, I was marking darts when she reminded me of the stray cat Isabel had charmed with bits of meat smuggled from the dining hall. Eventually, there was a basket attached to a rope, lowered from her window and pulled up once Puss was inside. But Puss was restless in her dorm room, meowing, rubbing up against bed and chair legs, leaping from bookshelf to windowsill to desk, eventually knocking over a vase of lilacs onto an unfinished prose composition. The ink ran. The paper rippled. Isabel snickered and complained furiously to the sisters: "I won't start again, not when the sanitation here is so lax we've got wild beasts in our rooms." She produced a soggy essay with a scattering of paw prints as proof. Kit mimicked Isabel's outrage in the sewing room, and we laughed, great quaking snorts.

When I hear footsteps coming around the side of the house toward the back stoop, I assume it is Tom and let out a sigh. But the man who comes into the backyard is not him. Even in the dim light, I can see he is not nearly so tall. There is a moment of fear when I think, If I am quick, I might manage to get Francis into the house, but then I see the man is wearing a constable's uniform. Fresh fear comes. I want to say "Where is Tom?" but press my lips closed.

"Mrs. Cole?" says the constable.

"Yes." I get up from the stoop.

"Tom asked me to come."

"He's all right, then?"

"He'll be a while. He wanted me to tell you that."

I suppose I ought to be thankful. Yet I am not. "What's happening?" I say.

"The Hydro was dredging around the intake gates, and the scow they were filling up with the sediment broke free from its tugboat and got pulled into the middle of the river. The men opened the hatches and dropped the anchor, and now they're caught on a ledge a short ways back from the brink."

I imagine Tom wading out to the scow, certain his legs will not be swept from beneath him. He will give me some nonsense about knowing it was safe, some hogwash about reading the current and working out the stability of the riverbed footholds beneath. "I can't explain it," he will say, "but sometimes I just know."

"The coast guard shot a line out to the scow," the constable says, "and rigged up a pulley and sling to cart the men back, but the lines got tangled up in the current. Tom was out, untangling the lines, when I left."

"He went into the river?" I ask. Francis stirs in my arms.

"He went out in a second sling, pulling himself hand over hand."

"I see," I say, but I do not. A scow is held back from the brink by a bit of rocky ledge and yet it serves as anchor to the lines Tom is dangling from. Should that scow shift in the torrent of the upper rapids, should the bit of rock give way, the scow along with the tangled lines, the pulley and sling, and Tom will be pitched over the falls.

A long while after the constable goes, I put Francis in his bed, and, with the first light of day, I walk across the empty lot to fetch Mrs. Mancuso from her house to watch the boys. She will be up, baking the *ciabatta* Mr. Mancuso prefers to eat warm.

F rom a ways off I see several lines strung from the roof of the Toronto powerhouse to a scow lodged midway between Goat Island and the Canadian shore. Ten yards from the scow, a man hangs from the lines, the torrent beneath him lashing at his feet. By the time I reach the crowd gathered at the powerhouse, the man has been hauled close enough to the shore for me to know he is not Tom but rather one of the rescued men. Beyond the man the scow is now an empty hull.

The crowd is whooping it up with far too much glee for anyone to have been lost, yet Tom is nowhere to be seen. Eventually the constable who came into our yard taps my shoulder from behind. "Tom is up top," he says, pointing to the roof of the powerhouse. "I can take you up."

As we walk, I catch words spoken in the crowd: "It's the wife, the riverman's wife."

The interior of the powerhouse is vast, empty except for a half dozen large drums housing the magnets and copper-clad rotors that make electricity. It is quiet, only the whir coming from the generators and our footsteps bouncing off the polished floor, echoing in the hollow space. Midway up the stairs the constable says, "He was out there a good two hours the first time, but the lines were a mess. He had to wait for daylight and go back. Shame you missed it, Mrs. Cole. You would've been bursting with pride."

I am alone in my disapproval. The others all sigh a great communal sigh and applaud when Tom Cole shows up with his waders and grappling hooks and rope. Everything will be all right. The riverman is here.

When we pass from the stairwell out onto the roof, one of the men from the scow is being helped from a sling attached to the line. He kisses the powerhouse beneath his feet, which I suppose seems as good as solid earth. Then he throws his arms around Tom, who is huddled in a blanket, looking cold and tired.

When he sees me, he lets the blanket fall from his shoulders. Then his arms are around me, squeezing me until my feet leave the roof. "Francis?" he says into my ear. "He's fine," I say back. Then, he makes a show of kissing me, and the dozen or so men on the roof applaud.

Is it glory he seeks, dangling above the falls, leaping from one cake of ice to the next? I am almost convinced of it, but when I say I would like to go home, he says he wants to wait on the roof awhile, until the crowd below thins out. And when a photographer from the *Evening Review* wants to come out onto the roof, the constable checks with Tom and then tells the photographer he cannot.

Tom speaks with the rescued men awhile, until a handful of the others on the roof work up the nerve to join the group. I pay little attention to the conversation that follows, talk of lifeline guns and pulleys and a riverbed just rough enough to snag a scow. Still, I manage to smile dutifully when it seems I should.

On the walk home I notice my pace is brisk. I notice myself ready to pounce. But my anger feels petty when Tom has been heroic, when lives have been saved. I reach for his hand, wondering if I should tell him yet again how it is for me when he is on the river, anesthetized to the risks, fueled by some notion of invincibility.

"Jesse would've been interested in all this," he says.

It is more than I can bear, his suggestion that I should have brought Jesse. "I'm not much interested in having him watch his father drown."

"Bess, that wasn't going to happen."

"Another line could have been shot out. Another pulley and sling could've been rigged up. You didn't need to go out."

"God, you're pretty when you're worked up," he says with a careful smile.

It is an effort to charm me from my mood, and any other day I would be pleased. Not today though. Today I fold my arms.

"We would have had to send for new lines," he says. "All that takes time."

"You're saying that there wasn't time, that the scow was set to go over the brink?"

"I knew what I was doing," he says. "I was sure."

I want to yell, to fall to my knees. Instead I breathe deeply, steadying myself. "But the lines holding you up were tied to the scow."

"That scow wasn't going anywhere. It'll be there until the bottom rusts out."

"But if you were sure it'd stay put, all the more reason to wait for new lines. Why didn't you just wait?" I keep up the pace though I am becoming short of breath.

"Those men had been out there half the night, and they were scared to death."

"You have a family," I say. "And I feel like an afterthought. Do you think I wasn't afraid? Think of me. Think of your sons, instead of two men you don't even know."

"Bess, I could just tell. I just knew."

"Fergus isn't out there with you, keeping an eye on things, if that's what you think." There is a mocking lilt in my voice.

He stops, waits for me to do the same. He looks me in the eye. "There's something."

"There isn't. You're alone." I spit the words, feel my throat constrict. "Fergus is gone. Dead. Dust." My voice breaks as I say, "Like Isabel," and Tom reaches for my hand but stops short as I jerk it away.

"Way back you told me you'd seen bits of silver—prayers—in the mist," he says.

"I was wrong," I say, resuming the march home.

We walk on in silence, his gait sluggish now, lagging my own furious stride.

Midmorning, I am alone in the kitchen, giving the final pressing to the pleated skirt of a dress for Mrs. Ross. The boys are with Mrs. Mancuso, and Tom has gone off to work. If we had been speaking, I might have told him not to go. He was shivering, despite a flannel shirt and knitted vest, despite a bowl of oatmeal and a mug of tea. The room is silent, except for a clunk when I roughly set the flatiron on the trivet, annoyed with myself for the sloppy job I am making of the pleats.

I pace the main-floor rooms, mulling over the morning, my argument with Tom. I hesitate in the dining room, empty except for a pine sideboard delivered just the other day. Tom's notebook is facedown, spread open on the sideboard, the way he left it last night. I leaf through pages of tables, columns of carefully printed numbers and dates, margins filled with notes, some underlined so heavily that the paper is nearly worn through.

As I close the cover, I am clear-eyed about what Tom saw when he stepped into our May Avenue house for the first time. He saw more house than he thought necessary. He saw a costly mantelpiece. He saw empty rooms, a kitchen without so much as a table, three bedrooms without so much as a single bed. He saw yet another tether strung between himself and the Hydro-Electric Power Commission.

He has said more than once that much of the Queenston-Chippawa power project is complete, that already men are being laid off. It seems he had said it clinging to the possibility he would one day finally be free from the place. But I had not wanted to hear. "Mr. Coulson's watching out for you," I had said, and Tom had stayed on.

So now there is the notebook full of tables, and I think I understand the rationale behind measurements better than he does himself. His penance for contributing to the Queenston-Chippawa power project would include making himself acutely aware of just how much damage was done, just how much he had caused his river to suffer.

I am back in the kitchen, taking another stab at the pleats, when Tom comes in the door. "Everyone's heard about the scow, and I was told to go home and get some sleep," he says. "I won't get docked for the time off."

"I know you go to work for me, for the boys," I tell him. "I know we're not an afterthought. I shouldn't have said what I did."

"I don't want you to be afraid," he says. He slips his arms around my waist, gently kisses my brow.

Mrs. Ross will not come by for another hour, and I have only a small section of skirt left to iron. I would like nothing better than to set the flatiron on the trivet, gently this time, and follow Tom upstairs, but there is the hollow rap of the door knocker.

I open the door to Mr. Coulson on the veranda, grinning, shaking his head, and then, a moment later, clapping Tom on the back. I offer tea, usher him into the kitchen—there is not yet seating for three in the living room—and thank my lucky stars the breakfast dishes are washed, even if the ironing board is set up in the middle of the room.

"Quite a feat this morning," Mr. Coulson says, taking a seat.

"I guess," Tom says, sitting down opposite him.

And then the conversation continues with Mr. Coulson asking questions and Tom offering precious few words in response, until Mr. Coulson says, "I expect those two fellows told you they were under contract with us."

"Those men, they had no business out in that scow," Tom says. "The only dredging they'd ever done was in some creek up in Alaska, looking for gold."

"We put the work to tender. We explained exactly what our requirement was. The specifics were laid out."

"Men are desperate. Men will say they know about tugs and scows and the river if it means a few dollars."

"Drury's got a commission investigating cost overruns, and they're breathing down my neck."

"Still," Tom says, hardening his gaze. "For the sake of a few dollars the Hydro could have lost a couple of men."

Mr. Coulson pushes himself back from the table, from Tom. "You might want to take it up with Leslie Scott. He signed off on the work order. Dredging is his bailiwick."

For a split second Tom looks perplexed, but then he says, "I see." It would have been Mrs. Coulson who told him my family spends more than the occasional evening with Kit and Leslie. Only last Saturday I had looked at the two of them—Leslie with his spectacles and hollow chest, Tom with his height and rolled-up shirtsleeves—and thought what an unlikely pair they were. Even so, they were talking up plans for a campout in the glen.

Mr. Coulson takes off his spectacles, rubs them with a handkerchief. He glances at his watch. "I'm due at the office," he says, standing up. Then he produces a stack of notes and holds it out to Tom.

He shakes his head. "No."

"You risked your life. You had the wherewithal to send for a lifeline gun and then the courage to go out to the men."

Tom's hands remain folded on the table.

"Take it," Mr. Coulson says. "Think of it as pay for a job well done. You've saved the Hydro a great deal of trouble. You saved the lives of two men."

Mr. Coulson sets the notes on the table, nudges them toward Tom.

After Mr. Coulson leaves, with only me escorting him to the door, Tom sits still a long while, and I pick up the flatiron and do my best to turn my attention to the pleats. Eventually he picks up the notes, counts them, and then counts them again. "A hundred dollars," he says.

"A hundred dollars?"

"Three weeks' pay. Six weeks', if Mr. Coulson hadn't decided I'm worth more to the Hydro than any other workingman."

"It's generous."

"I'm being paid to keep my mouth shut."

"You don't know that," I say, setting the flatiron on the trivet, giving up on the pleats.

"He practically came right out and said the Hydro would make a show of doing the right thing and sack Leslie if anyone kicked up a fuss."

"I think that's a bit of a leap."

It has not escaped me that Tom had dangled above the Niagara River just upriver from the brink, that he had done it to save the lives of two men who had ended up there because prudence had been swept aside for the sake of profit. Still, it seems Tom, with Leslie in mind, will not publicly lay blame, and among the sensations churning in my gut there is relief. Also, there is fear, even shame, that Tom spoke so harshly to the man I have grown used to assuming would catch us if we fell. And there is something new. Doubt. Has it always been that Mr. Coulson is really only looking out for himself?

ICE BRIDGE READY FOR ADVENTURERS

Adventurers from far and wide are expected to descend on Niagara Falls this weekend. Last week's weather proved just right for the formation of the ice bridge that townsfolk and excursionists anticipate all season. Expect coasting on the ice mound at Prospect Point, sleigh rides, and the usual shanties selling light fare, liquor, photographs, and curiosities.

Once again a path between the Canadian and American shores has been laid out, carefully avoiding hidden or impassable fissures and unstable portions of the bridge. For the first time in a half century the task of selecting the route fell to other than Fergus Cole. "I'll turn eighty soon enough, and Tom is more than ready for the job," said Mr. Cole, referring to his thirteen-year-old grandson. Fergus Cole went on to explain that his grandson had risen early Tuesday morning and announced the bridge had been frozen through overnight. "I listened hard, trying to hear the changed growl of the river for myself," the more senior Mr. Cole said. "No use in it, though, not with these old ears. It was time."

The shore-to-shore race for boys fourteen years and younger is scheduled for noon sharp on Sunday at the *Maid of the Mist* landing. Local favorites include Jack Gowland, Charles Standing, and William Hobson, along with last year's champion, the aforementioned Tom Cole.

28

At the market I moved a half dozen lemons from my shopping basket back into the crate. The day was sweltering and I was parched, and a glass of lemonade would have been just the thing once I reached home, but the lemons were not on sale and the price of sugar was still high at a dollar for ten pounds. It occurred to me I had become adept at scrimping, at planning meals around the cheapest cuts of meat, at saying no to a candy stick when the boys accompanied me to town.

I began the trudge home, wondering about Mrs. Reynolds, whether she had stopped by the house to pay for a gown as she had promised she would more than two weeks ago. Then my mind went to the money jar, empty in the cupboard, and I was not sure there was enough left in my change purse to pay for the block of ice we would need when the ice cart made the rounds. There was still the hundred dollars Mr. Coulson had given Tom, but it was in a sealed envelope, tucked behind *Mrs. Beeton's All-About Cookery,* exactly as Tom had left it the morning after rescuing the two men from the scow.

A walk home was as good a time as any to think about Miss Honey's wedding gown. The problem was, with ever more women buying ready-made, I had begun taking on projects I once would have passed up—alterations and housedresses and choir gowns, twenty-three of them, all exactly the same. Much of it had become drudgery, and my weariness was showing in even the most pleasurable of my work. I had said as much to Mother on the telephone a while ago, and she came back with, "Laundry, and pork and beans twice a week for supper are drudgery, too, but I've made a game of coming up with some new way of saving a few cents at least every week."

"It still sounds like drudgery," I said, and we both laughed. Inside I was filling with admiration. When Father lost his job, she had returned to dressmaking to keep our family afloat, and when that had not worked out as intended, she had come up with a new plan. Quietly she urged Father to restart in Buffalo, where she would adapt yet again, taking on the role of penny-pinching wife.

The scheme for Miss Honey's wedding gown still as vague as ever, I came to the spot on River Road where Tom and I once left each other pretty stones and beads, ferns and charmeuse, and finally the notes setting out how we would meet. I could have wept as I thought of that early love, so childlike, so pure, so ready to blossom into something I was no longer able to imagine being without.

From a ways off I saw Tom in the garden, directing Francis and Jesse in cutting a few stalks of rhubarb. Nothing appeared unusual about the boys' clothes, not from a distance. But their trousers were made from silk twill, which was durable and cool, and of low enough sheen to almost pass as cotton. And Francis's shirt was satin, sewn with the wrong side facing out and the more lustrous side hidden against his skin. The Cole children tumble and roughhouse not in cotton broadcloth and gabardine but in the leftovers from what I have made. Both were tanned and lean, and Jesse's shoulders were broad, likely because he swam like the dickens, even if he was only six years old. I could not look upon them without seeing Tom in their green eyes, in their watchfulness, their habit of looking west to see the weather the moment they set foot out of doors.

From time to time I passed the furniture shop Edward Atwell had once run, and I sometimes imagined what a life with him might have been like. There would have been kindness and consideration. There would have been plenty of sugar for the tea and eggs for breakfast each morning, and afternoons in the garden with the children, and never a moment given over to the dress I should be sewing if we were to make ends meet. I would not have known hardship. But I would not have known love.

I called out, "Hello," and then said to Tom, "Did Mrs. Reynolds finally pay up? I'm not sure there's anything left for ice."

And maybe those were the words that caused him to do what he did. I cannot say for sure, but in the evening, I was putting the salt cellar in the cupboard when the money jar caught my eye. It had been empty and now, curled inside, was a wad of notes, far too thick for Tom to have earned selling fish or even delivering a body to Morse and Son, far too thick even if Mrs. Reynolds had finally paid up. I stood there not fully convinced, until I had counted out one hundred dollars. I did not need to slide *Mrs. Beeton's All-About Cookery* from the shelf to know the envelope was no longer there.

I opened the back door and called out, "Tom," and he appeared from around the side of the house holding a giggling Francis upside down by his ankles. Tom set Francis on his feet and told him to go dig up a couple of worms. "The money from Mr. Coulson?" I said.

He placed a foot on the bottom step of the stoop and nodded.

"You're sure?"

"I've had a long while to decide about it," he said. "And I'm sure."

F or the six weeks since, Tom has been steadfastly mourning his river. With three generators operating, the river has dropped two feet. Standing waves and eddies have disappeared, dry riverbed is exposed, and boulders that were once islands have become part of the shore. It would be easy enough to say the ruin is the cause of his mood, except that the generators have been up and running for well over a year.

He began to walk the section of river between the Queenston powerhouse and Chippawa, where the water is first diverted, one autumn afternoon more than a year before any of the generators were switched on. It is a significant trek, and he makes it all the more so by climbing in and out of the gorge at the Devil's Hole Rapids, the whirlpool, and the *Maid of the Mist* landing. Etched into the cliff face at each point is a horizontal notch marking the height of the river on the day he began keeping track. For the longest time after the notches were first cut, he measured the drop in the river's height and recorded it in his small notebook once a month. But ever since he moved the hundred dollars to the money jar, the trek has become a daily event.

Now, when he manages a bit of time at home, he is exhausted on the chesterfield or sighing over the notebook at the kitchen table, oblivious to the boys, to me. He comes in for supper, late, and says, "The river will be down six feet or more once the rest of the generators are switched on," rather than "Hello." And if I tell him Jesse kicked Francis in the shins and made him fall down, he hardly seems to hear. "There won't be any wild strawberries or grapes along the shoreline in a year or two," he will say.

I miss the husband who practically sprinted home from work, the man who threw open the back door and announced he was home. As often as not I would be peeling carrots or potatoes, or washing up by the sink. He would put a hand on my cheek or thwack my bottom or pull a bouquet of wildflowers from behind his back, and I would smile and put my arms around his neck. There would be a kiss, never the perfunctory sort, always a kiss that said there was no place in the world he would rather be. The boys would come running, and he would gather them up into his arms and tickle them and jostle them until their laughter filled our house. Now it is I, on my own, kissing them good night and telling them stories that are not nearly as interesting as Tom's tales of Blondin and his tightrope, Annie Taylor and her barrel, Fergus and the day the falls stood still.

I am putting away the last of the supper dishes when I glance out the window and see Tom entering the yard. The boys, ever-hopeful, come running in their pajamas as Tom steps into the kitchen, looking hot and tired and not at all ready for the onslaught. "Daddy. Daddy's home," they call out.

"There's a roast chicken in the oven," I say, "overdone by now."

"The river's down another inch."

"Are we going for a hike on Sunday?" Jesse asks. "You said we would."

"I have three worms," Francis says, raising his fingers to show the count.

"Two are mine," Jesse says.

"Are not."

"You took them from beside the pump and it's my spot. It's my spot, Mommy. You said it was."

"Can you tuck them in?" I ask. "I've had enough."

"You can tell us the story about Great-grandpa and the gondolier with the cork suit," Jesse says, already halfway up the stairs.

"No. I want the one about when Captain Webb drowned," Francis says.

"Get a move on," Tom says to Francis, and then Tom is on the stairs with Francis on his heels, doing his best to keep up. As they round the landing, my last glimpse is of Francis, his hand held aloft, straining for Tom's. And I know the scene. I saw it once before, except Tom was just home from the war and it was Jesse trailing behind in the snow, his mittened hand reaching for Tom's.

Kit and I are in my sewing room with the door closed behind our backs, though there is no gown to fit, no darts to nip and tuck, no hem to mark. She is here because, unable to bear another day as wretched as the last, I asked her to come and help me sort out what to do. "I'm at my wits' end," I say. "He's up at the crack of dawn with twelve miles to walk and three trips in and out of the gorge to make, all before he goes to work. And on the mornings he cannot rouse himself early enough for the whole ordeal, he stays in bed, getting up just in time to make it to work. On those days he makes the trek afterward, wandering in at God only knows what hour. He used to take such pleasure in the river, in us, too, and now he's just so miserable. It's heartbreaking."

"Has he said what all the record keeping is for?" Kit asks.

"He says it's for himself. When I first saw the book, though, he said it bothered him that he couldn't say why the ice bridge broke up when it did. I know he'd been wondering about the intake gates opening and closing, and the river bobbing up and down, whether it might have weakened the moorings."

"I remember Leslie saying a couple of the directors were worried about the power companies being blamed. I don't think anyone thought it'd be justified, but truth be told there was some hand-wringing, mostly over what Tom might say. He's got a lot of clout."

I am silent, putting off by a moment the question that might finally settle my way of thinking about Mr. Coulson. "Do you think it's why Mr. Coulson offered him a job?" I finally say.

"It wouldn't have hurt."

"Is it the reason the reward was so large?"

Her shoulders rise as she sucks in a long breath, then fall as she exhales. "Mr. Coulson was on the telephone with Leslie even before Tom had the two men rescued from the scow," she says. "He wanted to know about their credentials, and then he tore a strip off Leslie for hiring a couple of buffoons even though it was Mr. Coulson who'd ordered him to take the lowest offer on tendered business. He said that Leslie had given Tom every right to accuse the Hydro of negligence, that he'd better hope no one drowned, or no amount of money would keep Tom quiet."

"Tom said he was being paid to keep his mouth shut. He said it when he was hired, and he said it again after the scow. I told him Mr. Coulson was indebted to my family, that he loved a hero, like everyone else." With that I stand up from the sewing bench and begin to pace.

"I thought about telling you what I knew," she says, "but it seemed disloyal to Leslie and I couldn't really see the point."

"After the ice bridge Mrs. Coulson wouldn't let up about Tom going to see Mr. Coulson. And there was that picture of Drury and Tom in the newspaper. He's a pawn, and it started way back."

"It seemed like saying something would belittle what he did. It was a mistake, not saying anything," she says, but I hardly hear. I am thinking about Isabel, about her pallor in the morning, about the tea dress that fit one day but not the next. It had been easier to shrug, to move the tea biscuits to the windowsill, than to piece together what I knew and face the facts.

"Tom's got to quit the Hydro," I say, knowing I will do whatever it takes to make it happen.

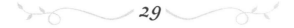

29

A t nine o'clock in the evening I put down the socks I am darning and follow Tom up the stairs. I climb into bed beside him without properly washing my face, with only the most cursory combing of my hair. Any delay and he would have been asleep.

He is on his back, and I snuggle up, my shoulder under his arm, my head resting on his chest, cheek against skin. He wraps an arm around me, and it gives me the courage I need. "You should resign," I say.

"Resign?"

"From the Hydro."

"It's work," he says, "and there isn't anything else." A flood of laborers was let go once the canal and forebay were excavated, and then a second round, once the concrete was poured, and a third, once the first of the generators was up and running. There are cutbacks everywhere, and when a job does come up, there are a hundred applicants, all willing to work for a third of what he makes at the Hydro-Electric Power Commission.

"We managed on just my dressmaking when you first got back from the war."

"We were living with Mrs. Andrews, and it was just the three of us."

"We'll put the house up for sale," I say. "You could get back to fishing and trapping, and sell what you caught. Jesse, too. It's what you did as a boy."

"Bess, you'd be miserable."

"Sadie managed all right."

"Sadie looked after herself from the age of thirteen. She ate nothing but apples and walnuts for weeks at a time. She wore the same buckskin dress every day, and she'd scraped it herself. When Fergus came along with a cabin and a rabbit twice a week and fish every other night, it was more than she'd ever had."

It hurts to be compared with Sadie and come up short, and I am on the verge of listing the hundred ways I have left my Glenview days behind. But how can I when, just three years ago, I had convinced the both of us I could not do without the May Avenue house?

"Remember that day at the whirlpool," he says, "the day Francis was born?"

I nod, thinking of myself in labor in his arms as he scrambled out of the gorge. I had been afraid until the moment he had promised to take the job at the Hydro.

"You said I should put my family first." He lifts my hand from his chest and kisses the base of my thumb. "You were right, Bess. A man needs to do what's best for his family."

"But you're not yourself anymore." I prop myself up beside him. "You're hardly here, and Jesse and Francis miss you so much. Me too. Listen to me, Tom. You're wearing yourself out with all the measuring, all the climbing in and out of the gorge."

"I know I haven't been pulling my weight," he says. "I'll figure something out for the boys."

"That notebook. You're tormenting yourself. And what for, Tom?"

He tilts his head back on the pillow, his eyes following suit, rolling upward so that he is looking at the ceiling. "I don't know," he finally says. "It's not like anything in that book will ever see the light of day."

Cheek back against his chest, I lie there listening to his heart, thinking about all those columns printed with dates and measurements, and margins scrawled with notes. Had keeping them to himself made his misery a whole lot worse? "I don't see why not."

"No one could care less," he says. "That's why not."

"I'm not so sure."

"I'm supposed to set myself up a soapbox on Clifton Hill and holler at the tourists walking by?"

"There are ways," I say.

"I'm dead tired, Bess. I just want to go to sleep."

"I could help."

"Just let me sleep," he says and lets go of my hand.

Early morning I open my eyes to blank sheet, to the hollow where Tom slept until he roused himself with time enough for all the measuring before setting off to work. I lie awake for a good hour, wondering what I could have said, waiting for the sound of the boys' feet on the floor. I think of him coming home earlier in the week, a dollar's reward money in his hand. He had gone into the upper river, after a dog this time. He stood there dripping on the kitchen floor, and when he finally spoke his voice quavered as though he were afraid. "There are two eddies between the spot where I went in after the dog and where we would have been sucked into the Toronto powerhouse. Either would have been enough to swing the two of us to shore. I missed the first one altogether and barely caught the second. I didn't get the current right."

A second later I am out of bed and in the boys' room. And there is Francis, curled into a ball, his thumb in his mouth. But there is no Jesse, only more blank sheet, another hollow, the place where he slept until Tom woke him with the news he had been craving for six weeks: They were going for a long hike. Twelve miles beginning in Chippawa, ending at Queenston Heights. Three times in and out of the gorge. And then a long trudge back to the house.

Once Tom is off to work and exhausted Jesse tucked back into bed and Francis sent to Mrs. Mancuso's, where he will not wake his brother, I telephone Cecil Randal at the *Evening Review*. "We're on May Avenue," I say, after he has agreed to come, "the house with all the fishing rods out front."

A half hour later I am sitting with Mr. Randal at the kitchen table, Tom's notebook open between us. "Tom's been keeping track for nearly three years, then?" he says.

I nod. "He says the river will have dropped six or more feet by the time all the generators are switched on."

"The hotel owners and the tour operators won't like it," he says.

"They might even kick up a bit of a fuss, but I can't see that anything will change. We've lived with blackouts and coal shortages and ever higher prices for electricity. People want the powerhouse. They voted for it. The money's been spent."

"You saw the picture of Premier Drury and Tom at the opening?"

"I did," he says.

"Tom was so humiliated," I say. "He can't stand everyone thinking he doesn't mind about all the water being siphoned off."

"But he works for the Hydro," Mr. Randal says. "There'll be trouble if we put all this in the newspaper."

"I expect you're right."

"You're sure."

"I am." And it is true. I am content to live in rented rooms, if it comes to that, and to eat whatever Tom is able to trap or catch on his line. I will sew, and when I have an idle moment, I will study the book where Sadie kept her recipes for groundnut root and wild leeks.

"And what about Tom? Is he sure?"

"He's been keeping track so he'd have proof," I say. It is almost not a lie.

By midafternoon the following day, I have been to the office of the *Evening Review* to collect one of the first papers off the press from Cecil Randal, and fairly well galloped back to May Avenue. Newspaper spread open on the kitchen table, I find the editorial, on page 2 no less.

BLEEDING THE RIVER DRY

According to Niagara riverman Tom Cole, the power companies are bleeding the river dry. And it is mighty hard to dismiss the warning when he has got a whole notebook full of facts and figures as proof.

A year before any of the generators were switched on at the Hydro's Queenston powerhouse, Mr. Cole cut notches marking the height of the river into the gorge wall at the Devil's Hole Rapids, the whirlpool, and the *Maid of the Mist* landing. At least once a month ever since, he has used the notches to track the river's height and recorded the results. His calculations show the river dropped nine inches with the first of the generators and just over two feet once all three generators were switched on. He expects the river will be down a full six feet with the other generators slated to begin operation in the next two years.

Alongside the figures, the margins of the notebook are crammed full of notes: "Heron gone from shallows at Hubbard Point." "No second eddy at Lower Steel Arch Bridge." "No standing wave at Colt's Point." "Seven more feet of dry riverbed at western flank of Horseshoe Falls." "Wild grapes missing from the northern shore of the whirlpool." "Six island boulders joined to shoreline at Foster's Flats." "Cliff face behind American Falls visible through veil of water." All this, plenty more, too, and the Queenston powerhouse is only a year and a half old, and operating at a third of the planned capacity.

Maybe it is time we reexamine the notion that says the river is ours to use as we see fit. It would be a mistake to wait until the falls are a mere trickle, a measly shadow of their former selves.

The editorial is just as Mr. Randal and I had discussed. Still, seeing it in black and white causes my hands to fly to my mouth. There is nothing to do but wait for Tom to come in from work.

I am bent over the sewing machine when I hear footsteps in the kitchen. I lift my foot from the treadle, listening, thinking that it is much too early for Tom, that the boys must have persuaded Mrs. Mancuso to fetch some particular toy. But Tom calls, "Bess?" up the stairs.

"In the sewing room," I call back down.

A moment later he is in the doorway, looking guilty with his head hung and his cap twisted in his hands. Even before he says so, I know he has been sacked, and I marvel at the speed with which Mr. Coulson got wind of the story. The first of the newspaper boys would barely have set foot on the street. I set down needle and thread, sorting out how to begin explaining what I must.

"Mr. Coulson told me I was finished at the Hydro," he says. "He called me to his office and said after all he'd done for me, I should be more grateful. He said I'd made him look like a fool."

"I showed Cecil Randal your notebook. He wrote an editorial." I pick up the newspaper from beside my sewing stool and hold it out to him. "Page two."

"You did what?"

"He copied out some of your tables and a whole lot of your notes," I say. "We worked out what he'd write."

With the newspaper still held aloft in my hand, Tom shuts his eyes and presses the heels of his palms against his closed lids. "What did you expect?"

"I expected the story to be printed in the newspaper," I say. "Then, I expected you to be sacked."

"Bess, you don't earn enough." His hands fall from his face to his sides, leaving his bewilderment plain to see. "You expected me to be sacked and you went ahead?"

"Yes," I say. "I'm relieved."

He cocks his head, furrows his brow.

"I really am," I say.

He sinks into a chair in the corner of the room and sits there a moment, very still. As silence swells in the sewing room, I begin to wonder if I have misjudged and press my lips between my teeth. "I'm going for a walk," he says, standing up and beginning to turn away. Then, thinking better of it, he swivels back toward me. He snatches the newspaper and strides through the doorway.

"Tom?"

"Leave me be for a bit," he says, not quite under his breath. "Just leave me be."

30

Niagara's Toronto powerhouse

Before I have managed to pace the kitchen twice, the telephone rings. When I pick up, I am thankful it is Kit on the line and say, "I was about to start calling around to your shops."

"Have you seen the newspaper?" It is typical Kit, cutting to the chase.

"It was me that spoke to Cecil Randal, not Tom."

"But, Bess, he'll be sacked." And then, always quick on the uptake, she adds, "You want him sacked."

I tell her that Tom was let go, that I had tried to convince him to resign before I went to Cecil Randal, that he would not budge.

"You went to the newspaper behind Tom's back. Wow. What'd he say?"

"Nothing." I sink into the chair beside the telephone. "He's furious. He left."

"I'll be over in a minute," she says.

I go back to wandering in the kitchen, keeping it up until the telephone rings again. This time it is Father on the line. "Is it true?" he says.

"What?"

"That Tom put a piece in the newspaper blasting the power companies?"

"It was me."

There is silence and then: "Good God, Bess. Mr. Coulson won't keep him on."

"It isn't right, someone like Tom, helping them siphon off half the river. It's ruining him." And then I am weeping because Kit is treating the situation like an emergency and Father is sounding alarmed.

"Ah, Bess. Don't cry. Things just have a way of working themselves out."

"But he left. Mr. Coulson sacked him, and when he got home I showed him the newspaper and he left." I do not attempt to keep my voice from breaking, to keep the sobs at bay.

"Bess. Bess. No need for tears. That Tom, he loves you like every father only wishes his daughter could be loved. There's no chance he's gone for good. He'll be back all right, sooner than you think, too."

And then Kit is at the door, so I say good-bye to Father and he says, "I'm telling you, Bess, I know what I know, not a speck of doubt."

The minute she takes in my tear-streaked face, her arms are around me. "I've been thinking about everything and, well, I think it'll all work out." She leans away from me. "It just isn't what anyone expects from you. He's going to need a bit of time."

We talk a long while, until the boys are back from Mrs. Mancuso's and supper is under way, and we have run out of angles and considerations, and repeated the most cogent of our thoughts a handful of times, and I am very nearly as certain as Father that Tom will come around. Then Kit steps back from the kitchen sink, where she is peeling potatoes, and says, "Know what, Bess?"

"What?"

"Promise you'll take this the right way."

"Promise."

"You're getting more and more like Isabel," she says.

I feel myself smile. "Tom always says she's still with me."

She stills, half-peeled potato in hand, then nods and turns back to the sink.

Tom comes home early in the evening, after Kit is gone, and the boys run from the kitchen to the front door with me following once I have dealt with a pot of milk warming on the stove. Any scrap of trepidation melts away the moment I see the three of them in the hallway, laughing and jostling. With Jesse draped over one shoulder, Tom scoops up Francis and holds him prisoner in the opposite arm. "You won't believe what happened," Tom says.

I lift my palms.

"I stopped in at the Windsor and Sean Garvey was working and he said one of the men from that group, a Mr. Bennett, was in a little earlier. You remember those lawyers and businessmen who were complaining about the Niagara Falls Park Commission kowtowing to the Hydro?"

"Go on. Of course I do." My fingernails are set to rupture the skin of my palms.

"Well, Mr. Bennett was asking around about how to get in touch with me. He had a copy of the story and he told Sean he wanted to talk to me about using it for their cause. And then a little later, when I showed up, Sean insisted on calling Mr. Bennett right then and there, and next thing I knew there were three of them from the group clapping me in the back at the Windsor Hotel. They want to see my notebook."

Then the boys are set down. I touch his chest and he does not flinch. I put my arms around his neck, pull him against me, and after a moment he hugs me back. We laugh and my feet leave the ground and I feel light-headed as he swings me around.

. . .

By eleven o'clock I have packed a small tin of lemon squares and a thermos of tea, and applied a bit of lipstick and decided on a cloche, and laughed aloud at my giddiness. I have settled on a pretty crepe de chine blouse and tapered skirt, though I imagine neither is suitable for a midnight row across the upper river. It is how we have decided to celebrate his freedom from the Hydro-Electric Power Commission, just the two of us, with the boys at Mrs. Mancuso's, finally tucked into bed for the night.

On the trolley heading toward the upper river, Tom and I sit very close, and I am reminded of the first time I snuck away with him on the Great Gorge Route, my first glimpse of the Devil's Hole and Whirlpool Rapids from the banks of the river. He had kissed me afterward, in the shadows of the Lower Steel Arch Bridge. My lips had parted to the warm wet of his mouth, and afterward, I was filled with a longing I was unable to shake. And here I am, eight years later, like a schoolgirl all over again.

By the time we reach Slater's Dock, on the far side of Chippawa, the river has widened to more than a mile across and the current has grown sluggish. We walk twenty minutes farther, hand in hand, along the riverbank. Tom points out Greater Bear and Lesser Bear high in the nighttime sky. "They were once a pretty maid and her son, or so the story goes," he says, "but Zeus had a jealous wife." He explains that, unlike the other constellations, Greater Bear and Lesser Bear never slip below the horizon, never sink into the cool water waiting there. It was Zeus's wife who came up with the punishment. As far as she was concerned, to be imprisoned in the body of a bear and flung high into the sky was not enough. No, Greater Bear and Lesser Bear were to spend all eternity wandering well above the horizon, pining for the water just out of their reach.

We come to a marshy bit of shoreline, and he drags a rowboat I had not noticed from the reeds. He had told me that it would be there, that he expected it belonged to a rumrunner, one of the men who rowed crates of bootleg gin and rye whiskey over to the American side.

Waves lap against the boat as we cross the river, and the sky is moonlit and full of stars. Tom rows masterfully, letting the current do much of the work.

"Remember the picnics in the athletic field?" he says.

"I do."

"You always brought me lemon squares."

"Remember the early days in the glen?" I say.

His head bobs in the darkness.

"You were always apologizing," I say.

"It was so soon after Isabel. I wasn't sure you were in your right head."

"You were the reason I got up in the morning."

"You're still the reason I do."

There are moments when it feels like my heart is not large enough to hold what I feel. Love wells in my eyes and I do not blink it away. I let it roll onto my cheeks.

He is a faded silhouette against his glittering river. Still, I can see the sheen that has come to his eyes.

A while later, we reach Grand Island, and he heaves the boat up onto the shore. We sit for a bit, sipping tea from the thermos, eating lemon squares. I watch him, gazing out at the river, at glittering crests and slick troughs, silver and black. And because it seems he is filled up, lost in the wonder of the river at night, I do not speak.

Eventually he comes back to me, to the grassy patch just beyond the riverbank, and spreads a blanket. He undoes the buttons of my blouse, the clasp of my skirt.

Afterward I lie with my hand on his belly, rising and falling with each of his breaths. Though his eyes are closed, the corner of his mouth is lifted in a soft smile that tells me that he has not drifted off, that he is wallowing in the pleasures of a few moments earlier. He moves a hand to his belly, threads his fingers with mine. His Adam's apple bobs as he swallows. The corner of his mouth lifts infinitesimally more.

I close my eyes, feel memory dissolve and slip away. I am in that place just before one forgets everything: who one is, even that one has a name. But he stirs, says, "Bess," just loud enough to call me back.

"Um."

"Why didn't you tell me what you were up to, with Mr. Randal, I mean?"

"You would've told me I shouldn't," I say.

He is quiet, long enough that I begin to wonder if he has fallen asleep, but then he says, "Suppose you're right."

WHIRLPOOL

September 1923 – October 1923

31

Whirlpool Rapids

I am stooped in the garden, picking tomatoes, thinking the crop will be the last we harvest at our May Avenue house, now that we have asked Mr. Brimley to come out later in the week and tell us what we might expect to get for it. With Tom making the rounds and as yet no luck, and me sewing like the dickens and only just managing to keep us afloat, we have got our eyes on a smaller place in Silvertown, which he assures me will heat up just fine with the wood he is being given as payment for clearing a lot adjacent Colt's Point.

As Tom and Jesse come into the yard, Jesse is the picture of unbridled vigor, his arms flapping this way and that, his feet kicking up as he trots backward, facing Tom.

When I say, "You're home," Jesse turns toward me and runs.

I open my arms, and a split second later he is in them saying, "Guess what."

He has half-knocked the wind from me. Though he is not quite seven, nothing of the toddler he once was remains. He is as tall as the nine-year-olds on the street and well-muscled, almost like a young man. This summer is the last I will catch him in my arms. "What?" I say.

"Muddy is going to take a barrel through the rapids on Labor Day and we're going to help." Muddy Sloane does little other than smoke and fish and talk about the barrel he has been reinforcing and waterproofing for the last umpteen years. Though a good decade Tom's senior, he lives with his mother and the dozen cats he claims keep him busy with their fondness for pike.

I fix my eyes on Tom, a few steps away. "Muddy was fishing at the whirlpool," he says.

"You're not serious," I say. The river was not something to be conquered. It was not something to be trivialized. I had heard him express the sentiment a hundred times. And only the summer before he had warned a Mr. Stephens his barrel would not survive a plunge over the Horseshoe Falls. Stephens went ahead and strapped his arms to the inside of his barrel. As ballast, he tied an anvil to his feet. Tom came home from the upper river dismayed. "He hasn't got a hope in hell, and I won't be a part of it," he said. When Stephens's barrel hit the plunge pool at the base of the waterfall, the anvil ripped through the floor of the barrel, taking him to his death. Tom recovered only an arm, tattooed with a message for Stephens's wife: "Forget me not Annie."

"Muddy's a friend," Tom says. "He should make out okay."

"What about Captain Webb?"

"He didn't have a barrel."

"Robert Flack was killed, and he had a boat," I say.

"Carlisle Graham made it through in a barrel five times and Bobby Leach, four. It's a whole lot different than going over the falls."

"Maud Willard suffocated," I say. Cozy in their beds, the boys had heard Tom tell the story time and again. Maud Willard, an actress from Canton, Ohio, came to the Niagara seeking fame as the first woman to shoot the Whirlpool Rapids. A Tuesday afternoon at a quarter past four, she climbed into her barrel, along with her dog, a fox terrier. By four thirty she was through the rapids, but her barrel was trapped in the whirlpool. Six hours later the barrel was finally cast to shore and the lid pried open. The fox terrier scrambled out, but Maud Willard lay battered and bruised, suffocated.

"But how can that be?" Jesse once asked. "Dogs breathe, too."

"There was an airhole in the barrel and the terrier blocked it with its snout."

"No one can know that," Jesse said, a dismissive pout coming to his lips.

"The dog's snout was a pulpy mess from being pressed up against the hole," Tom said.

"Was the dog hurt?" Francis asked, worry on his brow.

"His snout healed up, lickety-split."

"Not such a good idea, bringing a dog," Jesse said.

"Not such a good idea, shooting the rapids," Tom said.

I slip the tomato I am holding into the pocket of my apron and say to Tom, "Even if she hadn't suffocated, I don't think Jesse should be involved."

"Someone should have pulled her barrel out," Tom says.

Jesse is crouching within earshot, inspecting the garden, though it is rivers and rapids and water that interest him, not vegetables and soil. I ought to have sent him away, and now it is too late. I put my index finger to my lips, gesturing for Tom to shush. I take him by the shirtsleeve and lead him around the corner of the house. "You've always thought the stunters were fools," I say.

"It doesn't mean they deserve to die."

"You think Muddy will need help?"

"If he gets sucked into the whirlpool, yes."

"Not with Jesse," I say.

"There'll be things he could learn."

"He'll come away thinking of Muddy as a hero, like everyone else."

"We've talked about stunters," he says. "He knows what I think."

"It'll confuse him, you helping out."

He rocks back on his heels a moment, looking pensive. "All right," he says. "You're right. Not Jesse."

When I turn back to the garden, I nearly walk into Jesse, who has crept around the corner of the house. He raises his fists, begins pummeling my ribs. "I'm going," he says. "I'm going. I'm going. I'm going."

Tom scoops him up and throws him over his shoulder, and Jesse says, "Tell her I can go," and struggles to free himself. Tom is up the back stoop in a single step. Then, through the open kitchen window, I hear three thwacks and stifled sniffling and Tom saying, "Your mother is right, and if you treat her like that again, you won't fish for a month."

At supper Jesse is sullen, even when Tom says, "I've got something to show you, Jesse," and produces a piece of paper from his shirt pocket.

PRESERVE NIAGARA FALLS

In 1887 the Ontario legislature passed the Niagara Falls Park Act, vesting the Niagara Falls Park Commission with wide powers to restore and preserve the area around Niagara Falls. Despite the mandate, recent years have seen the Commission authorize unprecedented hydroelectric development with little concern for the harm done to the Niagara River and its environs. With the appointment of Philip William Ellis, former chairman of the Toronto Hydro-Electric Commission and longtime advocate of hydroelectric development at Niagara Falls, as chair of the Commission, all pretense of efficacy in fulfilling its preservation mandate has been lost.

WRITE TO
your Member of Provincial Parliament
and Premier Ferguson.
Insist on a renewed commitment
to the preservation of Niagara Falls
by the Niagara Falls Park Commission.

Friends of Niagara, c/o Mr. J. H. Bennett, River Rd., Niagara Falls, Ontario

"There'll be five hundred copies ready the week after Labor Day," Tom says, "all printed with the editorial from the newspaper on the back."

"It's wonderful," I say, patting his hand.

He puts the circular in front of Jesse and goes over the gist of it with him. Jesse does his best to feign indifference, though his gaze drops several times to the circular. "We'll be handing them out, and we've come up with a list of influential men and newspaper editors who'll be getting one in the post along with a personalized letter."

I pick up the circular. "It's a start."

"Mr. Bennett says that back in 1880, when folks were first lobbying for what turned out to be the Niagara Falls Park Act in Canada and the Act to Preserve the Scenery of the Falls of Niagara in the U.S., there was a petition signed by seven hundred men. It was addressed to both governments, and the list included members of parliament and Supreme Court justices and cabinet ministers and university presidents and bigwig businessmen like Molson and Redpath and Massey, and a long list of literary types—Emerson, Longfellow, Ruskin, a bunch of others I bet you'd know. Even the vice president of the United States signed his name."

Early morning on Labor Day, I feel Tom's lips on my cheek. Even though Muddy's run through the rapids is set for ten o'clock, we had agreed he would leave early, before Jesse was up. I roll onto my back and smile up at him. He takes my hand and gives it a squeeze, and then he is gone. I lie awake a long while, wondering exactly how far Tom would have gone to get Maud Willard's barrel out of the whirlpool. He had gone in after Isabel, already drowned. He was wet all the way through when he came to fetch me from Glenview. And no one can toss a grappling hook to the middle of the whirlpool, not even him. It has got to be three hundred yards across. What gamble would he make for Muddy Sloane, circling in the whirlpool, asking himself just how long his oxygen will hold out?

A while later I hear the boys stir. For three days, Jesse has moped around the house, with only the occasional slipup, once laughing at some funny thing I said, and another time returning my embrace before re-membering I was the enemy. Such resolve seems out of place in a child his age, and I have had moments of worry, when I stop whatever it is I am do-ing and ask myself if I have made a mistake. Tom says it is only that he is reminded of what he will miss at every turn; there are broadsheets pasted up all over Niagara Falls, and "Muddy Sloane" is on the lips of every boy in town.

But this morning Jesse flies down the stairs and delivers the bacon and toast to the kitchen table without being asked. He steps out onto the back stoop when his breakfast is done and looks to the west, then comes back into the kitchen and cheerfully says, "It's not going to rain and there's only a bit of wind, so the river won't be all that wild." He helps me wash up, chatting amiably as he often does about lures and bait and fishing holes.

I am upstairs opening windows and gathering coverlets to air on the clothesline when the strangeness of his behavior hits me full force. I call out, "Jesse," and, when there is no answer, I feel panic rise. I move to the top of the stairs and call out again. Still, there is no reply. I rush down the stairs, strewing bedding as I go.

Francis is in the kitchen, on top of the table, startled by my sudden appearance. His fingers are poised over the sugar bowl. "Where's Jesse?" I say.

"Outside," he says, snatching his fingers away from the bowl.

"Outside where?" My voice is stern, and he looks as though he could cry.

"He went to see Muddy."

"What?"

"Not with Daddy," he says, hopefully, as though that might make everything all right.

"Tell me what he said."

"He went to see the barrel."

"When did he go?"

"Today," he says, pleased with himself. We have been working on the concepts of yesterday, today, and tomorrow for quite some time.

I glance at the clock in the hallway and see it is ten minutes before ten o'clock. A barrel will make it from the *Maid of the Mist* landing through the rapids to the whirlpool in only a few minutes if it stays clear of all the boulders and eddies along the way. Jesse is likely at the whirlpool, away from Tom, who will be at the landing, preparing to send Muddy off.

From the kitchen window, I can see Mrs. Mancuso on her knees in the garden, digging up the first of her potatoes. I scoop Francis up and dash across the empty lot between our houses. "Jesse went to the whirlpool by himself," I say.

She begins to cross herself but thinks better of it and says, "There is crowd today." She takes Francis from me with a single stout arm and with the other shoos me away. "You, go," she says.

A few minutes later I am loping along River Road, avoiding the curious stares of the spectators gathered along the rim of the gorge. At Colt's Point, I take a moment to scan the stone beach far below. As Mrs. Mancuso predicted, there is a small crowd, locals who know how to access the passable parts of the riverbank. A neighbor might even be watching Jesse. And he knows to be careful. He has heard the stories: Captain Matthew Webb. Robert Flack. Maud Willard. Charles Stephens. He has seen the mangled bodies in the grappling hooks.

As I scramble down the ties of the old incline railway, my beating heart echoing in my ears, familiarity sweeps through me. The panic and pounding are the same, as is the derelict track. The only difference is the other time I was escaping the whirlpool after finding Isabel's lifeless body there. And now I am stumbling forward, into the gorge, toward endlessly swirling water, rather than out.

Eventually, I do not catch myself. I fall to my hands and knees, and pain shoots though my wrist. It is Tom's fault Jesse craves the river. I push myself up and wince as my wrist gives out. It is my fault, too, for not keeping a closer watch.

When I am nearly to the stone beach, I see a barrel, like a black coffin, trapped in the whirlpool, circling round and round, and I guess Tom is not far behind, making his way along the shoreline to the whirlpool. I see a man hurl a grappling hook. The throw is useless, pointless; the barrel is at least a hundred yards from the shore. The beach is shaped like a crescent, and at its downriver point, to my horror, I see Jesse stripped to his underwear and running headlong into the whirlpool. There is a rope tied around his waist and a second rope clenched in his fist. A moment later I notice two men on the beach, one letting out the rope tied to Jesse's waist, the other letting out the rope held in Jesse's fist. I try to call out, but his name is lodged in my throat.

For a moment the crowd stands in silent stupor, all but me. I am racing across the beach, tripping over stones, knocking into the elbows of the men in my path. Jesse is swimming with the current and takes several strong strokes, and someone begins to clap. Others join in, and soon enough someone calls out, "Swim. Swim." How I despise each and every onlooker, the men and women who come to watch, the people for whom a brush with death will mean a morning well spent.

I have almost reached the two men letting out the ropes when I overhear the gossip making its way through the crowd: "It's the Cole boy, the riverman's son."

"Pull him in," I call out. "Pull him in."

The men with the ropes glance at each other, uncertain.

"Pull him in," I say. "I'm his mother. Pull him in or I'll do it myself."

The older man, with a gray, bushy mustache, holds his rope out to me. "The boy said he'd give us a signal. He said if we pulled against the current, he'd be crushed."

"He's a child," I say.

"Look, lady," the younger man says, "the kid said he was going in whether we helped or not. He was a good ten feet from shore before we touched the ropes."

I sink to my knees, my torn, stained skirt puffed up around me, a billowing pillow ring.

"You want us to haul him in?"

I want Tom. Tom would know what to do. But he has yet to arrive.

I look across the whirlpool, to the end of the stone beach opposite me, and there he is, coming out of the woods. I watch him take in the situation in a single sweep. In an instant he is sprinting toward me, toward the ropes connected to Jesse. He is beautiful as he runs, his fists clenched, his tanned arms ripping through air, his green eyes flashing will.

I glance to Jesse, a few yards from the barrel, his arms tugging the water alongside him, his head lifting for breath every four or five strokes. "Tom will know what to do," I say.

"Tom Cole? The riverman?"

"Yes."

Just as Jesse moves within an arm's length of the barrel on the far side of the pool, Tom reaches the ropes. He grabs the rope tied around Jesse's waist and lets out more slack. He begins to speak in a low, steady voice, words Jesse cannot possibly hear. "Wait. Easy." The barrel heaves to a flatter bit of water. "Now." Jesse somehow manages to thread the rope that was in his fist through a grip on the outside of the barrel. "Clear out. Clear out." He uses his legs to push off the tossing barrel as best he can. Then he pauses, treading, water crashing over his head. "Swim," I say. But Tom only continues his hushed commands. "Nothing fancy, Jesse. A simple noose will do." It is a knot Jesse can tie in his sleep, a knot Tom taught him to make. "Haul it in," he says to the man holding the rope now tied to the barrel.

So far Tom has only let out rope as Jesse progressed away from the shore where we are on the opposite side of the whirlpool. Jesse was swimming with the current. But now he seems intent on the beach at the far point of the crescent, and, though his arms paddle furiously, he is losing ground to the current, being dragged away from the shore toward the mouth of the whirlpool.

"Kick," Tom says in his low, steady voice. And then a moment later, he is yelling, "Kick, Jesse. God damn it. Kick," and I taste bile in my throat. But when I look Tom is taking up rope, which means Jesse is on his way toward us, and for a moment I do not understand the panic in Tom's voice.

There is a crook in the Niagara River, an elbow of sorts. At the crook, water hurtling through the gorge is wrenched from its straight path and forced to circle counterclockwise, forming the whirlpool. The pool cannot accommodate an endless river. And so at its mouth, the exiting water is forced down, under the incoming flow. I have watched Tom throw in logs. I have watched them disappear. It is here, at the juncture of the incoming and exiting flows, that the water can strike a blow like a sledgehammer. It is here Captain Matthew Webb was last seen alive. It is here Jesse could be sucked from my sight.

Tom continues to pull in rope but is struggling to keep up with the slack as Jesse hurtles toward the mouth of the whirlpool.

I keep my eyes fixed on Jesse, as though my gaze is a lifeline of sorts. The crowd behind me lets out a cheer, and I search for the improvement in his situation that I missed. But it is only that the lid has been pried from the barrel, and that Muddy Sloane has stood up from crouching and tipped his cap to the crowd. At least that is what I surmise; I refuse to take my gaze from Jesse. Oh, if only Muddy Sloane were still circling endlessly in his barrel. If only Jesse were watching from the shore.

The oxygen in a barrel is sufficient for at least an hour or two. It is something Tom knows, something he might have told Jesse at the *Maid of the Mist* landing had I let him go. Or maybe it is something he and Jesse had discussed at great length, something Jesse knew even as he ran headlong into the pool. Like Tom, who chose not to wait for the coast guard at Fort Niagara to send new lines. Like Tom, who dangled needlessly above the upper rapids in the black of night. The scow was firmly lodged, he said. It would stay put in the upper rapids until the hull rusted through.

My last glimpse of Jesse, before he is pulled from sight, is the white underside of his foot.

I want to believe in the magic of cauls. I want to look at Tom's face and see him read his river and know Jesse will be pushed to the surface and floated to shore. But I am afraid to look.

Instead I glimpse his hands, which are letting out rope and more rope.

"Pull him in," I say.

"Not against the current. Not yet."

I force my gaze upward, from Tom's shoes to his chest. I glimpse his chin and see that he is counting. His chin is bobbing slightly, down, then up again.

"How long?" I say.

"I'll give him a couple of minutes."

Captain Matthew Webb's body did not surface for four days. Still, I begin counting as well.

There are ten plaques on Isabel's aluminum bracelet, and I twist the bracelet around my wrist in small intervals, using the plaques to mark off the seconds. I slide the bracelet around my wrist six times. Then twelve.

I have slid the bracelet around my wrist seventeen times when Tom touches my hair. "Believe in me, Bess."

I look up at his face, and I see tears in his green river eyes, or maybe it is only sweat. I cannot say for sure because before I can really look, he has abandoned the rope and is off, plunging into water that is thrashing and careening and wild.

Seconds later someone hollers, and I look in the direction of the voice and after that to the spot a couple of the men on the shore are pointing toward. And then I am taking in the rope Tom left beside me because it is Jesse, not twenty feet from the shore. I look for Tom, who has surely rescued his son from the green depths. But he is nowhere to be seen.

Jesse is on the stone beach without his underwear, coughing up water, gasping for breath. The skin around his waist is bleeding and raw. I throw my arms around him and try not to crush him. I try to remember he needs air. I push myself away and look into his terror-stricken eyes. Then he begins to sob, his fingers in my hair, pulling me close.

He sobs, in my arms, his face against my chest. I look past the crown of his head to the whirlpool. Where is Tom? I begin counting, again sliding Isabel's aluminum bracelet around my wrist.

I slide the bracelet around my wrist thirty times.

I stare, with narrowed eyes, at the grave-faced men who come to help. I bat away their hands.

I slide the bracelet around my wrist fifty times.

Then sixty. A hundred.

32

I sit at the whirlpool, alone, an afternoon to myself. I stay put, even as the light changes from high and white and clear to low and golden and soft. At one point a young couple appears on the stone beach, but they see me there and head back into the woods. They had come upon a private moment: the riverman's widow watching the water circle, endlessly so.

I stood here for three weeks, afterward. After Tom had gone in. For three weeks I threw any scrap of wood I could find into the pool. And sometimes I hit the bit of swirling green where I had glimpsed the white underside of Jesse's foot as he was pulled from sight. Sometimes the wood was sucked under and sometimes it bobbed up to the surface and broke through. Still, never once had it resurfaced at the spot where Jesse had reappeared.

Maybe it was only that the wind was different or that it had rained the night before. Or maybe the river had little to do with Jesse coming up where he had.

Once Jesse and I were home from the whirlpool, and Mrs. Mancuso was in place to intercept anyone who came to the door, I carried him up the stairs, in my arms, the way I had before he was able to manage the climb on his own. I laid him on his bed and wrapped a length of muslin around his waist and smoothed his still-damp hair from his eyes.

What to say to him?

He knew what had happened. He knew we would not find Tom at home. Men at the whirlpool had said, "He isn't coming up, ma'am. Let me help you get the boy home." And there were tears in people's eyes and on their cheeks. "I'm sorry," they said. "He was a good man."

And a constable had come to the stone beach, the same one who had come the night of the scow. "You're sure it was him? You saw him go into the pool?"

"Yes," I said. "I did."

"He went in after the boy?"

I nodded, almost imperceptibly. Jesse was huddled in my lap, and it seemed wrong to implicate him, though he was clever enough to have figured it out for himself.

As I sat on his bed that first awful night, Jesse gathered my skirt into his arms and held on for dear life. I stretched out alongside him and pulled him close and kissed his hair. "It's all right," I said into a tangle of curls. But it was not all right. I did not know how we would go on, not without Tom. He had only just begun teaching Jesse to row a boat and Francis to set a snare. He would see neither fall in love and marry. He would see neither hold a child of his own. Never again would he row with his wife across a lapping, moonlit river, beneath a starry sky.

Would Francis have anything more than the vaguest memories of his father? Tom had taken him to the river more times than I could count and taught him to predict whether a twig tossed into an eddy would circle endlessly or escape and be pitched downstream. These lessons he would keep. But would he remember Tom putting a warmed brick in his bed on a cold winter's night, or humming as he tinkered with his snares? Would he know a fellow ought to pull a chair out for a woman and take off his cap when it is time to eat? Jesse would remember more. And there is the rub. He would remember too much. His father went into the whirlpool after him. And then his father drowned.

When Jesse had lain quiet a good while, just when I thought he might have drifted off, he spoke. "I want to know about Isabel," he said. It was miles from what I had expected to hear. Truth be told, it was a relief. I had been dreading the questions I could not begin to answer, not even for myself.

He knew Tom had pulled Isabel's body from the whirlpool; it was a story we had never kept from him. He knew, too, how it was the bodies ended up circling there, in the whirlpool, before they were fished out. I had told him that she was not mangled, that only her dress was torn, a white tea dress I had made for her. These were details it had seemed important for him to know.

"She made up nonsense words to the hymns we sang at church," I said. "She held her hymnbook upside down."

"Her dress was ripped."

"It was a white tea dress. I made it for her. She was wearing it when she drowned."

"Is she a ghost?"

"There's no such thing."

"Is she in heaven?"

"I think so," I said, because just then, when surely he was really asking about Tom, it seemed best to lie. "And she's here and here." I touched my temple and then the spot just over my heart. "Here, too." I touched his temple, then his chest. "Like Daddy."

At that moment, I wanted faith and heaven and God as never before. I wanted my brokenhearted son to believe our existence was not trivial, something to be snatched away on a whim. I wanted him to believe his father would be with him, always, in the way Fergus had been with Tom.

Tears rose in my throat but did not come, because just then Jesse said, "She was in the whirlpool and she pushed me up."

"Isabel?"

"I was getting pulled down and I saw Isabel. Then she pushed me up."

"Jesse," I said, "Isabel isn't in the whirlpool."

"I was scared."

"Our imaginations can play tricks."

"There were pearls on her neck. Lots of them."

"Pearls?" I said. I had never once mentioned the choker Edward had given me, the choker I had buried with Isabel, not even to Tom.

"Yes," he said. "It was a necklace, a necklace with pearls."

There was a procession along Main Street and then Stanley Avenue to Fairview Cemetery. I had asked for a headstone to be put alongside

Sadie's and Fergus's, though the river had given up no body to bury there. It was a block of limestone, hauled out of the glen, carved with the words TOM COLE. RIVERMAN. BELOVED HUSBAND AND FATHER.

The day of the procession, the wind was westerly and harsh for early autumn. I had been to the whirlpool in the morning, and the standing waves were as high and as angry as any I had ever seen. I had thrown in several pieces of wood and watched them circle, or disappear and sometimes come up far from the spot where Jesse had reappeared.

Despite the drizzle and the wind, most of the town came out and formed a wide semicircle fifty-odd deep around the stone. There were friends from his years at the Windsor Hotel, laborers from the Hydro-Electric Power Commission, neighbors from Silvertown, associates from the Friends of Niagara, hundreds of acquaintances, hundreds more who felt compelled to come though their knowledge of Tom was limited to newspaper accounts and bits of lore traded on the streets. Many wore Save Niagara Falls buttons pinned to the lapels of their coats, and when I finally realized it, I remembered I had seen the same words scrawled on a placard leaning against the window of the Polish butcher and then again on a banner strung across the façade of Clark's Hardware, where Tom bought his lures.

I stood between the boys in a dress I had worn at Loretto and then again after Isabel died. It was out-of-date, and the elbows were shiny and threadbare. Mother had offered me the slightly less worn crepe suit she had brought for herself, but I shook my head and she knew to leave well enough alone. She stood beside Francis, with Father next in line, and held Francis's hand and picked him up when he began to cry. Mrs. Mancuso was ready with a handkerchief and a pocketful of sweets on Jesse's far side. But he did not cry or look up from the ground. Kit and Leslie were there, her face against the black of his jacket, his shoulders slumped, his chest as hollow as I had ever seen. I glimpsed Boyce Cruickshank at the rear of the crowd, his hands empty of the bouquet of yellow irises that had caught my eye as the procession filed past Isabel's grave. A new wave of sorrow came upon me, seeing him there, pining for what was gone, and I felt my knees go weak. Then Mother's arm was firm around my waist, reminding me that I must persist, for the boys, that as her daughter I could, now and always. Mrs. Andrews was home from Egypt and stood just behind me, sniffling and sobbing and blowing her nose. The evening before she had told me that I was the beneficiary named in her will, that she saw no reason to wait, not when the money was needed now. "Finances might be the furthest thing from your mind," she said, "but I thought you should know." I had my wits about me enough to know it was good news. Still, the practicalities of living seemed nothing in the face of what was lost.

I walk to the spot on the stone beach alongside where Jesse had come to the surface gasping for breath. I suppose everyone who has looked into the gorge from above and seen me here thinks I am still waiting for Tom. But I am not. I am merely remembering him.

I stood at this very spot for three weeks, tossing wood, always the same thought churning in my mind. When he touched my hair that final time and said, "Believe in me, Bess," what had he meant?

He was letting out rope and more rope. Nearly three minutes had passed since the white underside of Jesse's foot had slipped from sight. Then he touched my hair. He touched my hair so tenderly, like a loving husband might before setting off to war.

Believe in me, Bess.

As he waited on the shore, his son tethered to a rope, he surely knew going in after him meant almost certain death. Yet he dove into the pool. Had he thought there was a chance? In my darkest moments I wonder if Tom knew he would die but went into the whirlpool anyway. I have imagined what afterward would have been like, with Tom, without Jesse. And I might have blamed him. He had taught Jesse to love the river. He had held him in the current when he was just three years old.

Had Tom imagined what afterward would have been like and seen what I did? Had it edged him closer to the whirlpool? The day of the rockslide in the gorge and then again, after the ice bridge and the scow, he had said there were things he knew, things he could not explain. Would I have remained doubtful if he had not gone into the whirlpool, if Jesse had drowned, if afterward Tom had said he knew it would have been for naught?

. . .

He watched the gorge walls, predicted when ledges would collapse. He could forecast the weather with uncanny accuracy. He happened to be at the whirlpool when Isabel's body turned up. Some called it intuition or second sight. Some said his perception was just keener than most. I had wondered if, in his mind, the curious things he knew were things Fergus could see, things he whispered into Tom's ear. And I had scoffed.

Now there is the wood that never comes up at the spot where Jesse had. But it is impossible that the river should ever again be exactly as it was that awful day. There is also the choker Jesse was able to describe. But maybe the Atwells had gossiped, maybe all of Niagara Falls knows what I buried with Isabel. Maybe Jesse was told somewhere along the way. Maybe not.

I caught a pike the other day, the first of my life. Jesse had shown me how to cast, and Francis clapped as I reeled it in. Afterward they watched me gut it, astonishment on their faces, like paint on a clown's. "It's something Daddy taught me," I said.

"Me too," Jesse said.

Francis looked at his feet, and it seemed our happy moment had come to an end.

"I'll show you," Jesse said. "Other stuff, too, like where to camp and how to throw a grappling hook."

That night as I tucked Jesse in, I said, "You were a good big brother this afternoon." The words were sincere, planned, an introduction to the discussion that could no longer be put off. "You know you can't go down to the river, not by yourself, not with Francis, not without me, not yet."

"I want to do the measuring. I know where the notches are."

"Only if I'm with you. You know what can happen there."

He nodded and shifted over a smidgen from the center of the bed, making room for me to sit down. "Did I make Daddy drown?"

"No, Jesse." I swallowed hard. "I could say it was my fault for not letting you go with Daddy in the first place. And Daddy could say it was his fault for letting you think you could. And Francis could say it was his fault for not telling me sooner when you left."

"Was Daddy mad?"

"Not a bit. He was full of love. So, so full. That's why he went in." I threaded my arms around his neck and pulled him close.

"Daddy used to say Great-grandpa was with us, on the river."

"He could feel Fergus loving him."

"I'm going to be like Daddy," Jesse said, and I knew it was true.

Tom's eyes were the thing I noticed that long-ago day I first saw him. A sister out in front and a tail of paired-off Loretto girls trailing behind, we were making our weekly outing to the falls. I said, "Good day." He tipped his cap, and I thought his eyes were exactly like the river, green, full of vigor.

"You have Daddy's eyes," I said.

"Green."

"The color of the river."

"It's all the eroded limestone that makes it green," he said. "Daddy told me that."

M r. Bennett, from the Friends of Niagara, came to the house one day. He sat in the kitchen and drank the tea I offered and asked if I had noticed the placards and banners cropping up all over town. "Folks that keep their old newspapers are tacking 'Bleeding the River Dry' to their front doors," he said.

There have been obituaries in the Niagara Falls *Evening Review,* the St. Catharines *Standard, The Hamilton Spectator,* even *The Buffalo Evening News* and Toronto's *Globe,* all of which Father has managed to get ahold of and send along to me. Each covered the predictions and rescues, also the notches cut into the gorge wall, the drop in the river's height, and the disappearance of the heron from the shallows and the wild grapes from the shoreline. I lifted the teapot. "More?"

He held out his cup. "The circular with the newspaper story has been printed. We've been sitting on it."

"If you're waiting out of respect for Tom, it isn't what he'd want."

"It seemed best to ask."

"Thank you," I said.

. . .

I have stood at the brink of the falls, that thin line that separates eternity from time. I have looked for aberrations in the rising mist, those flecks of shimmering silver, those orbs of color a shade more intense than their surroundings that I had once seen from my window seat. I have counted to ten before opening my eyelids, and let my gaze become unfocused, and crossed and uncrossed my eyes, and waited in the mist until I was soaked through to the bone, until it finally occurred to me that faith is believing without proof. Someday I would stop needing proof.

I have imagined asking Kit if the fate of the choker is a secret between just the two of us, now that Edward is gone. I even parted my lips once to speak the words. But in the end, I pressed them shut.

The day when I will finally be ready to ask sometimes seems hazy and far off, though there are moments when it feels but a hairbreadth away. They come more and more, brief stretches when the answer holds little sway, usually when I am out canvassing, with Jesse quoting figures from Tom's notebook, and Francis marching along with his Save Niagara Falls button pinned to his coat, and one or two of the others from the Friends of Niagara Women's Auxiliary chatting away. For now I am content to wait, until I have grown unshakable in what I have come to know. To ask any sooner might be to snuff out the flickering sliver of light that says Isabel has been with us all along, that Tom is with us still.

Author's Note

William "Red" Hill (right)

BORN AND BRED IN NIAGARA FALLS, ONTARIO, I GREW UP awash in the lore of William "Red" Hill, Niagara's most famous riverman. I'd see the rusted-out hull of the old scow still lodged in the upper rapids of the river and be reminded of him rescuing the men marooned there in 1918. I'd see the plaque commemorating the ice bridge tragedy of 1912 and know he'd risked his life to save a teenage boy named Ignatius

Roth. I'd open the newspaper and read a story about his son Wes carrying on the Hill tradition and rescuing a stranded stunter.

When I set out to write a novel capturing the wonder I feel while standing at the brink of the falls, Red Hill's life was a natural place to find inspiration. Like my character Tom Cole, Red Hill was born with a caul and had an uncanny knowledge of the river, a knowledge he would pass on to his sons. It was said he could predict the weather simply by listening to the roar of the falls, also that he would wake in the night knowing he would find a body tossing in the river the following day. In his lifetime (1888–1942) he hauled 177 bodies from the river, rescued 29 people and hundreds of animals and birds, and assisted a handful of stunters. He was the only man alive to have been awarded four lifesaving medals—the first, at the age of seven, for saving his aunt from a flame-engulfed house; another for rescuing the whistling swans that were swept over the falls each winter onto the ice below; and two more for the ice bridge and scow rescues, both of which are retold in *The Day the Falls Stood Still*.

The ten turbines of the Queenston powerhouse all became operational in Red Hill's lifetime. Perhaps he saw the Niagara as diminished and, like Tom Cole, in some way mourned the river as it once was. Both men were spared the 1950 Niagara Diversion Treaty still in use today. With the drastically more lenient diversion limits set out in that treaty, the water plummeting over the Horseshoe and American falls now amounts to about 50 percent of the natural flow during the daylight hours of the tourist season and 25 percent otherwise.

There were aspects of Red Hill I did not incorporate into Tom Cole. Red Hill shot the lower rapids in a barrel three times, in one instance becoming trapped in the whirlpool. The oldest of his sons, Red Junior, lashed a rope around his waist and plunged into the water, eventually hauling his father's barrel to shore. According to local lore, Red Junior was paraded about on his father's shoulders, a hero. My riverman would not have lauded the daring. The Niagara was not a river to be mocked.

Red Junior and his brother Major both shot the rapids. Both attempted "the big drop." Major's trip was cut short when his barrel was tossed ashore in the upper rapids. Red Junior was not so lucky. In 1951 he plunged to his death in a barrel constructed of inflated rubber tubes, canvas, and fishnets. Corky, another of the Hill brothers, died in an accident while working in a hydroelectric diversion tunnel.

Red Hill's wife, Beatrice, was quoted as saying that she hated the river, that she was afraid of it. Perhaps rightly so.

Acknowledgments

A BIG, HEARTFELT THANK-YOU TO THE FOLLOWING: my agent, Dorian Karchmar, for believing in me, for pushing me, for astounding me with her extraordinary combination of editorial and business smarts; my U.S. publisher, Ellen Archer, and acquiring editor, Pamela Dorman, for saying yes; my editors, Kate Elton, Sarah Landis, Vanessa Neuling, and Iris Tupholme, for wielding hatchets or microscopes as necessary, always with generosity; my copyeditor, Susan M. S. Brown, for reading with diligence and skill; my first reader, Ania Szado (whose tears thrilled me), and early readers Brian Francis, Lesley Krueger, and my writers' group, for encouragement and helpful suggestions; my boys, Jack, Charlie, and William Cobb, for their unflagging curiosity, particularly when it comes to cork suits, lifeline guns, and severed, tattooed limbs; my husband, Larry Cobb, for food, water, shelter, and love, and for telling me all those years ago it was all right to depart the workforce to write fiction and then never once suggesting my "two-year" leave was long ago used up; my parents, Ruth and Al Buchanan, for everything that brought me to this, including their choice of Niagara Falls as a hometown; and the rest of the Buchanans and Cobbs, my big, boisterous, loving family.

I would like to express my gratitude for the generous assistance provided by Dr. Norman R. Ball, author of *The Canadian Niagara Power Company Story*; Sister Caroline Dawson, Loretto Niagara, IBVM; Sister Juliana Dusel, archivist, Loretto Archives, IBVM; Cathy Simpson, local history librarian, Niagara Falls (Ontario) Public Library; and Scott Tufford, author of numerous Niagara histories including one on Glenview.

Many books were helpful in researching this novel, particularly, on the topic of faith, Karen Armstrong, *The Spiral Staircase: My Climb Out of Darkness*, Vintage Canada, 2005; C. S. Lewis, *Surprised by Joy*, Fount, 1998; and Armand M. Nicholi, *The Question of God: C. S. Lewis and Sigmund Freud Debate God, Love, Sex, and the Meaning of Life*, The Free Press, 2002; on the topic of grief, Joan Didion, *The Year of Magical Thinking*, Alfred A. Knopf, 2006; and C. S. Lewis, *A Grief Observed*, HarperCollins, 2000; on the topic of cooking, Isabella Beeton, *Mrs. Beeton's All-About Cookery*, Ward, Lock & Co., 1915; and on the topic of Niagara Falls, Pierre Berton, *Niagara: A History of the Falls*, McClelland & Stewart, 1992; Andy O'Brien, *Daredevils of Niagara*, The Ryerson Press, 1964; Patrick McGreevy, *Imagining Niagara: The Meaning and Making of Niagara Falls*, University of Massachusetts Press, 1994; George A. Seibel, *Ontario's Niagara Parks: 100 Years*, The Niagara Parks Commission, 1985; Sherman Zavitz, *It Happened at Niagara: First Series*, The Lundy's Lane Historical Society, 1996; Sherman Zavitz, *It Happened at Niagara: Second Series*, The Lundy's Lane Historical Society, 1999; Sherman Zavitz, *It Happened at Niagara: Third Series*, The Lundy's Lane Historical Society, 2003; City of Niagara Falls Centennial Book Committee, *Images of a Century: The City of Niagara Falls, Canada, 1904–2004*, The City of Niagara Falls, Canada, 2005; and *Niagara Falls, Canada: A History of the City and the World Famous Beauty Spot*, edited by William J. Holt, The Kiwanis Club of Stamford, Ontario, Inc., 1967.

The newspaper account of Fergus's rescue of the workmen stranded on Ellet's bridge is taken nearly verbatim from a news report recounted in *Niagara Falls, Canada*, edited by William J. Holt. Grateful acknowledgment is made to The Kiwanis Club of Stamford, Ontario, Inc. for permission to reprint the account.

The description of the brink of the falls as "that thin line that separates eternity from time" comes from James K. Liston, *Niagara Falls: A Poem in Three Cantos*, printed and published for the author, 1843. Exact ownership of copyright is unknown.

An earlier version of chapter 5 appeared in *Descant* 138 (Fall 2007).

Grateful acknowledgment is made to the Toronto Arts Council for their award of a writers' grant.

Photo Credits

pp. iii and 1: Library of Congress, cph 3b15325 and 3b39941.

p. 5: Courtesy of Loretto Archives, Institute of the Blessed Virgin Mary, Toronto, Ontario.

p. 46: George Barker, Library and Archives Canada, PA-181218.

p. 55: Niagara Falls Public Library, Niagara Falls, New York.

pp. 71, 91, 236, 247, and 299: Niagara Falls (Ontario) Public Library.

p. 77: Niagara, copyright 1902 by A. Wittemann, Brooklyn, New York.

p. 102: Copyright unknown.

p. 159: William James Topley, Library and Archives Canada, PA-008929.

pp. 184 and 272: Photo courtesy of Ontario Power Generation.

p. 206: George Barker, Library and Archives Canada, PA-056072.

p. 279: Library of Congress, ppmsca 18039.